OXFORD WORLI

THE CRIMES

Donatien-Alphonse-François, Marquis de Sade, was born in Paris in 1741 into an old patrician family. He was educated at the Jesuit college of Louis-le-Grand and at military school at Versailles. The end of the Seven Years War in 1763 dashed his hopes of a military career, and that same year he reluctantly made the good match his impoverished father forced on him by marrying Renée-Pélagie de Montreuil, daughter of a recently ennobled but wealthy lawyer. Serious sexual misdemeanours brought him to the attention of the police and he was jailed twice for his excesses. In 1772, for attempted murder and sodomy, he was sentenced to death and his effigy was burned in his absence. In 1777, after years spent in not uncomfortable hiding, mainly at his chateau at La Coste near Avignon, he was jailed and not released until 1790. During his prison years study was his therapy and writing his salvation. It was now that he developed a coherent system of atheistical materialism and wrote plays, novels, and the stories of *Les Crimes de l'amour* (*The Crimes of Love*), which he published in 1800. In the 1790s, having no love for the *ancien régime* which had deprived him of his freedom, he played a minor role in the revolution. Jailed as a political moderate, he escaped the guillotine in July 1794 by an administrative accident. Describing himself as 'a man of letters', he tried to make a living from the novels (*Justine*, 1791; *Aline et Valcour*, 1795; *La Nouvelle Justine* and *L'Histoire de Juliette*, both 1797) which justified their obscenities by reference to a comprehensive system of sexual *realpolitik*. In 1801 he was jailed as the author of *Justine*, and in 1803 was transferred to the lunatic asylum at Charenton, diagnosed as suffering from 'libertine dementia'. He continued to write and even helped to stage plays for the inmates. His applications for release were consistently rejected, and he remained a captive until his death in December 1814. Against his wishes, he was given a Christian funeral, but was buried in an unmarked grave.

David Coward is the author of studies of Marivaux, Marguerite Duras, Marcel Pagnol, and Restif de la Bretonne, and of a *History of French Literature*. For Oxford World's Classics he has edited eight novels by Alexandre Dumas *père* and translated Dumas *fils*'s *La Dame aux camélias*, two selections of Maupassant short stories, Sade's *Misfortunes of Virtue and Other Early Tales*, Diderot's *Jacques le Fataliste*, and Beaumarchais's *Figaro Trilogy*. Winner of the 1996 Scott-Moncrieff Prize for translation, he reviews regularly for the *Times Literary Supplement*, the *London Review of Books*, and other literary periodicals.

OXFORD WORLD'S CLASSICS

For over 100 years Oxford World's Classics have brought readers closer to the world's great literature. Now with over 700 titles—from the 4,000-year-old myths of Mesopotamia to the twentieth century's greatest novels—the series makes available lesser-known as well as celebrated writing.

The pocket-sized hardbacks of the early years contained introductions by Virginia Woolf, T. S. Eliot, Graham Greene, and other literary figures which enriched the experience of reading. Today the series is recognized for its fine scholarship and reliability in texts that span world literature, drama and poetry, religion, philosophy and politics. Each edition includes perceptive commentary and essential background information to meet the changing needs of readers.

OXFORD WORLD'S CLASSICS

THE MARQUIS DE SADE

The Crimes of Love

Heroic and Tragic Tales, Preceded by an Essay on Novels

A Selection translated with an Introduction and Notes by

DAVID COWARD

OXFORD
UNIVERSITY PRESS

OXFORD
UNIVERSITY PRESS

Great Clarendon Street, Oxford OX2 6DP

Oxford University Press is a department of the University of Oxford.
It furthers the University's objective of excellence in research, scholarship,
and education by publishing worldwide in

Oxford New York

Auckland Cape Town Dar es Salaam Hong Kong Karachi Kuala Lumpur
Madrid Melbourne Mexico City Nairobi New Delhi Shanghai Taipei Toronto

With offices in

Argentina Austria Brazil Chile Czech Republic France Greece
Guatemala Hungary Italy Japan South Korea Poland Portugal
Singapore Switzerland Thailand Turkey Ukraine Vietnam

Published in the United States
by Oxford University Press Inc., New York

First published as an Oxford World's Classics paperback 2005
Reissued 2008

British Library Cataloguing in Publication Data

Data available

Library of Congress Cataloging in Publication Data

Sade, marquis de, 1740–1814
[Crimes de l'amour. English. Selections]
The Marquis de Sade, The crimes of love: heroic and tragic tales;
preceded by an Essay on novels: a selection/translated with an introduction
and notes by David Coward.
p. cm.—(Oxford world's classics)
Includes bibliographical references.
1. Erotic literature, French. I. Title: Crimes of love. II. Coward, David.
III. Sade, marquis de, 1740–1814. Idée sur les romans. English. IV. Title.
V. Oxford world's classics (Oxford University Press)
PQ2063.S3A65213 2005 843'.6—dc22 2004026058

ISBN 978–0–19–953998–7

13

Typeset in Ehrhardt
by RefineCatch Limited, Bungay, Suffolk
Printed in Great Britain by
Clays Ltd, Elcograf S.p.A.

CONTENTS

INTRODUCTION

THE MARQUIS DE SADE spent a third of his life under lock and key. Until 1794 he was jailed for his actions. After 1802 he was imprisoned for his writings. He never believed he had done anything wrong, and blamed his unjust captivity on the prejudices of his enemies. He was, however, jailed by every political regime he lived under, monarchical, republican, and imperial, as though no form of government could tolerate his provocations and excesses.

Even before he published a word, his name was associated with cruelty and perversion. His brushes with the law were widely reported and, as they passed from pen to pen, they turned into lurid travesties of the facts. In 1788 Restif de la Bretonne offered readers of *Les Nuits de Paris* glimpses of a 'monster' who cut up women, wallowed in blood, and was Caligula and Bluebeard rolled into one. When *Justine* was published in 1791 reviewers pronounced it 'odious', 'depraved', and 'monstrous', and compared it to a poisonous mushroom which, if tasted, would prove fatal. Restif claimed to have evidence that two hundred women had already died agonizing deaths at the hands of men who had read it, and he warned the authorities that if it were ever to fall into the hands of common soldiers, the fate of a further twenty thousand would be too gruesome to contemplate. Sade tried to make *The Crimes of Love* (1800) conform to the more conservative social climate inaugurated by Napoleon, but he was arrested in 1801 and deprived permanently of his liberty. Thereafter, Church and State continued to ban his books and moralists to think of him as the ultimate threat to everything civilization stands for. Was the Marquis de Sade the wickedest man in the world?

The Life and Prisons of the Marquis de Sade

Donatien-Alphonse-François de Sade was born in Paris in 1741. His family had been noble for three centuries, not long enough perhaps to warrant the patrician arrogance with which he treated his inferiors, but the line was certainly ancient and honourable. Its roots were in Provence. One ancestor, Louis de Sade, financed the construction of the famous bridge at Avignon in 1177: the family escutcheon was inscribed under the first arch and is still visible. Another, Laure de Sade, was the muse of Petrarch, an ideal of spiritual perfection. On his mother's side he was connected to the Great Condé, one of the seventeenth century's most celebrated generals, and he was born in the Condé palace and lived there with his Condé cousin, the Prince de Bourbon, until he was four. Unfortunately, his parents did not have the wealth to match their connections. In 1744, in the absence of his father, the spendthrift, womanizing Comte de Sade, a diplomat then on a mission to Germany, his mother decided that the boy should be sent to the family estates near Avignon, where he was cared for by his grandmother, assorted aunts, and an uncle, the licentious Abbé de Sade.

In 1750 he was enrolled at the Jesuit College of Louis-le-Grand in Paris. His progress was guided by a tutor, the kindly Abbé Amblet, to whom Sade, never overburdened with parental affection, always remained close. In 1754 he entered military college at Versailles. He was appointed sub-lieutenant in an infantry regiment the following year, became captain of cavalry in 1759, and saw active service in the Seven Years War. He also acquired a reputation for wayward, lewd behaviour, to the point that his father complained that he had become 'furiously combustible'.

His parents separated in about 1752, and the family's fortunes did not improve. The outbreak of peace in 1763 dashed Sade's hopes of a military career. His father overrode his wish to marry a Mademoiselle de Lauris, to whom he was genuinely attached, and instead arranged his marriage with Renée-Pélagie de Montreuil, daughter of a wealthy but recently ennobled middle-class family. Sade obeyed reluctantly and acquired money, a wife whose social origins he despised, and a mother-in-law whom he would learn to fear and hate.

He preferred the pleasure-haunts of Paris to home, and he soon attracted attention there. In October 1763, after subjecting Jeanne Testard, a fan-maker, to a night of sado-masochistic terror and—graver still—'horrible impiety', which included the desecration of a crucifix and other religious symbols, he was hauled before the justices, who jailed him briefly at the prison-fortress at Vincennes in eastern Paris. Unrepentant, he soon resumed his bad habits and consorted openly with expensive actresses, one of whom he passed off as his wife on a visit to his chateau at La Coste in the Midi. In 1767, on the death of his father, he inherited large debts and the title of 'Comte', which he never used, preferring to style himself 'Marquis'. By this time he was well known to the men who policed the capital's buoyant vice trade. On 16 October 1767 one of them predicted the worst:

It will not be long before more is heard of the horrors perpetrated by the Comte de Sade. He is presently moving heaven and earth to persuade Mademoiselle Rivière of the Opera to live with him and has offered her 25 louis a month on the condition that the days when she is not performing on stage she will spend with him at the little house he owns at Arcueil. The lady has refused because she is currently in receipt of the attentions of Monsieur Hocquart de Coubron, but Monsieur de Sade continues to pester her. Until such time as he can overcome her resistance, he has applied persistently this week to Madame Brissault [one of Paris's leading madams] asking her to furnish him with girls he can take to supper at his little retreat. But she has refused, for she knows all too well what he is capable of. However, he has probably approached others among her colleagues who are either less scrupulous or else do not know him, and one thing is clear: it will not be long before more is heard of him.

And so it proved.

On Easter Day 1768, in the Place des Victoires, he made an approach to Rose Keller, 36, who claimed to be a widow, an unemployed cotton-spinner reduced to begging for her bread:

Monsieur de Sade . . . going alone to his residence at Arcueil near Paris, chanced upon a beggar-woman whom he took with him to his house on the pretext that out of charity he wished to add her to his household, for his service. But when she arrived, he led her into an isolated room, bound her hands and feet, and stopped up her mouth to prevent her crying out. Taking a small knife, he made a number of incisions in various parts of her body and then melted some kind of Spanish wax into the cuts. Having done this, he calmly went out to take the air, leaving the victim of his ferocity under lock and key. However, she managed to free herself and jumped from the window without adding any more injury to herself than she had already sustained. All the villagers who saw her would have massacred the Comte de Sade if he had not fled. It is thought that he has lost his reason. His family has been granted an order for him to be detained at the chateau of Saumur, and the perforated woman has withdrawn the complaint she had made in court in consideration of a sum of money.

Like most reports of the 'Arcueil Affair' published at the time, this account in the *Gazette d'Utrecht* on 26 April was not altogether accurate. Rose Keller was in all likelihood a prostitute, the ordeal lasted some hours, and involved flagellation. Sade strenuously denied having bound his victim, claimed that she had exaggerated her injuries, and said the wax he had applied to her wounds was a healing balm. He took the view that whores were paid for their pains and therefore should not complain of maltreatment which was a condition of their employment. The court disagreed and imprisoned him. He later recorded his view of the judgement in a tale which satirized the legal profession, 'Le Président mystifié' (The Mystified President). The verdict had been handed down by judges more concerned for 'the swished backside of a common tart' than for 'a young army officer who, having spent the best years of his youth in the service of his king, found no honours waiting for him except a dish of humiliation served up by the greatest enemies of the country which he had very recently defended'. Sade's view of Rose Keller and his judges was as dim as his opinion of his somewhat distant military record was bright.

He remained behind bars for seven months, first at Saumur and then at Lyons, where he received treatment for haemorrhoids, from which he would suffer for the rest of his life. On his release, he kept out of trouble, and in the autumn of 1769 travelled through the Low Countries, but on his return his attempt to relaunch his military career foundered on his scandalous reputation and he retreated to La Coste. He showed little interest in estate management, but indulged his whims and took part in amateur theatricals and other amusements. He found time to seduce his sister-in-law under his own roof and then, in the summer of 1772, found himself in very hot water indeed, as the handwritten news-sheet, the *Nouvelles à la main*, reported:

24 July 1772: News comes from a great city in Provence that at a large gathering of people which he had assembled, a man of quality, showing only contempt for the duties which every man owes to society, took the barbaric pleasure of distributing lozenges designed to inflame the senses of the most frigid temperaments. In addition to the orgiastic eruptions provoked in persons of both sexes by the administration of a mixture of such elements, a number of accidents ensued which sent several persons to their graves. . . .

19 September: Readers will recall what occurred at Marseilles and the cruel effects of the lozenges distributed by the Comte de Sade. The case against the perpetrator of this atrocity now having been heard, together with that against his valet, he has been sentenced in his absence to be decapitated and his man to be hanged and then burned. They were both tried in this affair as poisoners. This is the same Monsieur de Sade who faced criminal charges some few years ago in Paris for having lured to a house at Arcueil a destitute woman on whom he purposed to carry out experiments in dissection. His family then succeeded in applying for his transfer to the prison of Pierre-Encize at Lyons and, observing that he had apparently regained his wits and been cured of his folly, was persuaded to restore his freedom to him. It is clear from the use he has made of it how wrong they were to have counted on the recovery of his reason, for all his criminal actions can only be imputed to madness.

Both men were in fact convicted for attempted poisoning and sodomy, a capital offence. The truth, though shocking enough, was again less garish than the many similar, very damaging accounts which circulated. The occasion was a private pleasure-party involving Sade, his manservant, and four prostitutes, one of whom became extremely ill after ingesting a strong aphrodisiac. No one died. The effigies of Sade and his valet were burned by the public hangman.

The Marquis fled with his valet and his sister-in-law to Italy. Now a wanted man, he was arrested in Piedmont at the request of the French government and imprisoned at Miolans in December 1772. He made a daring escape four months later and returned to La Coste, where he resumed his active and rather expensive pleasures, interrupted occasionally by the attentions of the authorities who, though they ordered a search of his premises in 1774, mostly let him alone. The following year a new scandal broke: Sade was accused of debauching five girls at La Coste and again absconded to Italy. When he returned late in 1776 it was to a catastrophic financial situation and an angry father, a weaver, who loosed off a couple of shots at him. By then his mother was terminally ill. Sade recalled what happened next in his novel *Aline and Valcour* (letter 67), in which his hero,

> who had been in hiding for a number of years, and was foolish enough to wish to do the *decent thing* and rush off to Paris to pay his last respects to a dying mother, made post-haste to the capital despite all the dangers. He had no sooner stepped inside the dead woman's room than his wife's family ordered the arm of the law to seize him by the scruff of the neck. He complained of such treatment but was laughed at and thrown into a

cell in the Bastille, where he whiled away the time agreeably by lamenting the loss of his liberty, the death of his mother, and the stupidity of his relations.

Sade's icy reference to his family was directed principally at his mother-in-law, Madame de Montreuil, whom he had at first liked and who had consistently used her influence with his judges on his behalf. But he had used up her patience with his excesses and his extravagance, which now threatened his family with financial ruin. At the time of his arrest Renée-Pélagie at La Coste had no money to buy food or fuel. Madame de Montreuil, deciding that her son-in-law needed to be restrained, applied for a *lettre de cachet*, an authorization signed by the king for removing from circulation (by prison or banishment) a father, son, brother, or any family member whose unruly, reckless, or criminal conduct constituted a danger to his family. Her next step was to bring pressure to bear on the court at Aix, which finally agreed to quash the death penalty it had passed on him in 1772. Sade expected to be freed, but to his chagrin the *lettre de cachet* would keep him in jail for the next dozen years, first at Vincennes and then, after 29 February 1784, at the Bastille.

Sade was a demanding, uncooperative prisoner. He disregarded cautions and warnings. The governor of the Bastille considered him 'violent and extremely difficult', and the tone of the many blistering letters he wrote was not calculated to win friends. To those in power he bit his tongue, but his contempt is obvious. To Madame de Montreuil, whom he dared not offend, he grovelled imperiously. He was waggish with his valet and orgy-mate, exchanged bantering intimacies with Mademoiselle de Rousset, a family friend, and treated his steward, Gaufridy, as a scoundrel who had his hand permanently in his master's pocket. He wrote frequently to Renée-Pélagie, his long-suffering wife, and to her he was contemptuous, suspicious, cruel, grateful, occasionally tender, and sufficiently insensitive to require her to procure the materials ('prestiges' was his word for them) he required for his onanistic practices. To judge by his correspondence at this time, his dominant mood was one of barely suppressed rage. He thought of himself as a rather grand, shackled Gulliver reduced to addressing Lilliputian oafs who did not rise much above his aristocratic boot-tops.

He complained incessantly of the conditions a man of his sort was forced to endure, and demanded fresh sheets, new breeches, and other necessaries. He wrote of his ailments—his breathing, indigestion, and eye-troubles—and ordered plain, wholesome food but also quantities of meringues, lemon tarts, and chocolate which, combined with his lack of exercise, made him grow very fat indeed. Sometimes it seemed that the balance of his mind was disturbed. To extreme irascibility he added the belief that the letters he received contained signals in a mathematical code ('there was no 17^3 in your last letter') which he could never quite decipher but surely contained the date of his release. When discussing his case he rarely moved beyond the infuriating injustice of his plight, at which he picked until it bled. His prison letters show that he found it difficult to be objective, and in them, as in his novels and the stories of *The Crimes of Love*, he never moves beyond the position that punishment, whatever the crime, is unproductive, for it neither persuades the criminal to repent nor does it rehabilitate him, but merely makes him resentful. But his argument never quite escapes the charge of special pleading: when Sade asserts that the ferocity of courts and prisons merely aggravate a man's vices, he is invariably thinking of his own case.

Like other prisoners of his rank, Sade was given privileges and lived in some style, both at Vincennes and then in the cell which occupied the whole of floor 6 of the 'Liberty' tower of the Bastille. 'Monsieur le six' ordered books, kept abreast of the news, and constructed a system of ideas which explained man and the world to his own satisfaction. He also began to invent fictions which expressed his iconoclastic philosophy, and which perhaps saved his sanity. Indeed, there is nothing to suggest that Sade was made mad by imprisonment. To look beyond his numerological obsession, supercharged sexual drives, and patrician outlook is to find a man of quick intelligence, intellectual curiosity, and cruel, barbed humour. Yet Sade the prisoner never seems admirable or attractive in any way. He shows none of the resilience of Henri Latude, who spent as long in the same jails, nor is he anywhere near as appealing as Choderlos de Laclos, author of *Dangerous Liaisons*, whose prison correspondence written during the Revolution reveal a very human, vulnerable face. Sade's testy, haughty letters are chronicles of frustration and impotence.

As the decade drew to a close he observed the dramatic rise in the political temperature with a mixture of apprehension and hope. On 2 July 1789, through an improvised loud-hailer fashioned from the tin funnel he used to slop out his cell, he appealed for help to passers-by in the rue Saint-Antoine beneath his windows, saying that the guards were killing the prisoners. Two days later he was hastily transferred to the asylum for the insane run by the Brothers of Charity at Charenton, just outside the city walls. In the rush he was forced to leave behind his furniture and 'fifteen volumes of manuscripts ready for the printer', notably *The 120 Days of Sodom*, which he never saw again.

In due course the Revolution abolished the *lettre de cachet*, its victims were amnestied, and Sade was released on 2 April 1790. Renée-Pélagie, who had remained loyal while he was in prison, refused to see him and they separated for good. More surprised than hurt, he promptly began an affair with Constance Quesnet which lasted until his death. She was 30 and had a 6-year-old son by a husband who had abandoned her. The couple were happy together, and Sade was genuinely grateful for the love and affection his 'good angel from heaven' brought him. Meanwhile he continued to demand money, sometimes with menaces, from Gaufridy who managed his estates. Styling himself 'a man of letters', he also tried to make his way with his pen, and submitted a number of plays to Parisian theatre managements, but with little success. But his novel *Justine*, suitably 'spiced', he claimed, at the request of the publisher, appeared in June 1791, and he turned one of the tales of *The Crimes of Love*, 'Ernestine', into a melodrama, *Oxtiern, ou les Effets du libertinage* (*Oxtiern, or the Effects of Libertinage*). It had just two performances, for audiences found the Count too villainous by half.

Sade rejoiced at the passing of the *ancien régime* and served the Revolution in its first, moderate phase as a constitutional monarchist. He played an active role in his local revolutionary committee, becoming its secretary in 1791, led a commission which looked into hospital conditions, and once addressed the National Assembly as head of a delegation of district representatives. But his fervour for the revolution waned as extremism grew. In August 1793 he sat on a committee which vetted aristocratic families, deciding which, for associating with émigrés, were guilty of counter-revolution, a capital offence. When the names of the Montreuils appeared before him, he could have sent his hated mother-in-law to the guillotine at the stroke of his pen. Instead, he succeeded in having both her name and her husband's removed from the list. Was it a glimpse of his better nature, the action of a gentleman, or of a patrician reluctant to allow the Revolution to meddle in his private family affairs? For despite parading his patriotic credentials—he missed no opportunity to remind the authorities of his heroic role on 2 July 1789, and wrote fulsomely in praise of Marat—he was no democrat. Not for one moment did he believe that the ransacking of La Coste by the liberated peasantry was an overdue compensation for centuries of feudal tyranny. Instead, he raged at Gaufridy and called the looters 'thieves' and 'bandits'. He approved of freedom, especially his own, but for him equality was a dangerous illusion, and fraternity so much misguided balderdash. For letting his moderation show, and because both his sons had emigrated, he was arrested in December 1793. After less than three years of freedom Sade was once more a prisoner.

He was then, according to prison records, 5 foot 6 inches tall, with fair or grey hair and eyebrows, a high forehead, light-blue eyes, medium nose, small mouth, round chin, and a full face. He suffered from ailments which included gout and digestive disorders. But at least long experience enabled him to cope with the uncertainty of not knowing his fate and the hope that the Revolution had forgotten him. It remembered on 27 July 1794, when his name was called and the dreadful invitation extended for him 'to kiss Madame la Guillotine', but he did not hear the summons, for such was the general confusion that he could not be traced in any of the four prisons which had housed him. The next day Robespierre fell, the Terror ceased abruptly, and by what might seem to some an act of the Providence in which he refused to believe, Citizen Sade escaped death by an administrative error. Freed in October 1794, he lived a retiring life, battling to have his name removed from the list of émigrés, caring for Constance on the pittance Gaufridy sent him, and doing what he could to promote his literary career. No theatre manager was willing to take his plays, but *Aline and Valcour* appeared in 1795 and *Le Philosophe dans le boudoir* (*The Philosopher in the Bedroom*) the next year. *La Nouvelle Justine, ou les malheurs de la vertu, suivie de l'Histoire de Juliette sa sœur, ou les prospérités du vice* (*The New Justine, or the Misfortunes of Virtue, followed by the History of Juliette, her Sister, or the Prosperities of Vice*) went on sale, probably in 1797. In that year he returned to Provence for the first time in two decades, and found La Coste, which had been sold in 1796, a looted ruin. He returned to Paris, where he continued to exist on the brink of destitution. In 1799 he was employed at 40 sous a day as a prompter in a theatre in Versailles, where, in a revival of *Oxtiern*, he played Fabrice, the stout-hearted innkeeper who foils the wicked Count.

Les Crimes de l'amour (*The Crimes of Love*) appeared in about September 1800. Although he had taken pains to purge his tales of anything that might give offence, the book was not well received and fell foul of the strict moral climate of Napoleon's new century. In March 1801 Sade was arrested as the author of two obscene works, *Justine* and *Juliette*, and languished in prison for two years. In 1803, for making advances to newly arrived male prisoners, he was interned once more at Charenton. While the authorities insisted that he was in full possession of his mental faculties, they judged him 'incorrigibly' vulnerable to his sexual manias, which amounted to 'a permanent state of libertine dementia'. Sade would never be free again.

At Charenton he was eventually joined by Constance, who continued to care for him. In 1804 he began a new novel, *Les Journées de Florbelle ou la Nature dévoilée* (*The Days of Florbelle, or Nature Unveiled*). The completed manuscript was seized by the police in 1807 and destroyed after his death. Until 1808 he was allowed to organize theatrical productions for the asylum inmates, which were also attended by members of fashionable Parisian society. Many applications for his release were made, but the authorities were immovable. His conduct did not change, but he became increasingly withdrawn: 'morose' was the word used by the few who visited the 'monster of depravity'. Nor did he stop writing, and took readily to the new fashion for historical novels. In 1812 he wrote *Adelaïde de Brunswick*, and in 1813 completed *Isabelle de Bavière* and published *La Marquise de Ganges*. Since 1811, despite his declining health, he had been receiving private visits from the 16-year-old daughter of a nurse who worked in the infirmary. He paid her for the last time on 27 November 1814, and died on 2 December at the age of 72. He had spent more than a quarter-of-a-century in captivity. Against the express instruction of his last will and testament, a mass was said for his soul and he was interred in the cemetery of the asylum at Charenton. Another wish, however, was respected: his family was only too happy to grant his request that 'all trace of my burial place shall disappear from the surface of the earth'. No name was engraved on his headstone.

The Wickedest Man in the World?

On 18 January 1766 the police were summoned to an incident in the Place des Victoires, where a gentleman was in dispute with a public coachman who had temporarily barred the way of his cabriolet. The gentleman, identified as the Marquis de Sade, had leaped down in a rage and set about the stationary horses with such violence that he snapped his sword, the broken end remaining in the belly of one of them. The justices accepted the arrangement whereby Sade paid the coachman 24 livres in final settlement.

Such incidents were not uncommon in eighteenth-century Paris, where the sword-carrying sons of the nobility drove recklessly through crowded streets and their elders ordered their coachmen to take their whip to anyone who got in their way. Nor was Sade's sexual behaviour unique or exceptional. The Duc de Richelieu, one of the great rakes of the age, once burned down a house to get at a woman who had refused his advances. As his revenge on a prostitute who had given him a venereal infection, one aristocrat inserted a bellows into her orifices and blew until she expired. In the 1760s police agents kept an eye on the activities of great gentlemen prepared to ruin themselves for a dancer, watched clerics of every rank who frequented the stews of Paris (Sade's uncle, the abbé, was one of them), and chronicled a wide range of sexual practices, which included the then fashionable vice of flagellation which, as one report commented, consumed more broom handles in the Paris area than were strictly required for cleaning purposes.

There is enough evidence to suggest that, for his mistreatment of Rose Keller, Sade was punished not for what he had done but for what he represented. His sentence was exemplary, designed as a warning to others like him not to overstep the tolerated limits. Sade was chosen, it has been suggested, because as an outsider, and not part of the regular company of libertines, he was more expendable than most. The 1772 verdict has also been shown to be less clear-cut than it seemed. Sade's trial was a skirmish in the wider political battle between the aristocracy, of which he was a member, and the lawyers of the *parlement* at Aix, representatives of the new nobility of law and commerce. Moreover, there was some truth in his belief that the attempts made by his mother-in-law, over-fearful for the good name and finances of the family, to save him from his excesses amounted to a form of persecution.

Yet in truth, Madame de Montreuil was less to blame than he imagined. When he had served two years at Vincennes, a family friend, Mademoiselle de Rousset, instituted discreet enquiries in Paris with a view to securing his early release. There she discovered the existence of an official file containing 'certain particulars which I believed were known to a few persons only', together with 'many other things which must remain shrouded in the deepest silence'. True or false, the contents of the dossier were so damaging that it was unlikely that any minister would ever recommend an early suspension of the *lettre de cachet* under which Sade was detained. She never told the Marquis of her discovery, which would have made him despair.

Sensationalized reporting, secret files, and the official determination to protect the public all helped to justify Sade's belief that he was treated badly by his judges and keepers. Was incarceration *sine die* a just punishment for 'indiscretions' indistinguishable from those committed routinely by his peers? He claimed he was a victim of the scandalous *lettre de cachet*, protested that his so-called 'crimes' were at most minor misdemeanours, and portrayed himself as a scapegoat for a society which preached virtue but practised vice. To Renée-Pélagie, on 20 February 1781, he wrote refuting the 'slanders' levelled at him and set out his defence: 'Yes, I admit I am a libertine. I have imagined everything that is capable of being imagined in that line—but I have most certainly not done everything I have imagined, nor ever will. I am a libertine, but I am neither a criminal nor a murderer.' In his favour, it should also be said that he never attempted to exploit the chaos of the revolution, when the breakdown of law and order gave free rein to 'sadists' high and low. On the contrary, he lived quietly throughout this period with a woman who clearly found him to possess qualities she admired and loved.

But it is a thin defence. To be capable of imagining such gruesome excesses is damning enough, but to admit to committing even some of those that he did imagine is sufficient to classify Sade as a dangerous sex offender. Various attempts have been made to analyse his compulsions, the diagnoses including a type of autism (his perception of other people not as sentient beings but as objects), and a frustrated Oedipal complex which made him particularly aggressive towards women. He has also been seen as a case of arrested adolescence; the symptoms include his tantrum-like defiance of authority, the incandescent rages exhibited not only in his novels but in his correspondence, and his regular threats to kill himself if he could not have his way. Readers suspicious of amateur psychology might prefer to think of him more simply as the most complete and callous snob. He looked down not only on whores and cab-drivers, but also on those, like Sartines, lieutenant of police, or Launay, governor of the Bastille, who had the power to give him orders but lacked the appropriate number of quarterings in their escutcheon. His patrician attitudes made it impossible for him to be a genuine convert to the revolution or to embrace any democratic vision of society. He never believed that his actions were really crimes, and attributed his continuing misfortunes to the 'prejudices of fools' and the vindictiveness of his enemies.

Sade was not, of course, the wickedest man in the world; his crimes are small indeed when set against those of Hitler or Stalin. But neither should he be seen as a symbol of resistance to injustice, a prisoner of conscience, a martyr persecuted for his commitment to free thought. He remains nevertheless a significant figure in the history of literature, ideas, and human psychology. Despite the relish with which he catalogued the horrors he imagined, he remained a lucid observer of himself. He was clearly aware of his nature, and possessed the singular ability to re-create its excesses in disciplined literary forms. The result forces us to look unflinchingly at human evil, the cruel impulses which drive the serial killer, the torturer, the terrorist, the dictator, the soldier with the power of life and death over the defeated enemy. Sade mapped the darkest areas of the human psyche with a completeness that has never been matched. It is in this sense that he could write, with justification, to his wife: 'I am a philosopher . . .'

'I am a philosopher . . .'

Sade's intellectual interests and literary pursuits pre-dated his incarceration in 1777. He once hinted that in the late 1760s he had a play staged in Bordeaux and had published—for money—two *libertin* novels, but none of these texts has been identified. At La Coste in 1772 he acted in a play, also lost, which he had written. On the other hand, a brief account of his travels in the Netherlands in 1769 and his well observed *Voyage d'Italie*, written in 1776, provide firm evidence of his long-standing literary interests. But it was in prison that he began to explore ideas and write in earnest. In 1782 he completed the 'Dialogue entre un prêtre et un moribond' ('Dialogue Between a Priest and a Dying Man'), which derided belief in God, and began *Les Cent-vingt journées de Sodome* (*The 120 Days of Sodom*), the most concentratedly gruesome of all his books. His prison years produced tragedies and comedies, a novel (*Aline and Valcour*), and all the short fiction he ever wrote. After his release from Charenton in 1790 he continued to write, and by his death had produced a dozen novels, most of them immensely long and rambling, fifty tales, and twenty plays, of which only one was performed.

Apart from the 'philosophical' *Aline and Valcour*, which contrasts utopia with dystopia, Sade's most famous novels show virtue, in the person of naive, god-fearing young women, tested to destruction by figures of unremitting evil, represented by a mixed cast of merciless and perverse aristocrats, churchmen, bawds, surgeons, and bandits all committed to sacrificing goodness to their insatiable sexual appetites. The action is intermittent and repetitive and the obscenity quickly becomes tedious. Plots are arranged to maximize the opportunities for fastidiously described scenes of torment and perversion, which bludgeon his martyred heroines (and the reader) into submission. At frequent intervals the horror stops and Sade inserts tirades into the mouths of his rapists and torturers who, warming to their theme in their rage and exultation, may express themselves in the crudest language. Through them he denounces God, the Church, and the law, and demolishes the taboos and moral restraints which are generally thought to raise human beings above the beasts of the field. At one level the novels were therapy for the prisoner, the imaginative outlet for the fierce sexual drives of a serial fantasist. At another, they constitute a coherent system of thought.

Sade was not a conceptual philosopher but rather a *philosophe*, an Enlightenment intellectual more committed to putting the discoveries of others to progressive use than in finding out new truths of his own. By the 1780s the 'philosophic' movement had built a strong rational case against both the 'superstition' that was religion and the political system to which it had given rise. Whole populations had been duped and enslaved by priests and governments. Yet even the most libertarian *philosophe* remained wary of liberty, and shared the view of both Church and State that human nature was not fit to be let off the leash. They believed that no society can function without laws to curb the basic human instincts and urges, always dangerous if unchecked. All social organization is, in this sense, a necessary unfreedom. When Voltaire remarked that if God did not exist He would have to be invented, he meant that the notion of a God who rewarded the good and punished the wicked was extremely useful to those charged with keeping unruly spirits in check. Like all liberation ideologies, eighteenth-century *philosophie* was an invitation to exchange one set of rules for another.

Sade begged to differ—he simply abolished all the rules. His starting point was his study of the life scientists and atheistical materialists who had begun the historical process of replacing religion by science as the key to our understanding of the world. He accepted their argument that what Christians called the Creation was an invention of self-serving priests, for the existence and contents of the universe are easily explained in non-transcendental terms. There is only one substance: gross matter. Evidence for the existence of atoms and molecules is abundant, but there is no trace of spirit or soul or any supernatural power. Matter exists, has certain properties, and is shaped into protean forms by physical laws through a constant process of decay and renewal. These natural forces account fully for the so-called 'creation' and make God redundant. The universe is indifferent to everything save its own flux and continuity, a never-ending, blind cycle of change, decay, and rebirth. In it, human beings have no privileged status but are subject to the same natural imperatives as all other material forms.

Sade was not the first to replace God by Nature, but no one else had ever been prepared to follow the argument to its logical conclusion: the law of the jungle. Sade, never a man for half measures, developed an uncompromising view of nature which dispensed with man's feeble rules. He abolished God, morality, and society and put natural law in their place. Since nature is the only power in the universe, everything that is and happens must be a requirement or a product of its processes. All our thoughts, actions, and desires are therefore natural for the reason that we think, perform, and feel them. They are the consequence of the physical arrangement of molecules of which we are composed: the self is the sum of our parts. Any attempt to control the workings of the self is by definition anti-natural. Theologians, moral philosophers, and legislators have therefore no business to tell us what to think, do, and want, for any attempt to promote 'civilized' values constitutes an unwarranted interference in the ways of nature. Jean-Jacques Rousseau, for example, was wrong to attempt to correct inequality, for we are all born different: inequality is part of nature's grand design and must not be touched. Similarly, philanthropists must not extend a helping hand to life's inadequates who, on the contrary, should be allowed to sink since they cannot swim. Do runts in the litter or the weakest of the pack survive?

It follows that society, with its rules and prohibitions, is a perversion of the natural order, for it not only constrains but criminalizes the instincts by which nature operates through us. Civilization is a conspiracy of the weak, who invented religion, morality, law, and love, to shackle the strong. In so doing they have meddled with the necessary indifference of nature which they name Evil, and to it have preferred the Good, which is an illusion. Priests invented Providence, moralists Virtue, philosophers Progress. Only Sade accepted that the universe is both eternal and infernal, and that the domination of the weak by the strong is nature's way. God is dead and each man, the sum of his natural urges, must be free to do whatever he can for as long as he can. He will seek pleasure and flee pain, and shall not be stopped in his rightful course by laws or misguided charity. Whereas tolerance is the virtue of the weak, the Sadean hero will thrive on murder, robbery, rape, sodomy, prostitution, matricide, and incest, ignoring all taboos and interdicts. He will be prevented only when outperformed by a stronger competitor, who will enslave him in turn.

The argument is hardly watertight. If all we do, think, and desire is legitimized by nature, then love, consideration for others, and selfless idealism are instincts no less natural than our most basic urges. And if a majority of 'weaklings' succeeds in creating a framework of equitable laws to tame the 'strong', then the society they create must also be natural, since it exists. The 'love' which impels Sade's tormentors to commit the 'crimes' he recounts in these stories is amputated of tenderness and entirely detached from the kindlier face of humanity. Even he at times recognized its aberrant pathology as a 'disorder of the imagination', a flaw which cannot be corrected (p. 239). His philosophy, therefore, hardly reflects the whole of human nature, but rather a personality deficient in its affective motors and compounded by arrogance of caste and male prejudice.

The Sade who chronicled the drives of raw, compulsive sexuality was exploring uncharted and very modern terrain. It was with some justification, therefore, that in 1788 he claimed that he was working 'in a completely original vein': 'from start to finish, vice triumphs and virtue is utterly humiliated . . .'

'A completely original vein . . .'

After 1789 literature, for long a central plank in the culture of the *ancien régime*, was annexed by the revolution. But while poetry turned into satirical verse and the theatre was appropriated for propaganda purposes, fiction, at a time when publishers had as little money to invest as readers had leisure to read, went through a lean period. But some kinds of novel remained viable, and after 1794 the market began to recover.

Novels of sentiment, often autobiographical, shed tears for broken lives, while women's fiction, already strong before 1789, continued to evoke the roses and thorns of love and the constraints of marriage. The sensational stories of the emerging market-leaders, Pigault-Lebrun and Ducray-Duminil, took their cue from the new melodramas playing in the Boulevard theatres, which showed widows and orphans at the mercy of convicts and misers, and reflected the violence of a decade of revolution. Nightmarish fantasies and dark deeds were perpetrated in the *roman noir*, or French 'gothic', which renewed a vein of writing dating back to the sixteenth century, styled *sombre* and *baroque*, which traded in horror and cruelty. It suited the bloodthirsty times and was influenced by atmospheric English models, notably Ann Radcliffe's *The Mysteries of Udolpho* (1794; trans. 1797), and *The Monk* (1794; trans. 1797), Matthew Lewis's 'terrifying' novel of Ambrosio who breaks his holy vow of continence with murderous consequences. Meanwhile the subversive *roman libertin*, more distinctively French, continued to thrive. The half-dozen very long books which Sade published between 1791 and 1797 made him the most productive of the pornographic authors who prospered in the favourable climate of violence and lawlessness, but unlike his rivals he did not set out to titillate for money: he had ideas to communicate, and he worked from a highly original theory of literature.

It is perhaps not surprising that the times were not conducive to serious reflection on the form and nature of fiction. The topic was not entirely neglected, however. Madame de Staël published an *Essai sur les fictions* in 1795 in which she divided fiction into three distinct types. 'Marvellous' and allegorical stories show the 'prodigious' exploits of superheroes, and illustrate abstract qualities like valour or heroism rather than the workings of individual human hearts. 'Historical' fictions show public, not private lives, and are therefore unrevealing about the working of personality. Only the third type, described as 'inventions based on truth', meets her criteria for the 'usefulness of fiction'. It deals not with ideas but with 'private life', and is concerned with ordinary human responses to familiar situations. Such fictions, 'where nothing is true and everything is true-seeming', illustrate human psychology in action and present virtue in the best possible light. By showing the behaviour of good people, they will teach the reader to love goodness; by showing the effects of crimes, they will inspire hatred of crime. Writing at around the turn of the century, the cosmopolitan Prince de Ligne based his own *Contes immoraux* (*Immoral Tales*, 1815) on real experience as observed by himself or reliable witnesses, deeming the exceptional and the fantastic to be vulgar. 'Monsters', he wrote, 'are for fairs'. In his first tale he has Satan remark that one of his faithful had sent him *Justine*, which he found too shocking to read, though in general he approved of novels which, while purporting to promote virtue, showed vice in action. But the staple narrative ploys of French fiction bored the Prince: intercepted letters, a misunderstanding, a shady bower, moonlight, a secret wedding, 'a handful of trite thoughts, a cartful of fine phrases, and very little happening'. His own tales, though, prove to be static conversation pieces which give generous space to the satire of manners.

Sade's views are altogether more interesting, for they reject the moral vocation of literature favoured by Madame de Staël and the winking naughtiness practised by the Prince de Ligne. At the Bastille he developed a cogent theory of fiction which he expressed in a 'draft Foreword' to a collection of tales planned in 1788 to alternate 'sombre' and 'facetious' registers (see Appendix I). He accepted that authors should 'conform to the tone and style of the age' in which they live, and accordingly, like both de Staël and de Ligne, preferred the 'true-seeming' to the true. But he did not share the former's interest in the full range of human passions, nor did he settle for the Prince's amused reportage of libertine manners. The writer's aim must be to capture nature, not serve morality, and Sade insisted that nature's truth was not to be subordinated to the artificial requirement that virtue be rewarded and vice punished. On the contrary, virtue was to be treated roughly and made to face terrifying threats, for only then would the reader be sufficiently involved to learn real lessons.

A dozen years later the 'Essay on Novels', published as a kind of preface to *The Crimes of Love*, sets out views which, though substantially the same, are considerably more sophisticated. Sade's survey of the genre from the earliest times reveals that the leaders and saviours of nations were first turned into heroes of fact before becoming heroes of legend. But history and myth do not satisfy the appetite for stories, which is born of a need to pray and a need to love. Stories in the 'praying' category are written out of fear and hope, and are no strangers to fantasy and wild imagination in their attempts to show man's relationship to the gods and cosmic powers which direct his life. The second kind are closer to the existential world. They show society as it is, and reveal the inner truth about people which is normally kept masked.

Having thus defined the usefulness of fiction in general as its unique ability to give readers an understanding of the universe and of themselves, Sade proceeds to identify different approaches adopted in the past by novelists to capture the truth, stating his unequivocal admiration for Rousseau's 'sublime' *Nouvelle Héloïse*, for the novels of Richardson and Fielding who wrote so accurately of the human heart, 'one of nature's most intricate labyrinths', and above all for Prévost, who 'invented the novel'—a master of his craft, an orchestrator of complex themes, a writer at ease in registers which range from the human passions to horror and the sublime.

The aspiring author must understand at the outset that writing is a calling, not a profession. It demands a deep understanding of the human heart, which is acquired by 'suffering and travel' and by listening, not speaking, when in company. As part of the crucial business of being 'true-seeming', documentary research may be needed—a very modern thought, expressed half-a-century before the Realists acted upon it. The novelist's imagination must strive to capture nature, not to defend virtue or promote a moral cause. Any moralizing should be placed in the mouths of the characters, not spoken by the author, whose major concern, on the contrary, must be to show virtue sorely tested. In his response to the critic Villeterque (reprinted here in Appendix II), Sade insists that the triumph of virtue, which had become a requirement of the genre, is dull, unrealistic, and ineffective, whereas to show virtue under duress provokes terror and pity, prompting indignation and tears which are as beneficial as the 'purging' catharsis Aristotle claimed as the purpose of tragedy.

Sade's reflections on the art of the novel are well-considered and more ambitious than those of his contemporaries. Urging 'boldness of invention', abandoning the assumption that literature meant showing virtue triumphant and vice defeated, jettisoning the episodic structure of fiction and replacing it with the concept of organic, unified form, Sade pointed the way ahead and set himself apart from novelists whose jaded imagination and lack of originality doomed them to repeat themselves and remain locked in their own times.

The Crimes of Love

Short tales had been popular in the thirteenth century, when the *fabliau* had turned a jaundiced, bawdy eye on human relationships. By the Renaissance more sophisticated varieties had become fashionable in the wake of Boccaccio and his imitators, and interest in the form revived after 1650 with the adoption of the model supplied by Cervantes's *Exemplary Tales* (1613). By the 1670s the longer *nouvelle* was becoming a major vehicle for the dissection of sentiment and it marked the beginning of the enduring French fascination with psychological analysis. Although Sade never wrote tales of sentimental love or 'gallant' amours, and while he despised the 'moral' tale made fashionable in the 1760s by Marmontel, his own short stories fit squarely into traditional categories. Posing as 'the French Boccaccio', he wrote bawdy *fabliaux* and 'facetious' *historiettes*, but his longer tales followed convention too. They were not only 'heroic and 'tragic', as the subtitle of *The Crimes of Love* describes them, but also 'historical' and 'modern', while 'Rodrigo' succeeds in being at once 'fantastic', 'allegorical', 'oriental', and 'philosophical'. Some purport to be 'national' (variously 'English', 'Italian', 'Swedish'), while a number drew on the old *genre sombre*.

This last had been most recently revived by Baculard d'Arnaud, author of *Les Épreuves du sentiment* (*The Ordeals of Sentiment*, 1772–80), a collection of tales of gore and horror which the 'Essay' commends almost as enthusiastically as Prévost's melodramatic *Clèveland*. From the outset Sade's imagination, darkened by his years as a prisoner, had been drawn to the dreadful, the sepulchral, and the cruel, as *The 120 Days of Sodom*, begun in 1782, makes abundantly clear. He had found his voice a decade before the English 'romance of terror' helped sensationalize French fiction in the 1790s. In the 'Essay on Novels' he denounces the use of ghosts and phantoms, since the supernatural was a child of superstition, which needed no encouragement. He was more impressed by Lewis's *The Monk* which showed decency and humanity sacrificed to the satisfaction of sexual appetite, a theme closer to his own preoccupations. He certainly exploited the tropes of the *roman noir* (bloodied corpses, sombre chapels, flickering candles, banditti) for their dramatic value. But if labels are to be attached to Sade, he was more baroque than gothic.

He claimed with a flourish that his approach was original: 'plots, narrative style, incidents, everything is of our own devising.' It is a boast better vindicated in these tales than in his longer and much less disciplined fiction. His young heroes, for example, might seem at first sight to be conventional types: Monrevel is valiant and chivalrous, Herman is a sensitive romantic hero, while Valmont, like his namesake in Laclos's *Dangerous Liaisons*, is a rake who falls in love. Sade's leading ladies also seem familiar: Mademoiselle Faxelange and Amélie de Sancerre, like Eugénie's mother, are sisters to any number of well-brought-up fictional heroines. But Sade does not rescue them from danger, reward them with marriage, and hold them up for our admiration. Instead, he shows how ill-equipped they are to deal with real evil. A few are made of sterner stuff: Gué gets the better of Franlo, while Henrietta Stralson, Ernestine, and Monrevel put up enough of a fight to earn our respect—but only at a terrible price. Sade's greatest originality was in redesigning the traditional villain, creating characters of both sexes who are unremittingly cruel and recognize no limitations to the realization of their desires. Franlo and Oxtiern, Franval and Rodrigo, the Countess of Sancerre and Eugénie (both darker by far than that other figure of evil in skirts, Laclos's Madame de Merteuil) obey no law but their own *realpolitik*, and they operate through lies, deception, and brute force. Winning, not honour, is their goal. They are not without psychological complexity: Franlo is a man of violence but he never ceases to be a gentleman, and he loves Faxelange truly. Oxtiern and Franval go from absolute villainy to absolute despair, while the Countess de Sancerre lives to mourn her crimes in a convent. Sade knew from the inside what it felt like to be both persecutor and victim, and his ability to empathize with both explains the depth he manages to give predators like Franlo or Rodrigo, who are cruelly, heroically, suicidally committed to desires which drive them as mercilessly as they drive their victims.

As to plot and incident, the crimes Sade devised for love to commit are kidnapping, fraud, deception, and murder, all tame ploys when set beside the horrible torments and grisly eviscerations which punctuate his novels. But if there is less wild invention here, the use he makes of incest as a dramatic subject tests his self-imposed discipline to the limit. Incest was a topic which fascinated his times: the *philosophes* had discussed it freely, and the frisson it produced had long made it popular in the theatre and the novel, where it had become a commonplace with authors desperate for a sensational twist to give their plot. They were happy to tease, allowing siblings, or children and parents, to love in ignorance of their true identities; but once the awful truth was revealed or one of the sinning parties died, the relationship ended and the danger disappeared. With Sade no hold is barred: Florville sleeps with her brother, son, and father. Franval and Eugénie reject all arguments against their mutual attraction, and to defend it reject the common decencies. But whether it is a cruel jest by fate or a driving motor of extreme behaviour, incest is used by Sade to show virtue under pressure from real danger and not from the trite threats of convention.

Sade's subtitle promises 'tales heroic and tragic'. From the author of *Justine* this is an earnest of his intentions, a pledge of good behaviour. His style is measured, and the sadism on offer is entirely psychological. There is no more physical violence than in the average adventure novel of the time, no overtly erotic acts, no hint of lewdness or bawdy humour. Instead of pictures of torture, he shows the psychological impact of sadism. He shows death, but not violent dying. He focuses on the reactions of Faxelange as she watches the prisoners being killed beneath her window, on Ernestine's feelings as she sees Herman executed, on the despair of Henrietta Stralson who is confronted by Williams's corpse. Such characters are 'heroic' but also 'tragic', for crime triumphs more often than not: of the eleven tales in the collection, only three end without the sacrifice of virtue. But the defeat of the good does not mean the victory of the bad. Franlo and Rodrigo are admirably defiant, but they die nonetheless. Oxtiern and Franval are defeated, but are redeemed by remorse. It is as if the true villain of the piece is always Love, not these heartless lovers: the predators are doomed, for they are ruled by their urges; and those they prey upon are condemned, for they cannot abandon the virtues which make them weak. Florville commits multiple crimes unwittingly, through no fault of her own. But the dark deeds committed by Granwel, Franval, and the Countess of Sancerre, though deliberate, are inspired by drives which seem the equivalent of some remorseless, physiological destiny over which they have no control. Who, then, shall we weep for? Florville, whose crimes are involuntary? Or Eugénie de Franval, who chooses with relish what Florville regards with horror? Sade insists that more is involved than the banal truth that love can bring both joy and regret. By divorcing 'love' from sentiment and redefining it as lust, he shows that the good and the bad are equally doomed, for to be human is to be a victim. Sade did not merely break with literary practice by showing 'virtue crushed by vice'. He reconnected with tragedy, as Racine had understood it.

Sade's tales move in time and space and reveal that the crimes of love are eternal and universal. In literary terms they are not without weaknesses. Certain narrative ploys are repeated (both Ernestine and Amélie are sent to their deaths in disguise), and all the tales spring from one basic situation, a plot laid against the innocent, which is sometimes even the same plot—'Lorenza and Antonio' is a doublet of 'The Countess of Sancerre'. But they are carefully controlled, and written with skills more usually associated with a dramatist. It is not surprising that some were turned into plays, for Sade proves to have a sharp ear for dialogue, excellent dramatic timing, and an ability to create suspense. Sometimes he strikes openly theatrical notes. His villains play roles, Amélie is persuaded to act out a scenario devised by her mother, and much is made of the moment when the mask drops and reveals the foulness beneath. Gestures and appearance are captured in neat stage directions, and much of the writing (the picture of Herman in prison, for example) is vivid and highly visual. Judicious use of décors borrowed from the *roman noir* create an atmosphere to match the suspense which, in large part, derives from the difficulty we have in believing that Granwel, Sancerre, or Oxtiern can *really* be as wicked as they threaten to be: will they carry out the threats they have made? Ultimately it is Sade's ability to convince us that they will indeed stop at nothing which gives these stories their power and makes us confront his utterly bleak assessment of the human condition.

Sade's Legacy

Although Villeterque, a dyed-in-the-wool puritan, savaged *The Crimes of Love* (see Appendix II), the *Journal de Paris* (28 October 1800) somewhat nervously commended the collection's deft use of history and the anonymous author's 'fertile imagination' which created 'a wide variety' of tales. But by this time Sade's reputation was such that it seemed he would never thereafter get a fair hearing.

After his death both Church and State silenced Sade's alarming voice by banning his books. Progressive spirits (Flaubert and Baudelaire among them) admired his gleeful demolition of society's moral, sexual, and social assumptions, though, and by 1900 he had begun to interest the new breed of psychologists, who were the first to edit his unpublished manuscripts. In 1909 the poet Guillaume Apollinaire called Sade 'the freest spirit that ever lived', and prophesied that his legacy would dominate the twentieth century, and indeed Sade's reputation has continued to grow since then. For the Surrealists his life and work were exemplary, for had he not liberated himself totally from the shackles of convention? They claimed he had fought for absolute justice and absolute equality, and said he had restored the vital force of primitive instinct and original sin to over-civilized, over-regulated modern man. After 1945 Sade became the embodiment of existentialist revolt. To the structuralists and post-structuralists of the next generation he symbolized transgression, the highest value of the age. His books became legally available once more during the permissive sixties and since then for publishers, advertisers, and film-makers he has become a name, a brand, short-hand for a product which never loses its allure or market. A bogey-man for the conservatively minded, 'the Divine Marquis' continues to be claimed by progressive intellectuals as the prophet of nature, the man who killed God, the apostle of freedom, the opponent of constraint, and the ultimate, most uncompromising defender of the rights of the self against the conspiracies which are morality and convention . . .

Yet this liberationist Sade is not easily identifiable with the author of books whose notoriety goes on being greater than their reader-ship. The stories of *The Crimes of Love*, though sedate by the standard of his novels, are bleak enough to show that the devout Sadean is not free at all. The strong are as absolutely constrained by Nature as the weak whom they despise. They are incapable of feeling anything but hate, rage, and lust. Closed to affection and tenderness, they have no free will, only urges; nor do they know desire, but only cravings which must be placated through a constantly repeated mechanical process of stimulation and sensation. There is temporary relief but no peace, for appetite is insatiable. There is no happiness, only fleet-ing exultation, perpetual dissatisfaction, an urgent need to begin again and the compulsion to increase the dose. The true condition of the Sadean hero is not freedom at all but the rage born of permanent frustration. Worst of all, it is not a lifestyle choice, but a curse. From the Chateau de Vincennes in 1782 Sade wrote to his wife explaining that 'the singularity of my pleasures' was a constitutional matter and beyond his control: 'We are no more capable of cultivating a particu-lar preference in such things than we are of standing ramrod straight if we were born with a hump, no more able to adopt this or that opinion as our creed than a man born with brown hair to become a redhead. That is my eternal philosophy, and I shall never change my mind.' And so, having survived the twentieth century as its 'freest spirit', the Marquis de Sade marches into the twenty-first, still ahead of the game, as sponsor of the gene for the modern form of that fate which we are no more able to avoid than Phèdre could elude Venus or Oedipus escape the cruelty of his gods.

NOTE ON THE TEXT

The first reference to Sade's stories is to be found in a provisional table of contents (Bibliothèque de l'Arsenal, ms 12456, *folio* 681) for an untitled two-volume collection of twenty tales, which included 'Miss Henriette Stralson, or the Effects of despair', 'The Countess of Sancerre', and 'Rodrigo, or The Enchanted Tower'. The same document, using some of these tales plus six others, draws up an alternative classification by subject—incest (6), sodomy (8), flagellation (5)—and notes that 'about six' have a 'dénouement de lumière', by which is meant a melodramatic climax or possibly an ending which suggested some philosophical idea or striking insight. Among these were 'Le Fatalisme', the original title of 'Florville and Courval', and 'Le Rival de son fils', which is probably 'Lorenza and Antonio'. The manuscript is not dated. However, in a letter of 15 January 1787 Sade asked his wife for information concerning 'Rodrigo', which was already written in 'fifteen or twenty pages'. This suggests that some at least of his tales had been composed by that time.

Another manuscript (BN. nouv. acq. fr., 4010), made up of twenty notebooks, contains, with the exception of 'Rodrigo', all the tales Sade had completed to date. To the titles mentioned in the earlier manuscript which would eventually appear in *The Crimes of Love* were now added the remaining six: 'Le Mariage trompeur' (the first title of 'Faxelange'), 'Dorgeville', 'The Double Test', 'Ernestine', 'Eugénie de Franval', and 'Juliette and Raunai'.

A third note mentions plans for a work to be entitled *Contes et fabliaux du XVIIIe siècle par un Troubadour provençal* (*Tales and Fabliaux of the Eighteenth Century by a Provençal Troubadour*). It was to contain a 'Foreword' (see Appendix I) and comprise thirty stories, sufficient to fill four volumes, each to be illustrated by an engraving. They would be so disposed as to alternate between the sombre and tragic on the one hand, and the light and even bawdy on the other. In the same note Sade recorded his intention to include a further sixteen shorter tales in a separate work, *Le Portefeuille d'un homme de lettres* (*The Portfolio of a Man of Letters*), which would also contain a number of historical and philosophical essays. Excluded from these plans were two tales which never proceeded beyond brief outlines, and a further eleven which have disappeared. In all, Sade completed about fifty tales, some little more than anecdotes and others having the dimensions of a novella (the longest, 'The Misfortunes of Virtue', provided the impetus for the two published versions of *Justine*). All these stories were written between 1786 and 1 October 1788, when he compiled a catalogue of his works. Sade's annotations of his manuscripts sometimes indicate the origin of his stories ('me', 'Amblet' (his old tutor), 'heard tell of it', 'my father', etc.), and sometimes supply dates of composition and revision.

Despite having compiled an imposing portfolio of work, Sade made no attempt to publish anything while he was a prisoner. But on his release from Charenton in 1790 he resolved to make his way as 'a man of letters' and began by exploiting what he had already written in prison, including about 'thirty acts' of plays which he tried to persuade reluctant theatre managers to stage. He also used 'Ernestine', his 'Swedish' tale, as the basis for *Oxtiern, or the Effects of Libertinage*, a melodrama performed twice with only modest success on 22 October and 6 November 1791. 'Rodrigo' found its way into *Aline and Valcour* (letter 38), where it inspired another 'Spanish' tale, 'Le Crime du sentiment, ou les Délires de l'amour' ('The Crime of Sentiment, or the Frenzies of Love'). It was also the starting point for a play entitled *La Tour enchantée* (*The Enchanted Tower*), which ended as a one-act *opéra-comique*, *La Tour mystérieuse* (*The Mysterious Tower*), of which Constance Quesnet deposited a copy at the Théâtre de l'Odéon in 1814 shortly before Sade's death.

But it was not until 1800 that Sade decided to collect the best of his tales into a book, which he prefaced with his 'Essay on Novels'. He made only minor revisions, some to emphasize his 'republican' sympathies, and others to modify a certain frankness of expression, principally in 'Eugénie de Franval', from which he omitted Eugénie's seduction by her father and the display of her charms to Valmont. More importantly, he dropped the subtitle 'ou les Délires des passions' from the collection, and opted instead to describe the tales simply as 'heroic and tragic', the better to respect the strict moral climate of the new century. The only collection of Sade's short fiction to be published during his lifetime was advertised in the *Journal Typographique et Bibliographique* of 8 July 1800 and published, in four volumes, probably in September, as: '*Les Crimes de l'amour. Nouvelles héroïques et tragiques, précédées d'une 'Idée sur les romans', et ornés de gravures, par D. A. F Sade, auteur d''Aline et Valcour'*, Paris, Massé, an VIII (1800).'

To each volume's title page was added an epigraph from Letourneur's prose translation (1769) of Edward Young's *Night Thoughts* (1742–5). The eleven tales were arranged as follows:

Volume I: 'Idée sur les romans'; 'Juliette et Raunai, ou la Conspiration d'Amboise, nouvelle historique'; 'La Double Épreuve'.

Volume II: 'Miss Henriette Stralson, ou Les Effets du Désespoir, nouvelle anglaise'; 'Faxelange, ou Les Torts de l'Ambition'; 'Florville et Courval, ou Le Fatalisme'.

Volume III: 'Rodrigue, ou La Tour Enchantée, conte allégorique'; 'Laurence et Antonio, nouvelle italienne'; 'Ernestine, nouvelle suédoise'.

Volume IV: 'Dorgeville, ou Le Criminel par Vertu'; 'La Comtesse de Sancerre, anecdote de la cour de Bourgogne'; 'Eugénie de Franval, nouvelle tragique'.

These stories, together with all Sade's surviving short fiction, were published by Maurice Heine in his edition of the complete *Histoires, contes et fabliaux* of 1926. *Les Crimes de l'amour* was also reprinted unabridged in Volume 10 of Sade's *Oeuvres complètes* (1966–7), which has been used to make this translation.

The present selection retains the 'Essay on Novels', which draws attention to Sade's literary preoccupations, and seven of the original eleven stories. Sade himself commended 'Ernestine', and remarked that no novel or short story depicted 'the escalations and miseries of libertinage' more effectively than 'Eugénie de Franval'. There was also a strong case for including both 'Faxelange' and 'Florville and Courval', and for preferring the latter to its shorter doublet, 'Dorgeville'. 'The Comtesse de Sancerre' is a more concentrated version of the theme which is treated at a more leisurely pace in 'Lorenza and Antonio'. 'Rodrigo' is included as Sade's only full-blown excursion into French gothic, and 'Henrietta Stralson' because it is Sade's most Richardsonian tale. 'Juliette and Raunai', a rather ponderous period piece, and the over-contrived 'Double Test' ('La Double Épreuve') have been discarded.

The footnotes in these stories are all Sade's own.

Appendix II gives the texts of a hostile review of the *Crimes of Love* by Alexandre-Louis de Villeterque, a contemporary man of letters, along with Sade's furious response, and a paragraph marking the end of the exchange.

SELECT BIBLIOGRAPHY

Works by Sade

Œuvres, ed. Michel Delon, 3 vols. (Paris: Gallimard, 'Bibliothèque de la Pléïade', 1990–97).

Les Crimes de l'amour, in *Œuvres complètes du marquis de Sade*, 16 vols. (Paris: Cercle du Livre Précieux, 1966–7), vol. 10. (The full text.)

Les Crimes de l'amour, ed. Gilbert Lély (Paris: Éditions 10/18, 1971). ('Idée sur les romans', 'Faxelange', 'Florville et Courval', 'La Comtesse de Sancerre', 'Eugénie de Franval'.)

Les Crimes de l'amour, ed. Béatrice Didier (Paris: Livre de Poche, 1972). ('Faxelange', 'Florville et Courval', 'Dorgeville', 'La Comtesse de Sancerre', 'Eugénie de Franval'.)

Les Crimes de l'amour, ed. Michel Delon (Paris: Gallimard, 'Folio', 1987). ('Idée sur les romans', 'Faxelange', 'Florville et Courval', 'Laurence et Antonio', 'Dorgeville', 'Ernestine', 'Eugénie de Franval'.)

Historiettes, contes et fabliaux, ed. Maurice Heine (Paris: Société du Roman philosophique, 1926). (Contains all Sade's surviving tales.)

Les Infortunes de la vertu, suivi des Historiettes, contes et fabliaux, ed. Gilbert Lély (Paris: Éditions 10/18, 1965). (Contains the first version of *Justine* and twenty-four tales not intended for *Les Crimes de l'amour*.)

The Misfortunes of Virtue and Other Early Tales, translated with an Introduction and Notes by David Coward (Oxford: OUP, Oxford World's Classics, 1992). (Contains the first *Justine*, the 'Dialogue between a Priest and a Dying Man', and twelve tales.)

Lettres inédites et documents, ed. Jean-Louis Debauve, préface et chronologie de Annie Le Brun (Paris: Ramsay/Pauvert, 1990).

Letters from Prison, translated with an introduction by Richard Seaver (London: Harvill Press, 2000).

Works About Sade

T. Airaksinen, *The Philosophy of the Marquis de Sade* (London and New York: Routledge, 1995).

Simone de Beauvoir, 'Faut-il brûler Sade?', in *Privilèges* (1955), translated as *Must We Burn Sade?, with Selections from his Writings*, chosen by Paul Dinnage (London: Arrow Books, 1990).

Laurence L. Bongie, *Sade, a Biographical Essay* (Chicago and London: University of Chicago Press, 1998).

Angela Carter, *The Sadeian Woman* (London: Virago, 1979).

Michel Delon, 'Dix ans d'études sadiennes (1968–1978)', in *Dix-huitième Siècle*, 11 (1979), 393–426.
Francine du Plessix Gray, *At Home with the Marquis de Sade* (London: Chatto & Windus, 1999).
Ronald Hayman, *De Sade: A Critical Biography* (London: Constable, 1978).
Maurice Heine, *Le Marquis de Sade* (Paris: Gallimard, 1950).
Pierre Klossowski, *Sade, mon prochain* (1947); translated as *Sade My Neighbour* (London: Quartet Books, 1992).
Alice Laborde, *La Bibliothèque du Marquis de Sade en 1776* (Geneva: Droz, 1991).
Françoise Laugaa-Traut, *Lectures de Sade* (Paris: Armand Colin, 1973).
Annie Le Brun, *Soudain un bloc d'abîme* (Paris: J.-J. Pauvert, 1986).
Jean Leduc, 'Les Sources de l'athéisme et de l'immoralité du marquis de Sade', in *Studies on Voltaire*, 68 (1969), 7–66.
Gilbert Lély, *Vie du marquis de Sade*, in *Œuvres complètes du marquis de Sade* (Paris: Cercle du Livre Précieux, 1966), vols. I–II.
Maurice Lever, *Donatien-Alphonse-François, marquis de Sade* (1991), translated by Arnold Goldhammer as *The Marquis de Sade: A Biography* (London: HarperCollins, 1993).
Colette Verger Michael, *The Marquis de Sade: The Man, His Works, and His Critics. An Annotated Bibliography* (New York: Garland, 1986).
Paragraph, 23: 1 (March 2000), special issue: 'Sade and his Legacy', ed. John Phillips.
Jean-Jacques Pauvert, *Sade vivant*, 3 vols. (Paris: Laffont, 1986–90).
John Phillips, *Sade: the Libertine Novels* (London and Stirling, Virginia: Pluto Press, 2001).
Neil Shaeffer, *The Marquis de Sade* (New York: Knopf, 1999; London: Picador, 2001).
Chantal Thomas, *Sade* (Paris: Éditions du Seuil, 1994).
Donald Thomas, *The Marquis de Sade* (1976; London: Allison & Busby, 1992).

Further Reading in Oxford World's Classics

Baudelaire, Charles, *The Flowers of Evil*, trans. James N. McGowan, ed. Jonathan Culler.
Constant, Benjamin, *Adolphe*, trans. Margaret Mauldon, ed. Patrick Coleman.
Diderot, Denis, *The Nun*, trans. Russell Goulbourne.
—— *Jacques the Fatalist*, trans. David Coward.
Laclos, Pierre Choderlos de, *Les Liaisons dangereuses*, trans. Douglas Parmée, ed. David Coward.

Lafayette, Madame de, *The Princesse de Clèves*, trans. and ed. Terence Cave.

Prévost, Abbé, *Manon Lescaut*, trans. and ed. Angela Scholar.

Rousseau, Jean-Jacques, *Confessions*, trans. Angela Scholar, ed. Patrick Coleman.

Sade, Marquis de, *The Misfortunes of Virtue and Other Early Tales*, trans. and ed. David Coward.

Voltaire, *Candide and Other Stories*, trans. and ed. Roger Pearson.

A CHRONOLOGY OF THE MARQUIS DE SADE

1740 2 June: birth in Paris of Donatien-Alphonse-François, son of the Comte de Sade (1702–67) and Marie-Éléonore de Maillé de Carman (1712–77), in Paris. He is brought up with his cousin, the Prince de Condé.

1744 Sent to Provence, where he is entrusted to his grandmother Sade, aunts, and an uncle, the licentious Abbé de Sade (1705–77).

1750 Attends the Jesuit Collège Louis-le-Grand in Paris, accompanied by a private tutor, the Abbé Amblet, of whom he grows fond.

1752 Probable date of formal separation of Sade's parents.

1754 24 May: enters an elite military school.

1755 14 December: sub-lieutenant in an infantry regiment. Sees active service in France and Germany in the Seven Years War, which he ends with the rank of captain (1759) and a reputation for lewd conduct.

1763 16 March: demobilized; April: affair with Mademoiselle de Lauris in Avignon; 17 May: marries Renée-Pélagie de Montreuil ('elle n'est pas jolie') in Paris; 29 October: jailed for two weeks at Vincennes for maltreating Jeanne Testard in a Paris brothel. The charge specifies 'extreme debauchery' and 'horrible impiety'; 13 November: released but confined for a period to the country estate of his wife's parents in Normandy.

1764 26 June: delivers a speech to the Dijon *parlement* as the newly appointed lieutenant-general of one of the Burgundy provinces, a post inherited from his father.

1765 Begins, among others, an affair with Mademoiselle Beauvoisin, a dancer. His name recurs in reports of police officers charged with repressing immorality.

1767 The death of the Comte de Sade leaves him with considerable debts. Sade does not take his father's title, and remains 'Marquis'; 27 August: birth of his son, Louis-Marie (d. 1809).

1768 Easter Sunday: encounter with Rose Keller, followed by the scandalous 'Arcueil Affair'. Imprisoned at Lyons, he is freed on 19 November and confined to his chateau at La Coste in Provence.

1769 2 April: returns to Paris; 27 June: birth of his second son, Donatien-Claude-Armand (d. 1847); September–October: travels through the Low Countries.

1770 His unsavoury reputation makes him unwelcome at court and blocks his military career.

1771 17 April: birth of a daughter, Madeleine-Laure (d. 1844); July–September: imprisoned for debt. Returns to La Coste with his wife and her sister, Anne-Prospère (1751–79), whom he promptly seduces.

1772 17 June: start of the 'Marseilles Affair'. Sade, accompanied by his valet and the infatuated Anne-Prospère, flees to Italy; 3 September: Sade and his valet are sentenced to death *in absentia* as poisoners and sodomites, and their effigies are publicly burned at Aix; 8 December: arrested and jailed at Miolans in Piedmont.

1773 30 April: escapes, and by the autumn is back at La Coste.

1774 January: eludes the authorities who, prompted by Madame de Montreuil, look for him at La Coste. Takes refuge in Italy, where he spends the summer; Winter: debauches with servants ('petites filles') at La Coste.

1775 July: facing prosecution for the *petites filles* affair, decamps to Italy.

1776 Summer: returns to La Coste and begins writing his *Voyage d'Italie*.

1777 17 January: after further debauches at La Coste, the irate father of Catherine Treillet fires two shots at Sade; 13 February: having arrived in Paris too late to see his mother before her death on 14 January, he is arrested and imprisoned at Vincennes.

1778 June: at Aix-en-Provence the death sentence passed in 1772 is lifted, but not the *lettre de cachet*, for which he continues to be detained; 16 July: during his return journey to Vincennes Sade escapes; 7 September: recaptured at La Coste. He is sent back to Vincennes, where he remains for the next six years.

1781 April: writes a comedy, *L'Inconstant*, first of a score of plays of which few have survived and only one was performed; 13 July: Renée-Pélagie granted permission to visit her husband. Sade is frequently angry, jealous, and abusive.

1782 12 July: completes the 'Dialogue Between a Priest and a Dying Man'. Begins work on *The 120 Days of Sodom*.

1783 Writes *Jeanne Laisné*, a tragedy. Experiences eye pain brought on by intensive reading.

1784 29 February: the prison of Vincennes is closed and Sade is transferred to the Bastille.

1785 Assembles what he has written of *The 120 Days of Sodom*, which he will never complete. Begins work on *Aline and Valcour*.

1786 Asks Renée-Pélagie to supply details of Spain and Portugal for his 'philosophical novel', *Aline and Valcour*.

1787 13 June: Sade loses control of the management of his affairs; late June–8 July: completes 'The Misfortunes of Virtue', the first version of *Justine*.

1788 First week of March: writes 'Eugénie de Franval'; 1 October: draws up a catalogue of his writings.

1789 Gives Renée-Pélagie *Aline and Valcour* to read; 2 July: from his cell window, Sade, using an improvised loud-hailer, calls for help and says that prisoners are being murdered; 4 July: transferred to the lunatic asylum at Charenton and forced to leave behind his furniture and a number of manuscripts.

1790 2 April: is freed from Charenton following the abolition of the *lettre de cachet* (13 March). The following day Renée-Pélagie refuses to meet him; 9 June: her request for a separation, a preliminary to divorce, is granted. Henceforth, Sade refers to himself as 'Citizen Sade, man of letters'; 25 August: the Comédie Française rejects Sade's comedy *Le Boudoir*, and in the autumn *Le Misanthrope par amour*, also a comedy, and his tragedy *Jeanne Laisné*. Begins a relationship with Marie-Constance Quesnet which will last until his death. Shows moderate sympathy for the new regime and frequents circles favourable to constitutional monarchy.

1791 Sade's financial plight deepens. After the failed flight to Varennes he publishes an *Adresse d'un citoyen de Paris au roi des Français* (*Address by a citizen of Paris to the King of the French*) which is critical of Louis XVI; June: *Justine, or the Misfortunes of Virtue*, published anonymously; 3 September: elected secretary of his District, the Section des Piques; 22 October: *Oxtiern, or the Effects of Libertinage*, performed at the Théâtre Molière.

1792 March: his comedy *Le Suborneur* is withdrawn at rehearsal, being judged 'too aristocratic'; 10 August: effective end of the monarchy; 17–21 September: in Paris political prisoners are massacred. The chateau of La Coste is pillaged by what Sade calls 'brigands' and 'thieves'.

1793 April: to justify the attack on his property, the *département* of the Bouches-du-Rhône adds Sade's name to the list of émigrés; August: saves the lives of his parents-in-law by ensuring that their names are removed from the list of émigrés; 15 November: heads a delegation to the Convention; December: the printer of the completed *Aline and Valcour* is arrested and Sade is imprisoned for 'moderation'.

The emigration of his sons Louis-Marie (September 1791) and Claude-Armand (May 1792) was also held against him.

1794 27 July: Sade condemned to death; 28 July: the fall of Robespierre ends the Terror, and Sade is saved providentially; 15 October: released from detention.

1795 Publication of *Aline and Valcour* 'by Citizen S***', and of *The Philosopher in the Bedroom*, which appears anonymously.

1796 Painful attacks of gout in the spring, followed by an illness which confines him to his bed in June and July; 13 October: sells the chateau of La Coste to Rovère, a supporter of the revolution.

1797 Summer: travels to Provence for first time for twenty years. Continuing efforts to remove his name from the list of émigrés, on which it has appeared by confusion with those of his sons. Publication of *The New Justine, or the Misfortunes of Virtue, followed by the History of Juliette, her Sister, or the Prosperities of Vice*.

1798 Spring: when Gaufridy, his agent in Provence, fails to send him income from his estates, Sade, reduced to penury, is forced to borrow money. Vain attempts to persuade the Théâtre Ribié to accept several plays, which may have included *Fanni, ou les Effets du désespoir, Henriette et Saint-Clair*, and *La Tour enchantée*.

1799 February: employed as a prompter in a Versailles theatre; 29 August: a newspaper reports Sade's death; 13 December: a new production of *Oxtiern*, in which Sade plays a minor role.

1800 January: having sold her dresses to buy food, Constance is obliged to seek work to support the family; 8 July: publisher's advertisement for *The Crimes of Love* appears in the *Journal Typographique et Bibliographique*; 18 August: the police seize a new edition of *Justine*. Fearing the worst, Sade again denies authorship; September/October: Publication of his *drame, Oxtiern, ou Les Malheurs de la vertu*, and *The Crimes of Love*; 22 October: appearance of Villeterque's review of *The Crimes of Love* in *Le Journal des Arts*. Sade's reply fails to halt references in the press which identify him as the author of *Justine*.

1801 6 March: arrested with his publisher and imprisoned on 3 April at Saint-Pélagie.

1803 14 March: after attempting to seduce male fellow prisoners, is transferred to Bicêtre and thence, on 27 April, to Charenton, to be detained at the family's expense.

1804 8 September: an official inquiry concludes that Sade is 'unreformable'.

1805 Easter Day: helps to serve mass.

1806 30 January: writes his will, which recognizes the part played by Constance Quesnet in saving his life during the Terror of 1794.

1807 5 June: the authorities confiscate *The Days of Florbelle, or Nature Unveiled*, an immense novel begun in 1804. After Sade's death the manuscript was destroyed.

1808 Organizes theatrical performances for the inmates of Charenton; 2 August: a new governor affirms that Sade is not mad and argues that he belongs in a secure prison rather than a hospital.

1809 9 June: death of Louis-Marie, his elder son, in an ambush in Italy.

1810 7 July: death of Renée-Pélagie. In a letter Sade describes his surviving son as astute but litigious, and observes that heaven had given him 'a daughter [Madeleine-Laure] steeped in stupidity and religion', and so unfitted to be a mother that 'it seems more than likely that she will leave this world in the same virginal state as that in which she entered it'.

1811 Start of ultimate liaison, with 16-year-old Madeleine Leclerc, daughter of a Charenton nurse.

1812 September–October: writes *Adelaide of Brunswick, Princess of Saxony*; 6 June: Napoleon definitively rejects Sade's application to be released;

1813 Publishes *The Marquise de Gange* and completes *The Secret History of Isabelle of Bavaria*.

1814 2 December: death of Sade. He is given a religious funeral and is buried, at his own request, in an unmarked grave.

1815 *Justine* and other works are banned.

1834 The word *sadisme* is formally lexicalized in Boiste's *Dictionnaire universel*.

1876 Publication of Krafft-Ebing's *Psychopathia sexualis*, where, together with 'masochism', the word 'sadism' acquired authority as a scientific term.

1904 The publication by Eugen Dühren (Iwan Bloch) of the newly discovered *120 Days of Sodom* marks the beginning of serious intellectual interest in the writings of Sade.

1909 Guillaume Apollinaire publishes a selection of Sade's works, calls him 'the freest spirit', and predicts that he will dominate the twentieth century.

1957 Jean-Jacques Pauvert found guilty of obscenity for publishing scholarly editions of various works by Sade, which, however, become widely available in the permissive 1960s.

1983 HM Customs, using the discretion allowed under the 1876 Act, permits translations of works by Sade, previously banned in the UK, to be imported.

THE CRIMES OF LOVE

AN ESSAY ON NOVELS

WHAT is ordinarily termed a novel (or *roman*) is a work of imagination inspired by the most extraordinary occurrences in the lives of men.

But why should this kind of composition be called a *roman*?

In which nation should we look for its beginnings, and which are the best-known examples?

And what, lastly, are the rules which must be followed if perfection is to be attained in the art of writing them?

These are the three questions with which we propose to deal. Let us begin by considering the etymology of the word.

Since there is nothing to indicate by what name such compositions were known to the peoples of antiquity, we should, it seems to me, attempt to discover why it was first given in France the name we give it still.

As is well known, the Romance language was a mixture of Celtic speech and Latin, and was in use during the first two dynasties of the kings of France.* It is not unreasonable to think that the kind of work we are considering, being written in that language, might well have been named after it, and that the term *roman* would have been coined to designate works dealing with the adventures of love, just as *romance* was used for plaintive lays inspired by the same subject. You will seek in vain an alternative etymology for the word, and since common sense offers no other possibility, it seems simplest to adopt it.

Let us now consider the second question.

In which nation should we look for its beginnings, and which are the best-known examples?

Standard opinion attributes its beginnings to the Greeks, from whom it was inherited by the Arabs, who passed it to the Spaniards, who transmitted it to our troubadours, from whom it was adopted by the authors of our old tales of chivalry.

Now while I see merit in this lineage, and sometimes find it convenient to use it myself, I am, however, most reluctant to apply it strictly. For surely such a linear process is difficult to impose on an age when travel was virtually unknown and communication so uncertain? There are fashions, customs, and tastes which do not need to be transmitted, since they are innate in all peoples and are by nature inseparable from the communities which give rise to them. Wherever men exist there are to be found inescapable traces of the same tastes, customs, and fashions.

Let us be in no doubt: it was in those lands which first acknowledged the existence of gods that novels first emerged, which consequently means in Egypt, patently the cradle of all religions. No sooner did men suspect the existence of immortal beings than they made them act and speak. Hence, from that moment on, all the metamorphoses, fables, parables, and novels—in short, all the works of untruth which took hold once untruth gripped the minds of men. This explains, once such fanciful notions took root, the appearance of books of fables. Once peoples, at first under the direction of priests, began slaughtering each other in the name of their non-existent divinities and then took up arms for king or country, the honour attached to heroism challenged the tribute paid to superstition. Not only were heroes very sensibly raised to take the place of gods, but the children of Mars were immortalized in song as once the children of heaven had been celebrated. The great deeds they had done were greatly exaggerated. Or perhaps when people wearied of them, they invented other personages who resembled them... and surpassed them, so that soon new fictions appeared which were certainly more plausible and infinitely more relevant to men than those which had proclaimed the fame of fanciful spirits. Hercules[1] was a great military leader who assuredly fought valiantly against his enemies: such a hero belonged to history. The Hercules who slew monsters and cleft giants in twain was a god, the fabulous shape and form of superstition—but a kind of superstition which was rational, since its purpose was to reward heroism: it was the gratitude accorded to those who had liberated a nation. Whereas the superstition which spawned non-created beings which had no material shape, grew out of the fears and hopes of deranged minds.*

[1] Hercules is a generic name made up of two Celtic words, *Her-Coule*, meaning 'Sir Captain'. *Hercoule* was the term which designated an 'army general', and this gave rise to many *Hercoules*. Subsequently, fables attributed the miraculous exploits of several to one such man. See Pelloutier's *History of the Celts*.*

In this way, each people had its gods and its demigods, its heroes, its true histories, and its myths. Thus, as we have seen, a thing might be true in terms of its heroes. But the rest was fabricated, legendary, a work of invention, a *roman*, because the gods spoke only through the mouths of certain men who, having much to gain from this absurd business, duly proceeded to invent the language of the spirits out of their own heads, using anything they considered suitable for convincing or frightening, in other words, anything that was mythical. 'It is widely accepted' (observes the scholar Huet*) 'that the term *roman* was formerly given to true histories and was subsequently applied to fictions. Here is irrefutable evidence for concluding that the second are derived from the first.'

Thus were novels written in every tongue, in every nation, which in style and specifics were based upon both the manners of each nation and the opinions adopted by those nations.

Man is subject to two failings inseparable from his very existence which is defined by them. Everywhere he must *pray* and he must also *love*—and there you have the basic stuff of all novels. Men wrote novels in order to show beings whom they *petitioned*; and they wrote novels to celebrate those whom they *loved*. The first kind, composed out of terror or hope, could not be other than brooding, sprawling, full of untruth and invention: such are those which Ezra chronicled during the captivity of Babylon. The second type is marked by refined taste and fine sentiments: such is Heliodorus' *Theagenes and Chariclea*.* But since man *prayed*, since he *loved* everywhere, novels appeared in every quarter of the globe which he inhabited, that is to say, works of fiction which showed either the fabulous paraphernalia of his particular faith, or the more real world of his love.

So we should not attach much importance to the business of locating the origin of this kind of writing in one nation in preference to another. We must allow ourselves to be convinced by what has just been said, viz., that all nations have used the term and have defined it in various ways according to their preference for love over superstition, or vice versa.

And now we pass to a brief consideration of the nations which have given the warmest welcome to this type of composition, of the works themselves, and of those who composed them. We shall then bring the story up to our own times, so that readers may be in a position to formulate their own views of the matter by comparison.

Aristides of Miletus is the earliest novelist mentioned by the writers of antiquity. Not one of his works, however, has survived. All we know is that his stories were called the Milesian Tales. A passage in the preface to *The Golden Ass* would seem to confirm that Aristides was a licentious author: 'It is in this style that I shall write,' says Apuleius at the outset of his *Golden Ass*.*

Antonius Diogenes, a contemporary of Alexander the Great, used a more polished style for *The Loves of Dinias and Dercillis*, a novel full of invention, enchantments, journeys, and very extraordinary adventures which Le Seurre copied in 1745 for an even more curious little work. For, not content with sending his heroes forth to travel through familiar lands, as Diogenes had done, he packs them off to the moon and then to hell.*

Next come the adventures of Sinonis and Rhodanis by Iamblichus; the loves of Théagène and Charicles which we have mentioned; Xenophon's *Cyropedia*; the loves of Daphnis and Chloé by Longus; and the amorous dalliance of Ismene and Ismenias, together with many, many more, some of which have been translated while others are now totally forgotten.*

The Romans, more given to censure and malice than to love or prayer, restricted themselves to a handful of satires, such as those of Petronius and Varro, which we should take care not to place in the category of novels.*

The Gauls, more inclined to the two above-mentioned weaknesses, had their bards who may be regarded as the first novelists of the part of Europe which we inhabit today. The business of these bards, so Lucan says,* was to compose poetry celebrating the immortal deeds of their nation's heroes and to sing them to the accompaniment of an instrument which resembled a lyre. Very few of these works are known today. After them we had the exploits of Charlemagne, attributed to Turpin, and all the romances of the Round Table, Tristan, Lancelot, Perce-Forêts, all written with a view to immortalizing real heroes or inventing new ones based on them who, since they were embroidered by the imagination, outshone the originals in the wonders they performed.* But how great a gap separates these long, tedious works, riddled with superstition, from the Greek novels which had preceded them! What barbarity, what coarseness followed the novels of such taste and agreeable invention for which the Greeks had supplied the model! For while there may well have been others before them, they are the earliest known to us.

Next followed the troubadours, and although they should be considered poets rather than novelists, the very large number of engaging prose tales which they composed nonetheless justly qualifies them to sit alongside the kind of writers of whom we speak. If confirmation of this is required, the reader has only to glance at the *fabliaux* which they wrote in the romance language during the reign of Hugues Capet, and which were avidly copied in Italy.*

That beautiful part of Europe, still groaning beneath the Saracen yoke, and still far distant from the time when it would be the cradle of the Renaissance in the arts, had virtually no novelists to speak of until the tenth century. The first appeared in that country at about the same time as our troubadours, whom they imitated, emerged in France. We do not flinch from taking pride in this: it was not the Italians, who were our masters in this art, as La Harpe (p. 242, vol. 3) states. On the contrary, it was in France that they mastered it. It was from our troubadours that Dante, Boccaccio, Tassoni, and even to some extent Petrarch learned to draft the stories they told. Nearly all the tales of Boccaccio were taken from *fabliaux* written in France.*

The same was not true of the Spanish, who were taught the art of fiction by the Moors, who themselves had acquired it from the Greeks and possessed Arabic translations of all Greek books of this kind. The Spaniards wrote delightful novels which were imitated by our authors. We shall return to them.

As the gallantry of love and war steadily assumed a new face in France, the novel made solid progress, and it was then—by which I mean at the beginning of the last century—that d'Urfé wrote his novel *L'Astrée*, and persuaded us, quite rightly, to prefer his charming shepherds and shepherdesses on the banks of the Lignon* to the implausible knights of the eleventh and twelfth centuries. A frenzy of imitation then took hold of all those to whom nature had given a taste for this kind of writing. The astounding success of *L'Astrée*, which still had readers as late as the middle of this century, went to everyone's head, and it was much imitated but never equalled. Gomberville, La Calprenède, Desmarets, and Scudéry* believed that they had improved the original by putting princes and kings in the place of the shepherds of the Lignon. Mademoiselle de Scudéry committed the same blunder as her brother. Like him, she attempted to add aristocratic tone to d'Urfé's creation and, like him, substituted dull heroes for his delightful shepherds. Instead of representing through the character of Cyrus the kind of prince described by Herodotus,* she invented Artamène who was more deranged than all the characters in *L'Astrée* combined—a lover capable of nothing save weeping from morning to evening, and whose languid posturings weary but do not interest. The same defects recur in her *Clélie*, where she gives the Romans, whom she misrepresents, all the excesses of the models which she imitated and which were never more garbled than they were by her.*

Here we would ask the reader to allow us to take a step backwards for a moment, so that we may keep the promise we made to cast a glance at Spain.

Certainly, if chivalry had inspired novelists here in France, to what pitch of excitement had it not also made heads spin on the other side of the Pyrenees? The catalogue of Don Quixote's library, amusingly drawn up by Miguel Cervantès, defines it exactly.* Be that as it may, the fact remains that the celebrated creator of the greatest madman who was ever hatched by the brain of a novelist had absolutely no rivals. His immortal work, known the whole world over, translated into every language, and to be identified as the very first novel of all, possesses to a greater degree than all the rest the art of storytelling, of linking adventures in the most agreeable fashion, and in particular of combining instruction and entertainment. 'This book', observed Saint-Evremond,* 'is the only one which I can reread without becoming bored, and the only one I wish I had written myself.' The same author's twelve 'exemplary' tales, full of interest, wit, and subtlety, confirm the place of this famous Spaniard in the front rank. Without him, perhaps we might never have had either Scarron's delightful novel nor most of those of Le Sage.*

After d'Urfé and his imitators, after the Arianes, the Cleopatras, the Faramonds, the Polixandres,* in short, all those sagas in which the hero, sighing through nine volumes, is only too glad to find a wife in the tenth—after, I say, all this nonsense which is quite unreadable today came Madame de La Fayette who, if too taken by the languid tone which she found in what preceded her, at least was much more concise. And in becoming more succinct, she became more interesting. It has been said, because she was a woman (as though her sex, naturally more delicate and more suited for the writing of novels, could not claim to succeed better than men at this sort of work)—it has been alleged, I was saying, that La Fayette was given unstinting help and wrote her novels only with the aid of La Rochefoucauld for her maxims, and Segrais for her style.* Be that as it may, no novel is more affecting than *Zaïde*, none more pleasantly written than *La Princesse de Clèves*. Ah, indulgent, charming lady, since the graces held your pen, why was not Cupid on occasion allowed to direct it?

Then came Fénelon, who tried to make himself interesting by reading a poetic lesson to his sovereigns, who paid no attention to it. Ah! Tender lover of Madame Guyon, your soul needed to love and your mind to write. Had you abandoned pedantry, I mean the arrogant urge to teach kings their business, you would have given us masterpieces instead of one book which no one reads any more.* This cannot be said of you, delightful Scarron, for until the day the world ends your immortal novel will make people laugh and your picturesque scenes will never grow old. *Télémaque*, which survived for only a hundred years, will perish under the ruins of its century which is now no more; but your actors from Le Mans, dear, kindly child of folly, will amuse even the soberest readers as long as there are men on this earth.

Towards the end of the same century the daughter of the celebrated Poisson, Madame Gomez, composed works which were no less amusing for all that they were written in a very different ink from that used by the writers of her sex who had preceded her. Her *Journées amusantes*, like her *Cent nouvelles nouvelles*, despite their numerous defects, will remain the perpetual core of the libraries of lovers of storytelling. Gomez was mistress of her art—no one should refuse her a commendation she so richly deserved.* Subsequently, Mademoiselle de Lussan, Mesdames de Tencin, de Graffigny, Élie de Beaumont, and Riccoboni emulated her. Their writings, brimming with delicacy and taste, unquestionably do honour to their sex.* Graffigny's *Lettres péruviennes* will always be a model of tenderness and feeling, and the missives of Lady Catesbi will be of perennial use to any who aim at elegance and lightness of style. But let us return to the century where we left it, for we felt impelled to praise these admirable women who gave men so many good lessons in novel-writing.

The hedonism of the likes of Ninon de Lenclos and Marion Delorme, of the Marquis de Sévigné and the Marquis de La Fare, the Chaulieus, the Saint-Evremonds, in short the whole of that charming society which had thrown off the languors of the god of Cythera* and now began to think, like Buffon, 'that the only good thing about love is the physical'*, soon changed the tone of novels. The writers who came after sensed that insipid adventures would not amuse a century poisoned by the Regent,* a century which had outgrown chivalric follies, religious excesses, and the worship of women. Finding it simpler to amuse or corrupt women than to serve them or place them upon pedestals, they created events, dramatic scenes, and conversations which reflected the spirit of the times more faithfully. They wrapped cynicism and immorality in an agreeable, playful, and sometimes even philosophical style, and at least pleased their readers if they did not instruct them.

Crébillon published *Le Sopha, Tanzaï, Les Égarements du cœur et de l'esprit*, etc. All were novels which flattered vice and made mock of virtue, yet when they appeared they were able to aspire to the greatest success.*

Marivaux, more original in his approach to painting reality, and more subtle, at least provided fully developed character-types, captivated the soul, and made the tears flow. But how could a writer possess such energy and yet write in such a precious, mannered style? He is the living proof that nature never grants a novelist all the gifts that are necessary for the perfection of his art.*

The aim of Voltaire was very different. Having no other purpose than to insert philosophy into his novels, he neglected the rest to implement his purpose. And how well he succeeded! Despite all the criticisms of them, will not *Candide* and *Zadig* always be considered masterpieces?*

Rousseau, to whom Nature had given in delicacy of sentiment what she had granted in wit to Voltaire, approached the novel from a quite different direction. What vigour and energy there are in *La Nouvelle Héloïse*!* Whereas Momus* dictated *Candide* to Voltaire, it was the god of love himself who lit up every burning page of *Julie* with his torch, and it may rightly be said that this sublime book will never have imitators. May this truth make the pens drop from the fingers of the multitude of ephemeral authors who, these last thirty years, have continued unceasingly to churn out bad copies of an immortal original. May they understand that if they wish to match it, they will need a soul of fire like Rousseau's and a mind as philosophical as his, two things which Nature never manages to bring off successfully twice in the same century

Meanwhile Marmontel offered us tales which he dubbed 'moral', not (as one esteemed critic has observed) because they taught morals but because they described our *mores*, even though this was done in a way which sailed a little too close to the manner of Marivaux. But this apart, what are these tales? Ridiculous balderdash written for women and children, which no one would believe came from the same pen which wrote *Bélisaire*, a work which alone makes the case for its author's greatness. How could the man who wrote chapter 15 of that book also aspire to the minor glory of furnishing us with sugary, rose-tinted tales?*

And then English novels, the vigorous works of Richardson and Fielding, appeared and taught the French that it is not by describing the tedious languors of love, or reporting the dull conversation of cliques and coteries, that success is achieved in this genre, but by creating strong, manly characters who, as the playthings and victims of that effervescence of the heart otherwise known as love, show both the dangers and miseries it generates. It is the only way to achieve the progression of plot and the workings of passion which are so well depicted in English novels.* It was Richardson and Fielding who taught us that only the deep study of the human heart, one of nature's most intricate labyrinths, can inspire the novelist whose work must show us man stripped bare, not only as he is or as he appears to be, for that is the task of the historian, but as he might be, as he might become after his vices are corrected and he has been subjected to the commotions of passion. If an author wishes to work in this genre, he must know all the passions and use their full range. From them we also learned that it is not always by showing the triumph of virtue that a writer wins over his reader; that while it certainly is to this that every effort must tend, this rule, which exists neither in nature nor Aristotle but is merely one which we would wish all men would respect for our benefit, is in no sense indispensable to the novel, nor is it even the principle which makes a work of fiction interesting. For when virtue triumphs, things being as they necessarily are, our tears dry up before they even begin to flow. But if, after it has been tested by the most severe trials, we finally see virtue crushed by vice, then our souls will inevitably be torn, and the book, having moved us immoderately and, as Diderot put it, 'made our hearts bleed from the back'*, will not fail to create the kind of interest which is the only guarantee of success.

Object if you will: what if, after twelve or fifteen volumes, the immortal Richardson had in the end *virtuously* converted Lovelace and made him *sedately* marry Clarissa? Would readers of the novel in this upside-down version then have shed the exquisite tears which it draws from every person of feeling? When a writer works in this genre, he must catch nature, he must capture the heart of man, that most singular of her creations, and not virtue, because virtue, however fine and necessary it may be, is only one of the manifestations of that astounding heart which every novelist must make his deepest study, and because the novel, if it is to be the faithful mirror of the human heart, must of necessity reflect all its crests and troughs.

Learned translator of Richardson, Prévost, in whose debt we stand for having enabled the beauties of that famous writer to pass into our language,* are you not also due on your own account some tribute of no less justified praise? And is it not with good reason that you may be called 'the French Richardson'? You alone possessed the art of devising intricate plots which keep the reader's interest over many volumes, by never allowing the main business to flag though it divides and diversifies;* you alone handled these intercalated episodes so skilfully that the main plot always gained rather than lost by their number and complexity. Thus the large number of events, for which La Harpe criticizes you,* is not simply something which enables you to produce the most sublime effects, but is at the same time the best evidence of the gentleness of your mind and the excellence of your genius. '*Les Mémoires d'un homme de qualité*' (to add to what we think of Prévost what others besides ourselves have thought), '*Clèveland, L'Histoire d'une Grecque moderne, Le Monde moral, Manon Lescaut* above all,[1] are full of affecting, prodigious scenes which strike and irresistibly conquer the mind. The situations found in these works, admirably managed, lead to moments when nature shudders with horror, etc.' And that is what is called writing a novel, and it is for

[1] What tears do we not shed as we read this exquisite book! How truly nature is painted here, how well the interest is sustained, how it grows by degrees! So many difficulties triumphantly overcome! What depth of philosophy was required to create such interest in a courtesan! Would it be too much to suggest that this book has a good claim to be considered our finest novel? It was in its pages that Rousseau understood that a heroine, for all her rashness and foolish ways, could still be capable of moving us deeply, and perhaps we should never have had *Julie* had it not been for *Manon Lescaut*.

this that posterity has guaranteed Prévost a place beyond the reach of any of his rivals.*

Then followed the writers of the middle of the century: Dorat, as mannered as Marivaux, as cool and with as little claim to be moral as Crébillon, but an altogether more agreeable author than either of those to whom we compare him; the frivolity of his times excuses his own, and he possessed the art of capturing it exactly.*

Charming author of *La Reine de Golconde*, will you allow me to offer you a crown of laurels? It is given to very few to have a more agreeable wit, and the century's most delightful tales are not as fine as this one story which will ensure your lasting fame. You are more engaging, more ingenious than Ovid, and since the Hero-Saviour of France, by summoning you back to the country of your birth, has demonstrated that he is as much the companion of Apollo as of Mars, strive to fulfil the expectations of this great man by pinning new roses in the hair of your beautiful Aline.*

D'Arnaud, Prévost's rival, may often be thought to have surpassed him.* Both dipped their pens in the Styx. But d'Arnaud sometimes tempers his with the sweeter flowers of Elysium, while Prévost, more forceful, never diluted the ink in which he wrote *Clèveland*.

R—— inundates the public. Since he needs a printing press at his bedside, it is the only one which is called upon to groan beneath the weight of his 'stupendous productions'. A style which is crude and pedestrian, nauseating adventures invariably set in the lowest company, and no merit other than a prolixity for which only spice-sellers will be grateful.*

Perhaps at this point we should by rights analyse the new novels whose only merit, more or less, consists of their reliance on witchcraft and phantasmagoria, by naming the best of them as *The Monk*, which is superior in every respect to the strange outpourings of the brilliant imagination of Mrs Radcliffe. But this essay would be too long. Suffice it to say, therefore, that this type of novel, whatever view might be taken of it, is assuredly not without qualities. It was the necessary offspring of the revolutionary upheaval which affected the whole of Europe. To those acquainted with all the evil which the wicked can bring down on the heads of the good, novels became as difficult to write as they were tedious to read. There was hardly a soul alive who did not experience more adversity in four or five years than the most famous novelist in all literature could have invented in a hundred. Writers therefore had to look to hell for help in composing their alluring novels, and project what everyone already knew into the realm of fantasy by confining themselves to the history of man in that cruel time. But this kind of writing posed many problems, and the author of *The Monk* was no more successful in overcoming them than Mrs Radcliffe. For an unavoidable choice had to be made: either to develop the supernatural and risk forfeiting the reader's credulity, or to explain nothing and fall into the most ludicrous implausibility. Were a book of this kind to be published that was good enough to achieve its aims without coming to grief on one or other of these reefs, then far from criticizing the means by which it has succeeded, we would hold it up as a model.*

Before we come to our third and final question: 'What are the rules of the art of writing fiction?', we should, I feel, respond to the eternal objection raised by those few atrabilious spirits who, to acquire a veneer of moral rectitude from which, in their hearts, they are far removed, are forever asking: 'What is the point of novels?'

What is their point? you crabbed hypocrites—for only you ask this absurd question. Their point is to portray you as you are, individuals puffed up with vanity who would like to escape the attention of the artist's brush because you fear the consequences. The novel, if I may express it so, is 'the picture of the manners of every age'. To the philosopher who seeks to know the nature of man, it is as indispensable as history. The historian's pencil can draw a man only in his public roles, when he is not truly himself: ambition and pride cover his face with a mask which shows only these two passions and not the man entire. The novelist's pen, on the other hand, captures his inner truth and catches him when he puts his mask aside, and the resulting sketch, which is far more interesting, is also much truer: that is the point of novels. Frigid censors all, who do not care for them, you are like the legless cripple who said: 'what is the point of portraits?'

So if it is true that novels are useful, let us not be afraid of setting down here some of the principles which we judge necessary if the genre is to be brought to the pitch of perfection. I am well aware of the difficulty of carrying out this task without drawing the general fire. Do I not make myself doubly vulnerable for not having performed up to standard, if I can demonstrate that I know exactly how that standard should be reached? But let us put such considerations to one side and subordinate them to our love of art!

The first and most important requirement is an understanding of the human heart. Now all discerning minds will certainly support us when we say that this crucial knowledge is acquired only through suffering and travel. You must have encountered men of all nations to know them, and you must have been their victim to know how to value them. The hand of misfortune, which elevates the character of those it brings low, gives its victim the right perspective from which to study others. He observes them from a distance, just as the passenger observes the angry waves break against the rocks on which the storm has driven his ship. But whatever the vantage-point at which he has been placed by nature or fate, if he wishes to know men, let him speak little when he is in their company. A man learns nothing when he talks; he learns by listening. Which is why those who talk the most are, in the ordinary run of things, fools.

You who would tread this thorny path should never lose sight of the fact that a novelist is a man of nature. Nature created him to be her portraitist. If he does not become the lover of his mother at the moment when she gives him life, then he must never write, for we will not read him.* But if he acquires the burning desire to write about everything, if he experiences a frisson as he unveils nature's bosom to draw from it his art and his models, if he has the talent and fire of genius, then he should follow wherever the beckoning hand leads him, for he has guessed the human riddle and will paint humanity's portrait. Governed by his imagination, he must yield to it and embellish what he sees. Any fool can pick a rose and pluck its petals, but the man of genius breathes its scent and paints its forms: that is the kind of author we will read.

But while I advise you to embellish, I forbid you to depart from what is plausible. The reader has every right to feel aggrieved when he realizes that too much is being asked of him. He feels that the author is trying to deceive him, his pride suffers, and he simply stops believing the moment he suspects he is being misled.

This apart, there is nothing to constrain you. Exercise as you see fit your right to make free with all the tales told by history, if jettisoning strict authenticity is necessary for the feast you will set before us. I say again: you are not asked to say what is actually true, only to tell us what seems to be true. To make too many demands of you would be to interfere with the pleasures we expect you to provide us with. But never replace the true with the impossible, and let what you invent be well expressed. You will be forgiven for substituting your imagination for the truth only on the condition that you observe the explicit injunction to embellish and astound. An author has no right to speak badly if he is free to speak of whatever he likes. If, like R——, you write only to say what everyone knows already, and were you, like him, to supply us with four volumes every month, then it would hardly be worth troubling to pick up a pen. No one forces you to ply the trade you follow. But if you do choose it, then acquit yourself to the best of your ability. And above all, you should not think of writing as a way of earning your living.* If you do, your work will smell of your poverty. It will be coloured by your weakness and be as thin as your hunger. There are other trades which you can take up: make boots, not books. Our opinion of you will not be any poorer, and since you will be sparing us acres of boredom, we may even think the better of you.

Once you have laid down the basic lines of your story, you must work hard to develop it, but without feeling that you must remain within the limits it seems at first to impose on you. If you accept those constraints you will produce thin, cold gruel. What we expect from you are flights of invention, not rule-bound exercises. Rise above your material, vary it, expand it: it is only as you work that ideas come. Why do you think that the idea which inspires you as you write is not as good as the idea dictated by your plan? I only ask one thing of you, which is to maintain the interest until the very last page. You will miss your goal if you disrupt your narrative with episodes which are unnecessarily duplicated or unconnected to the main story. But if you do include intercalated stories, you must work hard to see that they are even more polished than your main narrative: this much you owe the reader for taking him away from what interests him and offering him a sideshow. He may allow you to deflect him, but will never forgive you for boring him. And ensure that such episodes grow out of your tale and lead back to it. If you send your characters on a voyage, be sure you are acquainted with the countries where their travels lead them, and spin your tales with such magic that I can identify with them. Remember that I voyage at their side wherever you send them to, and that I may know more than you and will not excuse your errors in reporting manners and costumes nor forgive a geographical blunder. Since no one has forced you to devise such escapades, then either you must make your descriptions of your chosen localities authentic, or else you should stay at home. This is the only area of what you write where invention cannot be tolerated, unless the lands to which you transport me are imaginary. But even in such cases I still demand verisimilitude.

Avoid any display of moral earnestness. Morality is not something anyone wants in a novel. If the characters required by your plot are sometimes called upon to raise such matters, let them do so unaffectedly, without any hint of deliberate moralizing. It should never be the author who preaches, but his characters, and even then only when the circumstances leave him no alternative.

As to your denouement, it must be natural, not forced or contrived, and should emerge from the situation. Unlike the authors of the *Encyclopédie*,* I do not insist that 'it should satisfy the expectations of the reader', for what pleasure is left when he can guess what will happen? A denouement should be determined by the events which lead up to it, by the requirements of verisimilitude, by the working of your imagination. Follow these principles, which I make your wit and taste responsible for implementing, and if as a result you do not perform well then at least you will perform better than I have. For, as you will surely agree, in the tales you are about to read the boldness of invention which I have allowed myself does not always conform to the strict rules of the genre. But I trust that the extreme authenticity of the characters may be some compensation. Nature, far stranger than the moralists would have us believe, constantly overflows the limits which they have a vested interest in imposing on her. Unchanging in her designs, erratic in her manifestations, she is never at rest, and resembles the crater of a volcano which one moment shoots forth precious diamonds for the use of men, and now hurls balls of fire to destroy them. She is noble when she peoples the earth with the likes of Antoninus and Titus, fearsome when she spews forth the Andronics and the Neros,* but remains unfailingly sublime, majestic, and eternally deserving of our study, our pens, our respect, and our admiration, for her purposes are unknown to us and, slaves that we are to her whims and needs, it is not on our reaction to the hardships those purposes inflict on us that we should base our opinion of her, but on her greatness and her energy, whatever the effects they produce.

While the minds of men grow corrupt and a nation grows old, false ideas are eradicated because nature is more intensely studied and better analysed. Which is why it is so important to make known the lessons which nature offers. This injunction applies equally to all the arts. It is only through practice that they can be made perfect, and they will achieve their goal only through trial and error. It was surely excessive, during those grim centuries of ignorance when men were bowed down by the weight of religion, that he who tried to understand nature was punished by death and that the Inquisition's stake was the reward for genius. But in our present circumstances let us still take the same principle as our starting point. When man has tested his fetters, when, with fearless eye, he takes the measure of the barriers which impede his steps, when, like the Titans, he dares brandish his fist in the face of heaven and, armed with his passions as they once were with the lavas of Vesuvius,* he is no longer afraid to declare war on those who once made him tremble, when his *wrong-doings* no longer seem anything more than simple *errors* in the light of his subsequent discoveries, then should he not be spoken to with the same energy that he himself employs to direct his behaviour? In a word: are the men of the eighteenth century the same as the men of the eleventh?

Let us end with a positive assurance that the tales we publish here are absolutely new and in no way draw upon previously known models. Their originality might well be thought a merit in an age when everything seems to have been done, when the imagination of authors seems exhausted and incapable of creating anything fresh, and the public is offered only compilations, excerpts, and translations.

That said, 'The Enchanted Tower' and 'The Conspiracy of Amboise'* have some basis in history. But the reader will see from our frank acknowledgement of the fact how far removed we are from any wish to deceive him. In this kind of writing, authors must be original or leave well alone.

Here to be set against the various tales which follow is what may be found in the sources which we indicate.

The Arab historian* Abul-coecim-terif-aben-tariq,[1] a writer known to very few of our modern-day men of letters, recounts the following in connection with 'The Enchanted Tower':

[1] It would appear more likely that the name of this historian, unfamiliar to all the specialists we have consulted, should be written: Abul-selim-terif-ben-tariq.

Rodrigue, a decadent king and much given to the pleasures of the flesh, summoned to his court the daughters of his vassals and there abused them. Among their number was Florinde, daughter of Count Julian, whom he raped. Her father, who was in Africa, received the news by an allegorical letter written by his daughter. He raised the Moors and returned to Spain at their head. Rodrigue knew not which way to turn. His coffers were empty and there was no place to hide. He decided to search the Enchanted Tower near Toledo where he was told he would find vast amounts of gold. He entered and beheld a statue of Time holding a club poised to strike which, by means of words carved in stone, warned Rodrigue of the misfortunes which awaited him. The Prince continued on his way and found an immense tank full of water, but no money. He retraced his steps and ordered the tower to be shut up close and locked. A thunderbolt brought the building tumbling down, leaving only a ruin. Despite these dire portents, the King assembled an army, fought a battle near Cordoba which lasted one week, and was killed. No trace of his body was ever found.

That is what history supplied. Let the reader now peruse our story and he may judge for himself whether or not the multitude of events which we have added to this dry, bald anecdote justifies our contention that the story should be regarded as entirely ours.[1]

As to '*The Conspiracy of Amboise*', the reader may turn to Garnier's account and he will see how little we have borrowed from history.*

We had no source to guide us for the remaining tales. Plots, narrative style, incidents, everything is of our own devising. Perhaps the result is not of the very highest quality, but no matter. We have always believed, and will never cease to be persuaded, that it is better to invent, however feebly, than to copy or translate. He who invents may lay some claim to genius, and has at least some grounds for doing so. But what can the plagiarist claim? I know no viler trade, nor can I conceive an admission more humiliating than the confession

[1] This story is the same as that which Brigandos begins to tell in the episode of the novel *Aline and Valcour** entitled *Sainville and Léonore*, but is interrupted by the discovery of the corpse in the tower. The publishers of the pirated edition of this episode copied it word for word, but in so doing also reproduced the first four lines of the anecdote which are spoken by the gypsy chief. It is as important for us at this juncture as it is for those who buy novels to point out that the work published by Pigoreau and Leroux as *Valmor and Lydia*, and by Cerioux and Moutardier as *Alzonde and Koradin*, are one and the same and both literally stolen, sentence by sentence, from the episode *Sainville and Léonore* which fills about three volumes of my novel *Aline and Valcour*.

such men are forced to make when they themselves acknowledge that they have no wit of their own because they are obliged to borrow the wit of others.

As far as translators are concerned, God forbid that we should say anything to detract from their merits. Yet their sole purpose is to give comfort to our foreign rivals. Even if it were only for the honour of our country, would it not be better for those proud rivals to be told: *we too can create*?

Finally, I must reply to criticisms made of me when *Aline and Valcour* was published. It was said that my brush-strokes were too forceful and that I gave a far too odious picture of vice. Would you like to know why? It is not my wish to make vice attractive. Unlike Crébillon and Dorat, I harbour no dangerous plan to make women love men who deceive them, but on the contrary, to ensure that they loathe them. It is the only way of preventing them from being cheated. And with this in mind I have made those of my heroes who tread the path of vice so repulsive that they will certainly inspire neither pity nor love. In this I make bold to claim that I am a more moral writer than those who make their villains attractive. The pernicious novels of such authors are like certain fruits of America which, beneath the most brilliantly enticing exterior, harbour death in their flesh. Such low cunning on the part of nature, of which it is not for us to reveal the motive, is not to be imitated by man. In short, I shall never—I repeat, never—depict crime other than in the most hellish colours. I want the reader to see its naked face, to fear and hate it, and I know of no better way of achieving my objective than to show it in all its native horror. Woe to them who strew vice with flowers! Their intentions are less pure than mine and I shall never imitate them. In the light of this philosophy, there should be no more attempts to lay the novel entitled *J*——* at my door. I have never written books of that kind and I surely never will. Only fools or knaves, despite the truth of my denials, can still suspect me or repeat their accusations that I am its author. Accordingly, in future the most utter contempt is the only weapon which I shall use to counter their slanders.

MISS HENRIETTA STRALSON
or THE EFFECTS OF DESPAIR
An English Tale

ONE evening, at London's Ranelagh,* when the season was at its height, Lord Granwel, at thirty-six years of age the most debauched, wicked, cruel man in all England and unfortunately one of the richest, observed a pretty young woman he had never seen before pass close by the table where, with the help of libations of punch and champagne, he sat drowning his sorrows with three of his friends.

'Who is that girl?' Granwel promptly enquired of one of his guests. 'And how the devil can there be such a pretty little minx in London who has escaped my notice? I'd wager she's not yet sixteen. What do you reckon, Sir James?'

Sir James. 'A figure like Venus herself! Wilson, do you know anything about her?'

Wilson. 'I've come across her once before. She's the daughter of some baronet from Hereford.'

Granwel. 'Even if she was the devil's own daughter, God strike me down if I never have her!* Gave, I make you responsible for instituting enquiries.'

Gave. 'What's she called, Wilson?'

Wilson. 'Miss Henrietta Stralson. The tall woman you see with her is her mother. Her father is dead. She has been in love for ages with a man named Williams, a Hereford gentleman. They are to be married. Williams is in town to collect the inheritance of an elderly aunt which will be the entire extent of his fortune. Meanwhile, Lady Stralson wanted to show her daughter around London. When Williams's business is done, they will travel back to Hereford where the marriage is to take place.'

Granwel. 'May all the devils in hell make off with my soul if Williams lays a finger on her before I do!... I never saw a prettier little thing... Is this Williams here? I don't know the fellow. Point him out to me.'

Wilson. 'That's him there, bringing up the rear... Probably stopped for a word or two with some friends of his... He's caught up with them... Take a good look... that's him... there's your man.'

Granwel. 'The tall young fellow, very prettily made?'

Wilson. 'The very same.'

Granwel. 'Damn me, he can't be much more than twenty!'

Gave. 'True, your Lordship, he is a fine figure of a man... and a rival...'

Granwel. '...who I shall grind into the dust as I have many before him... Gave, on your feet: follow that angel... Really, she has made a deep impression on me... Follow her, Gave, try and find out all you can about her... Set spies on her trail... Have you got any money, Gave, are you in funds? Here are a hundred guineas—I don't want one left unspent tomorrow but I must know everything... Can I be in love?... What do you reckon, Wilson?... I'll say this, though: the moment I saw that girl, I felt a definite premonition.... Sir James, that divine creature shall have my fortune... or my life!'

Sir James. 'Your fortune, I grant you, but your life?... I hardly think you would ever feel like wanting to die for a woman...'

Granwel. 'No...' (And so saying, Granwel gave an involuntary shudder then went on): 'A figure of speech, my dear fellow. No one dies for trifling creatures like that. But truly, there are some who stir up a man's soul in the most extraordinary fashion!... Ho, waiter! Bring us some burgundy here! My brain is overheating and only burgundy can cool it down.'

Wilson. 'Is it true, then, that your Lordship really intends to stoop to folly and put a spoke in poor Williams's amours?'

Granwel. 'What do I care for Williams? What do I care for anything on this earth? Listen, my dear fellow, when this combustible heart of mine falls in love, there is no obstacle capable of preventing it from being satisfied. The more I fall in love, the more combustible it becomes. For me, having a woman is satisfying only by reason of the trouble I am put to on the way. Bedding a woman is the most prosaic thing in the world. Have one and you've had a hundred. The only way of avoiding the monotony of insipid triumphs is to achieve them by using only subterfuge, and it is on the ruins of a multitude of overturned prejudices that a man can find a modicum of entertainment in this business.'

Wilson. 'Would it not be better to try to please a woman, attempt to obtain her favours with love, rather than to succeed through violence?'

Granwel. 'What you say would be valid if women were more sincere. But since there is not one anywhere who is not false and faithless, we must treat them as we do the vipers which are used in medicine: cut off the head to have the body... take, whatever the cost, the few physical advantages they offer and eliminate any moral scruples to the point that you never even notice their effects.'

Sir James. 'That's the sort of talk I like.'*

Granwel. 'Sir James is my pupil and one day I'll make something of him... But here's Gave coming back. Let's see what he has to say...'

Then Gave, taking his seat after drinking a glass of wine, told Granwel:

'Your goddess creature has left. She got into a hired coach with Williams and Lady Stralson and the driver was told to go to Cecil Street.'*

Granwel. 'What? But that is so close to my house!... Did you have them followed?'

Gave. 'I have three men on the trail... three of the sharpest rogues who ever escaped from Newgate.'[1]

Granwel. 'Well, Gave? And is she pretty?'

Gave. 'She is the handsomest woman in London. Stanley... Stafford... Tilner... Burcley... they've all gone after her, they've all swarmed round her, and they all agree that there is not another girl to equal her anywhere in the three kingdoms.'

Granwel (eagerly). 'Did you hear her say anything?... Did she speak?... Did the honeyed sound of her voice reach into your vitals?... Did you breathe the air which she sweetened with her presence?... Well? Out with it!... Speak up, man! Do you not see that my head is in an absolute spin... that she must be mine or else I must leave England for ever?'

Gave. 'I did hear her, your Lordship... She spoke... She told Williams it was very warm at Ranelagh and said she preferred to leave than stroll there any longer.'

Granwel. 'And Williams?'

Gave. 'He gives every sign of being deeply attached to her... He

[1] A London prison.

never stopped looking at her... it was as though Cupid had tethered him to her footsteps.'

Granwel. 'He is a scoundrel and I hate him. I very much fear that circumstances might well force me to get rid of the man... Let us be off now, my friends. Wilson, I am obliged to you for your report. Let it remain our secret, or otherwise I shall spread the tale of your affair with Lady Mortmart all across London. And you, Sir James, I shall meet you in the park tomorrow and we shall go calling on that new girl they have at the opera... What am I saying? No, I shan't go... My mind runs on one topic... In the whole world there is only Miss Stralson and she fills my thoughts, I have eyes only for her... If I have a soul it is to worship her with... You, Gave, will come tomorrow and dine with me, bringing everything you can manage to discover about this divine creature... and sole arbiter of my fate... Farewell, my friends.'

His Lordship leaped into his coach and drove off furiously to the court, where his duties called him.

The few details supplied by Wilson about the beautiful vision who had turned Granwel's head could not have been more accurate.

Miss Henrietta Stralson, born in Hereford, had indeed come to see London, which she did not know, while Williams was settling his affairs. The whole party would then return home, where their tenderest wishes would be crowned by marriage.

It was not, furthermore, in the least surprising that Miss Stralson should have made such a favourable impression at Ranelagh, for to a captivating figure, the most gentle and alluring eyes, the most lustrous hair imaginable, and a face so fine-drawn, intelligent, and delicate, she added a delightful tone of voice, a moiety of wit, grace, and vivaciousness tempered by an air of virtue and modesty which made her many charms all the more piquant... When a girl has all this at seventeen... then obviously she can hardly fail to catch the eye. Accordingly, Henrietta had caused a prodigious sensation and in London the talk was only of her.

As to Williams, he was what is called a decent fellow, kind, honest, as little given to calculation as to deceit, who had adored Henrietta since childhood. He had set his heart on making her his one day, and in return offered sincere devotion, a pretty substantial fortune (if his lawsuit were to prove successful), a social rank a little lower than Henrietta's but honourable all the same, and a very pleasing face.

Lady Stralson was also an excellent person who, considering her daughter to be the most precious possession she had in the whole world, loved her as only a country mother can love. For all sentiments become corrupt in capital cities: the more we breathe their pestiferous air, the more our virtues decay and, since the corruption is general, we must either flee or be contaminated.*

Granwel, his head spinning with the effects of wine and love, had no sooner reached the King's antechamber than he became very aware that he was in no fit state to appear in the royal presence. He went home where, instead of sleeping, he devised the wildest and most extravagant plans for possessing the object of his desires. Having hit upon and rejected a hundred such schemes, each more frightful than the one before, the one he resolved upon consisted of driving a wedge between Williams and Henrietta, of trying if possible to tie Williams in so many legal knots that it would take him a very long time to get free of them, and meanwhile to seize whatever opportunities chance might offer to be with his inamorata, with a view to robbing her of her honour in London or else abducting her and carrying her off to one of his estates on the Scottish borders. There he would have total power over her, and nothing would prevent him from doing with her whatever he liked. This plan, suitably garnished with the most dreadful details, became for that very reason the one which appealed most to the wicked Granwel. And so, the very next day, all was set in motion to ensure its success.

Gave was Granwel's closest friend. Endowed with sentiments which were even more gross, he fulfilled on his Lordship's behalf a role which is so common nowadays, that of furthering the amours of others, multiplying their debauches, and profiting from their follies with scant regard for personal honour. You may be sure he did not miss the meeting arranged for the morrow. But that day he had little to report, only that Lady Stralson and her daughter were staying, as had been said, in Cecil Street, with a female relative, while Williams was at the Hotel Poland in Covent Garden.

'Gave,' said his Lordship, 'you'll have to answer to me for this Williams. I want you to call yourself by some Scottish name and wear Scottish clothes. Then you will drive in a rich carriage to the hotel where the clod is staying and make his acquaintance... then rob him... and ruin him. Meanwhile, I shall make the running with the ladies and you will see, my friend, that it will not take us a month to upset all the honest little plans made by these good country folk.'

Gave took good care to find no drawbacks in his master's plan. The enterprise called for the expenditure of large sums of money, and it became clear that the more his Lordship spent, the more lucrative its execution would become for the ignoble instrument of his villainous whims. Accordingly he made ready to act. For his part, his Lordship surrounded Henrietta with a large number of lesser agents who were to furnish him with an exact account of that charming young person's most trifling actions.

Miss Henrietta lived in the house of a cousin of her mother, a widow of ten years' standing, named Lady Wateley.

Much taken with Henrietta, although she had known her only since her arrival in the capital, Lady Wateley spared no effort to ensure that the object of her pride and affection should appear to the very best advantage. However, this kindly cousin, forced to keep to her room by a weakness of her lungs, had not only been unable to join the recent outing to Ranelagh but was even deprived of the pleasure of accompanying her cousin to the opera, where they were to go the very next day.

As soon as Granwel was informed of this theatregoing excursion by the spies he had placed in Henrietta's entourage, he resolved not to miss an opportunity to make the most of it. Further intelligence apprised him that a hired carriage would be used, since Lady Wateley needed her horses to fetch her physician to her. Granwel hurried at once to the owner of the carriage which was to be hired out to Henrietta, and without difficulty arranged for one of its wheels to break three or four streets from the point where it would pick up the ladies. Without pausing to think that such an accident could very well cost the life of the woman he loved (for he was concerned only with his stratagem), he paid handsomely for it to be executed and returned to his house in high spirits. From there he set out once more the moment he was informed that Henrietta was about to leave, and ordered the coachman who drove him to wait in the vicinity of Cecil Street until such and such a carriage would leave Lady Wateley's. The man should follow this carriage the moment he saw it and not let any other vehicle get between him and it.

Granwel was convinced that after leaving Lady Wateley's the ladies would go to the Hotel Poland and call for Williams. This they did. But the journey was not uneventful. The wheel broke, the ladies shrieked, one of the grooms broke a limb, and Granwel, to whom nothing mattered as long as he succeeded, drew up alongside their wrecked carriage, jumped out of his own, and offered his hand to Lady Stralson together with all the help his carriage could afford her.

'Really, Lord Granwel, you are too kind,' she replied. 'These hired London carriages are a disgrace. A person cannot go about in one of them without risking life and limb. There should be laws to put a stop to this scandalous state of affairs.'

Granwel. 'You will forgive me, Madame, if I do not complain. As far as I can see, neither you nor the young lady who accompanies you have come to any harm, and in the event I have acquired the inestimable advantage of being of some small service to you.'

Lady Stralson. 'You are too obliging, sir... But my groom seems to be in pain, and indeed I am very sorry for it.'

Immediately summoning two chairmen, his Lordship arranged for the injured man to be placed in their charge... The ladies gave orders that he was to be sent back whence he had come, and then stepped into Granwel's carriage which bore them off swiftly to the Hotel Poland.

It is impossible to describe his Lordship's feelings on finding himself seated next to the woman he loved, and with the circumstances which had brought them together taking on the appearance of a genuine service rendered.

'No doubt you were intending to pay a call on some lady also up from the country who is staying at the Hotel Poland?' he said to Henrietta when the carriage had set off.

'It's more than a visit to a country acquaintance, your Lordship,' Miss Stralson replied candidly. 'We go to call on the man I love... we are to see my future husband.'

Granwel. 'How disappointed you would have been, Mademoiselle, had this accident delayed the meeting you were so looking forward to. I reckon myself all the more fortunate to have had the pleasure of being of some service.'

Miss Stralson. 'Your Lordship is so kind to be concerned on our account. We are distraught at having put you to great inconvenience, and Mama will permit me to add that I fear we may have committed an indiscretion.'

Granwel. 'Ah, Mademoiselle, how unjust you are to view in such a light the greatest pleasure I have ever had! But if I myself dare risk an indiscretion, shall you not need my carriage to continue the other calls you have to make this afternoon? If so, may I be so happy as to know that you would be pleased to accept the use of it?'

Miss Stralson. 'That would be too great an imposition on our part, your Lordship. We were going to the opera. But now we shall instead spend the evening with the friend we are going to see.'

Granwel. 'It is a shabby way of repaying what you have acknowledged as a service to refuse me leave to continue it. Pray do not deprive yourselves of the pleasure you were anticipating. Melico[1] is singing today for the last time. It would be a dreadful shame to miss this opportunity to hear him. Besides, you must not think that I should in any way be inconvenienced by the offer I have made, since I am going to the performance myself. No more is involved than allowing me to accompany you.'

It would have been ungracious of Lady Stralson to refuse Granwel, and she did not do so. They arrived at the Hotel Poland, where Williams was waiting for the ladies. Gave, though he had arrived at the hotel that day, was not to begin playing his role until the next, and was thus not yet known to our young man who, as a consequence, was alone when mother and daughter arrived. He received them effusively and loaded his Lordship with civilities and thanks. But since time was growing short, they all removed at once to the opera. Williams gave Lady Stralson his arm, and Granwel, as a result of this arrangement which he had anticipated, was able to converse privately with Miss Henrietta, whom he found to be possessed of infinite wit, deep learning, refined taste, and everything which he might well have had great trouble finding in a young lady of more exalted birth who had spent her whole life in town.

After the performance Granwel escorted the two ladies back to Cecil Street. Lady Stralson, who had no cause but to be well satisfied with him, invited him inside to meet her cousin. Lady Wateley, who knew Granwel only slightly, nevertheless received him very grandly. She pressed him to stay to supper, but his Lordship, too canny to run before he could walk, said he had urgent business to attend to and left, more aflame with passion than ever.

[1] The celebrated Italian castrato.*

Ordinarily, people like Granwel do not go in much for sighing and pining. Obstacles rouse them to action but, in a soul such as his, obstacles which cannot be overcome extinguish rather than inflame the passions. And since persons of this sort need perpetual stimulation, then if all prospect of success is placed beyond reach, they simply find another object for their affections.

Granwel soon realized that working to drive his wedge between Williams and his bride-to-be might prove a long business, and that in the meantime he should also give some thought to setting the charming daughter against her mother, for he was convinced that his plan would come to nothing as long as the two women stood shoulder to shoulder. Once he had his entrée to Lady Wateley's house, it seemed impossible to him, when to his presence there was added the role of his spies, that anything that Henrietta did could escape him. This new stratagem of separating them now filled all his thoughts.

Three days after their visit to the opera Granwel called to enquire after the health of the ladies. But he was quite taken aback when he saw Lady Stralson appear in the parlour unaccompanied and offer her cousin's excuses for not being able to invite him upstairs. An indisposition was offered as the reason, and although Granwel was greatly irritated, he showed himself no less concerned for the health of the mistress of the house. But he could not refrain also from enquiring after Henrietta. Lady Stralson replied that she had been rather shaken by the accident and had not left her room since the day it happened. Shortly after this, his Lordship asked if he might call again and then took his leave, feeling very dissatisfied with his day.

Meanwhile Gave had struck up an acquaintance with Williams, and the day after the exasperating call his Lordship had paid on Lady Wateley he came to report on his activities.

'I have advanced your affairs much further than you think, your Lordship,' he told Granwel. 'I have seen Williams and also a number of men of business who are fully acquainted with his lawsuit. The inheritance he expects to get—which is the fortune he hopes to offer Henrietta—could very well be contested. In Hereford there is another nephew who is more closely related than he and completely unaware of his rights. We must write and tell this man to come immediately, befriend him when he is here, and ensure that the aunt's estate goes to him. Meanwhile I shall empty the pockets of the impertinent puppy who has dared set himself up as your rival. He has confided in me with a candour which does credit to his age, and has already told me all about his amours. He has even spoken of you, and of the kindness you showed his Henrietta the other day. He is well and truly snared, I assure you. You can leave this business entirely to me. I tell you, the dupe is firmly in our pocket.'

'This news goes some way to making up', said his Lordship, 'for yesterday's setback.'

And he recounted to his friend the manner in which he had been received by Lady Stralson.

'Gave,' he went on, 'I am head over heels in love and all this is taking a very lengthy turn. I cannot hold back indefinitely the violent urge I feel to have that girl... I have a new plan: listen well, then carry it out without delay. Tell Williams you are keen to meet the girl he loves. Say that since it is out of the question for you to go to her in the house of a lady you do not know, he must pretend to be ill and send urgent word to her that she must call for a sedan-chair and come to him at once... Get to work on that, Gave... go to it, but without neglecting the overall scheme, and leave me to act once you have set this new ploy in motion.'

Gave, the wiliest scoundrel in all England, succeeded so well in his efforts that, without losing sight of the main plan or forgetting to send word to Mr Clark, the other heir of Williams's aunt, that he was to come at once to London, he persuaded his friend to let him meet Henrietta in exactly the manner set out by Granwel. Miss Stralson was told that the man she loved was unwell. She wrote to him saying that she would find an opportunity to come and see him, using an imagined errand as a pretext. His Lordship was immediately informed from both quarters that on the Tuesday following, at four in the afternoon, Miss Henrietta would go out alone in a chair and make her way to Covent Garden.

'I worship her!' exclaimed Granwel, seeing his cup of joy overflow. 'And this time she shall not escape me! However violent the methods I have adopted to possess her may be, they do not fill me with remorse, since I am consoled by the pleasure she shall give me... Remorse! Can a heart like mine ever know the meaning of such a feeling? The habit of evildoing expunged it long ago from my calloused soul. A host of beautiful women, all seduced like Henrietta, deceived like her, abandoned like her, could tell her if I was ever moved by their tears, alarmed by their struggles, moved by their shame, restrained by their charms... Well, here is one more name to add to the list of the illustrious victims of my debauchery. And what use would women be if they were not good for that?... I defy anyone to prove to me that nature created them for any other reason. Let us leave the absurd mania for setting them on pedestals to the morons. By spouting such lily-livered nonsense, we have encouraged women to get above themselves. They observe that we set great store by the petty matter of *having them*, and accordingly think that they too are entitled to attach a great price to the same business and oblige us to waste on romantic elucubrations precious time which was meant only for pleasure... But what am I saying? Henrietta! Just one glance from your blazing eyes would rout all my philosophy and force me to bend my knee to you even as I swear to do you wrong!... What! Can it be that I am in love?... Begone!... Away, vulgar sentiment!... If there were a woman alive capable of making me feel it, I think I would rather blow her brains out than submit to her infernal arts!... No, no, weak, deceitful sex, you can never hope to fetter me! I have too often tasted of the pleasures you offer to be overawed by them. It is only by provoking the god of love that a man learns to desecrate his temple, and if he really wishes to destroy the creed of love, he cannot commit too many outrages against it...'

After these reflections, which were all too worthy of such a deep-dyed villain, Granwel sent out servants to hire all the sedan-chairs plying their trade anywhere near Cecil Street. He stationed men at every corner to ensure that no chair for hire approached Lady Wateley's residence, and ordered one, carried by two chairmen in his pay, to convey Henrietta, once they had her, towards St James's Park, to the house of a Madame Schmit who, for twenty years, had been a party to Granwel's secret affairs and to whom he had taken the precaution of sending word. Henrietta, without giving the matter a second thought or doubting the honesty of the public servants she assumed she was employing, put on her cloak and stepped into the chair which was offered her. She directed the men to take her to the Hotel Poland and, being unfamiliar with the streets, did not suspect for one moment during the entire journey that anything was amiss. She arrived at the house where Granwel awaited her. The chairmen, who had their orders, advanced up Madame Schmit's carriage-drive and did not stop until they reached her portico. The door opened...

Henrietta was astounded to find herself in a house which she did not know. She gave a cry, took several paces back, and told the chairmen that they had not taken her where she had instructed them to go...

'Miss Henrietta,' said Granwel coming forward at once, 'how thankful I must be to the good Lord above for giving me a second chance to be of service to you! I deduce from what you say and from what I see of the state of your chairmen, first, that they are drunk, and second, that they have mistaken their way. Is it not fortunate in the circumstances that it is at the house of a relative of mine, Lady Edward, that this minor mishap should befall you? Be so good as to come in, dismiss these rogues who cannot be trusted with your life, and allow my cousin's servants to procure a more reliable chair for you.'

It was difficult to refuse such an offer. Henrietta had met his Lordship only once before. She had no reason to complain of him, and now found herself in the hall of a house whose appointments did not suggest anything untoward. Even supposing there was some small risk in agreeing to the proposal which had been put to her, was there not even more danger in the prospect of remaining in the clutches of men who were not only drunk but, stung by the remarks Henrietta had addressed to them, were of a mind to abandon her there? So she entered the house, begging Granwel's pardon a thousand times. His Lordship himself sent the chairmen packing, and pretended to give orders to the servants to go out and find another chair. Miss Stralson proceeded further into the house where she was conducted by its mistress, and when she arrived at a charming salon the bogus Lady curtseyed and said to Granwel in a downright impudent tone:

'That's the style, your Lordship! To be honest I couldn't have supplied you with a prettier piece of goods.'

At this, Henrietta gave a shudder, her strength almost abandoned her, and she felt the full horror of her predicament. But she had enough presence of mind to control herself... her safety depended on it. She took her courage in both hands.

'What do you mean by those remarks, Madame,' she said, grasping La Schmit's arm, 'and who do people here think I am?'

'A very lovely girl,' replied Granwel, 'an angelic creature who very soon, I hope, will turn the most adoring lover that ever lived into the most fortunate of men!'

'Your Lordship,' said Henrietta, without releasing her hold on La Schmit, 'I see that my rash conduct has placed me in your power. But I appeal to your justice. If you take advantage of my situation, if you force me to hate you, you will certainly not gain as much as if you had trusted to the feelings you have started in me.'

'That is clever, but you will not get round me either by your bewitching face or the very subtle wiles which sustain you at this moment. You do not love me, you could never love me. But I do not aspire to your love. I know the man for whom your heart beats, and I reckon myself to be a happier one than he. He has no more than a trifling sentiment which I shall never obtain from you... But I have your delectable person which will fill my senses with an ecstasy of delights!'

'Stop, your Lordship! You have been misinformed. I am not in love with Williams. He has been offered my hand but I have not given him my heart. My heart is free and might love you as it might love any other man. But it will assuredly hate you if you insist on taking by force what you have it in your power to earn.'

'You do not love Williams? So why go calling on the man if you did not love him? Do you think I do not know that you were only going to see him because you believed he was ill?'

'Quite true. But I should not have gone at all if Mama had not insisted. Make enquiries. All I did was to obey her wishes.'

'Cunning vixen!'

'Your Lordship, acknowledge the feeling I now believe I can read in your eyes... Be generous, Granwel, do not force me to hate you when you could choose to have my respect.'

'Respect?'

'Heavens! Would you rather have my hate?'

'Hate would be no more than a warmer feeling which might make me feel something for you.'

'Are you really so ignorant of a woman's heart that you do not know what can come from gratitude? Send me home, your Lordship, and one day you will discover if Henrietta is ungrateful and whether or not she was worthy to have obtained your pity.'

'What! Me, show pity? Pity for a woman?' said Granwel, separating her from La Schmit... 'Me, relinquish the best opportunity I ever had and forgo the greatest of life's pleasures simply to spare you a moment's suffering?... Now why should I do that? Come here, you siren, come close, I will not listen to another word...'

And so saying, he tore away the kerchief covering Henrietta's lovely bosom and flung it to the far side of the room.

'God who art all goodness!' she cried as she threw herself at his Lordship's feet. 'Let me not be the victim of a man who is bent on making me hate him!... Have pity on me, your Lordship, I beg you! May your heart be touched by my tears and may it still hear the voice of virtue! Do not ruin an unfortunate woman who has done you no injury, in whom you inspired gratitude, and who might have felt more...'

As she said these words she was on her knees at his Lordship's feet, with her arms raised to heaven... Down her delicate cheeks coursed tears which, prompted by fear and desperation, fell on to her bare breasts which were many times whiter than alabaster.

'Where am I?' cried Granwel in bewilderment. 'What is this indescribable sensation which invades every fibre of my being? Where did you get those eyes which unman me? Who loaned you that beguiling voice whose every cadence melts my heart? Are you an angel from heaven or mere flesh and blood? Speak! Who are you? I do not know what I am saying, what I want, or what I am doing. All my faculties are swallowed up in you and allow me only to want what you want... Please rise, Miss Henrietta, get up, it is for me to fall at the feet of the god who enslaves me. Rise: your power is well and truly confirmed. It has become impossible... quite impossible for any impure desire to challenge it in my soul...'

And he returned her kerchief to her.

'Take this and cover your nakedness which intoxicates my senses. I have no need of anything to heighten the raging fever which so much beauty has stoked up in me!'

'Oh sublime man!,' exclaimed Henrietta, pressing his Lordship's hand. 'What reward do you not deserve for so generous a gesture?'

'What I wish to deserve, Mademoiselle, is your heart. That is the only reward to which I aspire, the only prize that would be worthy of me. You must never forget that once I held power of life and death over you and did not use it... And if that does not elicit from you the feelings I ask for, then remember that I shall be entitled to take my revenge, and that vengeance is a terrible thing in a soul such as mine... Please sit, Mademoiselle, and listen to what I have to say...

You have given me hope, Henrietta. You said you do not love Williams... you have allowed me to believe that you could love me... There you have my motives for desisting... and the reasons you must thank for your victory. I would rather deserve to be given freely what I could all too easily take by force. Do not make me regret this outbreak of virtue, do not force me to say that the faithlessness of men is a function of the deceitfulness of women, that if women always treated us as they should, we too would always behave as they would like.'

'Your Lordship,' replied Henrietta, 'you cannot possibly disguise the fact that in this unfortunate business the first wrong was committed by you. By what right did you seek to upset the settled pattern of my life? Why did you have me brought to a strange house, when I had entrusted myself to public servants in the belief that they would take me where I directed them? Given these certain facts, your Lordship, what entitles you to tell me what I ought to do? Should you not be offering me your apology instead of imposing conditions on me?'

And observing Granwel give a start of dissatisfaction:

'Nevertheless,' she went on quickly, 'your Lordship will perhaps allow me to explain? The first wrong you did can be excused, if you like, by the love you say you feel, and you have made amends for it by the noblest, the most generous of sacrifices... Of course I am grateful... I gave you my promise I would be, and have no intention of breaking my word... You should come and call on my family, your Lordship, I will urge them to treat you as you deserve. The habit of seeing you will constantly revive those feelings of gratitude you have planted in my heart. From this beginning you may conceive the largest hopes. I should go down in your estimation were I to say any more.'

'But how are you going to explain this incident to your friends?'

'In the most obvious way... as a mistake made by the chairmen who, by a most singular coincidence, delivered me a second time into the hands of a man who, having already once been of service to me, was only too delighted to be able to repeat his good deed.'

'And you solemnly declare, Mademoiselle, that you do not love Williams?'

'I cannot feel hatred for a man who has never behaved towards me except with plain, honest dealing. He loves me, of that I am quite sure. But he is my mother's choice, and there is nothing to prevent my sending him away.'

Then she rose to her feet.

'With your Lordship's permission,' she went on, 'I will now ask you to send out for a chair for me. This conversation, if prolonged, will arouse suspicion and might throw doubts on what I intend to say. Dismiss me now, your Lordship, and brook no delay in calling upon one who feels the sincerest gratitude for all your kindness and readily forgives you for devising so barbarous a plan in the light of the prudent, virtuous manner with which you choose to blot it from her memory.'

'Cruel girl,' said his Lordship, as he too rose from his chair, 'yes, I shall obey... But I am counting on your heart, Henrietta... I rely on it... Remember that, when betrayed, my passions reduce me to desperate measures... I shall use the same language as you: do not make me hate you. You would have run little danger from the hate you were forced to feel for me—but it will go hard indeed for you if you leave me no alternative but to hate you.'

'No, your Lordship, no. I will never make you hate me. I have more pride than you think, and I shall never do anything which would end my right to have your respect.'

At these words, Granwel sent for chairmen... there were many in the vicinity... they were announced... and his Lordship took Henrietta by the hand.

'Angelic creature,' he said, leading her off, 'do not forget that you have just won such a victory as no other woman but you could have ever dared dream of... a triumph which you owe entirely to the feelings you have started in me... and that if you ever betray those feelings, they will be replaced by all the crimes which my revenge can devise.'

'Farewell, your Lordship,' replied Henrietta as she stepped into the chair. 'You should never repent of a good deed. Remember, heaven and every just soul will be in your debt.'

Granwel went home in a state of inexpressible agitation. Henrietta returned to her mother looking so distraught that everyone thought she would faint.

Whoever reflects on the conduct of Miss Stralson will of course see at once that there was nothing but artifice and strategy in everything she had said to Granwel... and that she had stooped to these ruses, so foreign to her innocent nature, only so that she might escape the dangers which threatened her. We do not fear that in behaving in this way, our remarkable young woman has laid herself open to censure. The purest virtue must sometimes resort to less than blameless expedients.

When she reached her house, having no further reason for dissimulation, she told her mother and her aunt everything that had happened to her. She held nothing back of what she said in her efforts to escape, nor any of the promises she had been forced to make for the same reason. Apart from her imprudence in going out alone, no criticism was made of anything that Henrietta had done. But both her relatives were opposed to allowing the promise she had made to be honoured. They decided that Miss Stralson should take the greatest care to avoid Lord Granwel everywhere, and that Lady Wateley's door would remain firmly barred to whatever the scoundrel might attempt. Henrietta felt obliged to point out that such a course of action would greatly anger a man who might prove very dangerous when desperate; that in fact, if he had done wrong he had righted it like a gentleman; and that she believed in consequence that it would be better to allow him to call than make him angry. She felt justified in adding that such would also be Williams's opinion. But both ladies refused to change their minds, and orders were given accordingly.

Meanwhile Williams, who had waited all evening for Henrietta to come and, growing impatient when she failed to arrive, had left O'Donel (the name Gave adopted when he came to the Hotel Poland), begging his leave to go himself to find out the reason for a delay which gave him great cause for concern. He arrived at Lady Wateley's an hour after Henrietta had returned. When she saw him, she burst into tears... She took his hand and said to him tenderly:

'My dear, how near I came to being unworthy of you!'

And since she was at liberty to be alone for as long as she wished to speak with a man whom her mother already regarded as a son-in-law, they were left together to ponder all that had just happened.

'Oh Mademoiselle!' cried Williams when he had been told the full story, 'and it was on my account that you were to be dishonoured!... To give me a moment's satisfaction, you were almost reduced to becoming the most unfortunate of women!... yes, Mademoiselle, and all for a whim! I must tell you that I was not ill. A friend wished to meet you, and I wanted him to see what a fortunate man I am to possess the tenderness of such a beautiful woman. That is all the mystery there is, Henrietta. You see now that I am guilty twice over.'

'Let us say no more about it, my dear,' replied Miss Stralson. 'I am with you now and all is forgotten. But you do see, Williams,' she added, allowing her glance to ignite the sweetest of fires in the heart of the man she adored, 'you must see that I would never have seen you again if disaster had befallen me... You would not have wished to have any more to do with the victim of such a man and, in addition to my own grief, I should have known the despair of losing what I hold most dear in all the world...'

'You must not think that way, Henrietta,' Williams replied. 'There is nothing on this earth which will ever prevent you from being adored by a man who glories in your love... Since I shall worship you until the day I last draw breath, please believe that the sentiments you inspire rise above all human actions, and that it is as impossible for me not to feel them as it is for you to cease to be worthy of inspiring them.'

Then the two young people discussed the disastrous event with slightly cooler heads. They conceded that Lord Granwel was a very dangerous enemy, and that the course of action they had decided on would serve only to make him angrier. But there was no way of altering it, for the ladies would not hear of it. Williams spoke of his new friend, and such were the innocence and sense of security of those honest souls that they never suspected for one moment that the bogus Scotsman might be an agent in Granwel's employ. Far from it. Williams's favourable remarks about him made Henrietta wish to meet him. She was very thankful that he had formed so sturdy an acquaintance. But let us quit these right-thinking people who supped together, comforted each other, made plans for the future, and finally said goodnight... let us leave them there for a moment and return to their persecutor.

'By hell's pit and all the devils who dwell there,' his Lordship said when Gave came to see him the next morning, 'I do not deserve to live, my lad!... I am but a schoolboy, I am an utter fool, I tell you... I held her in my arms... I saw her kneel before me, and I did not have the courage to make her serve my appetites... I simply could not bring myself to humiliate her... She is no woman, my friend, she is a portion of the godhead come down on earth to wake in my soul virtuous feelings I never had before in my whole life. She led me to believe that she might love me some day, and I... I, who could never understand that loving a woman formed any part of the pleasure she gave me, I rejected the pleasure, which was there for the having, in exchange for an imaginary sentiment which torments and alarms me and which I do not yet understand.'

Gave took his Lordship severely to task. He made him fear that he had been the plaything of a mere chit of a girl. He told him roundly that such an opportunity would not come again in a hurry, for their quarry would now be on their guard...

'Yes, your Lordship,' he went on, 'remember that you will live to regret the mistake you have just made, and your leniency will cost you dear. Are you the kind of man who lets himself be carried away by a few tears and a pair of pretty eyes? And will the lethargy into which you have let your heart sink afford you the same quotient of sensual satisfaction which you ordinarily derive from the stoical indifference which you have sworn never to abandon? I tell you, your Lordship, you will rue your pity... upon my soul, you will regret it.'

'We shall soon know,' said his Lordship. 'Tomorrow, without fail, I shall call upon Lady Wateley. I shall study my clever Miss Henrietta, I shall watch her carefully, Gave, I shall read her feelings in her eyes, and if she is deceiving me then let her beware! I shall not lack new ways of making her fall into my clutches once more, and she will not always be able to count on her magic and witchcraft to escape again the way she did before!... As to you, Gave, continue ruining that damned Williams. When Mr Clark shows his face, send him to see Sir James, who I shall have put fully in the picture. He will advise Clark to pursue his inheritance on which another party has lodged a claim, and he shall have our full backing in his dealings with the judges... We can always undo all these arrangements if it is clear that my angel loves me, or press on with them hard if the infernal girl tricks me... But I repeat: I am a novice and I will never forgive myself for acting so foolishly. My stupidity must remain hidden from my friends, Gave. They would scoff without mercy and I should deserve every word of their mockery.'

They separated, and the next day—that is, the third after the interview at Madame Schmit's house—Granwel presented himself at Lady Wateley's in all his wealth and splendour.

Nothing had happened to change the ladies' resolve, and his Lordship was categorically refused entry... He stood firm and sent word that he must absolutely speak with Lady Stralson and her daughter concerning a matter of the greatest importance... The answer came back that the ladies he had asked for no longer lived at that address. He withdrew in a rage. His first thought was to seek out Williams, remind him of the service he had rendered Miss Stralson, giving the version he had agreed with Henrietta at La Schmit's, and then demand to be taken by him to see Lady Stralson or else, if his rival refused to do his bidding, they would settle their differences with naked blades... But this plan did not strike him as being sufficiently callous. His quarrel was with Miss Stralson alone... It was probable that she had not told her family what she had promised him she would say. She alone was responsible for the way he had been snubbed, and she alone was the person he should seek out and punish. It was to this end that he would direct his best efforts.

Among all the precautions they decided should be taken at Lady Wateley's, it was never suggested that no one should ever leave the house. Accordingly, Lady Stralson and her daughter did not fail to venture forth as was required by the business they had in London, and they even made forays designed to afford them pleasure or satisfy their curiosity. Lady Wateley, now somewhat recovered, accompanied them to the play, a few friends joined them there, and Williams also attended. Lord Granwel, well served by his spies, was kept fully informed of their movements and tried to turn every opportunity to advantage with a view to finding some way of satisfying both his vengeance and his wicked lusts. A month went by, however, without his being able to hit upon any such means, though on the other hand he never ceased to plot in the shadows.

Mr Clark who, on arriving from Hereford, was briefed by Sir James, had already set the matter of the inheritance in train with the powerful backing of Granwel and his friends. All this was a great worry to Williams, whose fortune the bogus Captain O'Donel, with his daily swindles, soon dilapidated to such an extent that he did not know which way to turn. But this approach proved to be too long-drawn-out for the liking of his impetuous Lordship, who continued to be no less impatient to have an earlier opportunity of humbling the unfortunate Henrietta. He was intent on seeing her on her knees before him once more; he wished to punish her for the stratagems she had used against him. Such were the evil schemes his cursed brain had hatched, when one day he was informed that the whole company residing under Lady Wateley's roof, none of whom had been much seen in society since Williams's affairs had taken such a disturbing turn, were nevertheless due the next day to go to Drury Lane, where Garrick, who was then planning to retire, was to perform *Hamlet* for the very last time.*

At that instant, Granwel's vile mind conceived the foulest plan that villainy could inspire. He resolved on nothing less than to have Miss Stralson arrested in the theatre and taken off that same evening to Bridewell.[1]

Let us throw some light on his unspeakable intentions.

A young woman named Nancy, a notorious courtesan, was newly come from Dublin. There she had committed numerous thefts and publicly ruined several Irish gentlemen before crossing to England where, though she was but recently arrived, she had already been guilty of a number of unpublicized misdemeanours. The police, armed with an order for her arrest, were actively working to apprehend her. Granwel got wind of this affair and went to see the officer who was to serve the warrant, and, discovering that the man was not personally acquainted with the young woman he had been ordered to arrest, had no difficulty in persuading him that she would be at Drury Lane that very evening, in the box which he knew would be occupied by Henrietta who, being there in the place of the courtesan who was being actively sought, would be at the mercy of his odious plans. He immediately offered to go bail for her, which meant that if the unfortunate prisoner agreed to his desires, she would be free... If she refused to do so, his Lordship would arrange for 'Nancy' to escape, confirm the opinion that Henrietta was one and the same as the Dublin adventuress, and thus ensure that his unfortunate victim's efforts to extricate herself would drag on interminably. The circle in which Miss Stralson moved gave him pause. But information would be laid before Lady Wateley, who had met Lady Stralson and her daughter for the first time when they had come to London... and knew she had relations of the same name in Hereford but might well have been misled as to the identity of these persons... so that there would be no difficulty in persuading her, said Granwel, that she had made a terrible mistake. What could she say or do to defend the two women and save them from the

[1] A prison for dissolute women.

arm of the law? This plan concocted in the head of Granwel was confided to Gave and Sir James, who both probed it and turned it this way and that and found nothing wrong with it, so that all were unanimous that it should be implemented at once. Granwel hurried off to the Justice of the Peace who was in charge of Nancy's case. He swore he had seen her the night before, and affirmed she would be at Drury Lane later that day in the company of honest ladies whom she had duped and to whose faces she had the impertinence to call herself a person of quality. The judge and his constable did not hesitate. The order was given and arrangements were made so that there would be no mistake in arresting the unfortunate Henrietta that same day at the play.

Granwel and his dreadful cohort did not fail to be at the theatre that evening. But as much from decency as from prudence, the members of this ignoble gang were to remain as mere bystanders. The box filled up. Henrietta took her place between Lady Wateley and her mother. Behind them sat Williams and Lord Barwill, a friend of Lady Wateley, a Member of Parliament and a man of the highest standing in London... The play ended. Lady Wateley decided that the rest of the audience should be allowed to leave first... It seems that she had some presentiment of the misfortune about to befall her friends. However, the constable and the men of the watch did not let Henrietta out of their sight for a moment, and Granwel and his cronies did not take their eyes off the constable. Finally, when the crowd had dispersed, the party left. Williams gave his arm to Lady Wateley, Lady Stralson walked alone, and Barwill squired Miss Henrietta. At the end of the corridor the officer stepped forward with his hand held high over the hapless young woman. He touched her lightly with his staff and ordered her to follow him. Henrietta fainted. Lady Wateley and Lady Stralson fell into each other's arms, and Barwill, seconded by Williams, fended off the men of the watch.

'You are making a mistake, you clods!' cried Barwill. 'Away with you, or I shall see that you are punished!'

This scene alarmed those spectators still in the theatre, who stared and crowded round... The constable, showing Barwill his warrant, informed him what sort of woman he took Henrietta to be. At that instant Sir James, prompted by Granwel, approached Barwill.

'Perhaps your Lordship would be good enough to allow me to point out', said the rogue, 'that you might well regret taking the side of a young woman you do not know. You may be in no doubt, your Lordship, that she is indeed Nancy from Dublin. I will swear an oath on it, if I have to.'

Barwill, who had known the two women for only a short space of time, turned to Lady Wateley, while Williams attended to Henrietta.

'Madame,' said he, 'here is a warrant and here is a gentleman whom I know to be a man incapable of deception. He tells me that the warrant is in order and that the constable has made no mistake. Would you be good enough to explain all this to me?'

'By all that I hold most sacred, your Lordship,' Lady Stralson promptly exclaimed, 'this poor girl is my daughter and not the wretched creature the police are looking for. Please, you must not desert us! Be our defender, get to the root of all this, your Lordship, protect us, be the friend of innocence!'

'Be off with you,' Barwill said to the constable. 'I shall be responsible for the young lady. I shall myself escort her to the Justice of the Peace forthwith. Go and wait for us at his house. There you will carry out whatever new orders you may be given. Until then I shall stand guarantor for Henrietta. Your task is finished.'

With these words the crowd broke up, the constable went his way, and Sir James, Granwel, and his accomplices went theirs. As he led the ladies away Barwill said:

'Let us go quickly and cease drawing attention to ourselves.'

He offered his arm to Henrietta and the rest of the company followed him. He and the three ladies got into his carriage, and they took only a few minutes to reach the house of the celebrated Fielding,* the justice in charge of the case.

This magistrate, taking account of the words of Lord Barwill, his long-standing friend, and after hearing the honest, candid answers of all three women, could not but conclude that he had been misled. To put this opinion beyond the reach of doubt, he set the description of Nancy against Henrietta's physical appearance and, on finding significant discrepancies between them, was effusive in offering the ladies his apologies and his good wishes. At this point they parted company with Lord Barwill, to whom they expressed their gratitude, and made their unhurried way home where Williams was waiting for them.

'Oh my dear,' said Henrietta, still very upset, when she saw him. 'What powerful enemies we have in this accursed town! I wish we had never come here!'

'There can be absolutely no doubt about it,' said Lady Stralson. 'This whole business must be laid at the door of that villain Granwel. I did not wish to air any of my ideas, out of circumspection, but my every thought merely confirms them. It is impossible not to suspect that the blackguard is hounding us in this way to pay off his score. And who knows', she went on, 'if he were not also responsible for saddling Williams with a new rival for his aunt's estate? We hardly knew this Mr Clark. At Hereford no one ever dreamed he was related to her, and now the man is succeeding and has the support of all London, while my unfortunate friend Williams may be on the verge of ruin! No matter,' continued the good, honest creature, 'even if he ends up poorer than Job, he shall still have my daughter's hand... This I promise, my dear... you have my word on it, Williams. For you are the only man my precious girl loves and I think of nothing save her happiness!'

Henrietta and Williams both flung themselves tearfully into Lady Stralson's arms, and overwhelmed her with the marks of their gratitude.

Yet Williams felt guilty, but did not dare admit it. Led astray by Gave, who masqueraded under the name of Captain O'Donel, he had, by gambling privately with this false friend or publicly in the assemblies into which he had been introduced by him, lost almost all the money he had brought to London. Knowing of no connection between Granwel and the Scottish Captain, he did not even remotely suspect that O'Donel was his Lordship's agent... He said nothing, sighed in silence, felt uneasy when offered marks of affection by Henrietta and her mother, and did not dare make a clean breast of his faults. He still hoped his luck might turn and perhaps restore his small fortune. But if it did not, and if, moreover, Clark were to win their lawsuit, then having made himself unworthy of the kindness he was shown daily, Williams, the hapless Williams, was resolved to do anything rather than abuse it.

As for Granwel, there is no need to paint his rage in words: it may be all too easily imagined.

'She is not a woman,' he repeated over and over to his friends, 'she is a creature of superhuman dimensions! Oh, I can strain my wit to mount plots against her, but she will always escape them!... Very well, let her continue... I advise her to do so... But if my star ever has the ascendant over hers, she will pay dearly for the tables she has turned on me!'

Meanwhile, all the heavy artillery calculated to bring poor Williams to his knees was drawn up in battle-order with even more art and dispatch than usual. The proceedings concerning the will had reached the point where a judgement was about to be given, and Granwel spared neither thought nor effort to back the case of Mr Clark who, since he conferred only with Sir James, never suspected whose was the hand which gave him such powerful support.

The day after the incident at Drury Lane, Granwel called upon Fielding to apologize for having been mistaken. This he managed with such good grace that the magistrate appeared to bear him no ill will, and the villain took himself off to devise new schemes, which, with greater success, might finally lure the hapless victim of his infatuation into his clutches.

An opportunity was not long in presenting itself. Lady Wateley owned a rather pretty country estate between Newmarket and Hosden,* about fifteen miles from London. She thought she would take her young niece there, to chase away the black thoughts which had begun to prey on her mind. Granwel, fully informed of every move Henrietta made, was told on which day she was to leave. He knew that the ladies were to spend a week on the estate, and return on the evening of the ninth day after their departure. He adopted a disguise, took with him a dozen of the ne'er-do-wells who roam the streets of London and will enter the service of any man for a few guineas, and galloped off at the head of these bravos to wait for Lady Wateley's carriage on the edge of a forest, not far from Newmarket and notorious for the murders committed there every day, through which the returning party would have to travel. The carriage arrived, it was halted... the traces were cut... the grooms were thrashed... the horses galloped off... the ladies fainted... Miss Stralson was carried unconscious to another carriage which stood waiting close by... Her kidnapper climbed into it after her, mettlesome steeds sprang into action, the carriage and its passengers arrived in London... His Lordship, who had neither revealed his identity to Henrietta nor spoken a single word to her during their entire journey, swept quickly into his town-house with his prey. He settled her in a sequestered chamber, sent his servants away... and unmasked himself.

'Well, fickle jade!' said he in a rage, 'do you know the man you thought you could betray with impunity?'

'Yes, your Lordship, I know you,' replied Henrietta bravely. 'Whenever disaster strikes, how can I avoid mentioning your name? You are the sole cause of all the misfortunes which have befallen me. Your only charm is your talent to cause me distress. You would not treat me differently if I were your most mortal enemy.'

'Cruel girl, was it not you who turned me into the most miserable of men by abusing my good faith? And by your duplicity, did you not make me the fool of the feelings I have conceived for you?'

'I believed your Lordship more just, for I imagined that before passing judgement on the accused you would at least allow them to speak.'

'And let myself be ensnared a second time in your damnable entanglements? Come now!'

'O most unhappy Henrietta! So you are to be punished for being too honest, too trusting! And it is the only man in the world you respect who will be the cause of all the calamities in your life!'

'What do you mean, Mademoiselle? Explain yourself. I am prepared to hear what you have to say in your defence, but do not think that you can play me for a fool... do not imagine you can abuse the love which is my fate and which has so surely worked to my shame... No, Mademoiselle, you will not pull the wool over my eyes a second time... Henrietta, I no longer feel anything for you, I see you now dispassionately, and the only desires you start in me are those prompted by crime and revenge.'

'Hold hard, sir, you make your accusations too lightly. A woman who set out to dupe you would have received you when you came calling on her, she would have encouraged you to hope, sought to placate you, and, if she had half the artifice you impute to me, she would have succeeded... Stop and consider the very different way in which I have behaved... and when you have deciphered my true motives, then you may condemn me, if you dare.'

'Come now! At our last meeting, you let me think that you were not indifferent to me. You yourself invited me to call on you... That was what placated me... it was on that condition that my heart turned delicate and cast out those other feelings which I see you do not approve of... Imagine! I did all I could to please you... I sacrificed everything in the hope of winning your heart, though had I heeded only my desires I would not have needed to possess it at all—and my reward was to have your door slammed in my face!... No, no, Miss Artful, you cannot hope to escape me again... you should not expect to, Mademoiselle, all your efforts will come to nothing.'

'Do with me what you will, your Lordship, I am in your power...' (and here she shed a few involuntary tears) '... but in taking me know that it will be surely at the cost of my mother's life... No matter. Use me as you will, I say, I shall not attempt to defend myself... But if you can hear the truth without suspecting me of deceiving you, then I would ask your Lordship if the occasions on which you were turned away do not utterly vindicate both the admission I made of my feelings for you and the fears that my friends felt of their power to harm me... For what would have been the point of turning you away if they had not been afraid of you? And would they have feared you had I not stated my feelings for you openly? Take your revenge, your Lordship, settle your account, punish me for surrendering too willingly to my sweet transgression... I deserve your anger... you can never give it too loose a rein... nor be too violent in expressing it.'

'Well now,' said Granwel, in a state of the most unbelievable agitation, 'did I not predict that this wily creature would again try to bring me to heel?... No, no, Mademoiselle, you have no right to speak of your transgressions, for they are all mine... I alone am guilty, and I am the one who must punish myself. I was a monster, that is clear, for I plotted against a woman who loved me from the bottom of her heart... I could not see it, I did not know... Ascribe it to the extreme humility of my character: how could I ever aspire to the proud thought that I might be loved by a woman like you?'

'You won't mind if I point out, your Lordship, that neither you nor I are given to sarcasm or jesting. You make me the unhappiest of women and I never wished that you should be the most unfortunate of men. That is all I have to say, your Lordship. Clearly you do not believe me. Please allow me my turn to have enough pride, humiliated though I am, not even to try to convince you. It is hard enough for me to have to blush for my behaviour in front of my family and friends, without being forced to regret it to the face of the man who drove me to it... You should not believe a word of what I say, your Lordship, I am the most duplicitous of women, and you ought not to allow yourself to see me in any other light... Do not believe me, I say...'

'But, Mademoiselle, if it is true that your feelings for me were really what you seem to be trying to convince me they were, then when you were not allowed to see me, what prevented you from writing? Did you not think how anxious I would be after the rebuff I had received?'

'I am not my own mistress, your Lordship. That is something you should never forget, for you will agree that a young person of my age, whose sentiments are a reflection of the tenor of her education, must devote all her attention to expunging from her heart any sentiments of which her family cannot approve.'

'And now that you are in effect free of your barbaric family, which was opposed both to your wishes and mine, will you agree here and now to be my wife?'

'What? At a time when my mother may be dying and I am kidnapped by your handiwork? Oh, please allow me to consider the woman who brought me into the world before I give any thought to my own happiness!'

'Make your mind easy on that score, Mademoiselle. Your mother is quite safe. She is at Lady Wateley's, and both are in as little danger as you. My orders that they should be given every assistance at the same moment that you were carried off were executed even more exactly than the plan which placed you into my power. You need have no anxiety on that score. You must not allow such worries to influence the clear answer I ask you to give me. Will you accept my hand in marriage, Mademoiselle, or do you refuse it?'

'Do you think that this is a matter which I can decide without the approval of my mother? It is not your mistress that I wish to be, but your wife. Should I be your wife legally if, being still dependent on my family, I were to marry you without their formal blessing?'

'But Mademoiselle, have you forgotten that you are in my power? That slaves are in no position to lay down conditions?'

'If that is how matters stand, your Lordship, I shall not marry you... I have no wish to be the slave of the man whom my heart has chosen.'

'Proud creature! Will I never succeed in taming you?'

'And what fine sentiment do you associate with achieving victory over a slave? How can what is gained through violence increase your self-regard?'

'It is not always the case that fine sentiment, of which so much is made, is so precious a thing as women imagine.'

'Leave such callous ideas to those who do not deserve to have the love of the persons they seek to dominate. Such odious maxims do not suit you, sir.'

'But Williams, Mademoiselle... as to friend Williams... I wish all the calamities nature inflicts on human kind would rain down on the scoundrel's head!'

'Do not call the best of men by such a name!'

'He has stolen your heart from me, he is to blame for everything. I know you love him.'

'I have already given you my answer on that subject and I shall go on saying the same thing. Williams loves me, that is all... Oh sir, you will never be as unhappy as you think as long as your plans are not threatened by anything more dangerous than him.'

'No, you Jezebel, no. I do not believe you...' (growing agitated) '...Come, Mademoiselle, make ready, I have given you plenty of time to reflect. As you can well imagine, it was not to be made a dupe by you for a second time that I brought you here. Matters stand thus: either you become my wife tonight... or my mistress!'

And so saying, he seized her roughly by the arm and dragged her to the pagan altar on which the brute intended to sacrifice her to his desires.*

'One word, your Lordship,' cried Henrietta, holding back her tears and resisting Granwel's onslaught with all her might, 'just one word, I implore you... What do you hope to gain by the crime you are about to commit?'

'All the pleasure it can give me!'

'Then you shall have that pleasure for just one day, your Lordship. Tomorrow I shall be neither your slave nor your mistress. Tomorrow you shall find only the corpse of the woman whose life you ruined... Oh Granwel, you do not know what kind of person I am or the lengths to which I am capable of going. If it is true that you have the slightest feeling for me, do you think you can justify my death with a fleeting gratification of your senses? The pleasures you are intent on taking by force I shall give to you: why do you not wish to accept them as the gift of my heart?... You are a fair-minded man, a man of feeling,' she continued, her head half bowed and holding her clasped hands out to her tormentor, 'take pity on my tears!... May my cries of despair reach once more into your soul... you will not repent of having heard them! Oh your Lordship! Behold before you, in the posture of a supplicant, a woman who gloried in the prospect of one day seeing you fall at her feet. You want me to be your wife? Very well! Act as though I were, and you will not dishonour the woman whose destiny it is to be so closely entwined with yours!... Return Henrietta to her mother, she implores you, and it will be with the tenderest, the most ardent feelings that she will repay you for your generosity.'

But Granwel was no longer looking at her but striding around the apartment... inflamed by love... tormented by sensual appetite... burning for revenge... yet stayed despite himself by feelings of pity born of love which her gentle voice, proud bearing, and freely flowing tears stirred in his heart... At certain moments he was ready to seize her again, at others he wanted to forgive her... and there was no way of telling to which of these two impulses he would surrender, when Henrietta, sensing his hesitation, said:

'Come, your Lordship, come and judge for yourself if I have any wish to deceive you. Take me to my mother yourself, come with me and ask her for my hand, and you shall see whether or not I am willing to serve your desires...'

'What an incomprehensible girl you are!' said his Lordship. 'Very well, yes! I shall yield to you a second time. But should you be so unfortunate as to decide to trick me again, then there is no human power capable of saving you from the effects of my vengeance... Mark me: it will be terrible!... It will mean shedding the blood of those you love best... there shall be not one, not a single one of those who are closest to you, who will not be slaughtered by my hand and left for dead at your feet!'

'I will submit to all your conditions, sir. Let us go now. Do not prolong the anxiety I feel for my mother. All I require for my happiness to be complete is her consent... to know that she is out of danger... and your desires shall be instantly gratified.'

His Lordship ordered the horses.

'I shall not come with you,' he told Henrietta. 'This is not the time for me to meet your friends—you see how much I trust you? But tomorrow, at noon exactly, I shall send a carriage for you and your mother. You will come to my house, you will be received by my family, the lawyers will be in attendance, and I shall be your husband before the day is out. Yet if I detect, either from you or your relations, the slightest hint of a rebuff, do not forget Mademoiselle, that you will not have in the whole of London a more mortal enemy than I... Now go. Your carriage awaits. I will not even see you to it. I cannot wait to be free of your eyes, which wreak such singular havoc in my heart that in them I see simultaneously everything which impels me towards crime and all that points me towards virtue.'

When Henrietta reached home she found the house in an uproar. Lady Stralson had received injuries to her head and arm. Her cousin Wateley had taken to her bed on account of the dreadful fright they had received. Two grooms had been almost crushed when the carriage had been stopped. Yet Granwel had been as good as his word. Once he had left the scene, the same men who had led the attack on the carriage became its staunchest defenders. They had rounded up the horses, helped the ladies back into the carriage, and escorted them to the gates of London.

Lady Stralson had shed tears far more bitter for the loss of her daughter than for the sudden hurts she had received. She could not be consoled, and the most serious measures were about to be taken for her recovery when Henrietta appeared and flung herself into her mother's arms. A few words clarified the situation but told Lady Wateley nothing new, for she had been in no doubt that the wicked Granwel was the sole perpetrator of this latest outrage. Miss Stralson related what had happened, and her account only served to deepen the general anxiety. Once his Lordship had formally asked for her hand, there would be no going back: Henrietta would have to become his wife the very next day... If they refused to accept his proposal, they would make a terrible enemy!

Faced with this appalling dilemma, Lady Stralson proposed that they should return at once to Hereford. But although this would be a decisive step, would it be enough to save the unfortunate mother and her daughter from the fury of a man who had sworn to pursue them to the ends of the earth if they did not keep their word? Would it not be better to lodge a complaint and call upon powerful protectors? But adopting this course would merely infuriate to the point of incandescence a man whose passions were terrifying and whose vengeance was to be dreaded. Lady Wateley was inclined to favour the marriage. It was difficult to imagine that Miss Henrietta could do better for herself: a lord of the very highest rank... with vast wealth... and surely the ascendant she had gained over him must convince Henrietta that she would be able to twist him around her little finger for the rest of her life?

But Miss Stralson's feelings did not allow her to share this view. Everything she had undergone had made Williams dearer to her and served merely to increase her detestation of the beast who pursued her so relentlessly. She declared that she would prefer to die rather than accept Lady Wateley's proposal, and added that the horrible position in which she had been placed of having to dissemble with Lord Granwel made him even more odious to her. They agreed therefore on delaying tactics, which meant, first, receiving his Lordship courteously and continuing to fan the flame of his love by allowing him to hope, whereas in reality they would put out his fire by postponing action indefinitely; and secondly, while all the foregoing was in train, completing the business they severally had in London, arranging for Henrietta to marry Williams in secret, and then returning to Hereford one fine day without Granwel suspecting a thing. Once there, they reasoned, if that dangerous man continued to stalk a woman who now had a husband, his actions would acquire a degree of gravity which would allow Lady Stralson and her daughter to seek the protection of the law. But would this plan really answer the purpose? Having been deceived twice already, would not a man as combustible as Granwel have grounds for believing that every effort was being made to deceive him a third time? And if this were so, what could they not expect to fear he might do? But these considerations did not enter the minds of Henrietta's friends. They resolved to keep to the plan they had adopted, and the next day Miss Stralson wrote to her persecutor to say that her mother's state of health was such as to prevent her honouring the promise she had given him. She earnestly begged his Lordship not to be angry, but on the contrary to call and console her for the regret she felt at being unable to keep her word and comfort her in the distress caused by her mother's illness.

Granwel's first reaction was one of vexation.

'I have been tricked again!' he cried. 'This is the third time I have been that deceitful creature's dupe!... And I had her in my power!... I could have forced her to satisfy my appetites... made her a slave to my will... But I allowed her to win... faithless jade... she has escaped me once more... But let us see what she wants with me... let us discover if it is true that she can use her mother's health as a legitimate excuse...'

Granwel arrived at Lady Wateley's and, never for one moment intimating, as will easily be imagined, that he was the instigator of the incident of the previous day, he merely observed that he had heard what had happened, and that the deep concern no one fortunate enough to have met Lady Stralson could help but feel for her had prompted him to call on her at once to enquire after her health and that of those persons who were close to her. This beginning was taken at face value, and the same tone was maintained. After a few moments Granwel took Henrietta to one side and asked if her mother's slight indisposition would place lengthy obstacles in the way of his happiness in becoming her husband, and enquired whether, despite this delay, he might not hazard a few proposals. Henrietta quieted him and begged him not to be impatient. She told him that although her mother and aunt pretended otherwise, they were nonetheless convinced that he was the sole cause of everything they had suffered the day before, and that in light of this it was definitely not the moment to open any such negotiations.

'Is it not a great deal', she went on, 'that we are allowed to see each other? Can you still accuse me of deceiving you when I have just arranged for you to have a permanent welcome in a house which you have filled with acrimony and gloom?'

But Granwel, who never believed that anyone had done anything for him at all unless his every wish was gratified, gave only a stammering sort of answer, saying to Miss Stralson that he was prepared to grant her another twenty-four hours. At the end of that time he would want to know exactly where he stood. Then his visit came to an end. This brief, quiet interlude will allow us to return to Williams, of whom we have lost sight in all of this.

Given the criminal attentions of Granwel and Gave, it would have been difficult for the poor young man's affairs to have been in a more parlous state than they were. A few days hence the court would deliver its verdict, and Mr Clark, who had the whole of London on his side, already considered himself, not without reason, to be sole heir to the estate which Williams was counting on to offer, together with his hand, to the lovely Henrietta. Granwel left no stone unturned in his efforts to ensure that the court's ruling was favourable to his designs. On this piece of chicanery, which had begun as a minor matter, he now placed his entire hopes for the success of his whole plan: would Henrietta be prepared to marry Williams if he were utterly ruined? And supposing that her niceness of sentiment would make her feel that she should, would her mother consent to it? Despite everything Granwel had learned from Miss Stralson at their last interview, he could hardly have failed to detect more diplomacy and circumspection than affection and truth in the words of the woman he loved. Moreover, he was kept informed by his spies, and was left in no doubt that the two young people went on seeing each other. He therefore decided to accelerate Williams's ruin, as much to discomfit both Stralsons as with a view to using Williams's undoing as his ultimate means of getting Henrietta in his clutches once more... And this time he swore she would not escape him again.

As for Captain O'Donel, after he had got all he could out of Williams, he had unceremoniously abandoned him and returned to Granwel's house, going out very little lest he be recognized. His protector had insisted he go on taking this precaution until the business in hand was concluded, which, according to his Lordship, should not take much more than a few days longer.

In the meantime Williams, reduced to his last four guineas and not even having the wherewithal to meet the expenses of the lawsuit which he would have to pay, resolved to go on bended knee to kind Lady Stralson and her adorable daughter and confess frankly what he had done. He was on the way to see them when the final bolts of the thundercloud which hung over his head were suddenly unleashed. The verdict was given, Clark was judged to be two degrees of kinship closer than Williams to the aunt whose estate was contested. At a stroke poor Williams was deprived of the small fortune he currently enjoyed and the larger one he had hoped to inherit one day. Crushed by so many reverses, unable to face the horror of his situation, he was ready to end his life. But he found it impossible to do the deed without seeing for one last time the only human being who made his life worthwhile. He hastened to Lady Wateley's. He knew Lord Granwel was a visitor there, and he also knew why. However troubling he found this circumstance, he dared not express his disapproval. Was it his place to try to impose his will in the precarious position in which he now found himself? It had been agreed, consequent upon the policy now directing whatever measures needed to be taken, that Williams should always come to the house secretly. It was therefore dark when he arrived, having chosen a time when all were quite sure that Granwel would not put in an appearance. As yet, no one had heard anything of his lost lawsuit. He told them, and at the same time added the ghastly news of his losing streak at the card table.

'Oh, dearest Henrietta!' he cried, flinging himself at the feet of the woman he loved, 'I have come to say farewell forever, to release you from your promise, and break with my life. Deal prudently with my rival, Henrietta, and do not refuse his proposal of marriage. He alone can now make you happy. The mistakes I have made and the reverses I have suffered no longer permit me to be yours. Become the wife of my rival, Henrietta—as your best friend I beg you. Blot out the memory forever of a poor wretch who is no longer worthy of your pity.'

'Williams,' said Henrietta, raising him to his feet and sitting him down at her side, 'I have never stopped loving you for one moment. How could you ever have believed that my feelings depended on the whims of fate? And how unjust a creature would I be were I to stop loving you because of your follies or your ill fortune? Believe me, Williams, my mother will never abandon you any more than I shall. I will take it upon myself inform her of what has happened to you—I want to spare you the distress of telling her yourself. But swear you will do nothing rash, Williams, and say that for as long as you are certain of my love nothing so terrible can ever happen that will tempt you to end your life!'

'Dearest Henrietta! Yes, I do so swear now on bended knee. What is more sacred to me than your love? What misfortune can I fear if I still have your heart? Yes, I shall live, because you love me, but do not ask me to marry you, you must never agree to join your fate to that of a miserable wretch who is no longer worthy of you! Become his Lordship's wife. If you do, although I would not greet the event without sadness, I could at least bear it without jealousy, and the magnificent life which so powerful a man would enable you to lead would, if anything could, console me for not having been able to aspire to the same bliss...'

It was not without shedding tears that the tender Henrietta heard these words, which she so disliked that she cut them short.

'But this is monstrous unfair!' she cried, taking Williams's hand in hers. 'Can I be happy if you are not? And would you be happy to know that I lay in another man's arms? No, my dear, I shall never desert you. I now have an additional debt to repay... one that your misfortune has laid upon me. Until this moment I was attached to you by love alone, now I am bound by ties of duty... It is my duty to console you, Williams... by whom would you prefer to be comforted if not by your Henrietta? Should it not be my hand that dries your tears? Then why would you deny me the pleasure of doing so? Had you married me with the fortune which you should have inherited, you would have owed me nothing, my dear. But now I can be joined to you by the chains of love and the bonds of gratitude.'

Williams bedewed Henrietta's hands with his tears, and so overpowering was the emotion which burned in him that he was prevented from finding words adequate to express it. Lady Stralson entered as the souls of our two lovers, lost in each other's arms, were ignited by the divine sparks of the love which consumed them. Her daughter told her what Williams dared not say, and ended her account of the matter by asking as a particular favour that her mother would not change the way of thinking she had always adopted.

When the excellent Lady Stralson knew everything, she threw her arms around Williams's neck and said:

'We loved you when you were rich and we shall love you even more now that you are poor! Never forget your two good friends, you may always look to them for comfort... You have acted rashly... you are young... you have no attachments... and you will put such foolishness behind you once you are married to the one you love.'

We shall not report the tender words which Williams spoke to express his affection. The reader who has a heart like his will know what they were and does not need them to be spelled out, while no number of words would explain his feelings to those whose souls are frigid.

'But Henrietta,' Lady Stralson continued, 'I greatly fear that behind all this I can again detect the handiwork of the terrible man who hounds us!... This Scottish Captain who succeeded in ruining our good friend Williams in such short order... and this Mr Clark whom we never knew was a relative of our dear friend's aunt... it all smacks of a conspiracy hatched by that reprobate... Oh, how I wish we had never come to London! This is a dangerous city, Henrietta, and we must leave and never come back!'

It is not difficult to believe that Henrietta and Williams were only too pleased to fall in with this suggestion. They therefore settled on a date and resolved that they would leave on the next day but one, but in such secrecy that even Lady Wateley's servants should know nothing of their intentions. When these plans were agreed by all the parties, Williams was about to leave when Henrietta stopped him.

'Have you forgotten, dear Williams,' she said, giving him a purse full of gold, 'that you told me of the sorry state of your finances and that it is for me alone to mend them?'

'Oh, Mademoiselle, you are too generous!'

'Williams,' said Lady Stralson, 'she reminds me of how remiss I am... Take her purse... take it... Today I shall allow Henrietta the pleasure of giving, but only on condition that she agrees not to deny it to me ever again...'

Reduced to tears, Williams left them in a welter of gratitude, saying:

'If I was meant to know happiness on earth, then it is most assuredly only with this respectable family that I shall find it. I have done wrong... I have received a terrible setback... but I am young... the army will offer me a way of redeeming myself... I will strive to ensure that my children never learn anything of all this: those precious fruits of my love shall always be the sole concern of my life, and I shall so wage war on fate that they will never feel the effects of my misfortune!'

The next day Lord Granwel paid a call on the woman he loved. He was received with the same self-control which he was ordinarily shown. But, too astute not to detect small variations in the behaviour of Henrietta and her mother, and too shrewd not to put them down to the revival of Williams's fortunes, he made enquiries. Although the planned departure and Williams's most recent visits had been kept secret, it was impossible that a whiff of something should not have leaked out. It could not be long before Granwel, most efficiently served by his spies, would know everything.

'Well now,' said he to Gave, once the latest reports had been brought to him, 'so I have been duped by that treacherous crew yet again! Even as Henrietta receives me at home, all she is thinking about is rewarding my rival!... Deceitful, faithless sex, how right we are to abuse you and despise you afterwards! Does a day go by when your manifold faults do not fully justify the reproaches levelled against you?... Oh Gave! The ungrateful vixen does not know what kind of enemy she has offended! I want my revenge to stand as the vengeance of my entire sex, I will make her weep tears of blood for the wrong she has done me and for the wrongs of all her kind!... Now Gave, in your dealings with that good-for-nothing Williams, did you acquire a specimen of his handwriting?'

'I have one here.'

'Good... Give it to me... Take the paper to Johnson: the rogue is well skilled in the art of forging all manner of hands. I want him to counterfeit Williams's and use it to write the note I shall now dictate to you.'

Gave wrote down the message and delivered the sample to Johnson, who copied it. The day before Henrietta was due to leave, at about seven o'clock in the evening, she was handed the following note by a man who assured her that it was from Williams who, he said, awaited her reply with the greatest impatience:

I am about to be arrested for a debt which amounts to more than all the money I can presently lay my hands on. There is no doubt that powerful enemies are at work. At most I may have a moment to embrace you for the last time. But I hope I might know that joy and receive your advice. Come to the corner of Kensington Gardens and bring a moment's solace to your luckless Williams, who is ready to die of his sorrows if you should deny him this small comfort.

On reading the note Henrietta was extremely distressed. Fearing that this latest imprudence would finally exhaust her mother's goodwill, she resolved to hide this new calamity from her, furnish herself with as much money as she could, and rush to Williams's aid... For a moment she reflected upon the risk she incurred in going abroad at such an hour... But what had she to fear from his Lordship? She believed he had been completely taken in by the strategy employed by her mother and her friend, Lady Wateley. The two ladies had not stopped receiving his visits, and Granwel himself had never seemed in a more settled humour... So what was there to be afraid of?... His Lordship might still take action against Williams, and perhaps he was the architect of this new disaster. But wishing to strike at a rival who was still greatly feared was not a reason for making a fresh attempt to abduct the woman of whose love he was sure.

Oh weak and hapless Henrietta, thus did your foolish thoughts run! Love whispered them to you and justified them. You did not pause to reflect that scales are never more firmly fixed on the eyes of lovers than when the ground is about to open beneath their feet!... Miss Stralson sent out for a sedan-chair and was taken to the appointed place... The chair stopped... the door opened...

'Mademoiselle,' said Granwel, handing her out of it, 'I am sure you were not expecting to see me here. I imagine you are about to say that the bane of your life seems to materialize at every turn.'

Henrietta gave a cry, then attempted to break free and run away.

'Not so fast, my sweet angel,' said Granwel placing the barrel of his pistol against her heart and indicating with a gesture that she was surrounded, 'you have no hope of escape, Mademoiselle, no hope at all... I am tired of being your dupe... I must be avenged... So keep your mouth shut, or I shall not be held accountable for your life.'

Miss Henrietta was carried in a faint to a post-chaise. His Lordship climbed in after her and, without stopping once, made good speed to the north of England, where Granwel owned a vast, isolated castle on the Scottish borders.

Gave remained at his Lordship's town-house. He had orders to keep his eyes open and provide accurate reports, to be carried by express couriers, of the latest news from London.

Lady Stralson noticed that Henrietta had gone out two hours after she had left the house. She had every confidence in her daughter's conduct, and at first was not unduly concerned. But when she heard ten o'clock strike, she shivered and the suspicion formed that new snares might have been set... She went at once to see Williams... Trembling, she asked him if he had seen Henrietta... On hearing the young man's replies, she became even more alarmed. She told Williams to wait for her and ordered her carriage to take her to Lord Granwel's house... She was told that he was indisposed... She insisted on being announced, feeling confident that his Lordship would allow her to enter when he heard her name. But the same answer was returned. Her suspicions grew stronger. She went back to Williams and both, filled with horrible foreboding, drove at once to find the Prime Minister, whom they knew was related to Granwel. They explained their predicament and demonstrated that the man who continued to disrupt their lives so cruelly, the man who was the sole cause of everything that had happened to them, the man who, in short, had abducted the daughter of one of them and the bride-to-be of the other, was none other than Lord Granwel...

'Granwel?' said the Prime Minister in amazement. 'But are you aware that he is a friend... a relative?... Whatever indiscretion I may suspect him to be capable of, I cannot believe he would stoop to commit such horrors...'

'It is he! He is the man, your Lordship!' replied Henrietta's distraught mother. 'Look into the matter and you will see if we are trying to deceive you.'

Men were dispatched immediately to Granwel's house. Gave, not daring to cross agents of the Prime Minister, told them his Lordship had left on a tour of his estates. This reply, added to his own suspicions and the complaint made by Henrietta's mother, finally opened the Prime Minister's eyes.

'Madame,' said he to Lady Stralson, 'go home with your young friend and be calm. I shall look into this matter. You may rest assured that I shall do everything in my power to return to you what you have lost and restore your family's honour.'

But all these measures had taken time. The Prime Minister had been reluctant to authorize any legal steps before he had first heard the views of the King, since Granwel's royal appointment made him answerable to the monarch. The delay had enabled Gave to dispatch a courier to his friend's castle, and as a result the events which we have still to narrate would run their course without impediment.

When Granwel reached his estate he had succeeded in calming Miss Henrietta to the extent of persuading her that she should rest a while. But he had taken the precaution of putting her in a room from which it was impossible to escape. However little inclined Miss Stralson was to sleep in her cruel predicament, she was much relieved to have a few hours of peace, and had been making no sound of any kind that might indicate she was awake when Gave's courier arrived. At that instant his Lordship knew that if he wished to succeed, then he would have to act quickly. He was prepared to adopt any means of achieving his end. However criminal this policy might prove to be, he was determined to stop at nothing, provided that he both got revenge and had his way with his victim. 'The worst that can happen', he told himself, 'is that I shall marry her and not be able to show my face in London again except as her husband.' But the way matters stood, as he judged from what Gave's courier had told him, he saw that he would not have time for anything unless he could dispel the storm-clouds which were gathering over his head. To this end, he quickly realized that he must do two things: smooth Lady Stralson's feathers and neutralize Williams. One abominable subterfuge, one more odious crime, would deal with both at a stroke, and Granwel, who never counted the cost when bent on satisfying his urges, had no sooner conceived his vile plan than his every thought was directed to its implementation.

Ordering the courier to wait, he went to see Henrietta. He began by making the most insulting propositions which, as on previous occasions, she warded off with practised ease. This was precisely what Granwel wanted. His aim was to make her deploy all her persuasive skills so that he might seem to be taken in by them once more, and then catch her in the same traps that she was by now accustomed to set for him. There was no art which Miss Stralson did not use in her efforts to overturn the plans which his Lordship outlined to her: tears, supplication, love, all were mobilized pell-mell against him, and after a long struggle Granwel, with every appearance of yielding, fell slyly to his knees before Henrietta.

'Heartless girl,' he said, bedewing her hands with the bogus tears of his remorse, 'your power is too great for me, you carry all before you, and I surrender now and forever... It is over, Mademoiselle... henceforth you shall find in me not a persecutor but your friend. My heart is nobler than you can possibly know and, like you, I too wish to prove that I am capable of the most extreme acts of courage and virtue. You know what I could by rights demand of you, all I could ask for in the name of love, and all I could obtain through violence. Well, Henrietta, I hereby renounce all my desires! Yes, I intend to force you to respect me, even some day to regret me perhaps... You should know that I was never your dupe, that pretend as you might I was not taken in, for you love Williams... Mademoiselle, it is with my blessing that you shall have him... Will this be enough to earn my pardon for all the suffering I have caused you?... By giving you Williams, and making good out of my own fortune the reverses which his finances have experienced of late, shall I find some small place in your heart, dear Henrietta, and will you then still say that I am your cruellest foe?'

'Oh, most generous benefactor!' exclaimed the young woman, only too glad to reach out for the illusion which momentarily flattered her hopes. 'What divinity has inspired this resolve in you? And why are you so pleased to change poor Henrietta's fate so expeditiously? You ask me what place you will earn in my heart. All the feelings of a grateful heart which do not belong to the unfortunate Williams shall be yours forever. I shall be your friend, Granwel... your sister... your confidante. Having no care other than to please you, I shall ask only one favour of you, which is that I might live the rest of my life near you and use every moment of it to show my gratitude... Oh consider, your Lordship... are not the feelings of a free heart preferable to those which you intended to take by force? You would have merely made a slave of a woman who will become your dearest friend.'

'Yes, Mademoiselle, you shall be that loyal friend,' stammered Granwel. 'I had so many bridges to mend with you that even with the sacrifice of my own feelings I still dare not think I have yet made full restitution. But I shall trust to time and my best behaviour.'

'What can your Lordship be thinking of? How badly you know me! Just as when attacked I defend myself, so repentance melts my heart and I no longer remember the injuries done me by anyone who takes a single step to obtain my forgiveness.'

'Very well, Mademoiselle, let all be forgotten on both sides, and give me the satisfaction of arranging here the wedding you want so much.'

'Here?' said Henrietta with an anxious start which she could not repress. 'But, your Lordship, I thought we would be returning to London!'

'No, no, my dear young lady, I regard it as a matter of honour not to let you go back to the capital except as the wife of the rival to whom I give you... Yes, by displaying you in this way, I want to show all England how dear my victory over myself has cost me. Do not object to my plan, for in it I shall find both my triumph and my serenity. Let us write to your mother and say that she is to calm her fears. Let us invite Williams to come here, celebrate this marriage at once, and then return to town the next day.'

'But, your Lordship, shall my mother be informed?'

'We shall ask for her consent. She is most unlikely to refuse and it shall be Lady Williams who will come and thank her in person.'

'Very well, your Lordship, I place myself in your hands. I feel such affection and gratitude that I would not wish to interfere in the arrangements which you are kind enough to make for my happiness. Do what you think fit, your Lordship, and I shall approve it all... I am so full of the sentiments which I owe entirely to you, too absorbed by feeling them and putting them into words, that I quite forget anything which interferes with my enjoyment of them.'

'But Mademoiselle, you must write.'

'To Williams?'

'And to your mother. Would what I say carry as much conviction as if you were to write yourself?'

The wherewithal was brought and Miss Henrietta wrote the two following notes:

MISS HENRIETTA TO WILLIAMS

We should both fall at the feet of the most generous of men. Come and help me express the gratitude which we both owe him. Never was there a nobler sacrifice, never was it made more graciously, never was it more complete! Lord Granwel wishes to join us in matrimony himself, Williams, and with his own hand tie our holy knot... Come quickly... Embrace my mother, obtain her consent, and tell her that soon her daughter will know the happiness of holding her in her arms.

THE SAME TO HER MOTHER

After a time of terrible anxiety follows the gentlest calm. Williams will show you my letter, most loved of all mothers! I beg of you, raise no objection either to your daughter's happiness or Lord Granwel's intentions—they are as pure as his heart. Adieu. Forgive your daughter who is so overwhelmed by feelings of gratitude that she can hardly express the sentiments which fill her for the best of mothers.

To these missives Granwel added two others, which assured Williams and Lady Stralson of the joy he felt on being able to bring together two young people whose most devoted friend he wished to be. He invited Williams to call on his London lawyer and receive the ten thousand guineas which he begged him to accept as a wedding gift. These letters breathed true affection, and bore such a stamp of openness and candour that it was impossible not to take them at face value. At the same time his Lordship also wrote to Gave and his friends instructing them to still public rumours, calm the Prime Minister, and spread the word that soon all London should see in what manner he righted the wrongs he had done. The courier galloped off with his dispatches, and Granwel devoted all his time to heaping kindness upon Miss Stralson in order, as he said, that she might do her best to forget all the wrong he had done her which lay heavy on his conscience... But in the depths of his black soul the monster exulted, because he had by means of a ruse at last triumphed over the woman who had for so long entangled him in her webs.

The courier sent by Henrietta's abductor reached London at the moment when the King had just advised the Prime Minister to set the wheels of justice turning against Granwel... But Lady Stralson, totally duped by the letters she had received, and believing their content all the more readily because she was so accustomed to Henrietta's habit of winning her battles with Granwel, hastened at once to see the minister. She begged him not to institute proceedings against his Lordship, gave him an account of what was happening, the furore receded, and Williams made ready to leave.

'Deal tactfully with his Lordship, who is a powerful and dangerous man,' said Lady Stralson as she embraced him. 'Enjoy the victory my daughter has won over him and come back quickly, both of you, to comfort a mother who loves you.'

Williams set off, but without collecting the magnificent gift which Granwel intended him to have. He did not even trouble to enquire if the money was there for him or not, for to have done so might have suggested that he had a doubt in his mind, and good people do not harbour such doubts.

Williams reached... God in heaven!... he reached his destination... my pen falters, it refuses to inscribe the detail of the horrors which awaited this tragic lover. Oh devils from hell! Appear and lend me your vipers that it may be with their glinting fangs that my hand shall trace the terrible events which remain for me to tell!

'My dear Henrietta,' Granwel exclaimed next morning as he entered his captive's room, looking happy and radiating good cheer, 'you must come and see the surprise I have gone to some lengths to arrange for you. Hurry, Mademoiselle, I did not want to let you see Williams until he was at the foot of the altar where he will receive your hand... Follow me, he is waiting for you there.'

'Here, your Lordship?... Heavens, he has come... Williams... is at the altar?... And I owe it all to you!... Oh sir, allow me to kneel before you... The feelings which you fill me with today are stronger than all the rest...'

Granwel, discomfited, replied:

'No, Mademoiselle, I cannot yet take pleasure from your gratitude. This is the last time it will draw blood from my heart. Do not show it, Mademoiselle, for after today it will make me suffer no longer... Tomorrow I shall have time to savour it at my leisure... But let us hurry, Henrietta. Williams loves you and aches to be yours—we must not keep him waiting any longer!'

Henrietta stepped out... feeling very nervous... very excited... she could scarce breathe. Never did the roses in her cheeks glow more brilliantly... Buoyed up by love and hope, she believed that she was moments away from happiness... They reached the end of an immense gallery which led into the chapel of the castle... Great God! What a sight was there!... This sacred place was hung with sable drapes and, upon a kind of funeral bier, surrounded by burning candles, lay the corpse of Williams pierced by thirteen daggers which still protruded from the bloody wounds they had just made.

'Behold your lover, you lying she-devil! See how my vengeance grants your loathsome vows!'

'False-hearted cur!' cried Henrietta, gathering up all her strength so that it would not fail her in this terrible pass... 'No, you have not deceived me! Every excess of vice has a natural place in your heart, and I would have been surprised only if I had found virtue there too. Let me die here, it is the last request I make of your cruel heart!'

'Your request shall not be granted just yet,' said Granwel with that icy self-assurance which is the special hallmark of all great villains... 'My vengeance is a dish that has been only half eaten; now the rest must be consumed. There you see the altar on which we shall make our vows come true. It is there that I wish to hear from your lips the oath you will swear to be mine for ever.'

Granwel was determined to be obeyed... Henrietta, who had sufficient courage not to break under the appalling strain... Henrietta, whose energy was awakened by the desire for revenge... checked her tears and promised to do all that was asked of her.

'Mademoiselle,' said Granwel when he was satisfied with her, 'you may believe every word of what I shall now tell you. Every vengeful impulse I ever felt has evaporated and my only thought is to make amends for my crimes... Follow me, Mademoiselle, let us leave this lugubrious display, everything waits in readiness for us at the temple. The ministers of religion and the common people have been gathered there for some time... Come, accept my hand without further ado... You will dedicate tonight to the first duties of a wife. Tomorrow I shall escort you publicly to London and shall return you to your mother as my bride.'

Henrietta turned and stared wildly at Granwel. She felt quite certain that this time she was not being deceived, but her embittered heart was no longer capable of being consoled by hope... Torn by despair... consumed by thoughts of revenge, she was capable of no other feeling but these.

'Sir,' said she, with the utmost calm which was bred of courage, 'I believe so completely in your unexpected change of heart that I am ready to grant you freely what you could easily obtain by force. Although our union will not have been sanctioned by Heaven, I shall nevertheless this very night satisfy you in the matter of all the duties you demand of me. I therefore beg you to postpone the ceremony until we reach London. I am reluctant on various counts to be married anywhere except in the presence of my mother. This must be a matter of complete indifference to you, Granwel, since I am prepared to submit to your desires.'

Although Granwel sincerely wished to be Henrietta's husband, he could not view her readiness to be his dupe a second time without a sense of gleeful exultation, and anticipating that after a night of sensual pleasure he might not be so patient, he agreed wholeheartedly to what she had proposed. The rest of the day passed quietly. No move was even made to touch the funereal decor, for it was essential to wait for the blackest shadows of night to gather before poor Williams could be buried.

'Granwel,' said Miss Stralson as she was about to retire, 'I beg you to grant me a second favour. After what happened this morning, will I be able to refrain from crying out for fear when I find myself in the arms of the man who murdered the one I loved? Will you agree that no light will illuminate the bed in which I shall... plight my troth? Must you not grant as much out of respect for my chastity? Have I not suffered enough to claim the right to be granted what I ask?'

'Make whatever arrangements you will, Mademoiselle,' replied Granwel. 'I should be unjust indeed were I to deny you in such matters. I fully understand the struggle that is going on in your heart and I am most anxious to do what I can to minimize it.'

Miss Stralson curtseyed and returned to her room, while Granwel, delighted with the success of his foul plans, silently congratulated himself on having at last routed his adversary. He got into bed, the torches were removed, and Henrietta was informed that her orders had been obeyed, and that she could now enter the nuptial chamber whenever she wished... And so she came... armed with a dagger which she herself had plucked from Williams's heart... She drew near... Pretending to feel her way, she stretched out one hand which located Granwel's body and with the other struck with the blade which it held. The villain fell to the floor blaspheming, cursing Heaven and the hand which had delivered the blow.

Henrietta hurried from the room and, trembling, made her way to the funeral chapel where Williams lay. In one hand she held a lamp and in the other the bloody steel which had been the instrument of her vengeance.

'Williams!' she cried. 'We were separated by crime but the hand of God will reunite us... All my life I loved you to distraction. Receive my soul! It will blend into yours, never to be parted from it more!'

And so saying, she turned her weapon against herself and fell convulsively upon the cold corpse on which, in an involuntary spasm, her mouth pressed her final kisses...

News of these dreadful events soon reached London. Granwel's passing was unlamented. For some time his excesses had made him odious. Gave, fearing to be involved in this appalling episode, fled at once to Italy, and the mourning Lady Stralson returned alone to Hereford, where she continued to weep for the two great losses she had suffered until such time as the Good Lord, touched by her tears, at last gathered her to His bosom and reunited her, in a better world, with those young people, so loved and so worthy of that love, who had been taken from her by libertinage, revenge, cruelty... in short by all the crimes which are spawned by the abuse of wealth, reputation, and above all, the neglect of the standards by which good men live and without which neither we nor those around us can ever be happy on this earth.

FAXELANGE
or THE FAULTS OF AMBITION

MONSIEUR and Madame de Faxelange enjoyed an income of some thirty or thirty-five thousand livres,* and lived for most of the year in Paris. Their union had been blessed but once, with a daughter as beautiful as the Goddess of Youth. Monsieur de Faxelange had fought for his country but had retired from military service when still a young man, and since then had devoted all of his time to caring for his family's affairs and bringing up his daughter. He was mild-mannered, not particularly intelligent, but a man of sterling character. His wife, who was about the same age, which is to say about forty-five or fifty, was a little more astute but, all in all, there was more honesty and decency about both husband and wife than guile and suspicion.

Mademoiselle de Faxelange had just attained her sixteenth birthday. She had one of those faces which are called 'romantic', because each feature expresses a general quality:* skin very white, fine blue eyes, mouth a little wide, figure graceful and slim, and hair which was beauty itself. Her mind was as gentle as her character: incapable of doing wrong, she was still at the stage where she was unable to conceive that wrong could be done. She was, in short, innocence and candour gilded by the hand of the Graces. Mademoiselle de Faxelange was cultured: expense had not been a consideration where her education was concerned. She spoke English and Italian fluently, played several musical instruments, and was a tasteful painter of miniatures. An only daughter and consequently destined to inherit her family's fortune, which was modest, she could expect to make a good marriage which, ever since she was eighteen months old, had been her parents' sole concern. But Mademoiselle de Faxelange's heart had not waited to hear what they had decided was to be her fate, and for more than three years she had no longer been mistress of her feelings. Monsieur de Goé, to whom she was distantly related and who often came to call on her on the strength of the connection, was the much-cherished object of her tender affections. She loved him with a sincerity, a delicacy which bring to mind the refined sentiments of times long past, which have been corrupted by our modern depraved manners.

Monsieur de Goé thoroughly deserved his good fortune. At twenty-three, he cut a handsome figure, had charming good looks, and his open, honest character matched that of his pretty cousin. He was an officer of dragoons, but not rich. He stood in need of a wife with a large dowry, just as a wealthy husband was required for his cousin who, although an heiress, was not possessed of a large fortune, as we have already observed. In view of this, both were quite aware that their hopes would come to nothing and that the love which burned within them was doomed to be consumed in sighs.

Monsieur de Goé had never informed Mademoiselle de Faxelange's parents of his feelings for their daughter. He anticipated a refusal and his pride prevented him from exposing himself to a rebuff. Mademoiselle de Faxelange, infinitely more timid than he, had also refrained from speaking of the matter, so that their innocent, virtuous intrigue, inspired by the bonds of true affection, was carried on in silence and secrecy. But come what may, they had vowed never to submit to alternative proposals and to love none but each other.

This was how matters stood with our two young lovers when a friend of Monsieur de Faxelange arrived one day, and asked his permission to present a visitor from a distant province who had been recommended to him by an acquaintance.

'This is not something I propose without good reason,' said Monsieur de Belleval. 'The man I mentioned owns immense estates in France and magnificent plantations in America. His sole purpose in coming to Paris is to find a wife. It may well be that he will take her off to the New World, and that is my only reservation. If this prospect does not alarm you unduly, then that apart, he is undoubtedly and in every respect the ideal husband for your daughter. He is thirty-two years of age, not particularly agreeable to look at—there is something rather grim in his cast of eye—but he is a man of noble bearing and uncommonly wide culture.'

'Bring him to see us,' said Monsieur de Faxelange.

Then turning to his wife, he added:

'And how say you, Madame?'

'We shall have to see,' she replied. 'If he indeed proves to be suitable, I would not hesitate to give the match my blessing, despite the pain the separation from my daughter would bring. I love her very much and her absence would make me miserable. But I shall not stand in the way of her happiness.'

Monsieur de Belleval, delighted with this initial reaction, suggested that a meeting be arranged. It was agreed that on the following Thursday Baron de Franlo would be presented to Madame de Faxelange.

Baron de Franlo had been in Paris for a month. He had taken the best apartment in the Hôtel de Chartres, where he kept a handsome carriage, two footmen, a valet, a large quantity of precious stones, a wallet bulging with letters of credit, and the finest wardrobe imaginable. He had never actually met Monsieur de Belleval. He did claim, however, to know a close friend of his. This friend had been absent from Paris for a year and a half, and was therefore in no position to be of help to him. He had gone to the house of this friend, where he was told that he was away but was advised, since Monsieur de Belleval was the friend's closest acquaintance, to pay him a call. Consequently it was to Monsieur de Belleval that he had presented his letters of introduction, and Monsieur de Belleval, to be of service to a gentleman, had not hesitated to read them and offer the Baron all the help he would have been given by his friend had he been in Paris.

Belleval was acquainted with none of the persons in the provinces who had furnished the Baron with references, nor had he ever heard his friend mention any of them. But then, he could not possibly know all of his friend's acquaintances. This thought removed any limit to the efforts he made on Franlo's behalf. He is a friend of my friend. Is that not more than enough for any gentleman to feel that his reason for wishing to be of service is amply justified?

Falling in with the Baron's wishes, Monsieur de Belleval took him everywhere. At the fashionable walks, at the theatre and in shops, they were invariably seen together. It was essential that their relations be thus made public to justify the interest Belleval took in Franlo and, since he fully believed him to be an excellent match, his reasons for introducing him to the Faxelanges.

On the day fixed for the expected visit, Madame de Faxelange, without forewarning her daughter, requested that she appear in her most elegant dress. She said that she was to behave as politely and pleasantly as possible to the person she would meet. If invited to do so, she must not need to be asked twice to display her talents, for their visitor was a man who had been personally recommended to them, and also because Monsieur de Faxelange and she had particular reasons for wishing to make him feel at home.

Five o'clock struck, the time that had been agreed. Monsieur de Franlo entered, duly escorted by Monsieur de Belleval. No man could have been better dressed or behaved more courteously or respectfully. Yet, as we have noted, there was something in this man's eyes which aroused instant revulsion, and it was only by carefully controlling his gestures and varying his facial expressions that he had learned to minimize this defect.

The conversation flowed. Various topics were aired and Monsieur de Franlo had something to say on all of them, and in so doing revealed that he was an immensely well-mannered and cultured man. The talk turned to the sciences, and Monsieur de Franlo spoke knowledgeably of all of them. Then it was the turn of the arts, and Franlo showed that he was acquainted with all its branches, there being none which at some time had not been his passion. When they talked of politics, he was no less deep: he had ideas about how the whole world should be run, and expressed his views without affectation or self-importance, imparting to everything he said an air of modesty which invited the indulgence of his listeners, indicated that he could be wrong, and intimated that he was far from sure that what he ventured to say was well-founded. Music was discussed. Monsieur de Belleval asked Mademoiselle de Faxelange if she would sing. Blushingly she obliged and, for her second song, Franlo begged leave to accompany her on a guitar which he saw had been left on a chair. He plucked the strings with all the grace and art imaginable and, in so doing, unostentatiously displayed rings of incalculable value which he wore on his fingers. Mademoiselle de Faxelange began a third song, an absolutely new composition, and Monsieur de Franlo accompanied her on the piano with all the assurance of the greatest masters. Mademoiselle de Faxelange was asked to read a few passages of Pope in English.* Franlo immediately continued the conversation in the same language, and amply demonstrated how well he had mastered it.

However, his visit ended without his having given any indication of what he thought of Mademoiselle de Faxelange, and her father, delighted with his new acquaintance, refused to let him go without first extracting his personal promise that he would come and dine with him on the following Sunday.

Madame de Faxelange, who showed less enthusiasm when they discussed their visitor that same evening, was not of the same mind as her husband. Her initial impression, she said, was that there was at first sight something so repellent about him that she felt that if he did indeed he want to marry her daughter, she would agree to the match only with the greatest reluctance. Her husband attempted to combat her prejudice. He said Franlo was most charming, and that it was hard to imagine a man who was more cultivated or had a more impressive manner. Surely faces did not come into it? Why should such things matter in a man? Besides, there was no reason why Madame de Faxelange should fear anything, for it was most unlikely that Franlo would do her the honour of seeking the alliance. But if by some chance this was indeed what he wanted, then it would be folly to let such an opportunity go by. Could their daughter ever expect to find a better match? None of this was enough to overcome a mother's prudence. She insisted that the face was the window of the soul, and said that if Franlo's soul was anything like his face, then he was most certainly not the husband who would make her darling daughter happy.

The day for him to come and dine arrived. Franlo, more elegantly dressed than on his previous visit, and even more knowledgeable and engaging, lent distinction and enjoyment to the proceedings. After dinner they sat him down to cards with Mademoiselle de Faxelange, Belleval, and another guest. Franlo had no luck, but behaved with amazing good grace. He lost very heavily: this is often a way of being agreeable in polite company, a fact of which our man was well aware. Afterwards there was music, and Franlo played three or four different instruments. The evening ended with a visit to the Comédie Française, with the Baron publicly giving his arm to Mademoiselle de Faxelange. Then the company went their several ways.

Matters continued on this footing for a month. During that time there was no mention of any proposal. Both sides were reticent. The Faxelanges were reluctant to take the initiative, while for his part Franlo, who wanted very much to succeed, was afraid of ruining his chances by appearing too eager.

Eventually, Monsieur Belleval called, this time fully authorized to conduct negotiations on Franlo's behalf. He made a formal declaration to Monsieur and Madame de Faxelange, stating that Baron de Franlo, a native of the Vivarais,* possessing three considerable properties in America and presently desiring to be married, had cast his eye in the direction of Mademoiselle de Faxelange and, through his representative, now asked the parents of this delightful young lady if he might be permitted to entertain some small hope.

The initial response, made for form's sake, was that Mademoiselle de Faxelange was still too young for there to be any thought of her being settled. But two weeks later the Baron was invited to a dinner, at which he was asked to give an account of himself. He said that he owned three estates in the Vivarais, each worth twelve or fifteen thousand livres a year; that his father, who had settled in America, had married a woman born in the place who had brought him a portion of almost a million; that both were now dead and he had inherited their properties; and that, since he had yet to claim his inheritance in person, he was determined to travel there with his bride, as soon as he found one.

This last proviso was not to Madame de Faxelange's liking, and she set out her fears. Against them, Franlo observed that nowadays people travelled to America as readily as to England; that the journey was vital to his interests; but that it would not last above two years, at the end of which time he undertook to bring his wife back to Paris; that consequently, the only outstanding issue was the matter of the separation of mother and her much-loved daughter, which, however, was quite unavoidable, since his plan was not to live permanently in Paris, where he did not feel comfortable in society, nor would he be as easy there as on his estates, where his wealth enabled him to play a prominent role. Then various lesser matters were discussed, and this first meeting closed with an invitation to Franlo to provide the name of some person well known in his part of the country who could be approached to supply further details, as was usual in matters of this kind. Franlo was prepared for such a request for assurances, approved this way of proceeding, advised in favour of it, and added that to his mind the simplest and speediest way forward would be to apply to the office of the Minister. This approach was approved. The next day Monsieur de Faxelange went to the Ministry. He spoke to the Minister himself,* who certified that Baron de Franlo, presently living in Paris, was not only most definitely a Vivarais man but also the worthiest and wealthiest. Monsieur de Faxelange, more enthusiastic about the prospect than ever, returned to his wife with excellent news. Not wishing to delay matters any longer, they summoned Mademoiselle de Faxelange that very evening and proposed Baron de Franlo as her husband.

For a fortnight past the charming young lady had been aware that certain plans were being made for her future, and, given the capriciousness by no means foreign to her sex, vanity had silenced her love. Flattered by Franlo's vast wealth and splendour, she imperceptibly transferred her preference from Monsieur de Goé to him. As a result, she replied that she was favourably inclined to accept what was proposed and would obey her family's wishes.

For his part, Goé had not been so indifferent as to be unaware of what was going on. He hastened to her house and was dismayed by the coldness of his reception. He spoke with all the heat of the passion he felt, expressed the tenderest affection and the harshest reproaches, told the woman he loved that he saw very clearly the reason for her change of heart which meant death to him. Never would he have suspected her, no never, of being so cruel and so faithless! His tears flowed and added conviction and force to the young man's bitter recriminations. Mademoiselle de Faxelange grew misty eyed, admitted she had been weak, and both agreed that the only way of repairing the damage done was to persuade Monsieur de Goé's parents to intervene. This plan was promptly pursued: the young man went down on his knees to his father, begging him to obtain the hand of his cousin for him, threatening to leave France for ever if what he asked was refused, and behaving in such a manner that Monsieur de Goé felt so sorry for him that the very next day he called upon Faxelange and asked for his daughter's hand for his son. He was thanked for the honour he did the family, but was told that it was too late and that troths had been plighted. Monsieur de Goé, who had only acted to oblige his son and was not entirely unhappy to see obstacles put in the way of a marriage which he did not find entirely suitable, returned home and coolly broke the news to his son, urging him at the same time to change his ideas and not stand in the way of his cousin's happiness.

Young Goé was furious and made no such promise. He went at once to call on Mademoiselle de Faxelange who, wavering constantly between love and vanity, proved on this occasion to be considerably less sympathetic and tried to persuade him to reconcile himself to the step she was about to take. Monsieur de Goé did his best to appear calm. He kept control of himself, kissed his cousin's hand, and left in a cruel state, which he felt all the more keenly because he was obliged to hide his feelings, though this did not prevent him from swearing that he would never love anyone else but had no wish to stand in the way of her happiness.

Meanwhile Franlo, prompted by Belleval that it was high time he thought seriously about winning the heart of Mademoiselle de Faxelange, given that there were rivals in the offing, spared no effort in making himself even more agreeable. He sent magnificent gifts to his future bride and, with the assent of her parents, she raised no objections to receiving the attentions of a man whom she was now required to think of as her husband. He took a charming house two leagues from Paris, and there, every day for a whole week, staged the most delightful entertainments for her benefit. In this way, by seasoning with skilful seduction the solemn steps which would finalize their union, he soon turned our sweet girl's head and eclipsed his rival.

And yet there were times when Mademoiselle de Faxelange was left remembering, when her tears flowed despite herself. She felt the cruel sting of remorse for having thus betrayed the first man who had awakened her feelings and whom she had loved so tenderly since she was a girl... 'What has he done to merit being cast off like this?' she asked herself in distress. 'Has he stopped loving me?... Alas, no, yet I have betrayed him... and for whom, dear God, for whom?... For a man I do not know... a man who has charmed me with his wealth... a man who may well make me pay a high price for the splendour for which I have sacrificed true love... Oh! The flattering words with which he turned my head... are they to be ranked with Goé's delightful turns of phrase... his sacred vows to love me always... the heartfelt tears which accompanied them!... Merciful heavens! What regrets I should have if I were about to be deceived!' Yet even as she was reflecting thus, the divine creature was being dressed for the fête and adorned with the presents Franlo had showered on her. She forgot her misgivings.

One night she dreamed that the man she was soon to marry, transformed into a wild beast, cast her into a pit filled with blood in which floated a mass of corpses. She cried out to her husband to help her, but in vain, for he would not listen... Goé appeared, pulled her out, and then abandoned her... she fainted... This dreadful dream made her ill for two days. But a new entertainment scattered these wild imaginings, and Mademoiselle de Faxelange, now thoroughly infatuated, reached the point almost of blaming herself for the impression left by her fanciful dream.[1]

All was finally being made ready and Franlo, eager to bring matters to a conclusion, was about to set a date when one morning our heroine received the following note from him:

The rage of a man who is a complete stranger to me will prevent my having the pleasure I had promised myself of inviting Monsieur and Madame de Faxelange and their lovely daughter to supper this evening. This man, who claims that I am depriving him of his life's happiness, wished to fight me and gave me a thrust of his sword which I hope to repay four days hence. But meanwhile I have been placed under strict medical supervision for twenty-four hours. You may imagine what a privation is it for me not to be able, as I had hoped this evening, to renew my vows of love to Mademoiselle de Faxelange.

From the Baron de Franlo

This note held no mysteries for Mademoiselle de Faxelange. She at once communicated its contents to her parents, and did so in the

[1] Dreams are deep impulses whose true significance is not recognized as often as it might be. One half of the population laughs at them; the other half believes in them; but there is no harm in paying them heed, even in believing them, in certain situations, as I shall explain. When we are waiting to see how some event or other will turn out, and if the way it will turn out for us personally occupies our every waking moment, then we will surely dream if it. Now the mind being entirely filled by this matter will almost invariably focus on an aspect of the matter we had not considered the day before, and when this happens what superstition, harm, or philosophical error would there be in including the possibility outlined in our dream among the number of other expected outcomes of the event and acting accordingly? It appears to me that to do so would be no more than common sense. For, in relation to the outcome of the event in question, the dream is just one of the ways the mind tries to open up and reveal some new aspect of the event. Whether this effort is made when we are asleep or while we are awake is immaterial: either way, it yields one of the possible answers, and whatever you do on that basis can never be an act of madness nor can it be said to be a form of superstition. Obviously, the ignorance of our forefathers led them to believe in some very absurd ideas; but does anyone believe that philosophy is without perils? If we analyse nature for long enough, we come to resemble the alchemist who ruins himself in his attempt to make a few ounces of gold. Let us prune and trim by all means, but take care that everything is not cut down, because there are in nature many strange things which we shall never understand.

belief that she was acting to protect the life of her former lover whom she was saddened to observe had compromised himself for her sake... after she had used him so cruelly. Coming from a man she still loved, such a bold, impetuous step was a serious challenge to Franlo's rights. But if the former had been the attacker, the latter's blood had been spilt, and Mademoiselle de Faxelange found herself in the unfortunate position of having to see everything from Franlo's point of view. As a result, Goé was put in the wrong and Franlo was declared to be in the right.

While Monsieur de Faxelange hurried off to see Goé's father and inform him of what was afoot, Belleval, Madame de Faxelange, and her daughter called upon Franlo to comfort him. He received them prostrate on an ottoman, dressed in the most stylishly informal clothes and with a face which looked so exhausted that it conferred a measure of attractiveness on his expression which at other times seemed so forbidding.

Monsieur de Belleval and his protégé made the most of the situation to encourage Madame de Faxelange to hurry matters along, for this business might have serious consequences—Franlo might be forced to leave Paris, and would he decide to go before the arrangements were complete?... This and many other reasons were promptly urged and energetically expressed through the friendly offices of Monsieur de Belleval and by Monsieur de Franlo's quick mind.

Madame de Faxelange was utterly convinced. Seduced like the rest of her family by the outward show of Belleval's friend, urged on by her husband, and observing that her daughter harboured only the most favourable views of the marriage, she was now disposed to accept it without demur. And so she ended her visit by assuring Franlo that the very first day the state of his health permitted him to stir abroad would be the day of his wedding. Our adroit bridegroom-to-be mentioned feelings of anxiety to Mademoiselle de Faxelange concerning the rival which this episode had brought to his attention. She offered him the most candid reassurances, but insisted on being given his word that he would never take action of any kind against Goé. Franlo promised and they separated.

The affair was soon settled through the good offices of Monsieur de Goé *père*. His son fully acknowledged what the violence of his love had led him to do. But when he saw that this sentiment did not please Mademoiselle de Faxelange and that he was cruelly cast aside by her, he agreed to place no further obstacle in her way. Monsieur de Faxelange, now easy in his mind, thought only of bringing matters to a conclusion. He needed to raise ready money at once. Monsieur de Franlo, who intended to travel directly to America, was optimistic that he could either restore or increase his estates there, and it was for this purpose that he intended to use his wife's dowry. The sum of four hundred thousand francs had been agreed on. It was a large amount and it would make serious inroads into Monsieur de Faxelange's fortune. But he had only one daughter and everything would be hers one day. This was a match which would not come again, and sacrifices therefore would have to be made. He sold possessions, took out loans, and in short had the money ready six days after the fracas involving Franlo and about three months from the moment the Baron had first set eyes on Mademoiselle de Faxelange. At last he appeared in public as her future husband. Friends, family, and guests foregathered. The contract was signed, and it was agreed that the ceremony should take place the next day and that two days later Franlo would leave, taking his money and his wife with him.

On the eve of that fateful day Monsieur de Goé sent his cousin a note beseeching her to grant him an interview in a secret location which he named, a spot where he knew Mademoiselle de Faxelange was free to walk. When she declined he sent a second message, assuring her that what he had to tell her was far too serious for her to refuse to see him out of hand. Our heroine, faithless, seduced, even dazzled, but unable to bring herself to hate the man she had once loved, finally yielded and made her way to the place appointed.

'I have not come here, Mademoiselle,' said Goé to his cousin the moment he set eyes on her, 'I have not come here to trouble what you and your parents call your life's happiness. But I claim to be a fair-minded man, and as such I am obliged to warn you that you are being duped. The man you are about to marry is a swindler. He will steal your money and he will then proceed to make you perhaps the unhappiest woman on earth. He is a rogue and you have been deceived.'

When she had heard him out, Mademoiselle de Faxelange told her cousin that before permitting oneself to blacken another man's character so foully, one should possess irrefutable proof of the charge.

'I do not yet have the evidence, that much I concede,' said Goé. 'But enquiries have been instituted and I hope to be fully informed in the very near future. In the name of all you hold most dear, you must persuade your parents to ask for a postponement.'

'Dear coz,' said Mademoiselle de Faxelange with a smile, 'your stratagem is plain for all to see. Your warnings are merely an excuse, and the postponement you ask for is only a way of deflecting me from an engagement which it is now too late to break. Admit your ruse and I will forgive you. But do not try to alarm me without good reason at a time when nothing can be done to change what has been settled.'

Monsieur de Goé, who in truth had only suspicions and no solid evidence and was merely playing for time, knelt before his cousin:

'I adore you,' he cried, 'and I shall idolize you until the day I die! My life's happiness is over and soon you will leave me forever!... It is true: what I said is only surmise. Yet I cannot put the thought out of my mind. It torments me even more than the despair of being separated from you... Please won't you try, on your day of glory, to remember the old days when we were children... those exquisite moments when you vowed that you would never love anyone but me... Ah, how quickly those instants of bliss have fled away, but how slowly will my grieving moments pass! What did I ever do to deserve to be rejected by you? Tell me, cruel girl, what did I do? Why have you turned your back on the man who loves you? Does the monster who has snatched you from my arms love you as much as I do? Has he loved you for as long as I have?'

Tears coursed down the cheeks of the unhappy Goé. He expressed his feelings by reaching for the hand of the woman he adored and by turns raising it to his lips and holding it to his heart.

It was difficult for the sensitive Faxelange not to feel a little moved by such a display of feeling... She shed a few tears.

'Dear Goé,' said she to her cousin, 'you must believe that you will always be dear to me. I have no choice but to obey—surely you see that it was impossible that we could ever have married.'

'We would have waited.'

'Oh, God! And build our future happiness on the misery of our parents?'

'We would not have wished to make them unhappy. We were young enough to wait.'

'And what guarantee did I have that you would have remained faithful to me?'

'Your sweet nature... your loveliness, everything about you... No man would ever stop loving as long as you were the one he loved... If only you still wanted to be mine... Let us run away to the end of the universe! Do you dare love me enough to come with me?'

'Nothing in the world would persuade me to do any such thing. Come, you must take heart. Forget me. It is by far the wisest thing you can do. There are many beautiful women who will console you.'

'Do not add insult to infidelity! Me, forget you, cruel girl? Do you really believe I could ever be consoled for losing you? No, you do not believe it, you never considered me base enough to dare think it for one moment.'

'My too unhappy friend, we must go our separate ways. All this talk causes me a distress for which there is no remedy, nor is there a cure for the pain you feel. We must part. It is the wisest course.'

'Very well, I shall obey. I see that this is the very last time in my life that I shall speak to you. No matter, I shall obey, faithless girl. But I ask two things of you. Will you harden your heart to the extent of denying my request?'

'What is it you want?'

'A lock of your hair and your word of honour that you will write to me every month, so at least you can tell me that you are happy... I shall be consoled if you are. But if ever that monster... Believe me, dear girl, yes, believe me when I say that I would go looking for you in the depths of hell to rescue you from his clutches.'

'You must not let any such fears trouble you, dear coz. Franlo is the most honourable of men. I find only sincerity and thoughtfulness in him... I see only that all his thoughts are plans for my happiness.'

'Oh God, where is the time when you said that your happiness would be possible only with me? Well? Will you agree to what I ask?'

'Yes,' replied Mademoiselle de Faxelange. 'Here is the lock of hair you wanted, and I give you my assurance that I shall write. Now let us go our separate ways, for part we must.'

In saying these words, she held out her hand to her cousin. But the hapless girl thought she was more fully recovered than was in fact the case. When she felt her hand bathed by the tears of the man she had loved so deeply, her sobs stopped her breath and she collapsed unconscious on to a chair. This scene took place in the apartment of a maid loyal to Mademoiselle de Faxelange; she hastened to attend to her mistress, whose eyes opened only to see her cousin on his knees before her, shedding tears of despair. She summoned up her courage, all her strength, and raised him to his feet.

'Goodbye,' said she, 'farewell. You must never stop loving one to whom you will remain dear until the day she dies. Do not reproach me for what I did, it is too late for that. I was infatuated... swept off my feet... and now my heart must listen only to its duty. But all the feelings which duty does not command will always be for you. Do not follow me. Farewell.'

Goé withdrew in a piteous state and Mademoiselle de Faxelange sought in sleep, which she solicited in vain, some relief from the remorse which racked her and left her with a sense of foreboding which she was unable to control.

However, the next day's ceremony and the celebrations which were calculated to highlight her beauty all helped to calm the weak-willed creature. She pronounced the fatal words which bound her forever... she was carried away by the occasion which occupied her whole attention for rest of the day. That night she consummated the ghastly sacrifice which separated her eternally from the only man who was worthy of her.

Next day she busied herself with the preparations for their departure. The day after that, with her parents heaping good wishes upon her, Madame de Franlo, carrying her dowry of four hundred thousand francs, climbed into her husband's post-chaise, which set off for the Vivarais. Franlo planned to remain there for six weeks, he said, before taking ship for America, which he would do from La Rochelle, where he had arranged his passage in advance.

The newlyweds' retinue was made up of two mounted grooms of Franlo's and a lady's maid for Madame, a woman who had been devoted to her since she was a girl and who, at the family's request, was to be allowed to remain in her service for the rest of her life. Additional servants would be engaged when they reached their destination.

They drove to Lyons without stopping, and until then our two travellers were accompanied by happiness, laughter, and refined pleasures. But at Lyons all that changed. Instead of staying at a hotel, as god-fearing people do, Franlo stopped at an out-of-the-way inn on the further side of the Pont de la Guillotière.* He ordered dinner and, two hours later, dismissed one of his grooms, got into a fiacre with the other, his wife, and her maid, arranged for a cart loaded with the baggage to follow, and went in search of a lodging for the night a league outside the town in a sequestered tavern on the banks of the Rhône.

This proceeding alarmed Madame de Franlo.

'Where are you taking me, sir?' she asked her husband.

'By God, Madame,' he replied brusquely, 'are you afraid I am about to do you an injury? To hear you, anyone would think that you had fallen into the clutches of some blackguard. We have to cross the river in the morning. To be on hand, it is my practice to spend the previous night by the water's edge. The boatmen wait for me here and in this way we waste much less time.'

Madame de Franlo said no more.

They reached a low tavern, the very sight of which struck fear into her soul. But imagine the hapless Faxelange's surprise when she heard the proprietress of this fearsome hostelry, who was even more terrifying than her premises, say to the supposed Baron:

'So there you are, Ripper, my lad! Where the devil have you been? Surely it didn't take you all this time to find that damned wench? Any road, a lot has happened since you've been gone. Old La Roche had his neck stretched at the gibbet at Les Terreaux* yesterday... Strong-Arm Jack is still in jug but maybe they'll do for him today. But no need to worry, none of the lads 'peached on you, and everything back there is still as it should be. There was a big raid a couple of days ago—six dead, but you didn't lose a single man.'

The unhappy Faxelange shuddered from head to toe. Put yourself in her place for a moment, reader, and you will appreciate just how terrible was the shock produced on her fine and trusting soul by such a sudden collapse of the illusion which had sustained her. Observing her dismay, her husband stepped close to her.

'Madame,' he said firmly, 'the time for pretence is over. I have deceived you, as you see, and since I would not like that prattlebox', he went on, glancing up at her maid, 'to let her tongue wag, you will understand,' he said, producing a pistol from his pocket and blowing the poor woman's brains out, 'you will understand, Madame, that this is my way of ensuring that she never opens her mouth.'

Then he reached out for his wife, who had almost fainted; he held her tightly to him and said:

'As for you, Madame, you may be easy in your mind. You shall receive only the very best treatment from me. You will retain all your rights as my wife, and you will also continue to enjoy the advantages that go with them. My comrades, you may rest assured, will always respect you as wife of their chief.'

Since the pretty creature whose history we chronicle was now reduced to the most desperate state, her husband made sure that she was properly taken care of. When she had recovered a little and looked in vain for the devoted maid, whose corpse Franlo had ordered to be thrown into the river, she again dissolved into tears.

'You must not allow the loss of a serving woman to upset you,' said Franlo. 'There was no way I could have let her remain with you. But I shall see to it that you want for nothing—even though you will no longer have her by your side.'

Observing that his wife now seemed a little less alarmed, he went on:

'Madame, I was not born to the trade I now ply. It was gambling which brought me to my present career of hardship and crime. I did not mislead you by passing myself off to you as Baron de Franlo, for both the name and the title were once mine. I spent my youth fighting for my country. At twenty-eight I had run through the money I had inherited three years before: all it took was that short space of time to complete my ruin. Since the man who had acquired both my fortune and my name is currently in America, I thought I might go to Paris for a few months, pull the wool over people's eyes, and make good what I had lost. My ploy succeeded beyond my wildest expectations. Your dowry cost me an outlay of a hundred thousand francs. So as you can see, I have gained a hundred thousand écus* and a charming wife, a woman I love, of whom I swear I shall take the greatest care for as long as I live. Please compose yourself, Madame, and hear the rest of my tale.

'When I could sink no lower, I joined a gang of robbers who were then terrorizing the provinces of central France:* let this be a dreadful lesson to young men who are tempted by the senseless passion for gambling.* As a member of the gang, I carried out a number of audacious undertakings and, two years after joining, I was accepted as its chief. I changed its area of operations. I moved to an uninhabited, steep-sided valley in the Vivarais mountains, virtually impossible to locate and where the gendarmes have never managed to penetrate. That, Madame, is the place where I live, and such is the estate that I shall make over to you. It is the headquarters of my gang and it is from there that my marauding parties set out. I send them north as far as Burgundy and south to the coast; they go east to the borders of Piedmont and west beyond the mountains of the Auvergne. I have four hundred men under my command, every one of them as determined as I am, and all ready to brave death a thousand times in the hope of living and getting rich. We do not kill many in our raids, in case the corpses give us away. We spare the lives of those whom we do not fear, and force the rest to follow us to our lair, cutting their throats there and nowhere else, but not before we have extracted everything they have with them and any information that might be useful to us. Our method of waging our war may be cruel, but our continuing safety depends on it. Is it right that a just government should allow the error a man makes by squandering his inheritance when he is so young to be punished by the appalling torment of having to vegetate for forty or fifty years in a state of abject poverty? Is it possible that one rash act can be enough to ruin him? That it can deprive him of his honour? Should he be left with no way out other than public disgrace or a debtor's prison, merely because he was unlucky? Such ideas turn men into criminals as you see, Madame, and I am living proof of it. If the law is powerless to deal with gambling, but on the contrary actually authorizes it, then at least it should not allow one player to strip another of all his money nor the winner to reduce the loser to the condition of a mere spectator at the gaming table. If, I say, the law does not make gambling an offence, then it should not, as it does, hand out such cruel punishments for the comparable crime which we commit when we strip a traveller in a forest. And why should the nature of the crime be important when its consequences are the same? Do you think that there is anything to choose between the gambler who holds the bank and robs you in the Palais Royal* and the Ripper who orders you to hand over your wallet in the Bois de Boulogne? They are one and the same, Madame, the only real difference between them being that the banker steals your money like a coward and the highwayman robs you like a man of courage.

'But let us return to you, Madame. It is my intention that you shall live under my roof in total peace and tranquillity. You will find a number of other women there, wives of my comrades, who will make a circle of acquaintances for you... a not very exciting one perhaps, for these ladies stand far beneath you in social graces and moral worth. But they will do what you tell them and organize your entertainments, which will keep you amused. As to your duties in my modest estates, these I shall explain when we arrive. But for this evening let us think only of your rest. You would be wise to sleep awhile, so that you are refreshed and ready to leave very early in the morning.'

Franlo ordered the hostess of the tavern to see that his wife was treated with every consideration and then left her with the old woman who, once she realized who she was dealing with, had changed her attitude. She now placed before her a dish of broth mixed with a little Hermitage wine.* Franlo's wretched wife swallowed a few mouthfuls to avoid offending her hostess, and then, asking that she might be left by herself for the rest of the night, she surrendered to the full force of her bitter anguish as soon as she was alone.

'Oh, dearest Goé,' she exclaimed through her sobs, 'see how the hand of God has punished me for betraying you! I am lost for ever, I shall be buried in an inaccessible mountain fastness and remain hidden from the face of the universe. I shall not even be able to inform you of the overwhelming misfortunes which will be my lot, and even if I were not prevented from doing so, would I dare to try after the way I treated you? Would I still deserve your pity? And you, father... and you, my worthy mother, who wept so bitterly while I, intoxicated by pride, was virtually unmoved by your tears... how will you learn of my terrible fate? At my age, to see myself buried alive with these monsters! For how many years shall I be able to endure this terrible punishment? Oh you blackguard! You seduced me, you deceived me!'

The mind of Mademoiselle de Faxelange (for her married name is offensive to us now) was awhirl with dark thoughts, remorse, and dreadful fears which were still beyond the calming reach of slumber when Franlo came and asked her to rise so that she could embark before first light. She did as she was bidden and clambered on to the boat, her head wrapped in scarves which hid the grief etched on her face and concealed her tears from the cruel man who had caused them to flow. A small shelter made of leaves and branches had been erected on the vessel where she could be quiet and rest. And Franlo—and this must be said in his favour—seeing that his sorrowing wife needed peace and calm, allowed her to enjoy both without disturbing her. Some vestiges of goodness remain in the soul of even the most hardened villain, and virtue stands so high in the eyes of men that the worst of them are forced to acknowledge its existence on innumerable occasions in their lives.

The respectful manner in which she saw she was treated nevertheless went some way to making her mind easier. She felt that, in her situation, she had no other course open to her than to humour her husband, and she let him see that she was grateful.

The boat was manned by members of Franlo's gang, and God knows what things they said! Our heroine, overwhelmed by despair, paid them no heed, and the same evening they landed just short of the town of Tournon,* on the west bank of the Rhône, at the foot of the mountains of the Vivarais.

The chief and his men spent that night as they had spent the previous one, in a low tavern nearby known only to them. Next day a horse was brought for Franlo. He mounted it with his wife, two mules carried the baggage, and four armed men formed an escort. They crossed mountains and travelled into the interior along precipitous tracks. Very late on the second day our travellers reached a small plain, about half a league across, hemmed in on all sides by impassable mountains and accessible only by the narrow trail used by Franlo. At the gorge which marked the beginning of this trail was an outpost manned by ten of these outlaws, who were relieved three times each week and kept a constant lookout night and day.

Once they emerged onto the plain they saw a wretched collection of a hundred or so huts, like those built by savages, prominent among which was a comparatively grand two-storeyed house entirely surrounded by high walls, which belonged to the chief. It was both his residence and the settlement's citadel, that is, the place where the powder-store, the guns, and the prisoners were kept. Two underground cellars, both deep and strongly vaulted, had been made for this purpose. Above them were three ground-floor rooms, a kitchen, a bedchamber, and a small office, and over them were a reasonably spacious apartment for the chief's wife and, at the far end, a safe room for storing booty. The domestic staff comprised one uncouth peasant and a girl who acted as cook: this was more than were to be found in any of the other dwellings.

Mademoiselle de Faxelange, worn out by fatigue and her distress, saw nothing of all this on the first evening. It was all she could manage to reach the bed to which she was shown and, falling into an exhausted sleep, was at least left undisturbed until the following morning when the chief entered her apartment.

'This, Madame, is your home,' said he. 'It is rather different from the three handsome estates which I promised you and the magnificent plantations in America on which you were counting. But take heart, my dear, I shall not always ply my present trade. I have not worked at it for long, and yet the safe room you see there already contains, including your dowry, something in the region of two millions in ready money. When I have four I shall move to Ireland, and set up there with you on the most sumptuous footing.'

'Oh sir,' said Mademoiselle de Faxelange as the tears coursed freely down her cheeks, 'are you sure that God will let you live in peace until that time comes?'

'Pshaw, Madame,' said Franlo, 'we do not concern ourselves with such matters. We follow the adage which says: "People who are afraid of leaves should stay out of the forest." People die all the time. Here I run the risk of being hanged; in Paris I would risk a sword-thrust. No situation is without its danger. The wise man sets it against what may be gained and makes up his mind accordingly. The threat of death which constantly hangs over our heads is the last thing that worries us. And what of honour, you will object? But men, unfair and prejudiced, have already stripped me of my honour: I had no money, so how could I have honour? Had I been locked up, I would have been regarded as a criminal. Is it not better to be a real criminal and enjoy the rights all men have—in other words, to be free—than to be thought a criminal and languish in chains? You should not be surprised if an innocent man turns to crime when he is disgraced; you should not be surprised if he prefers crime to prison, when both of these alternatives attract the same opprobrium. Law-makers, if you wish to reduce the number of crimes committed, you should order fewer punishments. A nation which has made honour its god may safely pull down its scaffolds and still govern its people as long as it can count on the sacred restraining influence of so glorious an illusion...'

'But sir,' Mademoiselle de Faxelange broke in here, 'when you were in Paris you gave every appearance of being a gentleman.'

'I had to seem so if I were to secure your hand in marriage. I succeeded, and now the mask has fallen.'

Such words and deeds horrified the wretched woman but, determined not to deviate from the resolve she had made, she did not contradict her husband. She even gave the impression that she agreed with him. And observing her to be less agitated, he asked her if she would like to visit the settlement. To this she agreed, and walked all round it. There were then only about forty men there, the others having gone marauding, and it was from their ranks that the men keeping watch on the pass were drawn.

Madame de Franlo was received on all sides with the greatest marks of respect and deference. She saw seven or eight women who were young and pretty enough, but whose appearance and manner all too clearly signalled the gulf between such creatures and herself. All the same, she returned the greetings they offered her, and when the tour was over dinner was served. The chief sat down at the table with his wife. But she could not bring herself to share the meal with the others. She excused herself, saying that she was still tired from the journey, and no one insisted. When it was over, Franlo turned to his wife and said it was time to complete her education, for he might perhaps have to leave the next day to go foraging.

'I do not have to warn you, Madame,' he said to his wife, 'that it is quite impossible for you to write to anybody from here. First, the means of doing so are strictly outlawed: you will never see pens and paper here. Even if you succeed in eluding my vigilance, none of my men would ever agree to carry your letters, and the attempt would cost you dear. I love you very much, of that you may be assured, Madame. But in our business sentiment always comes second to duty. Indeed, that is what makes our profession superior to all others. In the world outside, there is no duty that cannot be neglected for love. With us, the very opposite is true. No woman alive could ever make us forget what we are, for our very lives depend on the cautious way we go about our business. You, Madame, are my second wife.'

'What do you mean, sir?'

'I mean, Madame, that you are my second wife. The first, who preceded you, tried to write, and the words she penned were obliterated by her blood. She died as she wrote her letter.'

The reader may judge how the wretched woman felt on hearing such appalling stories and horrifying threats. But she managed once more to control herself and protested to her husband that she had no intention of disobeying his orders.

'That is not the end of it, Madame,' continued the monster. 'When I am not here, you alone will be in sole charge in my stead. Despite the trust that exists between the men and myself, you will appreciate that where our common interests are concerned I will always place my faith in you rather than in them. So when I send you prisoners you must search them yourself, and see that their throats are cut in your presence.'

'I, sir?' exclaimed Mademoiselle de Faxelange, recoiling in horror. 'You mean I must steep my hands in innocent blood? Ah, better a thousand times that you should shed mine than force me to commit such an atrocity!'

'I shall put this first reaction down to your weakened state, Madame,' answered Franlo. 'But it is quite impossible for me to excuse you this task. Would you prefer to be the ruin of us all rather than accept it?'

'Your comrades can do it.'

'And so they will, Madame. But since my letters will be addressed to you alone, it must be on your orders, as determined by mine, that the prisoners will be either locked up or slaughtered. Of course, my men will do the actual work, but it is vital that you should transmit my orders to them.'

'Oh sir! Could you not excuse me from...'

'Out of the question, Madame.'

'But surely I will not have to be present when these appalling things are done?'

'No... But it is vital you should take charge of the spoils and lock them up in our safe room. I shall not insist the first time, if that is what you really want. On that first occasion I shall take the precaution of sending a dependable man with the prisoners. But I cannot go on indulging you, and thereafter you must try to take full charge yourself. We are ruled by habit, Madame, there is nothing we cannot get used to.* Did not the ladies of ancient Rome dote on seeing gladiators fall at their feet? Did they not carry barbarity to the point of insisting that they die with style?* To accustom you to your duty, Madame,' Franlo continued, 'I have six men in the vaults waiting to be put to death. I shall go now and have them killed. The sight will familiarize you with such horrors and, two weeks from now, this aspect of the duties I expect you to perform will hold no terrors for you.'

Mademoiselle de Faxelange did everything in her power to avoid having to be present at so horrible a scene. She begged her husband not to make her watch. But Franlo said that it was clearly all too necessary, for it appeared to him that the business of training his wife to look with equanimity on what was to be a part of her general duties was far too important to be delayed a moment longer.

The six unfortunates were led out and had their throats cut without mercy by Franlo himself. His wretched wife, who was obliged to watch, fainted while the executions were taking place. She was carried back to her bed where, soon telling herself she must muster all her courage if she were to save herself, she saw that in fact, since she was no more than the mouthpiece for her husband's orders, her conscience could not be taxed with his crimes, and that given the opportunities she now had to encounter many newcomers, though they were in chains, perhaps she might yet find ways of saving their lives and escaping with them. And so the next day she promised her brutal husband that he would have every reason to be satisfied with her conduct. After spending the night with her, something he had not done since they left Paris in view of the lamentable state she had been in, Franlo left her the following morning to go on a raid, assuring her that if she performed her duties satisfactorily he would give up this way of life sooner than he had said and ensure that at least the last thirty years of her life would be happy and peaceful.

Mademoiselle de Faxelange was no sooner alone in the midst of all those robbers, than her anxieties returned.

'Alas!' said she to herself, 'if I were so unfortunate as to attract the lusts of these wicked men, who would prevent them from satisfying their desires? If they decided to loot their chief's house, kill me, and flee, what is to prevent them from doing so? Ah! God grant they will,' she went on, shedding copious tears, 'for the best thing that can happen to me is that they end my life as soon as possible, for it has no other future than to be stained by horror.'

Gradually, however, hope revived in her heart, which was young and stronger now as a result of all her sufferings. Madame de Franlo resolved to be courageous. This she judged to be clearly the best policy, and she made herself follow it. Consequently, she went out and inspected the lookout post, came back alone and visited each hut in turn, essayed a few orders and found that she was deferred to and obeyed. The women came to see her and she received them politely. She listened with interest to the stories some of them told of having been seduced and abducted as she had been, though they had once been honest enough but had been degraded by solitude and crime until they had become monsters like the men they had married.

'Oh, God!' she sometimes said to herself. 'How can people turn into such brutes? Is it possible that I myself might one day become like these wretched women?...' Then she would shut herself up in her apartment, weep, ponder her awful fate. But she could not forgive herself for having freely leaped into the abyss of her own accord through overconfidence and sheer blindness. All of this led her back to her dear Goé, and bitter tears flowed from her eyes.

A week had gone by in this manner when she received a letter from her husband, delivered by a detachment of a dozen men who brought four prisoners. She shook as she opened the letter, anticipating what it said, and was briefly tempted by the thought that she might kill herself rather than put the helpless prisoners to death. The four were young men, and by their faces it was clear to see that they were of good family and excellent character.

'You will lock up the oldest of the four in a cell,' her husband's letter read. 'The villain defended himself and killed two of my men. But he must be kept alive: he has certain information which I need to get out of him. Have the other three killed at once.'

'You've heard my husband's orders,' she said to the leader of the detachment whom she assumed was the dependable man of whom Franlo had spoken. 'So carry out his instructions.'

Saying these words in an audible whisper, she ran to her apartment to conceal her anguish and her tears. But unfortunately she heard the screams of the victims as they were massacred just outside her windows. It was too much for her delicate nature and she fainted away. When she regained her senses, the course of action which she had decided to follow gave her new strength. She knew she had only her own resolve to count on, and she went downstairs again. She ordered the stolen valuables to be locked away, she walked around the village, inspected the sentry post, and in a word appeared so fully in charge that Franlo's lieutenant, who was due to leave the following day to rejoin his chief, was able to give him the most glowing report of his wife... We must guard against judging her harshly: what other option did she have, since she had to choose between dying and behaving thus? And people do not kill themselves as long as there is hope.

Franlo was away for longer than he had anticipated. He did not return for a whole month, during which time he sent two batches of prisoners to his wife who continued to behave in the same way. At last he came, bringing with him vast sums from his pillaging foray which he justified endlessly, using specious arguments which his honest wife refuted. Finally, he turned to her and said:

'Madame, my justification is the same as that used by Alexander the Great, Genghis Khan, and every famous conqueror the world has ever seen. Their logic and mine are identical. But they had three hundred thousand men at their command, whereas I have only four hundred, and that is my crime.'*

'All that is very well, sir,' said Madame de Franlo, who at this point felt it wiser to pursue sentiment not argument. 'But if it is true that you love me as you have many times been kind enough to say you do, would you not be broken-hearted to see me die on a scaffold by your side?'

'You must fear no such calamity,' said Franlo. 'Our base here is well off the beaten track, and when I go on my forays I fear no man. But if we were ever found here, remember that I would have enough time to blow your brains out before anyone could lay a hand on you.'

The robber chief made a tour of inspection and, finding only reasons to give thanks for having such a wife, he was unstinting in his praise and compliments. He recommended her even more warmly than before to his men, and then left. His second absence returned his forlorn wife to the same duties, the same behaviour, the same atrocious interludes. It lasted more than two months, at the end of which Franlo returned to his base, even more delighted with his wife than ever.

The poor creature had now existed in a perpetual atmosphere of fear and horror for more than five months, watered by her tears and fed by her despair, when heaven, which never deserts the innocent, at last saw fit to deliver her from her tribulations through the most unexpected event.

It was October, and Franlo and his wife were dining in a pergola just by the door to their house when all of a sudden ten or a dozen shots were heard coming from the lookout post.

'We are betrayed,' said the chief, getting up from the table and reaching quickly for his gun. 'Here, Madame, take this pistol. Stay here. If you cannot kill any man who tries to get to you, use it to blow out your brains so that you don't fall into his hands.'

And so saying, he quickly summoned those of his men who were in the village and rushed off to defend the pass. But it was too late. Two hundred mounted dragoons had overcome the lookouts and, brandishing their sabres aloft, were riding down into the plain. Franlo and his men opened fire, but not having had time to organize them, he was immediately overrun and most of his companions were cut down or trampled under the horses' hooves. Franlo himself was seized, surrounded, and closely guarded by twenty dragoons whose responsibility he became. The rest of the detachment, their leader at its head, galloped towards Madame de Franlo. Picture the cruel state in which they found the wretched woman: hair dishevelled, features twisted by despair and fear, she stood with her back to a tree, holding a pistol to her heart, ready to end her life rather than fall into the hands of men she believed were the myrmidons of the law...

'Stop, Madame, stop!' cried the commanding officer as he leaped from his horse and threw himself at her feet, hoping by this action to persuade her to put down the gun. 'Stop, I say! Do you not recognize the unfortunate man who once loved you? He it is who kneels before you, he whom heaven has blessed by making him the agent of your deliverance. Put aside your weapon and allow Goé to hold you in his arms!'

Mademoiselle de Faxelange thought she must be dreaming. With growing certainty she recognized the man who spoke thus to her, and then fell lifeless into his open arms. The sight drew tears from everyone who was there to see it.

'Let us waste no time, Madame,' said Goé, recalling his fair cousin to life. 'We must make haste to quit a place that must be odious to you. But first, let us recover what is rightly yours.'

He broke into Franlo's coffers and from it took the four hundred thousand francs of his cousin's dowry, plus ten thousand crowns which he distributed among his dragoons, then sealed the room, freed the prisoners held by the scoundrel Franlo, chose eighty men to garrison the village, rejoined his cousin and the others, and persuaded her to leave without further delay.

As she was setting out for the pass, she observed Franlo in irons.

'Oh, sir!' said she to Goé, 'I ask on bended knee that this unfortunate man be pardoned. I am his wife... and I must tell you that I have the misfortune to be carrying within me the living testimony of his love. Furthermore, he has always treated me in nothing but the most honourable manner.'

'Madame,' replied Monsieur de Goé, 'I have no authority in these matters. I am merely the officer who commands these troops and am bound by my orders. This man is no longer my responsibility, and I could save his neck only by putting a great deal at risk. The Provost Marshal of the province is waiting for me at the other end of the pass. He will decide what is to be done with him. I shall not set his foot on the ladder to the scaffold: that is all I can do.'

'Oh, sir! Let him escape!' exclaimed this unusual woman. 'Your unhappy, weeping cousin implores you!'

'You are blinded by unwarranted pity, Madame,' Goé went on. 'The wretch will never mend his ways, and to save the life of this one man would cost the lives of more than fifty.'

'He is right,' cried Franlo, 'absolutely right, Madame. He knows me as well as I know myself. Crime is my element and I would only go on living so that I could resume my career. It's not my life that I want but a death that is not dishonourable. And so perhaps the kindly soul who is so interested in my case would be good enough to beg just one favour for me: permission to have my brains blown out by these dragoons'.

'Which of you lads is prepared to do it?' cried Goé.

But not one of them moved, for Goé commanded Frenchmen and it was unlikely that there were any executioners in their ranks.*

'In that case, give me a pistol,' said the villain.

Goé, greatly affected by his cousin's entreaties, walked up to Franlo and gave him the weapon he asked for. But was there ever such treachery? Faxelange's husband no sooner had what he asked for than he turned it on Goé and fired, though fortunately without hitting him.

His action enraged the dragoons, and their mood demanded revenge. Oblivious to everything except their fury, they fell on

Franlo and cut him to pieces in less than a minute. Goé led his cousin away, so that she hardly saw anything of this horrible spectacle.

They galloped through the pass. When they emerged, a gentle-spirited horse stood waiting for Mademoiselle de Faxelange. Monsieur de Goé gave the Provost an immediate report of the operation, mounted constables secured the lookout post, the dragoons withdrew, and six days later Mademoiselle de Faxelange, escorted by her rescuer, was restored to the bosom of her family.

'Here is your daughter,' the brave Goé said to Monsieur and Madame de Faxelange. 'And here is the money which was stolen from you. Now listen to me, Mademoiselle, and you will understand why I have delayed until now the explanation I owe of everything which concerns you.

'You had hardly left when the suspicions which I originally voiced merely as a way of keeping you here returned to torment me. I left no stone unturned in my efforts to follow the trail of your ravisher and find out all I could about him. I was fortunate enough to succeed on all fronts, and was not mistaken. I notified your parents only when I believed I was virtually certain of finding you. I was not refused the command of a troop of soldiers, which I requested to secure your release and simultaneously to rid France of the monstrous villain who had deceived you. In the end I succeeded. I have acted throughout from no motive of self-interest, Mademoiselle. The mistakes you made and your misfortunes have raised permanent obstacles between us. You will at least pity me... you will regret me. You will be left with only the memory of the feelings which you once denied me, and I shall be avenged.

'Goodbye, Mademoiselle. I have done my duty by our family and by my love, and now there is no course open to me but to separate from you for ever. Yes, Mademoiselle, I am leaving. The war presently being fought in Germany holds out the prospect of either death or glory. In the days when I could have hoped to lay my triumph at your feet I should have preferred the latter. But now all I seek is death.'

And with these words, Goé withdrew. Despite every effort to dissuade him, he fled, never to be seen again. Six months later news came that, during a desperate charge on an enemy position, he had been killed in Hungary while fighting for the Turks.

As for Mademoiselle de Faxelange, shortly after she returned to

Paris she was brought to bed of the unfortunate fruit of her marriage. Her parents had the child sent to a home for foundlings,* along with a large donation. When she had recovered, she begged her father and mother to allow her to take the veil at the Carmelite Convent.* In turn, her parents entreated her not to deprive them in their old age of the consolation of her presence. She yielded. But her health declined with each day that passed, undermined by regrets, withered by tears and sorrow, and blasted by remorse. She died four years later of consumption, a grim and terrible example of the avarice of fathers and the ambition of daughters.*

May the telling of this tale make the first more just and the second less foolish! If such proves to be the case, we shall not regret the pains we have taken to convey to posterity an episode which, although horrible in itself, might thus serve the good of humanity.

FLORVILLE AND COURVAL

or FATALITY

MONSIEUR DE COURVAL had just attained the fifty-fifth year of his age. Well preserved and in rude good health, he could still count on having another twenty years ahead of him. He had experienced nothing but unpleasantness from his first wife, who had deserted him long ago for a life of debauchery, and he had every reason to suppose her to be in her grave. Having received assurances to that effect which could not have been firmer, he conceived the idea of making a second marriage with a reasonable woman who, by the sweetness of her nature and the excellence of her principles, would help him forget his first disappointment.

As unfortunate in his children as in his wife, Monsieur de Courval had fathered only two—a daughter, whom he had lost in infancy, and a son who, at the age of fifteen, had deserted him as his mother had done, and regrettably for the same dissolute reasons. Believing that there was no way this monster could be brought to heel, Monsieur de Courval consequently decided to disinherit him and leave his property to the children he hoped to have by the new wife he was minded to take. He enjoyed an income of 15,000 livres.* He had been a man of business, and this was the fruit of his labours. He spent it like a gentleman, with a few friends who all liked and respected him and saw him sometimes in Paris, where he occupied a handsome apartment in the rue Saint-Marc,* but more frequently in his small but charming country property near Nemours, where Monsieur de Courval spent eight months of the year.

This honourable man disclosed his intention to these friends and, seeing that they approved, asked them most particularly to enquire among their acquaintance if there was a woman of thirty or thirty-five years of age, a widow or a spinster, who might answer to his requirements.

Two days later one of his former colleagues called and said he was pretty sure that he had found a suitable candidate.

'The person I propose', the friend said, 'has two things that count against her, and I must begin by telling you what they are so as to compensate afterwards with a review of her good qualities. Everyone seems sure that she has neither father nor mother living, but no one knows who they were or where she lost them. What is known', the go-between went on, 'is that she is cousin to Monsieur de Saint-Prât, a man of excellent standing, who acknowledges her, respects her, and will give you a favourable account of her which is above suspicion and thoroughly deserved. She has no fortune from her parents but has an allowance of four thousand francs from this same Monsieur de Saint-Prât, in whose house she was brought up and spent all her youth. So much for the first shortcoming, and now we turn to the second,' said Monsieur de Courval's friend, 'which is a liaison at the age of sixteen and a child now dead whose father she has not seen since. There you have the entire case against. Now for the positive side.

'Mademoiselle de Florville is thirty-six but looks scarcely twenty-eight. It would be difficult to imagine a women with a pleasanter and more interesting face. Her features are gentle and delicate, her skin has the whiteness of the lily, and her auburn hair reaches down to the ground. Her mouth is moist and most pleasingly set and is the image of a rose in springtime. She is very tall, but so prettily made and with such grace in her movements that no one could possibly complain of her height, which otherwise might lend a certain sternness to her appearance. Her arms, neck, and legs are all well shaped, and she has the kind of beauty which will not age for many years to come. As to her conduct, her extremely regular habits may well not please you. She has no taste for society, lives very quietly, is very pious and most conscientious in observing the duties of the convent where she lives, and if she edifies all who frequent her there with her religious virtues, she delights all who meet her with the charm of her wit and the grace of her personality. She is, in short, an angel come down to earth, whom heaven has set aside to make the happiness of your last years.'

Monsieur de Courval, delighted to find such a prospect, wasted no time but begged his friend to provide him with an opportunity to meet the person in question.

'Her birth is a matter which does not worry me in the least,' said he, 'for if she is pure in blood what concern is it of mine who transmitted it to her? The adventure she had when she was sixteen alarms me as little, for she has made up for her indiscretion with a goodly number of years of sober living. I shall marry her as though she were a widow. Since I have made up my mind to take only a wife of thirty or thirty-five, it would be asking too much to add to the specification a foolish clause making virginity a condition. Thus there is nothing in your proposal that displeases me. All I need do now is to urge you to let me see her.'

Monsieur de Courval's friend granted his wish in short order. Three days later he invited him to dine at his house with the person in question. Anyone would have found it difficult not to be won over on meeting this delightful woman for the very first time. Here was the wisdom of Minerva herself garbed in the beauties of Venus. Since she was acquainted with what was afoot she was all the more reserved, and her modesty, her discretion, and the nobility of her bearing when joined to so many physical charms, her sweet nature, and a mind as acute as it was well stocked, all this so turned poor Courval's head that he begged his friend to bring matters to the swiftest conclusion.

They met again two or three times, either at the same house or at Monsieur de Courval's or Monsieur de Saint-Prât's, until at the last Mademoiselle de Florville, being pressed very hard, declared to Monsieur de Courval that nothing could please her more than the compliment he was so good as to pay her, but that her finer feelings would not allow her to accept any proposal until she had first informed him personally of the adventures of her life.

'You have not been told everything, sir,' said the delightful creature, 'and I cannot consent to be yours unless you know more. To have your respect is too important for me to place myself in a position where I might lose it. I should certainly not deserve it if I took advantage of your misapprehension and agreed to be your wife, except on the condition that you first judge me worthy of the honour.'

Monsieur de Courval assured her that he did know everything, that it was no one's business but his own to worry about the kind of anxieties she spoke of, and that, were he so fortunate as to please her, then she need trouble herself no further on that head. Mademoiselle de Florville was firm. She stated categorically that she would not agree to anything unless Monsieur de Courval were in possession of all the facts which concerned her. There was therefore no choice. The only concession Monsieur de Courval could obtain was that Mademoiselle de Florville would travel to his property near Nemours, that preparations should be made for the marriage on which he was set, and that once Mademoiselle de Florville's story had been heard, she would become his wife the very next day.

'But sir,' said Florville agreeably, 'since your preparations may prove to be unnecessary, why make them? If, that is, I convince you that I was never meant to be your wife?...'

'That is something of which you will never persuade me, Mademoiselle,' replied the worthy Courval. 'I challenge you to try to convince me. So, pray, let us go—and do not try to oppose my wedding plans.'

There was no way Mademoiselle de Florville could be moved on this last point. All was made ready, and the coach set out for Courval. But at the insistence of Mademoiselle de Florville there were no other guests invited. What she had to say could only be revealed to the man who proposed to marry her. Accordingly no one was admitted, and the day after her arrival this beautiful and remarkable woman, after asking Monsieur de Courval to hear her out, related the events of her life in the following terms:

The History of Mademoiselle de Florville

Your intentions with regard to myself, sir, are of an order which precludes any deception. You have seen Monsieur de Saint-Prât to whom you have been told I am related, a fact which he himself has been good enough to confirm. And yet in this matter you have been comprehensively misled. I know nothing of my birth. I have never had the satisfaction of knowing who my parents were. A few days after I was born I was found in a green taffeta bassinet on the doorstep of Monsieur de Saint-Prât's town-house. A letter, unsigned, was pinned to the canopy of my cradle. It read simply:

> You are childless. Though you have been married ten years, each day you wish you had children. Adopt this infant. Her blood is pure. She is the fruit of the most chaste union, not the product of debauchery, and is well born. If this baby girl fails to please you, then you must have her conveyed to the hospital for foundlings.* Make no enquiries. None will succeed. It is impossible that you should know more.

The worthy couple with whom I had been left took me in at once, raised me, took every care of me, and I can truly say that I owe them everything. Since there was no indication of my name, Madame de Saint-Prât was pleased to call me Florville.

I had just reached my fifteenth birthday when I had the misfortune to see my benefactress die. Nothing can express the grief I felt at her loss. She had developed an affection for me such that on her deathbed she begged her husband to swear he would make me an allowance of four thousand francs and undertake never to desert me. These two requests were implemented to the letter, and Monsieur de Saint-Prât added to these kindnesses the favour of acknowledging me as a cousin of his wife and designating me as such in the papers granting the settlement which you have seen. I could no longer, however, remain in his house, as Monsieur de Saint-Prât gave me to understand.

'I have lost my wife and am still young,' that virtuous gentleman said to me. 'Your continuing to live under my roof would raise suspicions which neither of us would deserve. Your happiness and good name are dear to me and I would not wish to compromise either. We must separate, Florville. But I shall never abandon you as long as I live, nor do I wish you to live outside the family. I have a sister at Nancy, a widow. I shall send you to her. I answer for her affection as I do for my own. There, where I shall still be able to keep my eye on you, so to speak, I will continue to watch over your upbringing and your future happiness.'

I did not receive this news without shedding many a tear. This fresh increase of my sorrows was a bitter reminder of the grief I had felt at the death of my benefactress. But being absolutely persuaded by the excellent reasons for it given by Monsieur de Saint-Prât, I resolved to follow his advice and accordingly set out for Lorraine in the company of a lady of that region to whom I had been recommended, and who conveyed me into the hands of Madame de Verquin, the sister of Monsieur de Saint-Prât, with whom I was henceforth to live.

The tone of Madame de Verquin's household was very different from that of her brother. If in the one I had known only decency, religion, and morality, then frivolity, pleasure-seeking, and independence were, so to speak, at home in the other.

During my very first days there Madame de Verquin warned me that my prim and proper ways were not to her taste, adding that it was quite unheard of for anyone to arrive from Paris and behave with such gaucherie and display such ridiculous goody-goody ways, and that if I wished to continue on a good footing with her I should have to change my tune. This beginning alarmed me. I shall not attempt to make you think me better than I am, sir. But all my life I have found anything which departs from the path of religion and morality to be supremely distasteful. I have always been so opposed to what offends virtue, and the errors into which I have been led, against my will, have caused me such remorse that I confess it would be no service to me were I to be restored to fashionable company, for nature did not intend me to live in society where I feel awkward and shy. The most sequestered retreat is the haunt best suited to my general mood and way of thinking.

These reflections, still only half formed, being as yet unripe at the age I was then, did not preserve me from the evil counsels of Madame de Verquin, nor from the ills into which her blandishments would lead me. The same company which I saw perpetually, the boisterous entertainments that went on around me, the examples... the talk... I was swept up by it all. I was told I was pretty and was bold enough to believe it... and lived to rue doing so.

The Normandy regiment was then garrisoned in the town. Madame de Verquin's house was the meeting-place for the officers. All the young women gathered there too, and it was under her roof that all the town's amours were begun, ended, and took second breath.

It is very likely that Monsieur de Saint-Prât was unaware of the full extent of his sister's behaviour. How else, given the soberness of his own conduct, could he have agreed to send me to her, if he had known? This consideration made me hold my tongue and prevented my complaining to him. But if I am to be honest, perhaps I did not really care to. The impure air I breathed had already begun to contaminate my heart and, like Telemachus on the island of Calypso, perhaps I too would have paid no heed to the voice of Mentor.*

One day the unblushing Verquin, who had been for some time looking for ways of leading me astray, enquired if it was true I had brought a totally pure heart with me to Lorraine and whether there was not some lover in Paris I pined for.

'Alas, Madame,' said I, 'the thought that I might commit the faults of which you suspect me has never even entered my head.

Your brother will give you every assurance with regard to my conduct.'

'Faults!' Madame de Verquin broke in. 'If you have a fault it is that you are far too unspoilt for your age. I trust that it is a fault that you will try to correct.'

'Oh, Madame, is this the language I should expect to hear from a respectable lady like you?'

'Respectable?... Not another word, my dear, for I assure you of all the sentiments I should like to inspire respect is the very last: love is what I wish to arouse. Respect! I am not yet old enough for respect. Do as I do, my dear, and you will be happy... By the by, has Senneval caught your eye?' added the siren. She meant a young officer of seventeen who often came to call.

'Not particularly, Madame,' I replied. 'I can assure you that I view them all with the same indifference.'

'But that is exactly what you must not do, my sweet. From now on I want us to share our conquests... You must *have* Senneval. He is my handiwork. I took the trouble to train him myself. He loves you. You must *have* him.'

'Oh Madame, will you not spare me this? In truth, I do not care for anyone.'

'But you must. It is a matter I have already arranged with his colonel, my current amour, as you may have observed.'

'I beg you to allow me to act freely in this matter. None of my natural leanings inclines me to the pleasures to which you are so attached.'

'Oh, that will change! One of these days you will be as fond of them as I am. It is very easy not to like what you do not know. But no one should be allowed not to want to know what is made to be liked very much indeed. So there it is, it's all settled. Senneval, Mademoiselle, will declare his passion to you this evening and you will see to it that he is not left to languish, or I shall be cross with you... extremely cross.'

By five o'clock the company had assembled. As it was very hot, gaming tables were set up in the groves of the garden, and all was so carefully concerted that Monsieur de Senneval and I, finding that we alone did not play, were forced to converse with each other.

There is no point in hiding the fact from you, sir. The young man was agreeable and intelligent, and no sooner had he declared his feelings for me than I felt drawn to him by an impulse I could not control. When I later tried to account for this instinctive attraction, I found the matter quite impenetrable. It seemed to me that this inclination was not the product of an everyday sentiment, but that an obscuring veil concealed its true nature. On the other hand, at the very moment when my heart flew out to him, an unconquerable force seemed to hold it back, and in this turmoil... in the ebb and flow of ideas which I could not understand... I could not tell whether I was right to love Senneval or ought never to see him again.

He was given all the time in the world to say he loved me... Alas, he was given too much. For I was left with every opportunity to show that I was not indifferent to him. He took advantage of my confusion and insisted that I should confess my feelings. I was weak enough to say that I did not find him unattractive and, three days later, guilty enough to allow him to enjoy the fruits of his victory.

The malicious rejoicing of vice when it triumphs over virtue is a truly singular thing! I never saw anything to equal the exultation of Madame de Verquin the moment she learned that I had fallen into the trap she had prepared for me. She laughed at me, was vastly entertained, and at the last assured me that what I had done was the least complicated thing in the world, and the most reasonable. She added that I could receive my lover every night in her house without fear of the consequences... that she would not pry and that, being too occupied with her own affairs to pay any attention to my trifling business, she would not value my virtue at a lower rate since it was likely I would not look beyond one man while she, having to manage three, would continue at several removes from my reserve and modesty. When I attempted to take the liberty of observing that her dissolute conduct was odious, that it made short work of both delicacy and sentiment, and that it brought our sex down to the level of the lowest species of animal, Madame de Verquin burst out laughing.

'Spoken like a true heroine of romance!' she said. 'I admire you and do not in any way blame you. I know full well that at your age delicacy and sentiment are gods to which pleasure is sacrificed. The same does not apply at my time of life. To be undeceived about such chimerical phantoms is to slacken their hold, and more substantial sensual pleasures are preferable to the foolish nonsense which fires your enthusiasm. For why should we remain faithful to those who have never been faithful to us? Is it not enough to be the weaker sex without also becoming the most deluded? Any woman who tries to spoon delicacy into the mix is quite mad... Believe me, my dear, vary your pleasures for as long as your youth and looks permit, and jettison your illusion of constancy, a tedious, unassertive virtue which is unsatisfying to oneself and never deceives others.'

These arguments made me quail, but I realized at once that I had lost any right to counter them. I was dependent on the criminal protection provided by this immoral woman and I had no choice but to keep her sweet—the inescapable consequence of vice which, once we surrender to it, gives us into the power of persons for whom we would otherwise have nothing but contempt. I therefore accepted all Madame de Verquin's good offices. Each night Senneval gave me fresh proofs of his ardour, and six months went by in a state of such intoxication that I scarce had time to reflect.

Soon unwanted consequences opened my eyes. I discovered I was with child, and thought I should die of despair on finding myself in a state which vastly amused Madame de Verquin.

'Still,' she told me, 'we have to think of appearances. Since it would hardly be decent for you to be brought to bed in my house, the Colonel, Senneval, and I have made arrangements. He will give the subaltern leave, you will set out for Metz a few days ahead of him, he will follow in short order, and there, with his loving support, you will be delivered of the illicit fruit of your tenderness. Then you will both return here in the same manner as your going.'

I had no choice but to obey, as I have told you, sir. When we have, alas, done wrong, we are thrown on the mercies of others and are vulnerable to the whims of circumstance. We give rights over our person to all and sundry, and we must do everybody's bidding once we forget ourselves so far as to become the slaves of our passions.

All was arranged as Madame de Verquin had said. Three days later Senneval and I were reunited at Metz in the house of a midwife whose address I had been given as I left Nancy, and there I gave birth to a boy. Senneval, who all this time had shown the tenderest, the most delicate sentiments, seemed to love me at an even higher pitch now that I had, as he put it, doubled his existence. He was kindness itself to me, begged me to leave his son in his charge, swore that he would take the very best care of him for as long as he lived, and would not contemplate returning to Nancy until he had done his duty by me.

It was as he was about to take his leave that I tried to make him see how utterly miserable the fault he had made me commit would leave me, and proposed that we should make amends for it by being joined in marriage in the sight of God. Senneval, who was not expecting this suggestion, grew flustered...

'Alas!' he said, 'am I my own master in this? Since I am still not of age, would I not need my father's consent? What would our marriage amount to if it were not stamped with his formal approval? Besides, I am far from being a suitable match for you. You are Madame de Verquin's niece' (this was widely believed at Nancy) 'and could hope to do much better. Believe me, Florville, let us forget our foolishness. You may count on my complete discretion.'

His words, which were so unexpected, struck me cruelly and made me see the enormity of the mistake I had made. Pride prevented my replying, but did not make the pain less bitter. If anything had kept the horror of my conduct hidden from my own eyes, it was, I confess, the hope that I might one day atone for it by marrying my lover. I was so naive! I never thought, despite the perversity of Madame de Verquin, who should no doubt have warned me, no, I never for one moment dreamed that anyone could make a sport of seducing an unfortunate young woman and then of abandoning her! Nor did I imagine that honour, a sentiment which stands so high in men's eyes, was in reality without force where women were concerned, and that our weakness could be used to justify an insult which they would offer each other only at the risk of shedding their own blood. I therefore considered myself to be both the victim and the dupe of a man for whom I would have given my life a thousand times over. This appalling realization almost sent me to my grave. Senneval never left my side, he continued to care for me as before, but he never spoke again of my proposal, and I had too much pride to broach the reason for my despair with him a second time. In the end, when he saw that I was recovered, he went away.

I was resolved not to go back to Nancy and, knowing full well that it was the last time in my life that I should see my lover, all the wounds were reopened as he made ready to leave. However, I had strength enough to withstand this final blow... The cruel man galloped off, breaking free of my heart which brimmed with tears, whereas I did not see him shed one!

And there you see what happens to the promises of eternal love which we women are foolish enough to believe! The more affectionate we are, the more likely it is that our seducers will desert us... the unfeeling brutes... the more we try to keep them, the greater the chance that they will abandon us.

Senneval had taken his child and sent him away to a place in the country where it was impossible for me to find him... He had wanted to deprive me of the joy of loving and raising the tender fruit of our liaison myself. It was as though he wished I should forget everything that might still link us together. Forget I did, or rather I believed I did.

I resolved to quit Metz at once and never return to Nancy. However, I had no wish to fall foul of Madame de Verquin. For all her faults, the fact that she was so closely related to my benefactor was enough to oblige me to treat her with indulgence for the rest of my life. I wrote her the most guileless letter. I gave as my excuse for not returning to her town the shame I felt for the action I had committed, and asked her permission to rejoin her brother in Paris. She replied immediately that I was free to do as I pleased and that I could count on having her affection at all times. She added that Senneval was not yet back, that no one knew where he had gone, and that I was foolish to worry my head about all these trifling matters.

Once I received her letter I returned to Paris, and hastened to throw myself on the mercies of Monsieur de Saint-Prât. My silence and my tears soon informed him of my shame. But I took care to accuse no one but myself, and never spoke of the role played by his sister. A good and kindly soul, Monsieur de Saint-Prât had no inkling of the disorderly life she led and believed her to be the most respectable of women. I left him with his illusions intact, and this course, of which Madame de Verquin was not ignorant, meant that I remained on friendly terms with her.

Monsieur de Saint-Prât sympathized with me... made me see how wrong I had been, and in the end forgave me.

'My child!' he said with the solemn affection of the honest heart which is so very different from the odious exultation of crime, 'my dear girl, you see now the price that has to be paid for straying from the path of virtue!... The adoption of virtue is so necessary, it is so intimate a part of our existence, that only misfortune awaits us the moment we abandon it. Compare the tranquillity of the state of innocence you enjoyed before you left my house with the awful misery in which you have returned to it. Do the ephemeral pleasures you enjoyed as you fell from grace compensate for the torment which now lacerates your heart? It follows, child, that happiness lies only in virtue, and all the specious arguments of its detractors will never afford the smallest part of the joys it brings. Oh Florville, those who deny or resist those same sweet joys do so only out of envy, you may depend on it, out of the malicious pleasure of making other people feel as guilty and unhappy as they are themselves. They blind themselves and would like to blind everyone else; they are mistaken and would wish all to be mistaken. But if we could see into their hearts, we should find there only suffering and regret. All of these apostles of crime are wicked and desperate... we would not find one who is sincere, none who would admit—were he indeed capable of speaking the truth—that his corrupting talk or dangerous scribblings were directed solely by his passions. And indeed, where is the man who will coolly claim that the foundations on which morality is built can be shaken without the risk of adverse consequences? What man will dare to say that to do good, to desire good, is not of necessity the true goal of mankind? And how can the man who commits only acts of evil expect to be happy in a society whose best interest is served by the unceasing multiplication of good deeds? But will not this apologist of crime himself be left to quail and tremble when he finally uproots from all our hearts the only thing which he can count on to protect him? What will prevent his servants ruining him if they have ceased to be virtuous? What is there to stop his wife dishonouring him if he has convinced her that virtue serves no useful purpose? What will stay the hand of his children if he has stamped out the seed of goodness in their hearts? How shall his freedom and his property be respected if he has told those who govern: "Impunity walks at your side and virtue is nothing but an illusion!" Whatever sort of man this unfortunate may be, whether he be husband or father, rich or poor, master or slave, danger will attend him from every quarter, daggers will be raised against him on all sides. If he has dared eradicate from man the only obligations which serve to check his perversity, then we should be in no doubt: the wretch will sooner or later die the victim of his own abominable philosophy.[1]

'Let us set religion to one side for a moment, if you will, and consider only man in isolation. Who would be so foolish to believe that if he infringes all of society's rules the society he attacks can leave him in peace? Is it not in the interest of all men and the laws they pass for their own safety that they should always incline to crush all obstructive or harmful resistance? A degree of influence or well-filled moneybags may offer the evildoer a temporary flicker of prosperity, but how brief his candle! Exposed, unmasked, quickly transformed into the object of the hatred and contempt of the public, will he then find supporters to comfort him or apologists for his actions? No one would be prepared to own him. Since he has nothing more to offer them, they would cast him off as a heavy burden. Besieged by adversity on all sides, he would sink beneath the weight of opprobrium and misfortune and, no longer having a heart in which to find refuge, he would simply die of despair. But what is the absurd argument put up by our opponents? What sort of ineffectual attempt to weaken virtue do they undertake when they dare to say that any idea which is not universal is a delusion and that since virtues are local, none of them is real? Come now! So there is no such thing as virtue in general, since every nation has devised its own? Because different climates and different national temperaments have required different kinds of controls, and in short, since virtue has taken many different forms, there is therefore no such thing as virtue on this earth? You might as well doubt the reality of a river because it branches into innumerable different streams! What better proof is there that virtue is both real and indispensable than the need men have to adapt it to the infinite variety of human manners and customs and to make it the basis of all of them? Show me one nation which survives without virtue, just one where benevolence and humanity are not the basic cement which binds the whole! I will go further: if you can show me a gang of criminals which is not held together by a handful of virtuous principles, then I will abandon my

[1] 'Oh, my dear, never try to corrupt and deprave the one you love, for you never know where it all might lead,' a tender, loving woman said one day to the man who was attempting to seduce her. Permit me, adorable creature, to quote your exact words, for they define to such perfection the soul of a woman who, shortly afterwards, saved the life of that same man, that I would wish them carved in stone in the Temple of Memory, where your virtues surely give you a place.*

case. But on the other hand, if virtue can be shown to have its uses everywhere, if there is no nation, no state, no society, no individual who can survive without it, if, in a word, man cannot live happily or in safety without it, then am I wrong, child, to urge you never to turn your back on it? Surely you see, Florville,' my benefactor continued, clasping me to his heart, 'how low your first steps in waywardness have brought you? If you are still tempted to stray, if voluptuaries or your own weakness are even now spinning new webs to trap you in, think of the unhappiness your first wrongful steps brought you, think of a man who loves you like a daughter whose faults would break his heart... and you will find in such reflections all the strength required by the cult of virtue to whose fold I would have you return for ever.'*

Consistent with these same principles, Monsieur de Saint-Prât did not offer to let me stay under his roof. Instead, he proposed that I should reside with another relative of his, a woman as famous for the strict piety by which she lived as was Madame de Verquin for her laxness. This arrangement pleased me greatly. Madame de Lérince agreed to have me with the best will in the world, and I moved into her house the same week that I returned to Paris.

Oh sir! There was a yawning gap separating that respectable lady from the other whom I had left! If vice and depravity had established their dominion under the roof of the latter, the heart of the other was, so to speak, a haven for all the virtues. Just as I had been frightened by the debaucheries of the one, so I was comforted by the edifying principles of the other. I had found nothing but bitter disappointment and remorse by listening to Madame de Verquin; I met only with kindness and consolation by opening my heart to Madame de Lérince... Oh sir, permit me to describe her to you! She was adorable and I shall always love her. It would be a tribute which my heart owes to her many virtues, and I cannot resist paying it.

Madame de Lérince, then about forty years of age, was still very youthful in looks, and her expression of candour and modesty embellished her face more than the divine proportions with which nature had endowed it. Some said that a hint too much of nobility and loftiness made her seem distant upon a first acquaintance. Yet what might have been taken for pride softened the moment she began to speak. Hers was a soul so beautiful, so pure, she was so gracious of approach, so completely frank and honest, that you could not help being imperceptibly drawn to add the tenderest feelings for her to the veneration which she initially inspired. There was nothing fanatical or superstitious about Madame de Lérince's religion, for it was in her extreme sensitivity that the principles of her faith were to be found. The idea of the existence of God and the creed by which the Supreme Being was to be worshipped, these provided the most intense satisfactions of her loving soul. She freely admitted that she would be the unhappiest of creatures if some wicked philosophy ever forced her mind to abandon the respect and love which she had for her faith. Even more attached, if that were possible, to the sublime ethical teachings of that religion than to its observances and ceremonials, she made its admirable morality the rule by which she measured all her actions. No slanderous word had ever passed her lips, and she refused to offer any pleasantry which might be hurtful to her neighbour. Full of tenderness and kindly feeling for her fellow creatures, finding some good in them even when they were at fault, her sole occupation was either to conceal those faults discreetly or gently chide those who committed them. If they were distressed, she could think of no greater pleasure than to bring them relief. She did not wait for the poor to come to beg for her help, but went in search of them... she sniffed them out, and joy lit up her face for all to see when she had consoled a widow or provided for an orphan or made a poor family easier in its circumstances, or when by her personal intervention she had set those free of misfortune who had been dogged by it. There was no whiff of sternness or austerity in any of her proceedings. Provided the amusements in which she was invited to join were innocent, she was only too delighted to take part, and even devised entertainments herself for fear that others might find life tedious with her. Judicious... enlightened in her dealings with moralists... deep-thinking with theologians... she inspired novelists and smiled upon poets, surprised the lawmakers and the men of politics, and could play with a child. She possessed wit of all kinds, but the quality which shone brightest in her was most chiefly visible in the particular gift and admirable enthusiasm she had for bringing out or discovering wit in others. Living a retired life through choice, cultivating friends for their own sake, Madame de Lérince was, in short, a perfect model for both sexes, who ensured that all who lived within her circle enjoyed the same happy tranquillity... that heavenly bliss promised to the righteous man by the sacred God in whose image she was made.

I shall not bore you, sir, with the monotonous detail of my life during the seventeen years which I was fortunate enough to spend with this wonderful woman. Discussing moral questions and matter of faith, carrying out as many acts of charity as possible, it was with such duties that our days were filled.

'Men only take fright at religion, my dear Florville,' Madame de Lérince would say, 'because clumsy counsellors make them aware of its constraints without setting out its joys before them. Is there a man, when he lifts his eyes to contemplate the universe, who can be so absurd as to disagree that so many marvels can only be the handiwork of an all-powerful God? Once this fundamental truth is accepted—and what else does he need to be persuaded of it in his heart?—what cruel and barbaric individual would refuse to fall down and worship the benevolent God who made him? But the great diversity of religions creates a difficulty, for some find evidence of their falseness in their very multiplicity. But this is a specious argument! Is it not rather in the unanimous response of peoples in recognizing and serving a God, is it not in this tacit acknowledgement which is etched on the hearts of all men that we find even more conclusively than in the sublime organization of nature (if that be possible) the irrefutable proof of the existence of this supreme God? Come now! Man cannot live without adopting a God, he cannot examine his conscience without finding proofs of His existence in it, he cannot open his eyes without detecting traces of that God everywhere, and yet has he the temerity still to nurse doubts? No, Florville, no, there is no such thing as an honest atheist. Pride, obstinacy, and the passions, these are the weapons which attack God, who is unceasingly reborn in the heart or brain of men and women. And when each beat of that heart, when every insight of that brain leads me inescapably to this undeniable Being, shall I refuse to worship Him, shall I deny Him the tribute which He permits me to offer up in my weakness, shall I decline to humble myself before His greatness, shall I not seek His grace to help me endure the trials of life and to allow me one day to share in His glory, shall I not strive to be granted the blessing of spending eternity in His bosom, or shall I run the risk of spending that same eternity in a fearsome abyss of torments simply because I refused to accept the incontrovertible evidence of His existence that Almighty God has given me? My child, must not this dreadful alternative give pause for reflection? All you who stubbornly reject the illumination which God beams into your innermost heart, at least be just for once and, simply out of pity for yourself, yield to Pascal's irrefutable argument: "If there is no God, what difference does believing in him make, where is the harm in doing so? But if there is a God, what dangers do you not run by refusing to give him your faith?"* You unbelievers claim that you do not know what obeisance to pay this God, and say that the multiplicity of religions offends you. Well, examine them all, you have my consent, and afterwards come and say honestly in which you find the largest share of grandeur and majesty. Christians, deny if you can that the faith into which you were fortunate enough to be born emerges as the one whose attributes are the holiest and the most sublime. Go and seek elsewhere mysteries which are as great, dogmas as pure, and ethical values as comforting. Find in some other creed the ineffable sacrifice made by a God in favour of His creation, and discover therein promises which are more generous, a future which is more blest, and a God who is greater and more sublime! No, ephemeral philosopher, you cannot. No, seeker after pleasure, you cannot do it, for your faith changes with the physical condition of your nerves,* so that you are impious in the heat of your passions and credulous when they have cooled—I say you cannot. The God your brain rejects never ceases to be recognized by your heart. He walks constantly by your side, even as you slide down the slope of error. Only break the ties which bind you to wickedness and this holy and majestic God will never forsake the temple He has raised in your heart. Dear Florville, it is in our hearts far more than in our reason that we shall find the inescapable reality of God, who is apparent in and authenticated by all things. It is in that same heart that we must also find the inevitability of the creed through which we worship Him. It is your heart alone, my dear, which will soon persuade you that the noblest and purest religion is the one into which we were born. So let us practise that sweet and comfortable faith punctually and with joy. May it fill our most blissful hours here below. Let us cherish it and, led by its imperceptible hand to the end of our days, may it be in the path of love and delight that we walk until such time as we restore to the bosom of the Everlasting Father the soul which emanated from Him, which was made only to acknowledge Him, and which was given to us to enjoy only so that we should believe in Him and worship Him.'

This was how Madame de Lérince spoke to me, how my mind was strengthened by her counsel, how my soul grew purer under her saintly wing. But as I promised, I shall pass over all the banal details of what happened while I lived in her house and bring you to the nub. You are a generous, understanding man, sir. But now I must speak of my sins. Concerning the time it pleased heaven to let me live in peace and tread the path of virtue, I need do no more than thank God and hold my tongue.

I had not stopped writing to Madame de Verquin. I received letters from her regularly, twice a month. Now by rights I should have ended this correspondence. My reformed way of life and firmer moral outlook ought to have forced me to find some way of putting a stop to it. I owed it to Monsieur de Saint-Prât. But more insistent, I must admit, was the secret, unconquerable impulse which turned my thoughts to places to which I had been attached by people I had once loved, together no doubt with the hope that one day I might have news of my son, and all this committed me to persisting with a correspondence which Madame de Verquin had the good grace to maintain with regularity. I attempted to convert her and made much of the tranquil joys of the life I led. But she pooh-poohed them, saying they were delusions, always mocked or contested my good resolutions, and, as firmly attached to her own ways as ever, assured me that nothing on earth would make her change them. She told me of new girls she amused herself by turning into her proselytes. She said they were all more docile than I had been, and their many trips and stumbles were, according to this depraved woman, little triumphs which she never brought off without feeling an extreme pleasure, and the satisfaction of leading their young hearts into evil ways comforted her for her inability to do everything that her imagination devised. I often begged Madame de Lérince to lend her eloquent pen to the task of unseating my opponent. She said she would do so, with all her heart. Madame de Verquin responded, and her sophisms, some of them very forceful, obliged us to fall back on the somewhat less than victorious arguments of a tender heart which, as Madame de Lérince rightly claimed, infallibly contained all that was required to destroy wickedness and confound unbelief. From time to time I asked Madame de Verquin for news of the man I still loved. But either she could not or would not tell me.

It is now time, sir, we must now come to the second great catastrophe of my life, to a bloody tale which breaks my heart each time it resurfaces in my imagination, and which, by instructing you of what foul crime I am guilty, will doubtless make you abandon the fond plans you have conceived with regard to my person.

Madame de Lérince's house, although as strictly run as I have described it, nevertheless opened its doors to a few friends. Madame de Dulfort, a woman of middling years formerly in attendance on the Princess of Piedmont, often called to see us, and one day asked Madame de Lérince permission to present a young man who had been particularly recommended to her and whom she would be particularly pleased to introduce into a house where examples of virtue, of which he would be the constant recipient, would have the effect of educating his heart. My benefactress demurred on the grounds that she never received young persons, but overcome by her friend's pressing entreaties, she agreed that the Chevalier de Saint-Ange should come, and come he did.

Perhaps it was a presentiment, but let it be whatever you like, sir, the moment I saw the young man I was struck by a trembling in all my being whose origin I was unable to explain... I almost fainted... I did not bother to enquire much into the cause of this strange effect but attributed it to some internal malaise, and Saint-Ange ceased to have an impact on me. But if at that first meeting the young man had shaken me as I have said, something similar had also happened to him... This I learned from his own lips. Saint-Ange felt such respect for the house whose doors had been opened to him that he dared not forget himself so far as to give any hint of the passion which consumed him. Thus three months went by before he ventured to breathe a word of it to me. But his eyes spoke to me in a language so clear that it was impossible for me to mistake his meaning. Determined not to fall back into the kind of error to which I owed my ruined life, and shored up now by better principles, a score of times I was on the verge of informing Madame de Lérince of the feelings which I believed I detected in the young man. But, restrained by the thought of the pain I believed I should cause her, I chose to say nothing. It was a fatal decision, to be sure, since it was the cause of the hideous misfortune which I shall presently relate.

It was our custom every year to spend six months at a most agreeable country estate which Madame de Lérince owned at two leagues distance from Paris. Monsieur de Saint-Prât came often to see us there. Unfortunately for me, he was detained that year by the gout and could not attend. I say unfortunately for me, sir, because naturally having more confidence in him than in his cousin, I would have admitted to him certain matters which I would never have brought myself to tell other people, though admitting them might well have prevented the fatal disaster which occurred.

Saint-Ange sought Madame de Lérince's permission to join the party, and since Madame de Dulfort also asked for the same favour for him, it was granted.

We in our little company were all rather anxious to know who this young man was. Nothing emerged that was clear or certain about his life. Madame de Dulfort told us he was the son of a provincial gentleman to whom she was related. He himself, sometimes forgetting what Madame de Dulfort had said, let it be known that he was from Piedmont, a suggestion that drew some credibility from his way of speaking Italian. He had no occupation, though he was of an age to be usefully employed, and we took it that he had yet to make up his mind. Otherwise, he cut a very handsome figure, worthy of an artist's brush, behaved most civilly, spoke very respectfully, and gave every sign of having been given an excellent education. Yet running counter to all that was a prodigious hastiness, a kind of impetuousness of character which startled us at times.

Once Monsieur de Saint-Ange was in the country, his emotions having only grown stronger for having been constrained by the control he had tried to impose on them, he found it impossible to conceal what he felt from me. I trembled... and yet was sufficiently mistress of myself to respond by showing him nothing but pity.

'In truth, sir' said I, 'either you must have a very imperfect understanding of your own worth, or a great deal of time to waste, if you are prepared to spend it with a woman twice your age. But assuming I were foolish enough to listen to you, what absurd plans could you possibly have in mind for me?'

'To be joined to you by the holiest of unions, Mademoiselle. And you would have the lowest opinion of me if you imagined I had any other ambition!'

'In truth, sir, I shall certainly not offer the public the bizarre spectacle of a spinster of four and thirty who gives herself in marriage to a boy of seventeen.'

'But this is too cruel. If you felt in your heart one thousandth part of the love which consumes mine, would you even be aware of this footling disparity?'

'Make no mistake, sir, my heart is perfectly calm. It has been for many years and will, I trust, remain so for as long as it pleases God to allow me to continue on this earth.'

'So you even deny me the hope that I might some day make you think more fondly of me?'

'I go further. I forbid you to speak to me any more of this foolishness.'

'Florville, you are beautiful yet you seem determined to make my whole life a misery.'

'All I want is for you to be happy and at peace.'

'That I can never be unless I am with you.'

'Yes... until you put aside these foolish sentiments which you ought never to have had in the first place. Make an effort to overcome them, try to be master of your feelings, and you will regain your peace of mind.'

'I cannot.'

'You do not wish to. If you are to succeed, we must separate. If you do not see me for two years your agitation will subside, you will forget me, and you will be happy.'

'Never, never! Happiness for me can never be where you are not!'

But just then the others rejoined us, and our first conversation ended there.

Three days later Saint-Ange, having found the means of discovering me alone once more, insisted on resuming where he had left off at our previous meeting. This time I ordered him to be silent with such severity that his tears flowed in abundance. He left me abruptly, saying that I was driving him to despair and that he would take his own life if I continued to treat him thus... Then he stopped, came back, and said:

'Mademoiselle, you do not understand this heart which you despise... you have no conception... but I tell you, I am capable of the extremest measures, of undertaking such actions as you cannot imagine... yes, I would prefer a thousand times to commit them rather than give up all hope of finding my happiness with you!'

Then he withdrew, suffering torments of pain.

I was never more tempted to speak of this matter to Madame de Lérince than at that juncture. But I repeat: my fear of prejudicing the young man's interests held me back and I said nothing. For a whole week Saint-Ange studiously avoided me. He hardly spoke to me and avoided me at meals, in the drawing-room, during our common walks, no doubt to observe if this change in his behaviour would produce any effect on me. Had I shared his feelings, the stratagem would surely have worked. But I was so far removed from doing so that I scarcely gave any visible hint that I was aware of his tactic.

At the last, he approached me in a distant part of the grounds.

'Mademoiselle,' he said in the most agitated state imaginable, 'I have finally succeeded in composing myself. Your counsels have had on me the effect which you intended... you see how calm I have become once more... My only purpose in watching for this opportunity of finding you alone was to bid you an eternal farewell... Yes, I am about to leave you for ever, Mademoiselle... to go where you are not... never again will you see the man you hate... No, you shall never see him more!'

'Your decision pleases me greatly, sir. I am relieved to see you have at last come to your senses. But', I added with a smile, 'your conversion does not strike me yet as being very genuine.'

'Ah! But how must I appear, Mademoiselle, to convince you of my indifference?'

'Very different from how I see you now.'

'But at least, when I have gone... when you will no longer suffer the pain of having me in your sight, perhaps you will believe that I am reasonable and that all the efforts you took in that direction to make me so have succeeded?'

'Certainly, leaving now is the best thing you could do to convince me of it, and I shall not stop urging you to go.'

'So to you I am nothing but the most loathsome creature?...'

'You are, sir, a most personable young man who should have his mind on making conquests of quite a different order, and stop importuning a woman who cannot possibly listen to what you say.'

'But you shall listen,' he said furiously. 'Cruel you are, but whatever you may say, you shall hear the outpourings of my ardent heart, aye, and have my assurance that there is nothing in the world I would not do... to deserve you... or make you my own... To begin with,' he went on impetuously, 'do not believe in my so-called departure, it was a pretence designed to test you... You think that I could I leave you?... That I could tear myself away from the place which harbours you?... I would rather die a thousand deaths!... Hate me, faithless creature, loathe me, since that is my unhappy portion. But never hope that you can the kill in me the love which burns for you!'

Saint-Ange had worked himself into such a state as he pronounced these last words that, by some unwritten design which I have never been able to understand, he succeeded in stirring my emotions to such an extent that I had to turn my head aside to hide my tears, upon which I walked away, leaving him in the grove where he had managed to find me. He did not follow me. I heard him throw himself to the ground and give way to the most dreadful, frenzied lamentations... I myself, and I blush to admit it, sir, was quite certain that I had no feelings of love for the young man, but whether out of commiseration or by a recollection of things past, I could not help but give vent to my own emotions.

'Alas!' said I to myself as I surrendered to my sorrows, 'were not those the very words Senneval spoke?... It was those exact terms he used to express his feelings of love... also in a garden... in a garden like this... did he not say that he would love me always... and did he not deceive me cruelly?... Merciful heavens! He was the same age!... Oh, Senneval! Do you seek to deprive me of my peace of mind once more? Have you reappeared in this new, seductive shape only to push me a second time into the abyss?... Get away, you coward, get away from me... I hate even the memory of you!'

I wiped my tears away and shut myself up in my room until it was time for supper, when I went downstairs... but Saint-Ange did not appear. He sent word to say that he was unwell, and the next day was artful enough to show me a face on which was written nothing but calm... I was taken in. I genuinely believed that he had wrestled with himself and overcome his passion. I was deluding myself. Oh, the deceitful... But what am I saying, sir, I must not call him names... he may be entitled to my tears but he has no claim on my regrets.

Saint-Ange appeared so calm only because he had made all his plans. Two days went by in this manner, and as the evening of the third drew on, he publicly announced that he was leaving. With

Madame de Dulfort, his benefactress, he made various arrangements regarding their common affairs in Paris.

Then everyone retired for the night... Forgive me, sir, the confusion into which I have been thrown in anticipation of my account of that dreadful calamity. I can never see those events in my memory without experiencing a chill of horror.

As the weather was extremely warm, I had lain down on my bed virtually unclothed. My maid was outside my door and I had just blown out my candle... Unfortunately, my work basket had been left open on my bed, because I had been cutting pieces of muslin which I would need on the morrow. My eyes had scarcely begun to close when I heard a noise... at once I sat up straight... I felt a hand seize me...

'You will not run away from me again, Florville!' said Saint-Ange (for it was he). 'Forgive the violence of my passion but do not attempt to elude it... you must be mine!'

'Ignoble libertine!' I cried. 'Get out this instant or fear the weight of my anger!'

'All I fear is not having you, cruel that you are,' the ardent young man went on, and he leaped upon me so deftly and in such a state of furious passion that I became his victim before I was able to prevent it... Angered by such outrageous temerity and resolved to do anything rather than endure the rest, I worked free of his grasp and pounced on the scissors in the box at my feet. My head remained cool, despite my rage, and I tried to aim for his arm to wound him there, with a view much more to frightening him by this show of determination on my part than to punishing him as he deserved. But when he sensed what I was about to do, he increased the violence of his efforts.

'Get out, you villain!' I cried, attempting to wound him in the arm, 'Get out this instant and rue the shameful crime you have committed...'

Oh, sir! The hand of fate had directed mine... the hapless young man gave a cry and fell to the ground... I relit my candle at once-.. I leaned over him... Merciful heaven, I had struck him through the heart!... He breathed his last!... I flung myself on his bleeding corpse... Hardly knowing what I did, I clutched him to my heaving bosom... My lips, pressed to his, attempted to recall a soul which was even then departing... I bathed his wound with my tears...

'Ah! your only crime was to love me too much,' I exclaimed, distracted by my despair. 'Did you deserve to be punished like this? Did you have to lose your life by the hand of a woman for whom you would have willingly sacrificed it? Most unhappy young man!... living image of the one I loved... if loving you is all that is needed to restore you to life, then hear me, though I speak at this cruel juncture when you can tragically hear me no longer... hear me when I say that if your heart still beat I would give my life to revive it, that you were never indifferent to me, that I never saw you but I was troubled, and that what I felt for you perhaps burned far more brightly than the feeble flames which flickered in your heart!'

With these words, I collapsed senseless upon the body of the unfortunate young man. My maid ran in, for she had heard the noise. She tended me and then added her efforts to mine in an attempt to bring Saint-Ange back to life... Alas, all was in vain. We left the fatal apartment, carefully locked the door, took the key with us, and drove without delay to Paris, to the house of Monsieur de Saint-Prât... I ordered the servants to wake him, gave the key to the chamber of death into his keeping, and related my horrible adventure. He consoled and comforted me, and though he was ill, he had himself driven at once to Madame de Lérince's estate which was situated but a short distance from Paris, so that the night was long enough for all our toing and froing. My benefactor reached his cousin's house just as it was waking up, and nothing had yet transpired. Never did friends and relatives behave better than in that situation. In this, they were far from taking a leaf from the book of those stupid, unfeeling people whose only pleasure at such moments of crisis lies in repeating any tittle-tattle which will cast slurs or cause distress to themselves and those around them. The upshot was that the servants were hardly aware of what had happened.

'Well, sir?' interjected Mademoiselle de Florville at this juncture, breaking off on account of the tears which seemed as if they would choke her, 'Do you still wish to marry a woman capable of committing such a murder? Would you be prepared to take a creature in your arms who has deserved to feel the full rigour of the law? In short, a wretched female who is constantly tortured by her crime and has not spent one peaceful night since that cruel moment? No, sir, not one night goes by but that my unhappy victim appears to me, bathed in the blood which I let from his heart.'

'Compose yourself, Mademoiselle, pray be calm,' said Monsieur de Courval, adding tears of his own to those of this remarkable woman. 'Given the delicate soul which nature bestowed on you, I can well understand your feelings of remorse. But in this fatal incident there is not even the shadow of a crime. It was a terrible thing, no doubt, but that is all it was. There was no premeditation, nothing vicious was involved, merely your wish to protect yourself against the most odious assault... in short, a murder committed accidentally, in self-defence... Do not worry, Mademoiselle, be easy in your mind, I insist. The strictest court in the land would simply wipe away your tears. Oh, you were very much mistaken if you feared that any such thing would remove all the claims on my heart to which your many qualities entitle you. No, fair Florville, this incident, far from dishonouring you in my eyes, merely adds to the lustre of your virtues and makes you even worthier of finding a comforting hand which will make you forget your sorrows.'

'What you are so good as to say now,' replied Mademoiselle de Florville, 'Monsieur de Saint-Prât has also said to me. But the excessive kindness of both of you cannot drown out the clamour of my conscience: nothing can ever smooth away my remorse. But no matter, let us go on, sir, for you must be concerned as to how all this will end.'

Madame de Dulfort was, of course, distraught. Her young protégé, who had had so much to offer, had been too enthusiastically recommended to her for her not to deplore his loss. But she saw that there was good reason to keep silent about events, understood that a scandal which would ruin me would not bring her young man back to life, and accordingly said nothing. Madame de Lérince, despite the strictness of her principles and her extreme regard for propriety, behaved even more admirably, if that is possible, because caution and consideration are the distinctive marks of true piety. First, she let it be known in her household that I had been so foolish as to try to return to Paris that night, to enjoy the coolness of the nocturnal air; that she had been fully informed of my little whim, as it chanced that my going hence coincided very well with her own plans to dine in town that very evening; and she used this pretext as an excuse to send all the servants back to the capital. Once I was alone with Monsieur de Saint-Prât and his cousin, the priest of the place was sent for. Madame de Lérince's chaplain was, of course, as wise and enlightened as she. He made no difficulties about furnishing Madame de Dulfort with a death certificate, duly signed, and assisted by two of his attendants secretly buried the hapless victim of my fury.

When this was done, the house filled up again. An oath of secrecy was taken and Monsieur de Saint-Prât came and put my mind at rest by informing me of everything that had been done to bury my crime in the deepest oblivion. He gave the impression of wanting me to return to Madame de Lérince and continue on the same footing as before—she was willing to have me back—but I could not bring myself to do this. So he then recommended a change of scene. Madame de Verquin, with whom I had never ceased to correspond, as I have told you sir, was forever urging me to spend a few months with her. I mentioned this plan to her brother, he agreed to it, and a week later I set out for Lorraine. But the memory of my crime pursued me wherever I went, and nothing succeeded in calming my apprehensions.

I would wake in the middle of my sleep thinking I could still hear the moans and shrieks of the wretched Saint-Ange. I saw him lie bleeding at my feet, I heard him reproach me for my barbarity, vow that the memory of that dreadful deed would pursue me until my dying day, and say that I knew nothing of the heart I had broken.

One particular night Senneval—the faithless lover whom I had so little forgotten that he was the reason for my returning to Nancy—Senneval showed me two corpses together. One was Saint-Ange and the other a woman unknown to me.[1] He shed tears for both of them and showed me, not far from the spot, a coffin bristling with thorns which seemed to open to receive me... I woke in a state of the greatest agitation. A thousand confused thoughts crowded into my mind and a secret voice seemed to say: 'Yes, for as long as you shall live, this unhappy victim will force you to weep tears of blood that will grow more bitter with each passing day, and the pricks of your remorse will become not blunter but ever sharper.'

[1] Care must be taken not to lose sight of the words: *a woman unknown to me*, so that there is no confusion. Florville has still several griefs to bear before the veil lifts and allows her to recognize the woman she had seen in her dream.

It was in this state, sir, that I arrived at Nancy where a heap of sorrows awaited me. Once the hand of fate has singled us out, its blows multiply until we are crushed.

I was to lodge with Madame de Verquin as she had invited me to do in her last letter, in which she said she was greatly looking forward to seeing me again. But merciful heavens, in what circumstances would we both share that pleasure! When I arrived, she was on her deathbed! Who would ever have thought... O God! it was not two weeks since she had written to me... since she had spoken of her current entertainments and announced new ones to come. But such are the best-laid plans of mortals. It is at the moment when we conceive them, it is in the midst of our recreations, that implacable death snaps the thread on which our days are strung. Spending our lives without a thought for that fatal moment, living as though we shall live forever, we vanish into the dark cloud of immortality, uncertain of what fate awaits us there.

Would you allow me, sir, to break off the tale of my adventures for a moment to explain the loss of this woman to you and convey to you the fearsome stoicism which accompanied her to the grave?

Madame de Verquin was no longer young, being then fifty-two years of age. After growing heated in a vigorous dance, unwisely at her time of life, she threw herself into a pool to cool herself and immediately felt ill. She was carried to her room in a parlous state, a pleurisy appeared the next morning, and on the sixth day she was told that she had barely twenty-four hours to live. The news did not frighten her. She knew I was coming and gave orders that I should be welcomed. I arrived. According to the sentence pronounced by the doctor, she was due to die that same evening. By her command, she was moved to a chamber furnished in the finest taste and with every possible elegance. Casually attired, she reclined on a luxurious bed hung with lilac-coloured curtains made of heavy silk stuff which were agreeably enhanced with garlands of fresh flowers. Vases of pinks, jasmine, polyanthus, and roses brightened each corner of the apartment, while from other blooms she plucked petals, putting some into a basket and having the rest scattered throughout her apartment and over her bed. The moment she saw me, she held out her hand

'Come here, Florville,' she said, 'and kiss me on my bed of flowers... How tall, how beautiful you have grown!... I'll say this, my girl, virtue suits you... They have explained my condition to you... they have told you, Florville... they have told me too... a few hours from now I shall be dead. I would never have thought that when I saw you again it would be for so short a time...' (And seeing my eyes fill with tears): 'Come now, do not be foolish, you are not a child!... I take it you think I am desperately unhappy? But have I not enjoyed my life as much as any woman alive? I am merely being deprived of the years when I would have been obliged to give up my pleasures, and how should I have survived without my pleasures? Truth to tell, I do not regret that I shall not live to be older. The time would soon have come when no man wanted me. I never wished for a life which consisted merely of doing whatever was necessary so that I would not frighten them off. Death is to be feared, child, only by those who have faith. Heaven and hell hang over them, they do not know which will open to receive them, and their anxiety causes them infinite distress. But I, who hope for nothing, who am quite sure that I shall be no unhappier after my death than I was before I was born, shall fall quietly asleep in the bosom of nature, with neither regret nor pain, without remorse, without a care. I have asked to be laid to rest in my jasmine bower. A place for me is being made ready and there I shall remain, Florville, and the atoms released by my lifeless body will serve to nourish and produce the flowers I always loved above all others. Just think,' she went on, tapping my cheeks with a spray of that plant, 'next year, as you smell its blooms, you will inhale from their depths the soul of your former friend. And when the scent reaches the fibres of your brain, it will give you pretty fancies and force you to think of me once more.'*

My tears found a new course to flow down... I held the hands of the unfortunate woman and thought how I might replace her frightful, materialistic notions with others less impious. But no sooner did I intimate my intention of doing so than Madame de Verquin pushed me away with horror...

'Ah, Florville!' she cried, 'I beg you, do not poison my final hours with your foolish errors, but let me die in peace. I have not spent a lifetime detesting them only to adopt them on my deathbed...'

I held my tongue. What would my limping eloquence have achieved against so much firmness? I should have distressed Madame de Verquin without converting her, and common humanity forbade it. She rang, and immediately I heard a concert of sweet, melodious music which seemed to come from an adjacent room.

'You see', said this Epicurean, 'how I intend to die? Florville, is this not better than being surrounded by priests, who would fill my last moments with anxiety, alarm and despair?... I intend to show your true believers that we do not have to be like them to die in peace. I want to make them see that it is not religion we need if we are to die serene, but only courage and reason.'*

It began to grow late. A lawyer came into the room: she had sent for him. The music ceased, she dictated her last wishes. Childless, a widow for some years and consequently mistress of a considerable estate, she made bequests to friends and servants. Then she took a small casket from a writing-desk at the side of her bed.

'This is all I have left,' she said, 'a small sum in cash and a few trinkets. We shall use it to while away the rest of the evening. There are six of you here in this room. I shall divide my remaining fortune into six parts. We shall hold a lottery. You will draw lots and each of you will receive the prize you have won.'

I found it hard to believe that she could be so calm and collected. It seemed incredible to me to have so many things on one's conscience and reach the end of one's life in a state of calm which was the damnable product of atheism. If the gruesome death of certain wicked persons can strike fear into us, how much more fearful should we not be made by the spectacle of a heart so persistently impervious?

Meanwhile her wishes were carried out. She ordered a magnificent collation to be served. She tasted a number of dishes, drank wines from Spain and various liqueurs, her doctor having told her that in her present state nothing made any difference.

The lottery was drawn. We each received a prize of about a hundred louis in gold or gems. This little game was scarcely finished when she was shaken by a violent seizure.

'Well? Is this the moment?' she asked the doctor, with the same serenity which remained undiminished.

'I fear so, Madame.'

'In that case, approach, Florville,' she said to me, extending both arms, 'come and receive my last farewell. I should like to die in the bosom of virtue...'

She held me tight and her lustrous eyes closed for ever.

A stranger in that house, and having nothing to keep me there, I quitted the place immediately... and I leave you to picture in what state... and how much the scene I had witnessed had darkened my imagination still further.

There was too great a distance between Madame de Verquin's way of thinking and my own for me to love her sincerely. Besides, was she not the primary cause of the loss of my honour and of all the reverses I had suffered as a consequence? Yet that woman, sister to the only man who had truly taken good care of me, had never used me except in the best possible manner, and even in death she continued to serve me well. My tears were therefore quite genuine, and they grew more bitter as I reflected that, despite possessing admirable qualities, the wretched woman had brought disaster on herself unwittingly and that, having already been cast out of the bosom of the Almighty, she was doubtless even now undergoing the cruel punishment meted out for so depraved a life. The Lord's great goodness settled upon me nevertheless and blotted out these gloomy notions. I fell on my knees and ventured to pray the Lord God of all to pardon her waywardness. Though I myself stood in such great need of divine forgiveness, I dared beseech heaven to show mercy to others and, to make my voice as persuasive as it lay in my power to do, I added another ten louis of my own money to the prize I had won at Madame de Verquin's lottery, and arranged for the sum to be distributed immediately to the poor of her parish.

Meanwhile, her last wishes were carried out to the letter; the arrangements she had made were too well planned for them to go wrong. She was laid to rest in her jasmine grove over which was inscribed one word: VIXIT.*

Thus perished the sister of my dear friend and protector. Being possessed of a large portion of wit and knowledge, and favoured with charm and talent, Madame de Verquin, had she followed a different course of conduct, would probably have earned the respect and affection of everyone she knew. But she drew only their contempt, for her debauches had become more frequent as she grew older. Those who have no principles are never more dangerous than when they reach the age when they lose all sense of shame. Their hearts are gangrened by depravity, they refine and polish up their first offences and convert them into heinous crimes while still believing they are still at the stage of minor misdemeanours. But her brother's incredible blindness never ceased to amaze me. Yet such is the distinctive badge of a virtuous and candid heart: the good never suspect others of perpetrating wicked deeds which they themselves are incapable of committing. That is why they are so easily duped by the first rogue who sinks his claws into them, and why it is so easy and so despicable to trick them. All the insolent villain who attempts it achieves is to demean himself. He does not demonstrate that he has any talent for vice, but has rather provided an extra advertisement for virtue.

In losing Madame de Verquin, I had lost all hope of obtaining any word of my lover and my son. As you can appreciate, given the frightful state in which I found her, I had not dared raise the matter.

Devastated by this calamity and exhausted by a journey undertaken when my mind was in turmoil, I resolved to remain at Nancy for a while to recuperate, at the inn where I had taken a lodging, without seeing anyone at all, since Monsieur de Saint-Prât had seemed to indicate that I should disguise my name while I was in the town. It was from there that I wrote to my kindly benefactor, being determined that I should not stir from the place until I had received his reply:

An unfortunate young person who is nothing to you [I wrote], who has no other claim on you save upon your pity, is forever troubling the even tenor of your life. Instead of speaking only of the grief you must feel for the loss you have recently suffered, she ventures to speak of herself, to ask what your orders are, and to say that she will wait upon them, *etc.*

But it was written that misfortune would follow me wherever I went and that I should be eternally the witness or the victim of its baleful attentions.

I was returning one evening, rather late, after taking the air with my maid. I was attended only by this girl and a hired lackey who I had taken on when I arrived at Nancy. Everyone was already abed. Just as I reached my door, a woman of about fifty years of age, tall, still very handsome, who was known to me only by sight, since I had come to lodge under the same roof as her, suddenly stepped out of her room, which was next to mine and, clutching a dagger, burst into another close by... It was a natural reaction to want to see... I ran after her... my servants followed me. In the twinkling of an eye, before we had time to cry out or intervene... we saw the woman leap upon another woman, plunge her weapon into her heart a score of times, and then return to her own chamber in a daze and without noticing our presence. At first we thought that her wits had turned. We could not understand a crime for which we could see no motive. My maid and my lackey would have cried out, but a more imperious impulse, for which I could find no cause, obliged me to bid them keep silent and to lead them away with me into my chamber where, once inside, we immediately locked the door.

Soon we heard the most terrible uproar. The woman who had been stabbed had somehow managed to throw herself down the stairs, uttering the most ghastly shrieks. Before she expired she had time to name her assailant. And since it was known that we were the last people to return to the inn, we were arrested along with the guilty person. But since the victim's dying words gave no grounds for suspecting us, no action was taken against us save that we were ordered not to leave the inn until the trial was over. The murderess was led away to prison, but admitted nothing and defended herself with spirit. There were no other witnesses except myself and my servants, and we were required to give evidence... I was obliged to speak, and in so doing to take great care to conceal a secret feeling of unease which gnawed at me... I mean the thought that I deserved to die every whit as much as this woman who, through my forced testimony, was to finish on the scaffold; for while the circumstances were different, I was guilty of the same crime. I cannot say what I would have given to avoid having to make my cruel statement. I felt as I dictated it that as many drops of blood were being squeezed from my heart as I pronounced words. But everything had to be said. We repeated what we had seen. However convinced the court was that the crime had been committed by the woman, whose defence was that she had killed a rival—however certain the court was, I say, about who had done the deed, we were subsequently informed on good authority that it would not have been possible to find her guilty since a man had been involved in the incident. He had escaped, and suspicion might well have fallen on him. But our statements, especially that of my hired lackey who turned out to be an employee of the inn... a man known in the establishment where the crime had had taken place... our evidence, I say, which we could not have refused to give without compromising ourselves, sealed the wretched woman's fate.

The last time I faced her, the woman stared at me with an air of extreme amazement and asked me how old I was.

'I am thirty-four,' I replied.

'Thirty-four?... and you are a native of this place?'

'No, Madame.'

'Are you called Florville?'

'Yes,' I said. 'That is my name.'

'I do not know you,' she went on, 'but it is said in this town that you are honest and well thought of. That, unfortunately for me, is all I need to know...'

Then, continuing in a state of some agitation:

'Mademoiselle, in the midst of the horrors of my present predicament, you came to me in a dream. You were in it with my son... for I am a mother and most unhappy, as you can see... Your face was the same... you had the same figure... the same dress... and the scaffold stood there before me!'

'It was a dream,' I cried, 'only a dream, Madame!'

But then my own dream was recalled to my mind, and I was struck by the woman's features. I recognized her for the woman who had appeared with Senneval close by the coffin which bristled with thorns! My eyes filled with tears... The more closely I examined the woman, the more tempted I was to retract my statement... I wanted to ask to be allowed to die in her stead... I wanted to run away, but was rooted to the spot... When the terrible effect she was having on me was noticed, the authorities, who had no doubt of my innocence, simply separated us. I returned to my inn, overcome by many and varied feelings whose origin I could not identify. The following morning the wretched woman was led to her death.

That very same day I received Monsieur de Saint-Prât's reply: he urged me to return to him. Nancy could not but be most disagreeable to me after the harrowing scenes which had had recently been played out for me on its stage, and I left at once to make my way towards the capital, pursued by the new-minted ghost of that woman who seemed to cry constantly in my ear: 'Hapless creature! You send me to my death, yet you do not know who was cut down by your hand!'

Haunted by so many visitations and pursued by so much adversity, I begged Monsieur de Saint-Prât to find me some retreat where I might end my days in the most total solitude and in strict observance of the duties of my faith. He suggested the convent where you found me, sir. I took up residence there that same week and subsequently never left it, save twice a month to see my dear benefactor and to pay a brief call on Madame de Lérince. But heaven, intent on striking at me each day with telling blows, did not permit me to enjoy her company for long, and I had the misfortune to lose her last year. Her affection for me was such that she would not let me be parted from her at that painful time, and it was in my arms that she too breathed her last.

But who would have believed it, sir? Her death was nothing like as peaceful as that of Madame de Verquin who, never having hoped to gain anything, was not afraid to lose everything. Madame de Lérince appeared distraught as she saw the certainty of her hopes vanish. I did not recall detecting any regrets in a woman who by rights should have been besieged by them... yet this other, who had never done anything to be sorry for, was stricken by remorse. As she died, Madame de Verquin regretted only that she had not done enough wickedness; Madame de Lérince died mourning the good she had left undone. The first laid herself in a flowery grove, lamenting only the loss of her pleasures; the second would have preferred to die wearing sackcloth and ashes, rueing the hours which she had not devoted to the practice of virtue.

I was forcibly struck by these disparities, and a degree of laxness entered my thinking. Why, at times like these, I asked myself, why is peace not an entitlement for those who have lived a good life, since it clearly seems to be the reward of those who have led a bad one? But at that moment I was fortified by a heavenly voice which seemed to thunder deep in my heart, and I cried: 'Is it for me to question the will of the Almighty? What I have observed allows me to detect an additional merit: Madame de Lérince's fears enshrine the solicitude of virtue, whereas the cruel indifference of Madame de Verquin was her ultimate crime. Oh, if I am allowed to choose how I spend my last moments, may God grant that I should be afraid like the former rather than be misguided like the latter!*

And that, sir, was the end of my adventures. For the last two years I have been living at the Convent of the Assumption which my benefactor found for me. Yes sir, I have been there for two years, and in all that time I have not known one moment of peace, I have not spent a single night when the faces of the unfortunate

Saint-Ange and the wretched woman I condemned to death at Nancy have not appeared before me. Such is the state in which you have found me. These are the secrets I was obliged to tell you of. Was it not my duty to reveal them before I could respond to the feelings which you mistakenly have for me? You must judge now if it is possible that I could ever be worthy of you... It is for you to decide if a woman whose heart is riven by grief can add a few joys to the brief span of your life. Oh sir, believe me, stop living in a world of illusion! Let me return to the austere retreat which is the only place for me! Force me to leave it and you will be perpetually exposed to the dreadful spectacle of remorse, grief, and misfortune!'

Mademoiselle de Florville had not reached the end of her tale without experiencing a state of a violent agitation. Being by nature vivacious, sensitive, and delicate, it was impossible that the recital of her misfortunes should not have had a powerful effect on her.

Monsieur de Courval, who in the closing moments of her story had found no more plausible reasons than in its opening stages for altering his plans, did everything in his power to calm the woman he loved.

'I repeat, Mademoiselle,' he told her, 'there are a number of ill-fated, singular incidents in the story you have just told me. But I see nothing in it which should worry your conscience or damage your good name... an affair at sixteen, I agree... but there are many circumstances which speak in your favour... your youth, the blandishments of Madame de Verquin... a young man who was perhaps very attractive... whom you never saw again, is not that the case, Mademoiselle?' Monsieur de Courval went on, a whit anxiously... 'And whom in all probability you will never see again...'

'Oh, most surely never!' replied Florville, sensing the reasons for Monsieur de Courval's uneasiness.

'Very well, Mademoiselle, let us settle this matter now,' he went on, 'pray let us come to an understanding. You will please permit me to convince you without further ado that there is nothing in your history which could ever diminish in a gentleman's heart either the utmost admiration due to so many virtues or the homage owed to so many charms.'

Mademoiselle de Florville begged leave to return again to Paris to seek the advice of her benefactor for the very last time, promising most exactly that no opposition would be forthcoming from that quarter. Monsieur de Courval could not refuse to permit her to discharge so proper a duty. She left, and a week later returned, accompanied by Monsieur de Saint-Prât, whom Monsieur de Courval received with extreme courtesy. He declared in the least unambiguous terms how flattered he would be to be joined in marriage to a woman whom his guest had kindly taken under his protection, and begged him never to cease calling that admirable person his relative. Saint-Prât replied civilly to Monsieur de Courval's courtesies and continued to give him the most favourable idea of Mademoiselle de Florville's character.

Finally the day dawned which Courval had longed for, and the ceremony duly took place. When the marriage contract was read out, he was greatly surprised to note that Monsieur de Saint-Prât, without telling anyone, had, to mark the wedding, added four thousand livres to the allowance of that same amount which he already paid to Mademoiselle de Florville, and further made a bequest of a hundred thousand francs to be inherited on his death.

That remarkable woman shed a torrent of tears on learning of her benefactor's new kindnesses, and was deeply gratified to be able to offer the man who insisted on holding her in such high regard a fortune which was at least the equal of his own.

Good grace, undiluted joy, mutual assurances of respect and affection presided over the celebration of their marriage... that fatal marriage whose cheerfully lit torches were about to be snuffed out one by one by the Furies.*

Monsieur de Saint-Prât spent a week at Courval, as did the friends of the bridegroom. But husband and wife did not follow them back to Paris, resolving instead to stay in the country until the beginning of winter, which would allow them to arrange their affairs in such a way as to enable them to live in Paris on a comfortable footing. Monsieur de Saint-Prât had undertaken to find them a pretty house near his own so that they would see each other more often. Monsieur and Madame de Courval had been together almost three months, luxuriating in the prospect of these agreeable arrangements, and there was even confirmation of a pregnancy, news of which had been transmitted at once to the good Monsieur de Saint-Prât, when an unexpected event cruelly blighted the happiness of the happy couple and transformed the roses of marriage into funereal cypress.

Here my pen falters... I should ask my readers to excuse me, beg their leave to proceed no further... yes, and let them break off now if they have no wish to tremble with horror!... Mankind is so vulnerable in this vale of tears!... Fate is cruel and acts in the strangest ways... Why should the hapless Florville, that most virtuous of women, the sweetest and the most sensitive, prove, through an unimaginable concatenation of mischances, to be the most abominable monster ever spawned by nature?

One evening, as she sat with her husband, this tender and affectionate wife was reading an English novel of excessive gloominess, which was the cause of a considerable stir at the time.*

'I declare,' she said, tossing the book to one side, 'that here is a woman who is almost as unfortunate as I.'

'As unfortunate as you?' said Monsieur de Courval pressing his darling wife to his bosom. 'Oh Florville! I believed I had helped you forget your unhappiness... I see I was mistaken... Did you have to break it to me so unexpectedly?'

But it seemed that Madame de Courval had lost control of her faculties. She did not respond to her husband's questions. With an involuntary gesture she pushed him away in horror and fled far from him to a sofa, where she burst into tears. In vain the worthy man threw himself at her feet, in vain did he beseech the wife he worshipped to calm herself or at least tell him what was the cause of an outburst of such terrible despair. Madame de Courval continued to reject his overtures, to turn her head away when he tried to wipe away her tears, until matters reached the point where Courval, casting aside any lingering doubt that some fateful memory of Florville's old passion had flared up afresh, could not prevent himself from gently chiding her. Madame de Courval heard him out in silence, but at the last, rising to her feet:

'No, sir,' she said to her husband, 'no... you are mistaken in interpreting as you do the fit of anguish of which I have just been the victim. It is not memories that alarm me but presentiments which terrify me... I am here with you, sir and happy... yes, very happy... and yet I was not made to be happy. It is not possible that I should remain so for any length of time. The influence of my star is such that the dawn of happiness can never be for me any more than the lightning flash which precedes the thunder... that is what has made me tremble: I fear that we were not meant to live together. Today I am your wife, but perhaps I shall not be tomorrow... A secret voice cried out in the recesses of my heart that all my present happiness is no more than a ghostly shadow and will wither like the flower which opens and dies on the same day. Do not say, therefore, that I am capricious or that my love is turning cold, sir. I am guilty only of having feelings which are too sensitive, of possessing a gift for seeing everything in the most sinister light, which is a cruel after-effect of all my tribulations...'

Monsieur de Courval was on his knees before his wife, making every effort to calm her with reassuring words and gestures, though with no success, when all of a sudden—it was about seven o'clock on an October evening—a footman appeared and announced that a stranger desired urgently to speak to Monsieur de Courval... Florville gave a start... tears coursed unbidden down her cheeks, and she seemed stunned: she attempted to speak, but the words died on her lips.

Monsieur de Courval, more concerned for his wife's state than with the message he had been given, answered roughly that whoever it was could wait, and gave her all his attention. But Madame de Courval, fearing she might succumb to the secret impulses which she felt tugging at her... and wishing to hide what she was feeling in the presence of the stranger who had been announced, rose resolutely to her feet and said:

'It is nothing, sir. Really, nothing at all. Please have this stranger shown in.'

The footman went out and returned a moment later, followed by a man aged thirty-seven or thirty-eight, bearing on his face, which was otherwise pleasant enough, the marks of ingrained sorrow.

'Father!' cried the stranger, prostrating himself before Monsieur de Courval. 'Will you not recognize an unfortunate son who has been parted from you these twenty-two years, and has been most harshly punished for his cruel faults by misfortunes which have never ceased to befall him ever since?'

'What! You are my son?... Good God!... By what turn of events... ingrate... what is it has made you suddenly remember that I was still alive?'

'My heart! My guilty heart which despite everything has never stopped loving you! Listen to me, father... hear me out, for I have misfortunes to reveal to you that are greater than my own. Please be seated so that you might hear me. And you, Madame,' continued young Courval, turning to his father's wife, 'pray forgive me if, on this first occasion in my life when I can pay you my respects, I am forced to draw back the veil covering the most dreadful family tragedy, which can be hidden no longer from my father.'

'Speak, sir, speak out,' stammered Madame de Courval as she cast the wildest of looks at the young man. 'The language of misfortune is not new to me, for I have known it since childhood.'

The traveller stared at Madame de Courval, looked somewhat taken aback, and replied uneasily:

'You, unfortunate, Madame?... Oh merciful heavens, can you ever be as unfortunate as we are?'

They sat down. Madame de Courval's state cannot be easily conveyed... she fixed her eyes on the young gentleman... she lowered them to the ground... she heaved sighs of apprehension. For his part, Monsieur de Courval wept while his son tried to calm him by asking him to attend to what he had to say. Eventually the conversation took on a more orderly complexion.

'I have so much to tell you, sir,' said young Courval, 'that with your permission I shall pass over the details and give you only the principal facts of the case. I must insist that you give me your word, and Madame too, that you will make no interruption until I have set them all out before you.'

'I left your house, sir, when I was aged fifteen. My first impulse was to follow my mother, whom I was blind enough to prefer to you. She had been living apart from you for several years. I rejoined her at Lyons, where her dissolute ways so appalled me that I realized I should be forced to go away if I were to keep whatever feelings for her still remained to me. I journeyed on to Strasburg, where the Normandy regiment was quartered...'

Madame de Courval gave a start, but said nothing.

'I succeeded in attracting the colonel's attention,' young Courval went on. 'I told him who I was and he gave me a sub-lieutenancy. The following year I accompanied the regiment to the garrison at Nancy. There I fell in love with a relative of Madame de Verquin... I seduced the young woman, had a son by her, and then callously deserted his mother.'

At these words Madame de Courval gave a shudder, a muffled groan escaped from her lips, but she held firm.

'That wretched business was the cause of all my subsequent misfortunes. I gave the poor young lady's infant son into the keeping of a woman near Metz who promised me she would take good care of him, and shortly afterwards I rejoined my regiment. A harsh view was taken of my behaviour. Since the young lady had not been able to return to Nancy, I was accused of ruining her reputation. She had been too well liked not to have left an impression on the whole town, and there were those who were prepared to avenge her. I fought a duel, killed my opponent, and fled to Turin with my son, after first returning to Metz to collect him. I served a dozen years in the army of the King of Sardinia.* I will pass over the hardships I endured, for they are legion. It is only when a Frenchman goes abroad that he learns to regret France. Meanwhile my son grew and showed much promise. Having made the acquaintance at Turin of a countrywoman of mine who had travelled there to attend the French princess who had married into the court, and this worthy person having taken an interest in my misfortunes, I suggested that she might go with my son into France to complete his education, promising to arrange my affairs in such a way as to take him off her hands in six years' time. To this she agreed, escorted the hapless boy to Paris, spared no pains to give him a first-rate education, and kept me fully and regularly informed of his progress.

'I rejoined them a year earlier than I had promised. I arrived at the lady's house, anticipating the sweet comfort of embracing my son, of holding in my arms that token of a love which I had betrayed... but which still burned my heart... "Your son is dead," said my respectable friend through her tears. "He was the victim of the same passion which ruined his father's life. We had taken him to the country, where he fell in love with the most charming young woman whose name I have sworn never to reveal. Carried away by the violence of his feelings, he attempted to take by force what had been refused him by virtue... a chance blow, intended only as a warning, pierced his heart and left him for dead." '

At this juncture Madame de Courval fell into a kind of stupor, which for a moment prompted fears that she might have quite breathed her last. Her eyes seemed glazed and the blood no longer coursed in her veins. Monsieur de Courval, who could see all too clearly the secret chain which linked these awful events, interrupted his son and hastened to his wife... She recovered herself and said, with heroic courage:

'Let us allow your son to continue, sir. I may not yet have reached the end of my woes.'

All this time young Courval, who could not understand why the lady was so upset at matters which seemed to concern her only indirectly, but who detected something unfathomable in the expression on the face of his father's wife, stared at her in a state much affected by emotion. Monsieur de Courval took his son by the hand and, diverting his attention away from Florville, ordered him to proceed, concentrating on the essentials and omitting the details, because his tale contained mysterious particulars which were fast turning into matters of great interest to them all.

'Reduced to despair by the death of my son,' the traveller continued, 'and having nothing to keep me in France... except you alone, father, whom I did not dare to approach and from whose anger I fled... I resolved to journey through Germany... Unhappy parent, I now come to the cruellest part of what remains of the tale I have to tell you,' said young Courval, bathing his father's hands with his tears. 'I beg you to arm yourself with courage.

'On arriving at Nancy, I learned that a certain Madame Desbarres (this was the name which my mother had taken, under which to lead her dissolute life after she had given you to believe that she was dead)... I discovered that this Madame Desbarres had lately been sent to prison for stabbing a rival, and that she would in all likelihood be executed the very next day.'

'Oh sir!' exclaimed the hapless Florville, throwing herself into her husband's arms amid tears and the most heart-rending cries... 'Do you not see how the rest of my misfortunes will play out?'

'Indeed I do, Madame,' said Monsieur de Courval, 'I see it all. But I beg you to let my son finish...'

Florville controlled herself, but had almost stopped breathing. She no longer had one feeling which was not compromised, one nerve that did not twitch unbearably.

'Carry on, my boy, proceed,' the wretched father said. 'I shall explain all this to you presently.'

'As you wish, sir,' young Courval went on. 'I enquired as to whether there was not some misunderstanding about the names. But alas, it proved all too true that the murderess was indeed my mother. I asked to see her, permission was granted, and I fell into her arms... "I die guilty," the unfortunate creature said, "yet fate has played a most odious role in the circumstances which have brought about my death. Suspicion was to have fallen on another party, a man, and indeed it would have, for all the evidence was against him. But a woman and her two servants, who had come quite by chance to the inn, observed me commit the crime, though I did not see them, my mind being then distracted by my main business. Their testimony was the sole reason for the sentence of death passed on me. But it matters not. Let us not waste on vain recriminations the few moments I have to speak to you. I have secret matters of great moment to tell you, so listen well, my son. The moment my eyes are closed for good you must find my husband and inform him that, of my many crimes, there is one of which he knew nothing but which I must at last admit to... Courval, you have a sister... she was born the year after you... I loved you dearly and feared that a sister would injure your prospects because, if she were to be married one day, her portion might be subtracted from the fortune that should rightly be yours. To safeguard your inheritance intact, I resolved to be rid of the girl and do everything in my power to ensure that henceforth my husband should harvest no further fruit from our union. My reprobate life led me into other wickednesses, which prevented my putting these new criminal intentions into practice by inciting me to commit others, more terrible still. But for the girl I had no pity, and was determined that she should die. I was about to do the infamous deed, being assisted in it by the wet-nurse whom I rewarded handsomely, when this creature told me she knew of a man, long married, whose daily wish was to have children but who never could. She would take my child off my hands without crime coming into it, and manage the business in such a manner that she would perhaps be happy. I accepted at once. That same night my daughter was deposited on the man's doorstep, and a letter placed in her cradle... When I am dead, make all haste to Paris, beg your father to forgive me, to refrain from cursing my memory, and take the child back under his roof."

'With these words, my mother embraced me and tried to calm the dreadful agitation into which I had been plunged by all I had learned from her lips... Oh, father, she was executed the next day!... A terrible illness then brought me close to death's door, and for two years my life hung by a thread. I had neither the strength nor the courage to write to you, but when my health returned my first thought was to come to you, kneel at your feet, beseech you to forgive your hapless wife, and reveal the name of the man from whom you may ask for news of my sister. His name is... Monsieur de Saint-Prât.'

Monsieur de Courval started, all his senses turned to ice, his faculties deserted him... his condition gave cause for alarm.

As to Florville, who had suffered the torment of a thousand cuts in the last quarter of an hour, she now rose to her feet with the serenity of one who has decided what must be done.

'Well, sir,' she said to Courval, 'now do you believe that there can be in all the world a criminal more vile than the wretched Florville?... Senneval, you see in me your sister, the girl you seduced at Nancy, the woman who murdered your son, the wife of your own father, and the ignoble creature who sent your mother to the gallows... Yes, gentlemen, those are my crimes. Whichever of you I look at, I behold horror personified: either I see my lover in my brother or I see my husband in my father, and if I pause to consider myself, I see only the execrable monster who stabbed her own son and sentenced her mother to death. Can you believe that heaven will ever have enough torments to inflict on me, or do you imagine I can survive for another moment these calamities which rack my soul?... No! Yet there is still one crime I must commit, one which will avenge us all.'

Whereupon the wretched woman, reaching for one of Senneval's pistols, took hold of it impulsively and blew out her brains before anyone had time to guess what she intended to do. She died without saying another word.

Monsieur de Courval fainted away. His son, his mind full of so many horrible pictures, called for assistance as best he could. It was too late for Florville, who was beyond help, for the shadow of death had already spread over her brow and her twisted features were a hideous combination of the cataclysm of violent death and the convulsions of despair... She lay in a pool of her own blood...

Monsieur de Courval was carried to his bed, where he lay for two months in a state near to death. His son, whose condition was no less parlous, was nevertheless sufficiently blessed for his loving care to recall his father to life. But both, after seeing so many strokes of fate cruelly heaped upon their heads, resolved to flee the society of men. A strict, solitary retreat keeps them far from the eyes of their friends for ever. There, clothed in piety and virtue, they quietly live out their sorry, painful lives, which were given to them only so that they and those who will read their deplorable history might be persuaded that it is only in the darkness of the grave that man will find the peace which the wickedness of his fellows, the tumult of his own passions, and, above all, the inevitability of his fate shall eternally deny him in this life.

RODRIGO
or THE ENCHANTED TOWER
An Allegorical Tale

RODRIGO, king of Spain, was the most knowledgeable of all princes in the art of varying his pleasures, and the least scrupulous in his methods of procuring them. Believing the throne to be one of the safest places from which to enjoy them with impunity, he had been prepared to do anything to secure it for himself. Since he had only to remove the head of one child to achieve his goal, he damned the infant without a twinge of conscience. But Anagilde, mother of the hapless Sancho, the boy in question whom Rodrigo, his uncle and guardian, was resolved to kill, had the good fortune of discovering the conspiracy which had been mounted against her son and was clever enough to circumvent it. She fled to Africa, offered to hand over to the Moors the rightful heir to the throne of Spain, told them of the criminal plot which had deprived him of it, implored their protection, but died along with her unfortunate son just as she was about to have her wish granted.

Rodrigo, now King Rodrigo, entirely safe from anything which might threaten his peace of mind, devoted every waking hour to his pleasures. To multiply stimulants that would excite his senses, he hit on a plan for luring the daughters of all his vassals to his court. The pretext he gave as a cover for this wicked scheme was to secure their loyalty by taking and holding these hostages. Did any resist? Did any demand that their children be returned? If any did, such acts of rebellion were quickly declared to be crimes against the state, punishable by death. Under a reign so cruel, there is never a middle path to tread between cowardice and corruption.

Among the young girls who in this manner embellished the King's decadent court, Florinde, aged about sixteen years, stood out from her companions as the rose catches the eye among ordinary flowers. She was the daughter of Count Julian, on whose services Rodrigo had relied in his attempt to block the negotiations of Anagilde in Africa. But the death of Don Sancho and his mother had made the Count's efforts pointless. He could have returned, of course, and might have done so had not Florinde been so beautiful. For Rodrigo no sooner spied that enchanting creature than he sensed that the Count's return would be an obstacle to his desires. He wrote ordering him to remain in Africa and, anxious to have full enjoyment of a treasure whose possession her father's absence seemed to guarantee, and indifferent as to the means by which he might have it, he ordered Florinde to be taken one day into the innermost court of his palace and there, more eager to plunder her favours than to show himself worthy of them, Rodrigo, having conquered, soon had no other thoughts than for new crimes to commit.

He who perpetrates an outrage may well be quick to forget what he has done. But they who have suffered at his hands are justified at least in remembering the wrongs he has done them.

Florinde, reduced to despair and not knowing how she might inform her father of what had happened, had recourse to an ingenious allegory which historians have handed down to us. She wrote to the Count saying that 'the ring which he had so warmly enjoined her to care for had been broken by the King himself; that throwing himself upon her, with a dagger in his hand, his Majesty had broken the gem whose loss she deplored; and that she begged to be avenged'. But she died before she could receive a reply.

However, the Count had understood his daughter's meaning perfectly. He had returned to Spain and implored his vassals to help him. They promised to serve him. Back in Africa once more, he persuaded the Moors to support his plan of revenge, telling them that a king capable of such a horrible act must be easy to vanquish, and giving them proof of Spain's weakness by citing its depopulation, the hatred which his subjects felt for their master, and in a word set out all the persuasive arguments his embittered heart could devise. His listeners did not hesitate to offer their help.

Emperor Muza, who then ruled over that country of Africa, first sent out a small corps of troops in secret to confirm what the Count had stated. These soldiers joined forces with the Count's discontented vassals, received their help, and were very quickly reinforced by other soldiers, the success of whose mission Muza believed was virtually guaranteed. Spain was gradually filled with Africans. Rodrigo was still safe. But what could he have done? He had no soldiers and not one fortress left, for they had all been pulled down to deny his Spanish subjects safe refuges from which they might have withstood the exactions of their king. And to make matters worse, the royal coffers were empty.

But the danger grew greater and the hapless monarch was on the point of being turned off his throne. At this juncture he recalled an ancient monument in the vicinity of Toledo, called the Enchanted Tower. The general opinion was that it contained treasure. The King travelled there as quickly as he could, with the intention of laying his hands on it. But there was no way into the gloomy keep. An iron gate, secured by numberless locks, defended the entrance so stoutly than no man born of woman could gain access to it. Over this fearsome gate these words were written in Greek: 'If you fear to die, do not approach.' Rodrigo was not afraid. For him his kingdom was at stake, and since all other hope of raising money had been completely dashed, he had to break down the gate. Therefore he approached.

As he reached the second step, an awesome giant appeared. It placed the point of its sword against Rodrigo's stomach and cried:

'Halt! If you wish to see this place, you must come alone. None, whoever they may be, shall accompany you.'

'That is of no account,' said Rodrigo, proceeding, and leaving his attendants behind. 'I come in search of help or death!'

'You may perhaps find both,' replied the apparition, and the gate clanged shut behind him.

The King walked on, while the giant who went on before spoke not a word to him. When they had climbed more than eight hundred steps, they finally reached a great hall lit by an infinite number of torches. All the victims who had been sacrificed by Rodrigo were gathered under its roof, and there each was seen to undergo the punishment to which he had been sentenced.

'Do you recognize these unfortunates?' asked the giant. 'This is how despots should be shown their crimes. The new atrocities they inflict make them forget the old, and they only see one at a time... But gather them all together like this and perhaps they might be made to quake. Behold what rivers of blood are here shed by your hand, simply as a means of serving your passions. With one word, I could set all these poor souls free. With one word, I could throw you to them.'

'Do as you please,' said proud Rodrigo. 'I have not come so far to quake with fear.'

'Follow me, then,' continued the giant, 'since your courage is equal to the wickedness of your crimes.'

Rodrigo proceeded from there to a second hall, where his guide showed him all the young women who had been dishonoured for his cowardly pleasure. Some tore their hair, others attempted to turn daggers against themselves. A few who had already died by their own hand lay in pools of their own blood. From the midst of these unfortunates the King saw Florinde rise up, looking exactly as she was on the day he had violated her...

'Rodrigo!' she called to him. 'Your terrible crimes have brought the enemy into your kingdom. My father is working to avenge me, but he can never restore my honour or my life. I have lost both: you are the sole cause of it. You will see me once more, Rodrigo, but you should dread that fatal moment, for it will be your last. To me alone has fallen the honour of avenging all the wretched women you see here.'

The proud Spaniard turned his head away and followed his guide into a third hall.

In the middle of this room stood an enormous statue of Time. It was armed with a club with which it struck the ground once every minute, with such a horrendous noise that the entire hall shook.

'Wretched Prince!' exclaimed the statue. 'Your evil star has led you to this place. You shall at least learn the truth here: know that you will soon be stripped of your crown by foreign powers so that you may be punished for your crimes.'

At that instant the scene changed. The vaulted ceiling vanished and Rodrigo rose through it. Some invisible, airy power bore him aloft with his guide until they stood atop the towers of Toledo.

'Behold your fate!' said the giant.

The King at once looked down over the plain below and saw the Moors contending with his people, who seemed so completely overcome that very few could be observed who were still capable of running away.

'What have you decided now you have seen this sight?' the giant demanded of the King.

'I wish to return to the Tower,' answered proud Rodrigo. 'I intend to carry off all the treasure it contains and then return to take my chance with fortune. This spectacle has not made me fear defeat.'

'To this I agree,' said the spectre. 'Yet pause to reflect. Appalling ordeals await you and you will not have me at your side to give you courage.'

'There is nothing I shall not undertake,' said Rodrigo.

'Very well,' replied the giant. 'But remember that even though you vanquish all enemies... even though you carry off the treasure you seek, you will still not be certain of victory.'

'No matter,' said Rodrigo. 'My victory will be even less certain if I cannot field an army and am attacked without the means of defending myself.'

No sooner had he spoken these words than in the twinkling of an eye he found himself once more inside the tower with his guide, in the same room where stood the statue of Time.

'Here I shall leave you,' said the apparition as it was about to disappear. 'Ask the statue where the treasure you seek is to be found and it will tell you.'

'Where must I go?' asked Rodrigo.

'Back to the place whence you came, to be a trial to all mankind,' replied the statue.

'I do not understand. Speak more clearly.'

'You must go down into hell.'

'Then show me the way and I shall go with all convenient speed.'

The earth shook and opened. Unable to save himself, Rodrigo was cast into it and fell ten thousand fathoms below the surface of the land. He got to his feet, opened his eyes, and found himself standing on the bank of what seemed a burning lake on which horrible creatures sailed in iron boats.

'Do you wish to cross the river?' cried one of these monsters.

'Must I?' asked Rodrigo.

'Yes, if it is the treasure you seek. It is located sixteen thousand leagues from here, beyond the deserts of Taenarus.*'

'And where am I now?' asked the King.

'On the banks of the Agraformikubos, one of the eighteen thousand rivers of hell.*'

'Ferry me across, then!' exclaimed Rodrigo

A sailing craft drew close and Rodrigo jumped aboard the blazing boat. He could not stand on its deck without feeling eruptions of searing pain, but it conveyed him in a trice to the other side. Here was perpetual darkness: that savage place had never known the beneficent rays of the sun. Informed of the way he was to take by the grim ferryman who set him ashore, Rodrigo advanced across burning sands along trails hedged by everlastingly burning bushes, from which at intervals sprang fearsome beasts that have no like on earth. Gradually the land narrowed until all he could see before him was an iron span bridging the two-hundred-foot divide to the next part of the terrain, separated from where he stood by ravines six hundred fathoms deep, at the bottom of which flowed various streams of the river of fire that seemed to have its source there. For a moment Rodrigo looked hard at the bridge he must cross, and realized that he would surely die if he fell. There was nothing he could cling to, no rail to give him support. 'After all the dangers I have already come through,' he thought, 'I would be a poltroon not to dare go any further... So best foot forward!' But he had scarcely advanced a hundred paces when he began to feel dizzy. Instead of shutting his eyes to the perils which surrounded him, he gazed at them in terror... He lost his balance, and the hapless man was pitched into the abyss that lay beneath his feet. For a few minutes he was quite stunned, but then stood up. He could not explain how he was still alive, but had the impression that his fall had been so smooth and his landing so gentle that it could be nothing else but the result of some magic power. How could it be otherwise, since he had lived to tell the tale? He collected his wits, and the first thing he saw in the fearsome valley into which he had been transported was a column of black marble on which he read these words: 'Be brave, Rodrigo! Your fall was necessary. The bridge over which you just crossed is the symbol of life. Is not life, like that bridge, beset by dangers on all sides? The good man reaches the other side without mishap; but monsters such as you fall. Yet since your courage urges you forward, go on your way—you are only fourteen thousand leagues from the treasure. Travel seven thousand of them to the north of the Pleiades and the rest with Saturn at your face.'

Rodrigo walked forward to the edge of the river of fire which snaked and twisted its course a thousand ways through the valley. Eventually one of its tortuous loops forced him to halt, and there seemed no means by which he might cross. Then a fierce lion appeared. Rodrigo looked it in the eye.

'Let me cross this river on your back,' he said to the animal.

The monstrous creature immediately prostrated itself at the

King's feet. Rodrigo climbed on to its back, the lion leaped into the river, and ferried the King to the other bank.

'Thus do I return good for evil,' said the lion as it was about to lope away.

'How so?' asked Rodrigo.

'Behold in me the symbol of your most mortal enemy,' replied the lion. 'You persecuted me in the world, and I do you service in hell... Rodrigo, if you succeed in remaining master of your kingdom, remember that a sovereign is worthy of the name only when he makes all his people happy. It is to improve men's lot, not to use them as the instruments of his vices, that Heaven raises him above all others. Learn the lesson of benevolence from one of the species commonly thought to be the most ferocious on earth. Know that I am less fierce than you, because hunger, that most imperious of needs, is the only reason for my cruelty, whereas yours was ever inspired by the most execrable passions.'

'Prince of creatures,' said Rodrigo, 'your words are pleasing to my mind but find no response in my heart. I was born to be the plaything of the passions you tax me with. They are stronger than I am... they carry me along. I cannot fight my nature.'

'Then you shall die.'

'Such is the fate of all men. Why do you think the prospect should frighten me?'

'But do you know what awaits you in the next life?'

'What do I care for that? I have it within me to defy any power that opposes me.'

'Proceed, then. But remember: your end is nigh.'

Rodrigo walked on. Soon he lost sight of the banks of the river and came to a narrow path which led between sharp-toothed rocks whose tops touched the clouds. Unceasingly, huge slabs of stone hurtled down vertically on to the path, either only narrowly failing to crush the King or barring his way. Rodrigo overcame these perils and finally debouched on to an immense plain where there was nothing to guide his steps. Worn out by exhaustion, his throat dry with thirst and hunger, he threw himself down on a heap of sand. Swallowing his pride, he called upon the giant who had taken him down through the tower. Immediately six human skulls materialized before his eyes and a stream of blood flowed at his feet.

'Tyrant!' thundered a voice he did not know, nor could he see the creature from which it emanated. 'This is what you devoured to satisfy your appetites when you lived in the world! Use more of the same to feed your needs now that you are in hell!'

And Rodrigo, proud Rodrigo, feeling disgust but not pity, hauled himself to his feet and continued on his way. The stream of blood dogged his steps, widened as the King advanced, and seemed to be his guide through this savage wilderness. It was not long before Rodrigo saw shadowy figures cresting the surface of the stream... He recognized them. They were the shades of the unfortunate women he had seen as he entered the tower.

'This river is your handiwork!' one of them cried out to him. 'Rodrigo, you see us floating on a tide of our own blood, the wretched blood that was shed by your hand! Why do you not wish to drink of it now? It satisfied your thirst well enough when you were in the world. Are you more squeamish here than in the gilded halls of your palace? You must not complain, Rodrigo. The spectacle of the crimes of the tyrant is the punishment which the Eternal Lord decrees shall be meted out to him.'

Enormous serpents leaped up out of the depths of the river and increased the horror represented by those hideous shades which danced upon its surface.

For two whole days Rodrigo followed the banks of the blood-red river, until at last, peering though the twilit gloom, he made out the end of the plain. It was bounded by an immense volcano and there seemed no way of circumventing it. As Rodrigo advanced he was surrounded by rivers of molten lava. He saw huge quantities of it spewed forth by the crater, which sent it soaring beyond the clouds. Now his only guide was the flames which leaped up all around him. He was covered with ash and could barely walk.

Confronted by this new difficulty, Rodrigo summoned up the apparition.

'Cross the mountain!' cried the same voice which had spoken before. 'On the other side of it you will find creatures with whom you may speak.'

It was no mean undertaking. The burning mountain, which ceaselessly belched rocks and flames, seemed to be a thousand fathoms high. Every track or trail teetered on the edge of a precipice or else was filled with lava. Rodrigo gave himself new heart, his eye measured the distance to his goal, and he was carried to it by the sheer power of his will.

Everything our poets have said about Etna is as nothing compared with the horrors which Rodrigo now beheld. The mouth of the abyss was three leagues in circumference. He observed huge masses of debris ready to rain down on his head and obliterate him. He made haste to cross this fiery furnace, and on reaching the other side found a gentle slope down which he directed his steps. There herds of animals unknown to him and monstrous in size pressed round him on all sides.

'What do you want of me?' the Spaniard asked. 'Are you here to guide me or to prevent me from going any further?'

'We are the symbols of your appetites,' an enormous leopard cried out to him. 'They laid siege to you as we do, and like us they prevented you from seeing where your life on earth would lead you. Since you could never master them, how will you overcome us? It was one of these passions which brought you to these infernal regions where mortal man never before set foot. Follow where it so impetuously leads you, and make speed where fortune beckons. It awaits your coming to reward you. But you will find other enemies more dangerous than we, whose victim you may become. So forward, Rodrigo, advance, there are flowers at your feet! Follow this plain for six hundred leagues more and you shall see what lies at the end of it....'

'Unhappy mortal that I am!' cried Rodrigo, 'that is the language in which my cruel passions spoke to me in the world! They cajoled and terrified me by turns, and I listened to their weasel clamour without understanding what they said.'

Rodrigo walked on. Gradually the land fell away and led him imperceptibly to a subterranean grotto. At its portal he spied an inscription which bade him enter. But the further he went, the narrower the passage became, until he found that it had dwindled to no more than one foot wide. Its sides bristled with daggers and more were suspended above his head. He felt their points prick him and was aware of being cut, of being covered in his own blood. His courage was about to desert him when a consoling voice urged him to persist:

'You approach the moment when you shall find the treasure,' cried the voice, 'and the success of the great venture you shall attempt with it will be a matter for you alone to accomplish. If in the midst of the flatterers who led you astray your conscience had pressed you, if it had pricked you as these dagger-points now lacerate your flesh, had your finances been in order and your coffers full, you would not be exposed to the trials you now have to suffer to make good the chaos you created... So step out, Rodrigo. Let it not be said that your resolve deserted you and your courage let you down. They are the only virtues you have left. Put them to good use. You are not far from the end.'

At last Rodrigo spied a glimmer of light. Imperceptibly the passage widened, the daggers disappeared, and he found himself at the entrance to the cave. There he found a fast-flowing river on which he had no choice but to embark, for there was no other way to take. A small boat was moored and ready and he embarked at once. A momentary calm brought temporary relief to his sufferings. The river down which he travelled was overhung by the most delightful fruit-trees. Orange, musk-pear, fig, peach, coconut, and pineapple intermingled and hung down at random, presenting him with as many of their cooling fruits as he could wish for. The King seized his opportunity and meanwhile was regaled by a delightful chorus of innumerable songbirds, which hopped on the branches of these heavily laden trees. But the few pleasures allowed him were doomed to be interspersed with cruel pains, and nothing would happen to him now that was not a reflection of his life. Words cannot describe the speed of the craft which bore him between the river's heavenly sweet banks. The further it went, the faster it travelled. Soon cataracts, prodigious in height, came into Rodrigo's view, and in them he discovered the cause of his accelerating progress. He saw that he was the puny plaything of the torrent which bore him onwards and was about to carry him over the most terrifying waterfall. He had barely a moment to take this in when his boat, dropping more than five hundred fathoms, was swallowed up in a deserted valley where the river which had transported him frothed and roared. There he heard the same voice which had spoken to him from time to time:

'Oh Rodrigo!' it cried, 'you have just seen a reflection of your former pleasures. They began as pleasant fruits which momentarily slaked your thirst. But where did those pleasures lead you? See, proud monarch, like this boat, you fell into a pit of suffering from which you will emerge only to sink back into it shortly. Now you must follow the narrow, gloomy trail which leads between these two mountains whose tops are hidden in the clouds. At the end of the pass, when you have travelled two thousand leagues, you shall find what you seek.'

'Merciful heaven!' cried Rodrigo, 'am I doomed to devote my whole life to this agonizing quest?'

It felt to him as though he had been journeying through the bowels of the earth for upwards of two years, although it was not yet one week since he had first entered the tower. Meanwhile the sky, which had been constantly in view since he emerged from the cavern, was gradually overcast by the blackest clouds, which were rent by the most terrifying shafts of lightning. The thunder crashed and its detonations re-echoed around the mountain peaks which hung over the track the King was negotiating. It was as though all the elements were preparing to join forces. Unceasingly the lightning struck the rocks round about, dislodging large boulders which rolled down and came to rest at the feet of our luckless traveller, constantly putting new obstacles in his path. An awesome storm of hailstones accompanied these dangers and so beat down on him that he was forced to stop. An innumerable host of spectres, each more macabre than the next, descended from the clouds and danced around him: each of these shades presented Rodrigo with an image of one of his victims.

'You will see us in many different shapes,' cried one of them, 'for we shall not cease to come to you and claw at your heart until it becomes the prey of the Furies* who lie waiting to avenge the crimes you committed against us.'

In the meantime the storm doubled in intensity, bolts of fire leaped continuously from the sky, while across the horizon lightning flashes slanted, clashing and criss-crossing at all angles. The very earth produced great gouts of flame which rose two thousand fathoms into the air and fell back as burning rains. Never did Nature in angry mood serve up more magnificent horrors.

Taking shelter under an overhanging rock, Rodrigo cursed Heaven, offering up neither prayer nor repentance. Then he stood up and looked around him. He shuddered when he saw chaos everywhere and found in it only new fuel to stoke his blasphemy.

'Irresponsible, cruel being!' he roared into the clouds. 'How can you judge us when the example of turmoil and catastrophe is given by your own hand? But where am I?' he went on, seeing that the path had petered out. 'And what is to become of me in the midst of this devastation?'

'See the eagle perched on the rock under which you sheltered,' cried the voice he was by now accustomed to hear. 'Go to it. Sit on its back. It will bear you on fleetest wings to the place where your steps have for so long been leading you.'

The monarch obeyed. Within three minutes he was high in the air. The proud bird which bore him now spoke.

'Rodrigo, consider whether your pride was unjust... Behold the whole earth spread out at your feet. Observe the small corner of the globe of which you were master. Does it make you feel proud of your rank and power? Reflect, for that is how the petty potentates who fight each other for the world must look in the eyes of the Everlasting Lord, and remember that it is His prerogative, and His alone, to require men to pay Him homage.'

Still rising through the air, Rodrigo was eventually able to make out some of the planets which fill space. He saw that the Moon, Venus, Mercury, Mars, Saturn, and Jupiter, close to which he passed, were worlds like ours.

'Peerless bird,' he cried, 'are these worlds inhabited in the same way as ours?'

'They are peopled by better beings,' the eagle replied, 'who are moderate in their passions, which they do not seek to satisfy by tearing each other to pieces. Only happy peoples dwell there and tyrants are unknown.'

'And who governs these peoples?'

'They are governed by their own virtues. People who have no vices need neither laws nor kings.'

'Are the people of these worlds more dear to the Eternal One?'

'All things are equal in the sight of God. This multiplicity of worlds spread throughout space, which a single act of his goodness created and which a second could destroy, adds neither to His glory nor His happiness. But if the conduct of those who inhabit them is a matter of indifference to Him, is it any less necessary for them to act justly? And does not the just man always find his reward in his own heart?'*

Gradually our two travellers drew near to the Sun and, without the magical protection surrounding the King, it would not have been possible for him to withstand the power of the rays in which he was bathed.

'How much bigger that luminous globe seems than the others!' said Rodrigo. 'Monarch of the skies, will you not tell me something about a star to which you can fly at will?'

'This sublime, blazing furnace of light', intoned the eagle, 'is thirty million leagues from our planet and we are now just one million miles from its orbit. You see how high we have risen in such a short time. It is a million times larger than the Earth and its rays reach it in eight minutes.'[1]

'Is this star, whose proximity frightens me, always the same size?' asked the King. 'Is it possible that it never varies?'

'It is never the same,' continued the eagle, 'for comets fly into its sphere and restore its strength.'

'Explain to me the celestial workings of everything I see,' Rodrigo went on. 'My priests are superstitious and devious and they taught me nothing but fables and never told me one single truth.'

'And what truth could you hear from rogues who live only because they lie? Listen to me now,' the eagle continued as it flew on. 'The common centre towards which all the planets gravitate is almost exactly at the middle of the Sun. This star gravitates towards the planets. But the gravitational pull which the Sun exerts on them is stronger than the force which they exert on it by as many times as it exceeds them by volume of matter. This august star changes its position constantly, to the extent that it is more or less attracted by the planets, and though it draws only marginally closer to the planets, the Sun is nevertheless able to correct the misalignment produced by the way the planets act upon each other.'

'And so', said Rodrigo, 'it is this constant deflection of the Sun's course which maintains the order of nature. Which means that disorder is necessary to the maintenance of all heavenly bodies. If evil has its uses in the world, why would you wish to eliminate it? And who can affirm that the general order of things is not dependent on the disorder of our daily conduct?'

[1] It would take a cannonball twenty-five years to cover the same distance. But all this is explained by the theory of gravity of Newton who, however, as is well known, has many hostile critics today. The truth is that although we know nothing we must at least appear to know more than our predecessors.

'Puny monarch of the smallest fragment of all these planets,' exclaimed the eagle, 'it is not for you to scrutinize the ways of the Everlasting God, and still less to justify your crimes by invoking the incomprehensible laws of nature. What appears as disorder to you may be only the means by which He creates order. Do not deduce from this probability any kind of moral consequence. Nothing proves that what shocks you in your analysis of the workings of nature is really disorder, and your experience must convince you that the crimes of men produce only evil.'*

'And are the stars also inhabited? By how much have their spheres increased in size in the time we have been drawing nearer to them?

'Do not doubt that they too are worlds. And although these luminous globes are four hundred thousand times further away from our Earth than our Sun is from us, there are yet more suns above them which we cannot see but which are also inhabited like the stars and all the planets which you now observe. But we are nearly at the end of our journey and I shall fly no higher,' said the eagle as it began its descent to earth. 'May what you have seen, Rodrigo, give you some understanding of the greatness of the Everlasting God. May you see what your crimes have deprived you of, for they debar you from ever drawing close to Him...'

As it spoke these words, the eagle landed on the top of one of the highest mountains in Asia.

'We are a thousand leagues from the place where I found you,' said the divine friend of Jupiter.* 'You must climb down this mountain alone. At its foot you will find what you seek.'

Whereupon it disappeared.

In a few hours Rodrigo completed the descent of the sheer rock face on which the eagle had set him. At the base of the mountain he found a cave sealed by a grating guarded by six giants, each one more than fifteen feet tall.

'What was your purpose in coming here?' asked one of them.

'To carry off the gold which is assuredly in this cave,' said Rodrigo.

'To do that,' said the giant, 'you will first have to kill us all.'

'I am not frightened by my small chance of victory,' replied the King. 'Have weapons brought, that I may borrow them.'

At once equerries equipped Rodrigo with arms. The proud Spaniard made a spirited attack on the first giant who stepped forward, and a few minutes sufficed to dispatch him. A second advanced; he cut him down in the same way. And in less than two hours Rodrigo had overcome all his foes.

'Tyrant!' cried the voice which on occasion came to him. 'Enjoy your last glorious exploits. The success which awaits you in Spain will not be as brilliant as this triumph. The decrees of fate have been fulfilled and the treasure of the cave is yours—but it will serve only to destroy you.'

'What! Have I conquered only that I might be vanquished?'

'Seek no more to probe the mind of the Everlasting God. His decrees are immutable, they are incomprehensible. Know only this: that when a man prospers unexpectedly, it is merely a present sign of future disaster.'

The cave opened. Inside, Rodrigo saw millions... Then a light sleep overcame his senses, and when he awoke he found himself at the door of the enchanted tower, surrounded by all his court and fifteen wagons loaded with gold. The King embraced his friends. He told them it was impossible for any man to imagine what he had seen. He asked them how long he had been away from them.

'Thirteen days,' he was told.

'Merciful heavens!' exclaimed the King. 'I feel as though I have been travelling for five years.'

And so saying, he leaped on to an Andalusian steed and galloped off to return to Toledo. But hardly had he gone a hundred paces from the tower when he heard a clap of thunder. He turned and saw the ancient monument borne up into the air like an arrow. This did not deter the King from riding any the less hard towards his palace. By now all the insurgent provinces had already opened their gates to the Moors. Rodrigo raised a formidable army, marched at its head against his enemies, faced them near Cordova, attacked them, and thus began a battle which lasted one week... It was without doubt the bloodiest encounter ever seen in the two kingdoms of Spain.* A score of times fickle victory promised to bestow her favours on Rodrigo, and twenty times she cruelly took them back again. At the end of the last day, just as Rodrigo, having assembled his entire force, seemed about to place the laurel crown upon his head, a hero appeared who challenged him to single combat.

'Who are you,' the king asked him imperiously, 'that I should grant you such a favour?'

'I am captain of all the Moors,' returned the warrior. 'I am grown weary of all the blood which we have shed. Let us spare the rest, Rodrigo. Must the lives of the subjects of empires be sacrificed to the fleeting interests of their masters? Let kings fight each other when argument divides them, and their quarrels will not last so long! Name the place, proud Spaniard, and measure your lance against mine. Let the spoils of victory go to whichever of us prevails... Will you agree to this?'

'I am your man,' answered Rodrigo. 'I much prefer the prospect of fighting a single opponent such as you than to go on fighting to overcome these countless waves of men.'

'So I do not seem to you to be a redoubtable adversary?'

'I never saw a feebler.'

'It is true that you already vanquished me once, Rodrigo. But you are no longer in the heyday of your victories, you are not ensconced now in your palace in the midst of your ignoble pleasures, you no longer shed the blood of your subjects to slake your appetites, you no longer rob them of their daughters' honour...'

At these words the two warriors took to the field, watched by both armies... They bore down on each other, they clashed heatedly, exchanged furious blows.

At the last Rodrigo was brought low. His valiant opponent made him bite the dust, and then, as he threw himself on his fallen foe, he cried:

'Know your conqueror before you die, Rodrigo,' the warrior said as he raised his helmet.

'Merciful heavens!' cried the Spaniard.

'So you tremble, coward? Did I not say that you would see Florinde again at the moment you drew your last breath? Heaven, outraged by your crimes, allowed me to leave the country of the dead to punish you and end your life. See how she whose honour you once ravished now tarnishes your glory and withers your laurels! Die, too unhappy King! May your example teach the monarchs of this world that only virtue can validate their power, and that he who abuses his authority, as you have done, will find sooner or later punishment for his wickedness in God's divine justice.'

The Spaniards fled and the Moors occupied the land. And so began the period which made them masters of Spain, until a new reversal of fortune, prompted by a similar crime, expelled them from the country forever.*

ERNESTINE

A Swedish Tale

AFTER Italy, England, and Russia, few European countries seemed as interesting to me as Sweden. But if my imagination was ignited by the wish to see the celebrated regions which once gave birth to all the Alarics, Attilas, and Theodorics*—I mean those heroes who led vast hordes of troops and, confronting the ambition of the imperial eagle which sought to cover the world with its wings, made the Romans tremble even unto the gates of their capital—if, on the other hand, my soul yearned to take flight in the homeland of Gustavus Wasa, Christine, and Charles XII*—whose fame is of a quite different order, since the first[1] achieved renown for his enlightened philosophy, so rare and precious in a monarch, and for the commendable good sense which casts aside religious systems when they seek to thwart both the authority of the government, to which they should be subordinate, and the good of the people, which is the sole purpose of lawmaking; the second for her greatness of soul which led her to prefer solitude and her library to the vain pomp of royalty; and the third for his heroic prowess which earned him the everlasting appellation of Alexander—if, I was saying, I was stirred by all these different motives, did I not also long more fervently still to see and admire a people, so wise, sober, and magnanimous which may be called the model of the north?

It was with this purpose in mind that I left Paris on 20 July 1774 and, after travelling through Holland, Westphalia, and Denmark, arrived in Sweden in about the middle of the year following.

After I had spent three months in Stockholm my curiosity was first whetted by the celebrated mines of which I had read so many descriptions. There I imagined I might perhaps stumble across adventures similar to those reported by the Abbé Prévost in the first

[1] Observing that the Catholic clergy, despotic and seditious by nature, were encroaching on the power of the throne and ruining the people by the onerous vexations which they invariably impose when not obstructed in their exactions, Gustavus Wasa introduced Lutheranism into Sweden after ordering the vast wealth stolen by the priesthood to be returned to the people.

volume of his anecdotes.* And so I did... but with very different results!

I therefore travelled to Uppsala, on the River Fyris which divides the town in two. For long Sweden's capital, Uppsala is still today its largest city after Stockholm. I stayed there for three weeks and then moved on to Falun, ancient birthplace of the Scythians:* the inhabitants of this capital of Dalecarlia still retain its customs and costume. Leaving Falun, I journeyed on to the mine at Taperg, one of the largest in Sweden.*

Mines, for so long the state's major source of revenue, soon became dependent on the English, because of the debts contracted by their owners with a nation which is always quick to extend a helping hand to those it believes it can some day gobble up, once it has wrecked their trade or undermined their power through loans made at extortionate rates.

Once I reached Taperg my imagination began to work, even before I had descended into those subterranean regions where high finance and the greed of a few men swallow up the lives of so many others.

Since I was not long returned from Italy, I imagined at first that these underground passages would resemble the catacombs of Rome or Naples. I was wrong. Though they were far deeper, I found them no less desolate but much less fearsome.

At Uppsala, to guide me in my peregrinations, I had been supplied with a man of considerable erudition who was a student of literature and very well read in it. Fortunately for me, Falkenheim (such was his name) spoke perfect German and English, the only northern languages by which I could communicate with him. With the aid of the former of these two tongues, which we both preferred to use, we were able to converse on all manner of topics, and thus I had no difficulty in hearing from his lips the anecdote which I am about to relate.

By means of a basket and a rope rigged in such a way that our descent was entirely without risk, we were lowered to the bottom of the shaft and very quickly found ourselves 120 fathoms under the surface of the earth. Once there, I was extremely surprised to see streets, houses, chapels, taverns, bustle, activity, policemen, judges—every advantage, in short, that the most civilized town in Europe could supply.*

When we had examined these strange dwellings, we stepped

into a tavern where Falkenheim ordered the host to bring us refreshment, viz., a very drinkable beer, dried fish, and a kind of Swedish bread made with the bark of pine and birch mixed with straw and a few wild roots, and the whole kneaded with oatmeal: is anything more required to satisfy our basic needs? The enquiring spirit who travels the world in search of knowledge must habituate himself to all customs and religions, in all times and in all climates, sample every kind of bed and food, and leave the self-indulgent, indolent city-dweller to his prejudices and his luxury... that shocking luxury which does not stop at meeting real needs but must create artificial appetites every day to the detriment of our pocket and our health.

We had almost finished our frugal meal when one of the miners, dressed in a blue coat and blue breeches, with a wretched small blond wig on his head, came up and greeted Falkenheim in Swedish. Out of deference to me my guide answered in German, and immediately the prisoner (for such he was) began expressing himself in that language. Realizing that this manner of proceeding was intended for my benefit alone, and being convinced that he knew from which country I hailed, he offered me a compliment in French, which he spoke very correctly, and then enquired of Falkenheim if there was any news from Stockholm. He mentioned the names of several persons from the court and talked of the King, maintaining at all times a degree of ease and freedom which prompted me to pay him closer attention. He asked Falkenheim if he thought that some day there might be some reduction in his sentence, to which my guide replied by shaking his head sadly and giving him his hand in sympathy. At once the prisoner moved away, with a desolate look in his eye, having refused to share any part of our meal despite all our urging. A moment later he came back and asked Falkenheim if he would be good enough to deliver a letter which he would now go and write without further delay. My companion gave his assent and the prisoner left.

As soon as he was gone, I turned to Falkenheim.

'Who is that man?' I said.

'One of the highest-ranking noblemen in Sweden,' he replied.

'You surprise me.'

'He is very fortunate to be here. The clemency shown by our sovereign might be compared with the generosity of Augustus to

Cinna.* That man is Count d'Oxtiern,* one of the senators most hostile to the King during the revolution of 1772.[1] After peace was restored he committed crimes for which there was no precedent. When the courts passed sentence on him, the King, recalling the hatred he had formerly shown, had him brought before him and said:

'Count, my judges have ordered your death... as you ordered mine a few years ago, which is why I have decided to spare your life. I want to make you see that the heart of the man you considered unworthy to sit on the throne is not without qualities.'

Oxtiern fell at Gustavus's feet and wept copious tears.

'I only wish I could save you altogether,' said the King, raising him to his feet. 'But the enormity of what you have done makes that impossible. I am sending you to the mines. You will not be happy, but at least you will be alive. Now, go.'

'Oxtiern was brought to this place: you have just seen him. Let us go now, it is late,' Falkenheim went on. 'We shall collect his letter on the way.'

'Wait, sir!' said I to my guide. 'You have more than whetted my curiosity, and if we have to spend a whole week here in the bowels of the earth, I shall not leave until you have told me why this wretched man was cast into this place for ever. A criminal he may be, but he has an interesting face. The man is surely not yet forty? I should like to see him freed. He might become an honest man once more.'

'Honest, him? Never... never.'

'Please, sir, indulge me.'

'Very well,' said Falkenheim. 'In any case, the delay will give him enough time to finish his correspondence. Let us send word that there is no hurry and move into that back room. It will be quieter there than sitting here next to the street. Still, I shall be sorry to tell you these things, for they will somewhat alter the feelings of pity which the villain has roused in you. I would much prefer him to retain your sympathy and you to remain in ignorance.'

'Sir,' said I to Falkenheim, 'the mistakes which men make teach me to know Man. The study of Man is the sole object of my travels. The further he strays from the limits imposed on him by the law or nature, the more valuable he becomes to study and the more deserving

[1] It is worth remembering that in this revolution the King made common cause with the popular party, while the senators opposed the people and the King.*

he is of my curiosity and my compassion. Virtue has no need to be enshrined in a creed, for it confers happiness of itself, and so it should: a thousand arms will open and embrace the virtuous man who is plagued by adversity. But no one wants anything to do with a criminal... we feel as uncomfortable to see his tears as we are to shed ours for him, word spreads, we take fright, he is banished from every heart, and through pride we cast out a man whom our humanity should incite us to help. So where, sir, could there be a mortal more interesting than a man who was raised to a great height but was suddenly cast down into a pit of woes, a man born to favour and fortune who now knows only disgrace, is surrounded by nothing but disaster and poverty, and in his heart feels only the sharp thorns of remorse or the serpents of despair? Only a man like that, my dear fellow, can deserve my pity. I will not repeat what foolish people say, "it is his own fault," or what the cold-hearted claim when they try to justify their lack of charity, "he is too guilty by half". Look, I am not interested in what laws he broke, the rules he disregarded, or what he actually did. He is a man and was therefore weak. He is a criminal and therefore wretched, and I feel sorry for him. So speak, Falkenheim, speak, I am impatient to hear what you have to say.'

And so my worthy friend began to speak in this wise:

During the early years of this century a gentleman, Catholic by faith and German by birth, was obliged, as a result of a piece of business which in no way dishonoured him, to leave his country. Knowing that, although we have abjured the errors of popery, they are nevertheless still tolerated in our provinces, he came to Stockholm. Young and upstanding, with a taste for the military life and an appetite for glory, he attracted the attention of Charles XII and had the honour of accompanying him on several of his campaigns. He was present at the unfortunate reverse at Poltava, followed the King as he retreated to Bender, shared his time with the Turk, and returned to Sweden with him. In 1718 the state was deprived of its royal hero when he was killed under the walls of Frederikshald, in Norway.* By then Sanders (such is the name of the gentleman I speak of) had been promoted colonel, and it was with this rank that he retired to Nordkoping, a commercial town which stands fifteen leagues from Stockholm on the canal which connects Lake Vättern to the Baltic in the province of Ostrogothy.* Sanders married and had a son, who was well received by both Frederick I and Adolphus-Frederick.* Advancement came to him as a result of his merit, he rose to his father's rank, and, though still young, he too retired to Nordkoping, the town of his birth, where he married, as his father had done, taking for his wife the daughter of a merchant of modest means, who died a dozen years later after giving birth to Ernestine, who is the subject of this tale. Three years ago, when Sanders was about forty-two years of age, his daughter was sixteen and rightly considered to be one of the most beautiful women Sweden had ever seen. She was tall, pretty as a picture, with a proud, aristocratic bearing, the most lustrous and vivacious black eyes, and very long hair of the same colour, a very rare phenomenon in our latitudes, despite which she boasted the finest and whitest skin. People said they saw a resemblance to the beautiful Countess de Sparre,* the well-read friend of our learned Christine, and it was quite true.

Sanders's young daughter had not reached her present age without giving her heart and making her choice. But having often heard her mother say how cruel a thing it was for a young wife who loved her husband to be constantly separated from him by the duties of a profession which required him to move from town to town, Ernestine, with her father's approval, had made up her mind in favour of young Herman,[1] who was of the same religion as she, and who, having decided to make his way in commerce, was learning the business in the bank owned by the late Monsieur Scholtz, Nordkoping's foremost merchant and one of Sweden's richest.

Herman, born into a family of the same middling station, had lost both his parents when very young. Shortly before his death his father had recommended him to his former associate, Scholtz. He lived in Scholtz's house and, having earned his confidence by his honesty and industry, he had been made, when its head died without issue, director of the firm's finances and accounting, though he was not yet twenty-two years of age. Young Herman then became responsible to his master's widow, a haughty, imperious woman who, despite the recommendations in Herman's favour made by her late husband, seemed to have made up her mind to rid herself of the

[1] We feel it necessary to point out that each letter is heard in these northern names, so that they are not to be pronounced negligently, in the French fashion, as Hermang, Sandaire, Scholt, but as though they were written Herma*nn*, Sander-*ss*, Scholt-*ss*, and so on.

young man if he failed to measure up to the plans she had for him. Herman, a perfect husband for Ernestine, being as handsome a man as she was a beautiful woman, and as much in love with her as she with him, also proved, quite understandably, attractive to the widow Scholtz, who was still a very comely woman despite her forty years. But since his affections were engaged elsewhere there was no question that he would respond to his employer's feelings for him, and, though he was left in no doubt about what these were, he decided that the prudent course would be to behave as if he were unaware of them.

However, this development alarmed Ernestine Sanders. She knew Madame Scholtz to be a bold, enterprising woman, with a jealous, passionate nature, and the thought of having her as a rival made her extremely uneasy. Moreover, she knew herself to be a much less attractive prospect as a wife for Herman than Madame Scholtz. On her father's side her expectations were nil, though it was true they were rather better from her mother, yet they were as nothing compared with the considerable fortune which Madame Scholtz could bring to the young man who managed her accounts.

Sanders fully endorsed his daughter's choice. Having no other child, he worshipped her and, knowing that Herman had some money, intelligence, and a steady character, and was furthermore loved by Ernestine, he had no thought of placing any obstacle in the way of so suitable a match. But Fortune does not always favour what is right. It seems that her pleasure is to thwart the best-intentioned schemes of men, so that from her inconsistency they might learn lessons which will teach them never to take anything for granted in a world where instability and chaos are the most dependable laws.

'Herman,' Widow Scholtz said one day to Ernestine's young man, 'you are now sufficiently trained in our business to make a decision. The funds your parents left you have more than sufficiently increased in value, thanks to my husband's stewardship and mine, for you to live very comfortably. Buy a business, my dear. I intend to retire soon. We shall settle our account with each other at the first opportunity.'

'As you wish, Madame,' said Herman. 'You know that I am trustworthy and disinterested. I am as easy in my mind about the moneys which you are holding for me as you can be regarding those which I manage for you.'

'But Herman, have no plans for setting up on your own?'

'I am still young, Madame.'

'That makes you all the more attractive a proposition for some older woman. I am sure there must be one who you would make very happy.'

'I would need to have a much larger fortune behind me before I considered such a step.'

'A woman could help you to make it.'

'When I marry, I want my fortune to have been made, so that I would have nothing else to do but give my full attention to my wife and children.'

'Does that mean that there is no woman you prefer to another?'

'There is one alive whom I love as a mother, and all my efforts will be dedicated to her service for as long as she wishes to accept them.'

'I am not talking about sentiments of that sort, my dear. I am grateful for them, of course, but they are not the feelings that are needed in a marriage. Herman, I am asking if you do not have your eye on some person with whom you would like to share your life?'

'No, Madame.'

'Why are you forever going to see Sanders? What is it that you always have to do in his house? He is a military man, you are in trade. Stick to people of your own sort, my dear, and have nothing to do with those who aren't.'

'Madame, you know that I am a Catholic. So is the Colonel. We meet to pray... and go together to the churches where we are allowed to worship.'

'I have never had anything against your religion, though I am not a Catholic myself. I am absolutely convinced of the uselessness of all that nonsense and, as you know, Herman, I have never interfered in any way with your beliefs.'

'Well, Madame, there it is: religion. That is why I sometimes go to see the Colonel.'

'Herman, there is another reason for your frequent visits, and you are hiding it from me. You are in love with Ernestine, a little girl who, in my view, has neither looks nor wit, though the whole town talks of her as though she were one of Sweden's marvels. Oh yes, Herman. You are in love with her, I tell you, you love her, I know it.'

'Mademoiselle Ernestine Sanders does think well of me, I believe. But her birth, her position... Did you know, Madame, that her grandfather, Colonel Sanders, was a friend of Charles XII and an honourable gentleman of Westphalia?'

'Indeed I do.'

'Well, Madame, would such a person be a suitable party for me?'

'Herman, I assure you that she would be totally unsuitable for you. You need a mature woman, a woman who thinks of your future, who would help you make your fortune, in short a woman of my age and position.'

Herman blushed and looked away... Since tea was brought in at that moment, the conversation was interrupted, and after their lunch Herman returned to his counting house.

'My dearest Ernestine!' said Herman to Mademoiselle Sanders the next day. 'It's true! That cruel woman has plans for me. I have absolutely no doubt on that score. You know how ill-tempered and jealous she is, how high her credit is in this town:[1] Ernestine, I fear the worst.'

And as the Colonel returned home at that very moment, the two young people communicated their apprehensions to him.

Sanders was an old soldier, a man of practical good sense who, not wishing to make trouble for himself in the town, and realizing that the protection he offered Herman was certain to align Widow Scholtz and all her friends against him, he considered it his duty to advise the young lovers to submit to circumstances. He pointed out to Herman that the widow on whom his livelihood depended was really a much better match for him than Ernestine, and that at his age he should take more account of money than pretty looks.

'Dear boy,' the Colonel went on, 'it is not that I refuse you my daughter's hand... I know you, I respect you, you are adored by the girl you love. I give my consent on those grounds, of course. But I would be most unhappy to think that I should have any hand now in encouraging you to do something you might regret later. You are both young. At your age all you can see is love, you think that it is possible to live on love. That is an error. Love grows weary without money, and the choice made by love alone is soon followed by regret.'

'Father,' said Ernestine throwing herself at Sanders's feet, 'dear, most respectable father, do not dash my hopes of being united with

[1] Since Nordkoping is a town totally devoted to business, it follows that a woman like Madame Scholtz, who ran one of the most profitable banks in Sweden, should occupy the highest rank in society.

my beloved Herman! From the day I was born you have promised me I should marry him... The prospect makes me so happy, and if you deny me now you will kill me. I have given my heart and it is so gratifying to know that my father approves of its feelings. Herman will find in the love he feels for me all the strength he needs to resist the Widow Scholtz's blandishments. Dear father, do not abandon us now!'

'Get up, child,' said the Colonel. 'I love you... with all my heart... If Herman makes you happy, and since you are both agreed, then worry no more, you shall have no other husband... In any case, in reality Herman does not owe that woman anything. His honesty and hard work have cancelled any debt of gratitude, and he has no reason to feel obliged to sacrifice himself to please her... But you must try not to fall foul of anyone...'

'Sir,' said Herman, embracing the Colonel, 'now that I have your blessing I can call you father. Words cannot express how deeply indebted to you I am for the promises which your heart has made! Yes, I shall be worthy of what you have done for me. My only concern shall be for you and your dearest daughter, and the sweetest moments of my life shall be devoted to comforting you in your declining years. Father, you must not worry... we shall not make enemies. I have not reached any sort of understanding with Madame Scholtz. If I draw up a full and clear statement of her accounts and ask for mine in return, what can she say?'

'Oh, my dear boy! You do not know the sort of people you think you can defy!' continued the Colonel, who felt troubled by vague apprehensions beyond his control. 'There is no kind of crime which a malicious woman will not commit when she sets out to have her revenge for the slights a man makes against her beauty. This wretched woman will shoot the poisoned arrows of her rabid fury so high that they will fall on us, and it will be wreaths of cypress that we will gather, Herman, not the roses you hope for.'

Ernestine and the man she loved passed the rest of the day putting Sanders's mind at rest, extinguishing his fears, promising that he would be happy, and in general painting him uniformly pretty pictures. There is nothing as persuasive as the eloquence of lovers: they reason with the logic of the heart, which was never a match for the logic of the brain. Herman supped with his devoted friends and left early, his soul intoxicated by hope and joy.

About three months passed in this way without any further moves on the part of the widow, and without Herman's daring to take it upon himself to propose that they should part company. The Colonel gave the young man to understand that there was no harm in the delay. Ernestine was young, and her father was not averse to adding to the small dowry she would have the legacy of his aunt, a Widow Plorman who lived in Stockholm and, being full of years, might die at any moment.

However, Widow Scholtz, growing impatient, and far too astute not to guess at her young bookkeeper's quandary, made the first overtures by asking him if he had thought about what she had said to him the last time they had spoken together.

'Yes,' replied Ernestine's intended, 'and if Madame wishes to discuss a statement of our accounts and the ending of our association, then I am yours to command.'

'As I recall, Herman, that was not exactly the matter which we discussed.'

'What was it, then, Madame?'

'I asked you if you wanted to set up in business for yourself, and if you had chosen a wife who would help you to run it.'

'I believe my answer was that I wanted more money behind me before I married.'

'You did say that, Herman, but I did not believe it. And at this moment every expression on your face suggests that you lie in your heart.'

'Oh, deceit has never dishonoured my heart, Madame, as you know very well. I have been close to you since I was a boy and you were kind enough to take the place of the mother I lost. Do not fear that my gratitude will ever fade or die.'

'You are always talking about gratitude, Herman. I had hoped you might show me sentiments which were rather more tender.'

'But Madame, is it within my power to...?'

'Villain, is this what I get after all the care I have lavished on you? Your ingratitude has made the scales fall from my eyes. Now I see it plainly... I have wasted my labours on a monster! I will hide it no longer, Herman. When I was left a widow, I hoped I might marry you. The order I have put in your affairs... the way I have made your capital grow... the way I have treated you... my eyes, which doubtless gave me away... everything, you deceiver, everything surely convinced you of the strength of my feelings? And is this how they are received? With indifference and contempt?... Herman, you do not know what sort of woman you have so mortally offended... No, you have no idea what she is capable of... You may find out when it is too late... Now, get out!... Yes, go!... Make up your account, Herman, and I shall supply you with a statement of mine, and then we shall go our separate ways... we shall part company... You will not have any trouble in finding somewhere else to live. No doubt Sanders's house stands ready and waiting for you.'

Since the evidence of his eyes left him in no doubt of Madame Scholtz's mood, it was very plain to our young lover that it was vital to conceal his feelings for Ernestine, so that the fury and vengeance of this dangerous woman would not be turned against the Colonel. Herman therefore merely returned a soft answer, saying that his benefactress was mistaken and that his wish not to marry before he was richer did not mean that he had any plans for the Colonel's daughter.

'Listen to me,' Madame Scholtz replied, 'I know what goes on in your heart as well as you do. Your indifference to me would surely not be so obvious if you were not in love with someone else. I may not be as young as I was, but do you think that I am so unattractive that I cannot still find a husband? Yes, Herman, you would love me if it were not for this other woman whom I hate and who will feel the force of my vengeance for your contemptible treatment of me.'

Herman shuddered. Colonel Sanders, a retired army man of modest means, was far from enjoying the same standing in Nordkoping as Widow Scholtz. Her credit was spread far and wide while he, already forgotten, was regarded by men who, in Sweden as elsewhere, judge people by the yardstick of favour or wealth—he was no longer regarded, as I was saying, as anything more than a private citizen who could be brushed aside by influence and money. Madame Scholtz, like all contemptible souls, had wasted no time in making this calculation.

So Herman now went much further than he had previously done and, throwing himself on Madame Scholtz's mercy, begged her to calm herself, assured her that there were no feelings in his heart which could ever lessen his awareness of all he owed to a person from whom he had received so many benefits, and beseeched her to postpone the separation with which she threatened him. Given what

Widow Scholtz knew to be the current state of the young man's thoughts, it is difficult to imagine what more she could have expected. Trusting to time and her seductive powers, she recovered her composure.

Herman did not fail to give an account of this latest conversation to the Colonel who, wise as always, but still fearful of the displeasure and dangerous character of Widow Scholtz, tried once more to make the young man see that he would be far better advised to submit to the will of his benefactress than to persist with his plans for Ernestine. But once more, both young people resorted to the arguments which they believed most likely to remind the Colonel of the promise he had made them, and persuade him to give his word never to break it again.

Matters had been at this stage for six months when Count Oxtiern, the villain you have just met in the chains which have kept him shackled now for more than a year, and which he will wear for the rest of his life, was obliged to travel from Stockholm to Nordkoping to withdraw a large sum of money deposited with Madame Scholtz by his father, whose entire estate he had just inherited. Madame Scholtz, aware of the Count's rank in society—for he was the son of a senator and a senator himself—had made ready the finest apartment in her house and prepared to receive him with all the splendour her wealth allowed.

The Count arrived, and the very next day, in his honour, his elegant hostess held the grandest supper, followed by a ball to which the town's prettiest women were invited. Ernestine was not forgotten, and it was with some trepidation that Herman saw that she was quite determined to attend. Could the Count set eyes on her and not pay her the attentions which were her due? What might not Herman have to fear from such a rival? And supposing disaster did strike, would Ernestine be strong enough to resist, would she refuse to become the wife of one of Sweden's greatest noblemen? Out of this ill-fated ball would there not come a confederacy ranged against Herman and Ernestine, and led by Oxtiern and Widow Scholtz? And what misfortunes should Herman not fear for himself? How could he, who was weak and defenceless, hold out against the weapons of so many enemies sworn to end his precarious existence?

He spoke his thoughts to Ernestine. She, an honest, perceptive, tactful girl who was ready to sacrifice her idle pleasure to the fears which consumed him, suggested to Herman that he should say no to Widow Scholtz's invitation. The young man was more or less of the same opinion. Yet since in their little circle of right-thinking persons nothing could be done without Sanders's agreement, they asked his advice. He took a very different view. He pointed out that to reject Madame Scholtz's proposal would inevitably lead to a breach with her, that being a shrewd woman it would not take her long to discover the real reasons for his refusal, and that in circumstances where it seemed vital to treat her with even greater circumspection, the inevitable result would be to provoke her fury.

Ernestine then ventured to ask Herman what it was exactly that he feared. She did not disguise the deep hurt which such suspicions caused her.

'Oh my own sweet!' said the remarkable young woman, pressing Herman's hands in hers, 'if the most powerful men in Europe were present at the ball and they all fell madly in love with your dearest Ernestine, do you not see that all their assembled devotion would be no more than a fresh laurel in my true conqueror's crown? Oh Herman, there is nothing to fear. This heart of mine which you have subjugated could never love another. If I had to live with you in slavery, I would prefer my fate to the throne of Sweden itself. All the advantages that earth can offer would mean nothing to me in the arms of any but the man I love!... Herman, be fair: how can you think that if I attend the ball I shall set eyes on another mortal who would be your equal? Let my heart be the judge of your worth, my dear, and you will always be the most lovable, as you are the most loved, of men.'

Herman smothered Ernestine's hands with kisses, and stopped talking about his fears, but could not stop thinking of them. There come into the heart of a man in love certain presentiments which deceive very few. Herman felt them but said nothing, and fair Ernestine appeared at Madame Scholtz's ball like a rose surrounded by thorns. She had decided to wear the traditional costume of the women of her country, and was dressed in the Scythian style. Accoutred thus, her face, noble and proud, appeared to singularly better effect, her graceful, supple figure was conspicuously set off by her tight, smooth-fitting jacket which showed the lines of her body, her lovely hair cascading over the quiver at her back and the bow she held in one hand—all this made her look like Cupid disguised as

Bellona:* it was as though the arrows she carried with such grace could not fail to make the hearts which they pierced the slaves of her divine power.

If the worried Herman did not observe Ernestine's entrance without a pang of apprehension, Oxtiern on the other hand did not see her without experiencing an emotion so intense that it was several minutes before he could speak. You have seen Oxtiern, a fine-looking man... but did nature ever conceal such foulness inside such a deceptively attractive shell? The Count, an exceedingly rich man and recently master of his entire fortune, did not imagine that there were any limits to his impetuous appetites. Any obstacle placed in their way by reason or circumstances simply became additional fuel to fire their combustibility. Having neither principles nor virtue, still steeped in the prejudices of an arrogant caste which had lately taken up arms against the sovereign himself, Oxtiern imagined that there was nothing which could apply the brake to his passions. And of all the passions which inflamed him, love was the most incendiary. But this sentiment, which can become almost a virtue in a noble soul, can become only the source of many crimes in a heart as corrupt as Oxtiern's.

This dangerous man had no sooner set eyes on our beautiful heroine than he made up his wicked mind to seduce her. He danced with her a number of times, sat next to her at supper, and made the feelings she inspired in him so clear that the whole town was left in no doubt that she would shortly become either Oxtiern's wife or his mistress.

It is impossible to convey Herman's cruel state of mind while all this was taking place. He had been present at the ball, but seeing Ernestine the object of such dazzling attention, how could he have dared approach her, even for a moment? She had not changed in the way she felt about him, but is any young woman proof against pride? Will she not surrender for one brief moment to the heady thrill of public adulation? And by demonstrating that she can be adored by all men, does not her vanity, which is flattered by those around her, weaken the firm intention she had beforehand to listen only to the gallantries of one man? Ernestine could see very clearly that Herman was anxious. But Oxtiern was bound to her chariot wheels, the whole company showered her with praises, and she was not aware, as she ought to have been, of all the hurt she was inflicting on her unhappy

Herman. The Colonel was also treated with great honour. The Count conversed with him at length and volunteered to use his influence on his behalf in Stockholm. He assured him that he was far too young a man to have retired, that he should find himself an opening in some regiment and rise to the top of his profession as his talents and birth qualified him to do, and added that he would serve him at court in this as in any other ambition he might have, insisting that Herman should not fear to overtax him, for he would regard as a personal pleasure any and every favour that such a gallant man enabled him to perform. The ball ended at dawn and all the guests retired to their homes.

The next day Senator Oxtiern asked Madame Scholtz to tell him all there was to know about the young Scythian maid whose image had not been absent from his senses since the moment he had first seen her.

'She is the prettiest girl we have here in Nordkoping,' said the woman of business, delighted to observe that the Count, by putting a spoke in the wheel of Herman's amours, might well restore the young man's heart to her. 'It is true, Senator, there is not another girl in the whole country who can compare with her.'

'The whole country, Madame?' exclaimed the Count. 'Her like does not exist in the whole of Europe!... But what does she do?... What does she think?... Who loves her?... Who worships the divine creature?... What sort of man is it who thinks he can compete with me for her charms?'

'I will say nothing of her family, since you know that she is the daughter of Colonel Sanders, a man of sound worth and quality. But what you perhaps do not know and, given the feelings which you clearly have for her, you will be grieved to learn is that she is about to marry a young accounts manager who works for me. She is madly in love with him, and he is at least as much in love with her.'

'Ernestine cannot marry a man like that!' cried the Senator. 'An angel like her cannot become the wife of a ledger-clerk!... This shall not be, Madame, it must not happen. You must join forces with me to prevent this ridiculous match. Ernestine was born to shine at court, and I intend that she shall be presented there under my name.'

'But she has no money, Count!... she is the daughter of an impoverished gentleman... a military man who came up through the ranks!'

'She is the daughter of the gods!' cried Oxtiern, beside himself, 'And she should dwell where they live!'

'But Senator, you will break the heart of the young man I told you of. Such intense affection as his is rare, and feelings are not ordinarily so sincere.'

'The least of my worries, Madame, is having a rival of that species. Can such lowly creatures be allowed to become a threat to my amours? You shall help me to find a means of sending the fellow away, and if he does not have the good grace to go of his own accord... then leave him to me, Madame Scholtz, just leave it all to me and we shall be rid of the knave.'

Widow Scholtz approved of the plan, and far from allowing the Count's ardour to cool, she merely pointed out various obstacles of the kind which are easily overcome and, being overcome, act as a spur to love.

But while all this was going on in the widow's house, Herman was on his knees before the woman he adored.

'Oh Ernestine, I told you so,' he exclaimed through his tears, 'I warned you, I knew that cursed ball would bring us nothing but grief! Every compliment the Count lavished on you was like a dagger which he thrust into my heart. Can you be in any doubt now that he worships you? Has he not made it perfectly obvious?'

'How can you be so unfair? Do you think', the Colonel's daughter replied trying her best to calm the only object of her affection, 'that I am the least interested in the fulsome compliments which that man thought fit to heap on me, since my heart belongs to you alone? Did you think that I was flattered by his attentions?'

'Yes, Ernestine, I did, and I was not wrong. Your eyes shone with pride because he was so attracted by you, and you paid no attention to anyone else.'

'I do not care at all for this rebuke, Herman, I am hurt to find you so critical. I thought you were sufficiently understanding to know you had no cause for alarm. Well, tell your fears to my father, and if you wish our marriage to be celebrated tomorrow, then I consent.'

Herman immediately seized on the suggestion. Accompanied by Ernestine, he went to see Sanders and, throwing himself into the Colonel's arms, asked him to promise by everything he held most dear that he would place no more obstacles in the way of his happiness.

Since it was less counterbalanced by other sentiments, pride had made considerably more progress in Sanders's heart than in Ernestine's. The Colonel, a plain-speaking man of his word, had no wish whatsoever to break the promises he had given Herman, but he was dazzled by the prospect of Oxtiern's patronage. He had seen for himself how his daughter had conquered the Senator's very soul, and friends had made him see that if the Count's passion were to be followed by the honourable consequence which he had no reason to doubt, then clearly the outcome would be to make his fortune. The matter had preyed on his mind all night. He had made plans. He had surrendered to ambition. In short, the juncture was hardly propitious for Herman, who could not have chosen a worse moment. But Sanders was not minded to give the young man a blank refusal, for such behaviour was contrary to his nature. In any case, was it not possible that he was building his hopes on sand? What guarantee was there that the dreams he had fed on that night would become reality? So he fell back on the arguments he normally used: his daughter's youth, the money Aunt Plorman was expected to leave, his fear of unleashing upon himself and Ernestine the vengeance of Widow Scholtz, who now, with the backing of Senator Oxtiern, would be even more of a threat than ever. Besides, was it sensible to set a date when the Count was in town? There seemed no sense in drawing attention to themselves, and if doing so meant firing up Widow Scholtz's wrath, then the time when she enjoyed the Count's backing was obviously the moment when she would be at her most dangerous. Ernestine was more insistent than ever. In her heart she felt a twinge of guilt for the way she had behaved the night before, and she was only too glad to be able to prove to Herman that if she had committed faults, loving him less was not one of them. The Colonel hesitated and, unaccustomed to refusing his daughter's entreaties, asked only that she wait until the Senator had gone, and promised that afterwards he would remove every obstacle and if necessary even go to see Widow Scholtz to calm her, or persuade her to agree to a basic audit rather than the full rendering of accounts without which Herman could not decently part company with his employer.

Herman went away feeling dissatisfied yet reassured by the sentiments of the woman he loved, but still consumed by a brooding anxiety which nothing could allay. He had not been gone long when the Senator called on Sanders. He was accompanied by Widow

Scholtz, and had come, he said, to do his duty by a true soldier whom he was so very happy to have met on his travels, and asked his leave to pay his compliments to the lovely Ernestine. The Colonel and his daughter accepted his civilities politely. Widow Scholtz, concealing her rage and jealousy because now she could see any number of schemes which would serve the cruel impulses of her heart, sang the Colonel's praises and was extremely charming to Ernestine, so that the conversation was as pleasant as could be expected in the circumstances.

Several days passed in this way. During this time Sanders and his daughter and Widow Scholtz and the Count called on each other, dined at each other's tables, and never once was the hapless Herman invited to any of these agreeable occasions.

Meanwhile Oxtiern let slip no opportunity to speak of his love, and it was becoming impossible for Mademoiselle Sanders to be left in any doubt that the Count felt the most ardent passion for her. But Ernestine's heart was her protection and her abiding love for Herman shielded her from any possibility that she might be caught for a second time in the toils of her own pride. She refused to listen, she said no, never appeared anything other than constrained and inattentive in the gatherings at which she was forced to be present, and never returned home without begging her father not to make her go to any more. But it was too late.

As I have already told you, Sanders no longer had the same reasons as his daughter to be wary of Oxtiern's bait, and was quickly hooked. There had been secret discussions between Widow Scholtz, the Senator, and the Colonel. In the end, the unsuspecting Sanders was dazzled. The smooth-tongued Oxtiern, without ever committing himself, without promising marriage, but merely making it seem that it would all come down to that in the end, had completely won Sanders round. He made him agree to reject Herman's proposal, and even persuaded him to quit the backwater that was Nordkoping and settle in Stockholm, where he would enjoy the influence the Count guaranteed him and the favours which he intended to heap on him.

Ernestine, who in the meantime had seen much less of her lover, nevertheless still continued to write to him. But knowing him to be capable of taking matters into his own hands, and wanting to avoid open confrontation, she did her best to hide what was going on from him. Besides, she was not yet absolutely certain that her father had weakened. Before she said anything on that score to Herman, she decided to find out the truth.

One morning she went in to the Colonel's room.

'Father,' she began respectfully, 'they say the Senator intends to stay in Nordkoping for a long time. But you promised Herman that you would allow us to marry soon. May I ask if your view is still the same?... and why is it necessary to wait for the Count to leave, to celebrate a wedding which we all want so much?'

'Sit down, Ernestine,' said the Colonel, 'and listen to me. As long as I believed that you would find happiness and a settled future with young Herman, it must have been clear, daughter, that far from raising any objection, I was only too ready to agree to what you wanted. But since a better prospect now awaits you, Ernestine, why do you ask me to sacrifice your future?...'

'A better prospect, you say? If it is my happiness you seek, father, do not imagine I shall ever find it anywhere except at dear Herman's side, for only there will it be certain. But no matter, for I think I know what you have in mind... and I tremble! Ah, you must not make me the victim of your plans!'

'But Ernestine, my advancement depends on those plans.'

'Oh, father! If the Count will not further your career unless he obtains my hand in marriage... then so be it. You will, I concede, enjoy all the honours you have been promised. But the man who sold them to you will never enjoy the reward he expects, for I would rather die than be his.'

'Ernestine, I believed that you had a sweeter nature, I thought you loved your father more.'

'And I, revered father, thought that your daughter was more precious to you, that... Oh why did he have to travel here... with his ignoble temptations?... We were all happy before that man came... There was just one obstacle in our way, and we could have overcome it. I feared nothing as long as I had my father's support. But you will abandon me, and now all I can do is die...'

And Ernestine, distraught and overcome by misery, uttered a despondent groan which would have softened the hardest of hearts.

'Listen, my girl, listen to me before you start to grieve,' said the Colonel as he stroked away the tears from Ernestine's cheek. 'The Count intends to make me rich and successful, and although he has not said in so many words that he will ask for your hand in return, it is really not too difficult to guess that this is what he really wants. It is certain, so he says, that I will be taken back into the service. He wants us to go and live in Stockholm, where he has promised we shall lead the most enviable life. As soon as I arrive in town, he tells me that he will, personally, meet me with a paper guaranteeing me a pension of a thousand ducats[1] which is due for my years of army service and my father's, which he says the Court would have agreed to pay me long ago had we then had a friend in the capital to put our case. Ernestine, are you prepared to lose all these advantages? Do you really want to ruin your future and mine?'

'No, father,' Sanders's daughter replied firmly, 'I do not. But I would ask one favour of you, which is that before you do anything you set a test for the Count which I am sure he will not refuse to undertake. If he seriously intends to do everything he says he will to help you, and if he is sincere, then he will go on being a true friend without asking anything for himself. If he lays down conditions, there is every reason to fear what he might do. From that moment he would be serving his personal interest, and his actions would perhaps be false. He would no longer be your friend but my seducer.'

'He will marry you.'

'He will do no such thing. But listen to me, father, if the Count's sentiments for you are genuine, they must be kept quite separate from whatever he might feel about me. He ought not to want to make you happy in the certain knowledge that in so doing he would make me unhappy. If he is good and kind, then he should render you all the service he can without demanding me as his price. To find out what he has in mind, tell him that you accept his offers but that you ask him as an earnest of his generosity to me to give his blessing, before he leaves Nordkoping, to the marriage of your daughter with the only man on earth she could ever love. If the Count is a fair-minded, honest, disinterested man he will agree. If it is his intention to sacrifice me in return for serving you, he will give himself away. He must be made to respond to your suggestion. Coming from you, it will be no surprise to him, since you have said he has not yet asked for my hand in so many words. If his answer is to make it the price of his benevolence, then he is more interested in serving his own

[1] The Swedish ducat is worth a few sous less than our crown.

interests than yours, for knowing I am already spoken for, he will try to force me against my will and my feelings. If he does, then he has a wicked heart and you should be wary of all his offers, whatever the gloss he tries to put on them. An honourable man would not want to marry a wife whose love he knows he can never have. It cannot be at the daughter's expense that he will accommodate the father. The test is infallible and I beseech you to try it. If it succeeds... I mean, if we are convinced that the Count's intentions are utterly honourable... then we must do whatever he says, in which case he will have advanced your career without undermining my happiness. We shall all be content, father, every one of us, and you would be spared any feelings of regret.'

'Ernestine,' the Colonel said, 'it is quite possible for the Count to be an honest man and still intend to oblige me only on the condition that you should be his wife.'

'Yes, if he did not know I was already promised elsewhere. But once told that I am, if he then persists in making his offer of service to you conditional on coercing me, his behaviour will be pure selfishness and finer feelings are excluded from it. Which means that we should be very suspicious of his blandishments...'

And throwing herself into the Colonel's arms, Ernestine exclaimed through her tears:

'Oh father! Do not deny me the test I ask for,' do not refuse me, father, I beg you, do not be so callous as to sacrifice a daughter who loves you dearly and whose only wish to is to live for you. Poor Herman will die of grief. He will die hating us, I would quickly follow him to the grave, and you will have lost the two persons who are closest to your heart.'

The Colonel loved his daughter. He was a magnanimous man with a generous spirit. The only criticism that could be made of him was that he possessed the kind of trusting nature which, though it makes an upright man such easy prey for scoundrels, nonetheless reveals all the candour and sincerity of a truly noble soul. He promised his daughter that he would do exactly as she asked, and the very next day spoke to the Senator.

Oxtiern, who was wilier than Mademoiselle Sanders was shrewd, had of course made arrangements with Widow Scholtz to cater for all eventualities. He returned the most satisfactory answer to the Colonel.

'My dear fellow, did you seriously imagine', he told him, 'that I had a personal interest when I offered to oblige you? All other considerations aside, you must learn to know my heart better. Why, it brims with the desire to help you. Of course I love your daughter. Nothing would be gained if I tried to hide the fact. But if she does not think that I am the man to make her happy, then I would be the last to try to force her against her will. I shall take no hand in tying the knot of her marriage, as you seem to wish, for my involvement would be too painful. I shall sacrifice myself, but may I at least be allowed to prefer not to have to do the deed by my own hand? But this marriage will take place, I shall see to it personally. I shall put Widow Scholtz in charge. If your daughter would prefer to be the wife of a bookkeeper rather than the consort of one of Sweden's leading senators, then she is free to choose. But you must not fear that her choice will in any way prejudice me in what I propose to do for you. I shall be leaving almost immediately. As soon as I have settled one or two matters here, one of my carriages will call for your daughter and you. You will travel to Stockholm with Ernestine. Herman can follow and marry her there, or if he prefers, he can wait until you have settled into the post I have in mind for you, in which case he will make a better marriage.'

'Worthy friend,' said Sanders, taking both the Count's hands in his, 'you are too generous! The service which you are pleased to render us will be all the more precious because it is disinterested and because it is such a costly sacrifice... Oh, Senator! This is the very highest manifestation of human generosity! In this age of ours when virtue is a rare commodity, your great kindness should incite men to build temples in your honour.'

'My dear fellow,' said the Count, returning the Colonel's handshake, 'the honest man is always the first to enjoy the good deeds that he does. Is that not what he needs to make his happiness complete?'

The Colonel had no business more pressing than that of giving his daughter an account of the important conversation he had just had with Oxtiern. Ernestine was moved to tears and believed that the road ahead was now smooth. Fine souls are trusting, and are easily convinced by promises of what they themselves are capable of doing. Herman was not quite as credulous. A few careless remarks which Widow Scholtz let slip, in her exultation at seeing her vengeance so surely served, prompted suspicions which he communicated to

Ernestine. The sweet girl reassured him. She made him see that a man of Oxtiern's background and standing was incapable of deceiving her... Innocent creature! Little did she know that vices, when buttressed by birth and wealth and thus made bold because they are untouchable, grow all the more dangerous in consequence. Herman said that he wished to have the matter out with the Count personally. Ernestine forbade him to take the law into his own hands. The young man protested that he had no intention of doing so. But at bottom he heeded only his pride, his love, and his courage, and he loaded a pair of pistols. The very next morning he was shown into the Count's apartment and, standing at the foot of his bed:

'Sir,' he began boldly, 'I believe you to be an honourable gentleman. Your name, your rank, your wealth, all assure me that you are. I therefore ask you, sir, to give me your word, in writing, that you categorically give up any claim you may have expressed with regard to Ernestine. If not, then I shall expect to see you accept one of these two pistols so that we may try to blow each other's brains out.'

The Senator, somewhat taken aback by the compliment, first began by asking Herman if he had thought seriously about what he was doing, and if he believed that a man of his rank owed any kind of apology to an inferior such as he.

'Please keep a civil tongue, sir,' replied Herman. 'I did not come here to be insulted, but on the contrary to demand satisfaction for the affront you have offered me by attempting to seduce my fiancée. An inferior, you say? Senator, a man has the right to require another to make amends for depriving him of his property or doing him a wrong. The prejudice which sets one class above another is an illusion. Nature created men equal. There is not one of us who did not come into the world poor and naked, none whose life is preserved or ended differently from all the rest. The only distinction I recognize between them is that which virtue makes. The only man born to be despised is he who uses the rights granted him by spurious convention to cultivate vice with impunity. Get up, sir. Were you a king I would still demand of you the satisfaction I am due. Give it me, I say, or I will blow your brains out if you do not look lively and defend yourself.'

'One moment,' said Oxtiern as he dressed. 'Sit down, young man. I would like us to take breakfast together before we fight... Will you refuse me this one favour?'

'As you wish, Count,' replied Herman. 'But I trust that afterwards you will take up my invitation in the same spirit...'

The Count rang, breakfast was served, and, having given orders that he was to be left alone with Herman, the Senator, after the first cup of coffee, asked him if what he was bent on doing had been concocted in concert with Ernestine.

'Absolutely not, Senator. She does not even know I am here. She even went so far as to say that it was your intention to be of use to me.'

'If that is the case, what motive can you have for behaving so rashly?'

'Fear of being duped, the sure knowledge that, being in love with Ernestine, I can never give her up, the urge to discover how matters stand.'

'You will know that very soon, Herman, and while I should have nothing but harsh words for the temerity of your action—and although your ill-considered conduct ought really to change my plans for the Colonel's daughter—I will nevertheless keep my word. Yes, Herman, you shall marry Ernestine. I gave my promise and it shall be kept. I am not standing down in your favour, young man; I am not the kind of man who would make way for you in anything. The truth is, Ernestine can persuade me to do anything, and it is to her happiness that I sacrifice my own.'

'Such generosity...'

'You owe me nothing, I tell you. What I have done is for Ernestine: the only gratitude I expect will come from her.'

'Please allow me to add my own share, Senator, and by the same token allow me to apologize profusely for being so hasty. But, sir, may I really count on your word? And if it is your intention to keep it, will you refuse to give it me in writing?'

'I will write anything you like, but there is no point. Besides, your unjust suspicions will merely add to the foolishness with which you have seen fit to act.'

'It would be helpful for Ernestine's peace of mind.'

'She is less suspicious than you. She believes me. But no matter, write I shall and gladly—but the note will be addressed to her. To proceed otherwise would be improper. I cannot help you and humble myself to you at the same time.'

And the Senator, seating himself at a writing desk, wrote the following lines:

Count Oxtiern hereby promises to allow Ernestine Sanders to make her choice freely, and to use his best efforts to enable her to taste the joys of marriage without further delay—whatever the cost to one who loves her, whose sacrifice will soon be as inevitable as it will be painful.

Poor Herman, far from understanding the note's cruel meaning, snatched it up, kissed it with fervour, repeated his excuses to the Count, and ran as fast as he could to bring Mademoiselle Sanders the sorry trophy of his victory.

She was very angry with him. She accused him of not trusting her, and added that after what she had said he should never have gone to such lengths with a man who so far outranked him, that there was every reason to fear that the Count, who had only yielded out of prudence, would on reflection be minded to take extreme measures which might prove fatal for both of them and, in any case, certainly very harmful to her father. Herman reassured her and showed her the note... which she too read without understanding its ambiguous phrasing. They conveyed the news to the Colonel, who was even more disapproving of the young man's behaviour than his daughter. But they were soon reconciled, and our three friends, full of confidence in the Count's promises, went their separate ways easy in their minds.

Meanwhile Oxtiern, after the scene with Herman, had gone down at once to Widow Scholtz's apartment and had told her what had happened. The wicked woman, more convinced than ever by the action the young man had taken that it was now impossible to imagine that she would ever make him hers, committed herself more strongly than ever to the Count's cause and promised to serve him until the wretched Herman had been completely destroyed.

'I know an infallible way of undoing him,' said the unfeeling shrew. 'I have a second set of keys to his money-chest, though he does not know it. Soon I shall have to pay out a hundred thousand ducats against promissory notes issued by Hamburg merchants. All I have to do is show that he has sticky fingers and he will either have to marry me or have his life ruined.'

'If the latter is the case,' said the Count, 'you must let me know at once. You may rest assured that I will act as best befits our joint vengeance.'

Then the two rogues, only too cruelly united by their interests, revised their final arrangements so that their underhand schemes would be as foolproof and as villainous as they wished.

When their plans were finalized Oxtiern called on the Colonel and his daughter to say farewell. In front of Ernestine he kept a check on his feelings, and expressed not his love and true intentions, but all the nobility and disinterestedness which his hypocrisy allowed him to muster. To Sanders he repeated his most fulsome offers of service, and persuaded him to agree to make the journey to Stockholm. The Count offered to have an apartment in his town house made ready for them. But the Colonel said that he would prefer to lodge with his cousin, Madame Plorman, whose estate he expected would be left to his daughter, adding that it would be a friendly gesture which would give Ernestine a good reason to humour a lady who could improve her prospects very materially. Oxtiern endorsed the plan, and it was agreed that they would travel by carriage, since Ernestine was afraid of the sea. And then they separated with the warmest protestations of affection and regard for each other. Herman's rash initiative was not mentioned.

Widow Scholtz kept up her pretence with Herman. Aware of the need to remain on the same footing with him until the affair she was plotting was made public, she never spoke of her feelings and continued to treat him, as before, with the same trust and kindly interest. She did not tell him she knew all about his foolish scene with the Senator, and our upstanding young man believed that since the confrontation had not ended greatly to the Count's advantage, he had kept it carefully concealed.

However, Herman was only too well aware that the Colonel and his daughter would soon be leaving Nordkoping. But having complete trust in Ernestine's love, the Colonel's friendship, and the Count's promises, he was in no doubt that the first withdrawal Ernestine would make on her credit with the Senator would be to persuade him to reunite them without delay. Mademoiselle Sanders endlessly assured Herman that such was her plan, and indeed she was most sincerely committed to it.

A few weeks had gone by in this fashion when there arrived in Nordkoping the most magnificent carriage, escorted by grooms charged with delivering a letter to Colonel Sanders from Count Oxtiern. They were to wait upon the Colonel's orders concerning the journey he was to make to Stockholm with his daughter. The carriage had been sent to him for that purpose. The letter informed Sanders that, through the Senator's good offices, Widow Plorman had agreed to place the finest apartment in her house at the disposal of her two relatives, that they were both free to come whenever they chose, and that the Count would wait until they arrived before telling his friend Sanders the outcome of the action he had taken on his behalf. As to Herman, the Senator went on, he felt it would be only right if he were left to conclude his business quietly with Madame Scholtz. When he had done so, with his affairs then being in a healthier state, he would make an even more suitable match and could present himself and ask for Ernestine's hand. Everyone would gain by this arrangement. Meanwhile the Colonel, by then enjoying a pension and perhaps an army promotion, would be better placed to help her financially.

This proposal did not please Ernestine. It started suspicions in her mind which she immediately communicated to her father. The Colonel said that he had not for a moment thought that Oxtiern had ever intended to proceed differently. Besides, Sanders went on, how could Herman possibly leave Nordkoping before settling his affairs with Widow Scholtz? Ernestine shed a few tears and, still torn between her love for Herman and her fear of harming her father's interests, did not dare express her extreme reluctance at the prospect of not taking advantage of the Count's offers until such time as Herman would be free.

And so they had to make up their minds to go. The Colonel invited Herman to dine at his house so that they could say their farewells. Herman accepted, and the following cruel scene took place in a mood of tearful emotion:

'My dearest Ernestine,' wept Herman, 'I must be parted from you and know not when I shall see you again. You leave me to face a cruel enemy, a woman who conceals her feelings which are far from being dead. Who will help me deal with the avalanche of troubles the shrew will bring down on my head when she sees that I am more determined than ever to follow you... when I tell her that I shall never belong to any other woman but you?... And you, my God, where are you going?... To live under the thumb of a man who loved you... and loves you still... whose sacrifice is more than dubious. He will make you love him, Ernestine, he will dazzle you, and all poor Herman, abandoned and alone, will have left are his tears!'

'Herman will always have the heart of Ernestine,' said Mademoiselle Sanders, clasping his hand. 'Does he have any cause to fear that he will be deceived, seeing that he is the possessor of such a treasure?'

'Oh, may I never lose it!' cried Herman falling on his knees before the beautiful girl he adored. 'May Ernestine never yield to the blandishments which will be offered to her, and never forget that there is only one man on earth who loves her as I love her!'

And the hapless young man had the audacity to beg Ernestine to allow him to pluck, from her rose-red lips, a precious kiss which would serve as the pledge he demanded for her promise. Ernestine, virtuous and discreet, who had never before granted so much, felt obliged to make a concession to the circumstances. She leaned forward into the arms of Herman who, inflamed by love and desire, and succumbing to the sorrowing joy which can only find expression in tears, set the seal of the love he had sworn on the most beautiful mouth in the world, and from that mouth, whose imprint lingered on his, was vouchsafed the most exquisite words of love and constancy.

Yet the hour, the fatal hour of the departure, struck. For two hearts who love truly, what difference is there between the bell which rings for their separation and the knell that tolls for their death? When we part from the one we love, it is as though the heart is fractured or rent in twain. That organ, as though physically attached to the departing beloved, seems to shrivel at that cruel moment. We want to flee, we turn and come back, we separate, we kiss, we cannot bear to end it. But since end it we must, all our faculties are numbed, and we feel as though we have been abandoned by the life-force which sustains us. What remains is inert, and it is only in the person who has gone from us that we feel that we still live.

It had been agreed that the passengers should board the carriage once dinner was over. Ernestine turned to look at Herman: she saw that he was weeping, and felt her very soul had split in two.

'Oh, father!' she cried, bursting into tears. 'You see what I sacrifice for your sake!'

And throwing herself once more into Herman's arms, she cried:

'I have never stopped loving you and I shall go on loving you until my dying day. Here, in the presence of my father, I swear that I shall belong to no man save you. Write to me, think of me, pay heed to no one but me, and consider me the lowest of creatures if another man but you should ever receive either my hand or my heart.'

Herman was by now in a state of considerable agitation. Bending low, he kissed the feet of the woman he loved, and it was as if through his burning kisses his soul, whose stamp they bore, his entire soul which pulsed in those kisses of fire, would hold Ernestine in its spell...

'I shall never see you again... never again!' he told her through his sobs. 'Father, let me go with you. You must not let Ernestine be taken from me. But if that is what my fate must be, alas, then take your sword now and plunge it into my heart!'

The Colonel managed to calm the young man, and gave his word that he would never attempt to place obstacles in the way of his daughter's wishes. But when love takes fright, there can be no reassurance. Herman was only too well aware that few lovers had ever parted in such cruel circumstances, and despite all his efforts to prevent it, his heart reached breaking-point. The moment of departure could no longer be postponed. Ernestine, desperately unhappy and with her eyes welling with tears, took her seat next to her father in the coach which bore her out of the sight of the man she loved. At that moment Herman imagined he saw death wrapping its dark wings around the dismal carriage which had deprived him of his most precious possession. His melancholy cries called out to Ernestine, his distraught soul followed her, but then he saw no more... everything grew dim and was lost in the thick black shadow of night, and the unhappy young man returned to the house of Widow Scholtz in a state of distress sufficiently obvious to exasperate still further the jealousy of that dangerous monster.

The Colonel reached Stockholm early the next day, and at Madame Plorman's door, where the carriage halted, he found Senator Oxtiern, who handed Ernestine down. Although the Colonel had not seen his relative for a number of years, he was not the less well received for that. But it was easy to see that the Senator's protection had played a highly significant part in the warmth of the welcome. Ernestine was admired and made much of. Her aunt said aloud that she believed that her charming niece would eclipse all the most beautiful women in the capital, and that very same day arrangements were made for her to enjoy every pleasure possible, so that she would be dazzled and intoxicated and thus forget her beloved Herman.

Madame Plorman's house was isolated by its situation, and its owner, who was old and avaricious by temperament, saw very few people. It was perhaps for that reason that the Count, who already knew her, had not been unhappy about the choice of residence the Colonel had made.

Under Madame Plorman's roof lived a young officer in the regiment of Guards who was by one remove more closely related to her than Ernestine, and therefore had a better claim than she to the estate. He was called Sindersen, an upright, decent man, but naturally enough hardly well disposed to relatives who, though more distantly connected to his aunt than he was, nevertheless seemed to believe they had similar claims on her. These circumstances created a certain coolness between him and the Sanderses. However, he was polite to Ernestine and civil to the Colonel, and beneath the social veneer known as courtesy succeeded in disguising the hostility which naturally occupied pride of place in his heart.

But let us allow the Colonel to settle in, and return to Nordkoping, while Oxtiern leaves no stone unturned in his efforts to amuse the father, dazzle the daughter, and work for the ultimate success of the perfidious plans which he hopes will end in triumph.

A week after Ernestine's departure the Hamburg merchants arrived and asked for the one hundred thousand ducats which Widow Scholtz was holding for them. The money was assumed to be safely locked up in Herman's strongbox. But the villainy had already been committed, for thanks to the second set of keys, the money had disappeared. Madame Scholtz, who had invited the merchants to dinner, immediately informed Herman that he was to produce the full sum, for her guests wished to travel on to Stockholm later that same evening. Herman had not checked the strongbox for some time but, knowing that the money was inside, opened it with complete confidence only to fall almost in a faint when he realized that he had been robbed. He ran at once to his employer.

'Oh, Madame!' he exclaimed in bewilderment, 'We have been burgled!'

'Burgled you say? No one has broken in, and I can answer for the honesty of everyone here.'

'But someone must have got in, Madame, it cannot be otherwise, for the money is not there now... and you surely have every confidence in me?'

'I did once, Herman, but when love turns the head of a young man like you, there is no vice that will not creep into his heart in the wake of his passion... You young fool! Think hard about what you may have done. I need that money at once. If you are guilty, admit it. But if you have done wrong and insist on denying it, you may not be the only one I shall drag into this disastrous business... Ernestine sets off for Stockholm at the precise moment when my money disappears... who knows if she is still in the kingdom?... She went ahead... you planned to run away together!'

'No, Madame, no! You cannot seriously believe what you have just said,' Herman replied firmly. 'You cannot believe it, Madame. A criminal does not ordinarily begin his career by stealing such large sums, for in the heart of man the path to major crimes is invariably paved with vices. What have you ever seen me do until now that might lead you to think me capable of such a breach of trust? If I had stolen your money, would I still be here in Nordkoping? Did you not warn me a week ago that you would have to disburse this sum? If indeed I took it, would I have the effrontery to remain here calmly and wait until my shame was made public? Is such behaviour plausible? Do you really suppose that I am capable of it?'

'It is not for me to look for the grounds by which you might be exonerated, since I have suffered a loss on account of your crime, Herman. I go by one simple fact: you were in charge of my strong-box, you alone were responsible for it, and it is empty when I need the cash which should be in it. The locks have not been damaged and none of my employees has disappeared. It follows that this theft, which has left no sign of forcible entry or any visible trace, can only be attributed to the person who had the keys. For the last time, Herman, consider. I will keep the merchants here for another twenty-four hours. Tomorrow, either I have my money or I shall have to seek redress in the law.'

Herman withdrew in a state of despair far easier to imagine than to describe. He burst into tears and took heaven to task for allowing him to live long enough to have to endure so many misfortunes. Two choices presented themselves: flee, or blow out his brains. But no sooner had they taken shape in his mind than he rejected them in horror... To die without clearing his name... without undoing the suspicions which would devastate Ernestine: could she ever come to terms with the fact that she had given her heart to a man capable of such villainy? Her delicate nature would not bear the weight of his infamy and she would die of grief... To run away would be to admit his guilt: how could he agree to look as though he were the perpetrator of a crime he was so incapable of committing? Herman much preferred to accept his fate, and accordingly wrote letters asking for the protection of the Count and the support of the Colonel. He was confident of obtaining the former and had no doubts of the latter. So he wrote telling them of the terrible catastrophe which had befallen him, convinced them of his innocence, and above all gave the Colonel to understand how badly the affair could turn out for him, since it involved a woman so eaten up with jealousy that she would not fail to seize the opportunity to destroy him. He asked to be sent his advice quickly, given the urgency of the situation, and then surrendered to the will of Providence which, he was bold enough to think, was just and would not abandon an innocent man.*

You may easily imagine what an anxious night the young man spent.

Early next morning Widow Scholtz sent word that he was to attend her in her apartment.

'Well,' she said, giving an impression of candour and benevolence, 'are you ready to confess the error of your ways? Have you finally made up your mind to tell me the reason for your singular behaviour?'

'I have come to offer my person as my only defence, Madame,' the young man replied courageously. 'I should not have remained in your house if I were guilty. You gave me plenty of time to run away, and if I were the thief I would have done so.'

'Perhaps you would not have got very far without being followed and your escape would have been sufficient to condemn you. Running away is what a very inexperienced criminal would have done. By remaining, you show me one who is not a beginner.'

'We will make an audit of the accounts whenever you wish, Madame. Until you find errors in them, you have no right to speak to me in this manner. But I am quite entitled to ask you to wait until you have stronger evidence before you question my honesty.'

'Herman, is this the thanks I get from a young man I raised... and in whom I placed my fondest hopes?'

'You do not answer, Madame. Your prevarication surprises me and almost raises doubts in my mind.'

'Do not make me angry, Herman, do not make me lose my temper when what you should be doing is to try and soften my heart...' (And continuing with some warmth): 'Are you unaware, you callous villain, of the feelings I have for you? But now that you do, can you think of anyone more willing to conceal your wrongdoing?... Why should I hound you when I am prepared to spill my own blood to undo the wrong you have done?... Listen, Herman, I can put everything to rights. I have in the banks I deal with ten times the sum required to make good your mistake... Admit that you did it, that is all I ask. Agree to marry me and everything will be forgotten.'

'And in so doing I would buy misery for the rest of my life, the asking price being a horrible lie?'

'Misery for the rest of your life, you unfeeling wretch? Is that how you regard the married state I seek, when it would take just one word from me and you would be ruined for ever?'

'You are quite aware that my heart is not mine to dispose of, Madame. It belongs entirely to Ernestine. Anything which would interfere with our intention of spending our lives together can only be anathema to me.'

'Ernestine?... You can leave her out of your reckoning. She is already married to Oxtiern...'

'Married?... But that cannot be, Madame. She gave me her word and her heart. She would never deceive me.'

'What has been done was agreed in advance. The Colonel was a party to it.'

'God in heaven! Very well, I shall find out the truth for myself. I shall leave immediately for Stockholm... I shall see Ernestine... I will learn from her lips if you are misleading me... What am I saying? Is Ernestine capable of betraying the man she loves? No, never!... If you believe that, then you cannot know how pure her heart is! It is more likely that the sun will cease to shine than for such treachery to cast a shadow on her soul.'

And with these words, the young man would have rushed from the house had not Madame Scholtz detained him.

'Herman, you will ruin yourself. Now listen to me, for this is the last time I shall speak to you like this... Do I need to spell it out? There are six witnesses who are prepared to testify against you. You were seen carrying my money out of the house and what you did with it is known. You had doubts about Count Oxtiern's motives. With the hundred thousand ducats, you intended to carry off Ernestine and take her with you to England... The legal machinery has already been set in motion. But I repeat: one word from me and it will be stopped again... Here is my hand, Herman. Accept it and everything is put right.'

'But this is a tissue of horrors and lies!' cried Herman. 'Deceit and contradiction are audible in every word you have said. If, as you claim, Ernestine is the Senator's wife, then I had no reason to steal the missing money for her, and if I did steal the money for her, then it is not true that she is married to the Count. Since you can tell such outrageous lies, it is clear that this is all a trap set by your spiteful heart to ensnare me. But I am confident that I shall find a way of restoring my honour which you would strip from me. And the means by which I shall convince the world of my innocence will at the same time prove you guilty of all the crimes you have committed so that you would have your revenge against me for spurning your advances.'

He had nothing more to say. Avoiding Widow Scholtz's arms, which reached out to detain him once more, he rushed into the street at once with the intention of travelling to Stockholm... Poor wretch! He did not suspect for one moment that chains were already being made ready to hold him... Ten men laid hands on him as he stepped though the door and dragged him off unceremoniously to the felons' prison, observed by the unforgiving harridan who had engineered his ruin and now, as she watched him being led away, seemed to take pleasure from the utter misery which her unbridled fury had inflicted on the unfortunate young man.

'Very well,' said Herman when he found himself in the abode of crime... and too often of injustice... 'at this instant I challenge heaven to invent misfortunes which would lacerate my soul more savagely. You, Oxtiern, double-dealing Oxtiern, you alone are responsible for this plot. I am here because I am the victim of jealousy, your accomplices, and your wicked self... This is an example of how men may from one moment to the next fall into the deepest pit of humiliation and misfortune! I imagined that only criminal acts could bring a man so low... But no... all it takes to be guilty is to be suspected...* all that is required for a man to be crushed is that he should have powerful enemies!... But you, my own Ernestine, whose loving pledges continue to comfort me, is your heart at least still mine in my misfortune? Are you as innocent as I? Did you have a hand in any of this?... My God, what odious suspicions! I feel more oppressed by the fact that I can think such thoughts for one moment, than bowed down by all my other woes... What? That Ernestine should be guilty... that Ernestine should betray the man who loves her?... No, deceit and hypocrisy were never hatched out in the secret recesses of her delicate soul!... And the tender kiss which lingers still... the only kiss I ever received from her, is it possible I gathered it from a mouth sullied by lies?... No, no, dear heart, no... we have both been duped... The monsters will make the most of my predicament to blacken me in your mind!... Celestial angel, do not let yourself be taken in by the cunning of mortal men, and may your soul, as pure as the godhead from which it emanates, be as impervious as its model to the iniquities of this world!'

Then suffering, dark and silent, took possession of the unfortunate Herman. As the full horror of his fate sank in, the helplessness he felt grew to such a pitch that he began to struggle against his chains. One moment he fretted to be free so as to make haste and vindicate himself, the next to run and throw himself at Ernestine's feet. He rolled on the floor and made the vaults ring with his piercing lamentations... Then he stood up and flung himself against the doors which barred his way, attempting to break them down with the weight of his body, tearing his flesh, bleeding profusely, before collapsing once more against the prison bars which he had not even begun to loosen. And it was only by his sobbing and weeping... by the buffetings of despair... that his downcast soul clung on to life.

There is no plight on this earth to be compared with that of a prisoner whose heart blazes with love. The fact that he is denied any means of knowing if his sentiments are requited immediately releases, in the most agonizing form, the dark demons of his passion. Cupid's darts, which in the world outside give such sweet pain, are now transformed into the sting of serpents and torment him. His mind is clouded by innumerable fancies. One moment uneasy, the next at peace, now trusting, now suspicious, fearing and desiring the truth, hating and loving the idol of his heart, forgiving her then believing her capable of the worst treachery, his soul, like the waves of a storm-tossed sea, is a soft and yielding thing into which every passion sinks, the better to consume it.

Assistance was forthcoming. But what a sorry service they did him by holding to his lips the bitter cup of life, of which all that now remained was gall!

Knowing that he must defend himself, and acknowledging that the burning desire to see Ernestine again which raged within him could only be satisfied by demonstrating his innocence, he decided to conduct his own defence. An investigation had begun, but since the case was too important for a lesser court like Nordkoping, it was decided that it should be heard before the Stockholm justices. There the prisoner was transferred... happy... if anyone can be happy in such cruel circumstances... for he had the consolation of breathing the same air which gave life to Ernestine.

'I shall be in the same city,' he said with satisfaction, 'and I may be able to let her know what has happened... they will certainly have kept the truth from her... I may even be able to see her! But come what may, there I shall be less exposed to the charges brought against me. I cannot believe that those who come into contact with Ernestine are not as pure as her own fine soul, for the light of her virtue shines on everyone around her... it is like the rays of the sun which gives life to the world... I have nothing to fear if I am where she is.'

Foolish lovers, such are your dreams! They are a consolation, and that is no small thing. But let us leave poor Herman to them and find out what was happening in Stockholm to the persons who interest us.

Ernestine, kept constantly amused and enrolled in a round of parties and excursions, had not, however, forgotten her dear Herman. To the new entertainments designed to turn her head she gave only her eyes; but her heart, still full of Herman, beat for him alone. She wished him there to share her pleasures, for they seemed insipid without him. She wanted him to be near, she saw him everywhere, and the illusion, a bubble invariably pricked, made the truth even more cruel. The poor girl was entirely ignorant of the lamentable condition to which the man who ruled her thoughts so despotically had been reduced. She had received only one letter from him, which he had written before the Hamburg merchants had arrived, and measures had been taken to ensure that thereafter she would receive no others. When she spoke of her anxieties, her father and the Senator blamed the delay on the press of important business for which the young man was responsible, and sweet Ernestine, whose delicate nature shrank from pain, allowed herself to be gently carried along by whatever seemed to calm her fears. If new worries surfaced, they soothed them in the same way, the Colonel in good faith and the Senator by deceiving her. But reassured she was, and meanwhile a pit for her to fall into was being dug beneath her feet.

Oxtiern also kept Sanders occupied and had introduced him to several ministers. This mark of esteem flattered the Colonel's pride and gave him the patience to wait patiently for the outcome of the promises of the Count, who constantly reminded him that however sincere he was himself in his determination to oblige him, everything at court took an unconscionably long time.

This dangerous, devious man, who, had he been able to succeed by other means than the crimes he planned would not have needed to stoop to them, made an effort from time to time to return to the language of love when he spoke to the young woman he was set on corrupting.

'I sometimes regret having given a helping hand,' he said one day to Ernestine. 'I sense that the power of your glance is imperceptibly undermining my resolve. With my honest self I want you to marry Herman, but in my heart I do not. Oh God! Why did the hand of nature invest so many graces in the adorable Ernestine and so much weakness in the heart of Oxtiern? I would serve you better were you less beautiful, or perhaps I should not be so much in love if you were not so inflexible!'

'Count,' said Ernestine in alarm, 'I thought you had left such feelings far behind you. I cannot believe that they still have some claim on your attention.'

'You are unjust to both of us if you think that the impression you make can ever fade or, alternatively, if you imagine that if that impression was made on my heart it will not last for ever!'

'But can it be consistent with honour? And was it not by a sacred vow that you promised to bring me to Stockholm only to help my father's prospects and hasten my marriage with Herman?'

'You always speak of Herman, Ernestine! Really! Will that unavoidable name never be expunged from your memory?'

'Of course not, Senator. I shall go on saying it for as long as the dear thought of the man who bears it inflames the heart of Ernestine. Perhaps this will make you understand that only death will put an end to it. But Count, why do you postpone the promises you made me? You said I should soon see the gentle and only object of my affections again. Why has he not come?'

'His accounting with Widow Scholtz—that is the likeliest reason for the delay you find so hard to bear.'

'And shall we have him once that business is done?'

'Yes. You shall see him, Ernestine... I promise to let you see him whatever the cost to me... whatever the place... You shall certainly see him... And what shall be the reward for all my efforts?'

'You will experience the pleasure of having made them, Count. To a kind heart, that is the best reward of all.'

'It comes at a high price, Ernestine, if it must be earned at the cost of the sacrifice which you demand. Do you think there are many people who would be capable of making it?'

'The greater the sacrifice, the greater the esteem in which I shall hold you.'

'Oh, esteem is too cold a word to be a proper return for the sentiments I have for you!'

'But if it is the only return you will get from me, should you not be satisfied with it?'

'Never, never!' said the Count, darting a furious look at the unfortunate creature... (Then getting up to leave) 'You do not know what sort of man you drive to despair, Ernestine... you are too blind... No, you do not know this heart that beats, you have no idea to what extremes your contempt and your disdain may lead it!'

It will not be difficult to believe that these last words struck alarm into Ernestine. She reported them at once to the Colonel who, still filled with confidence in the Senator's integrity, was far from persuaded by the interpretation Ernestine put upon them. The gullible Sanders, ambitious as ever, occasionally resuscitated the plan whereby the Count would be preferred to Herman. But his daughter invariably reminded him of his word. The honest, upright Colonel felt bound by it, yielded to Ernestine's tears, and swore to keep on reminding the Senator of the promises he had made to both of them, or else he would take his daughter back to

Nordkoping if he felt that Oxtiern had no intention of being sincere.

It was at this juncture that each of these good people, all too basely duped, received letters from Widow Scholtz, from whom they had parted on the best of terms. The letters apologized for Herman's silence, saying that he was in the best of health but, being extremely busy auditing an account in which there were certain irregularities which were attributable solely to his distress at being separated from the woman he loved, he was obliged to have recourse to the pen of his benefactress to send news to his dearest friends. Through her, he begged them not to be anxious, because before the week was out Madame Scholtz herself would bring him to Stockholm and Ernestine.

These letters went some way towards calming her, but were not entirely reassuring.

'It does not take long to write a letter,' she said. 'Why should Herman not bother to take the trouble? He should know I would have more confidence in a single word from him than in twenty letters from a woman we have every reason to mistrust.'

Sanders continued to reassure his daughter. Ernestine, naive and unsuspecting, yielded to the efforts the Colonel made to calm her, but then her anxieties would return to torture her mind, like red-hot pincers.

Meanwhile Herman's case proceeded. But the Senator, who saw the presiding judges often, had recommended they use extreme discretion. He had proved to them that if any hint of the trial were to get out, Herman's accomplices—those who were already in receipt of the moneys—would flee abroad if they had not done so already, and because of the precautionary measures they would take, none of the spoils would ever be recovered. This specious reasoning persuaded the magistrates to maintain the strictest silence. And all this was done in the very town where Ernestine and her father were residing, without either of them knowing and without there being the remotest possibility that they ever would.

Such, more or less, was how matters stood when, for the first time in his life, the Colonel was invited to dine with the Minister of War. Oxtiern could not accompany him, having, he said, twenty dinner guests himself on that day. But he did not leave Sanders ignorant of the fact that he had arranged the invitation personally and, when he told him of it, was very insistent that he must not refuse to go. The Colonel made up his mind not to be late, although the pernicious dinner would add nothing to his future happiness. And so he dressed with all dispatch, left Ernestine in Widow Plorman's care, and drove to the Minister's residence.

He had not been there an hour when Ernestine saw Widow Scholtz walk into her room. The formalities were brief.

'Be quick,' said her visitor, 'and we shall hurry round to Count Oxtiern's house. I have just left Herman there and rushed here to let you know that your benefactor and your intended both await your coming with equal impatience.'

'Herman?'

'That's right.'

'But why did he not come with you?'

'His first duty was to the Count. It was only proper that he should pay his respects. The Senator, who loves you, is standing down in the young man's favour. Surely you can see that Herman owes him a debt of gratitude?... Would it not be churlish not to acknowledge it?... But as you see, both have sent me here as a matter of the greatest urgency... Today is the day of many sacrifices, Mademoiselle,' Widow Scholtz continued, giving Ernestine a look of bogus encouragement. 'Come and you will see them all performed.'

The hapless girl, torn between her burning desire to run to the place where she had been told Herman was, and the fear of taking a serious risk by going to the Count's house alone in her father's absence, hesitated as to which course she should follow. And as Widow Scholtz continued to urge her, Ernestine decided that in the circumstances she should seek the advice of her Aunt Plorman and ask that she, or at least her cousin Sindersen, should accompany her. But the latter was not at home and, when consulted, Widow Plorman replied that the Senator's palace was far too respectable a destination for any young woman to fear anything by going there. She added that surely her niece knew what the house was like, since she had been there several times with her father, and that besides, since she would be going there with a person of the years and standing of Madame Scholtz there was clearly no danger. She added that she would have gladly joined the party if she had not, for ten years past, been made a prisoner in her own house by horrible sufferings which prevented her ever going out.

'But there is absolutely no risk, niece,' Madame Plorman went on. 'It will be perfectly safe for you go where you are wanted. I shall tell the Colonel the moment he gets back so that he may come to you at once.'

Ernestine, delighted by a piece of advice which accorded so completely with her own assessment, climbed eagerly into Widow Scholtz's coach, which bore them both to the palace of the Senator, who came out to the portico to greet them.

'Ernestine, you look charming,' he said, giving her his arm. 'Come and taste your triumph, savour the sacrifices which I and Madame here shall make, come and be convinced that in the hearts of good and kindly people generosity will always prevail over all other sentiments...'

Ernestine could no longer contain herself. Her heart raced with impatience, and if it is true that the prospect of happiness makes a woman more beautiful, then never was Ernestine more deserving of the tribute of the whole universe than at this moment... Yet a few discordant circumstances gave her cause for alarm and modified the sweet emotions which filled her heart. Although it was still the middle of the day, no footmen appeared anywhere in the house, which was filled with a lugubrious silence. No one spoke, all doors were shut carefully after they had gone through them, and the dimness increased the further they went. All these precautions so alarmed Ernestine that she was almost ready to faint when she reached the room where she was to be made welcome. At last she arrived. The room, very large, gave on to a public square outside. But the windows were shut tight on that side, and only one, which overlooked the rear of the house, was partially open and allowed a little sunlight to enter through the closed shutters. When Ernestine entered the room there was no one there. The defenceless girl hardly dared breathe, but seeing that her safety was dependent on her courage:

'Sir,' she said with considerable composure, 'what is the meaning of this? This empty house, the frightening silence, the doors you lock so carefully, the windows which let in so little light... all these precautions seem intended to intimidate me. Where is Herman?'

'Sit down, Ernestine,' said the Senator, motioning her to a chair between him and Widow Scholtz. 'Stay calm and listen to me. A great deal has happened, my dear, since you left Nordkoping.

Unfortunately, the man to whom you gave your heart has demonstrated that he was unworthy of it.'

'Heavens, you are frightening me!'

'Your Herman is nothing but an embezzler, Ernestine. We need to establish whether you had a hand in the theft of a large sum of money from Madame Scholtz. Suspicions have been voiced about you.'

'Count,' said Ernestine rising from her chair with as much dignity as firmness, 'this subterfuge is all too transparent... I realize how rash I have been... I am undone... I am in the power of my worst enemies... I cannot escape the fate that awaits me...'

Then, falling on her knees and raising her arms to heaven:

'Lord most high,' she exclaimed, 'I have no protector but Thee! Do not deliver me in my innocence into the hands of crime and wickedness!'

'Ernestine,' said Madame Scholtz, raising her to her feet and making her sit, despite her protests, on the chair she had vacated, 'this is no time for praying to God but for supplying answers. The Senator is not trying to trick you. Your Herman stole a hundred thousand ducats from me, and was about to run off with you when fortunately the facts came out. Herman has been arrested, but the money has not been recovered. He denies having taken it, and that is what makes people think it was already in your possession. Meanwhile Herman's position has taken a decided turn for the worse. Witnesses have testified against him. Several persons at Nordkoping saw him leave my house at night carrying bags under his coat. So his crime is proved beyond any doubt, and your Herman is in the custody of the law.'

Ernestine. 'Herman guilty! Ernestine under suspicion! And you believed all this, sir?... You actually believed it?'

Count. 'Ernestine, we have no time to discuss this business now or to think of anything except how to find the speediest solution. I did not mention the matter to you and tried to spare you unnecessary anxiety, and it was for that reason that I explored every avenue before resorting to the step I have taken today. You are a suspect, that is all they have against you, which is why I was able to ensure you were spared the horror and mortification of a prison cell. I owed it to your father and to you, and I did what was necessary. But as to Herman, he is guilty... and there is worse, my dear. I can scarce say the words without a shudder: he has been sentenced to death...'

Ernestine (turning pale). 'Herman, sentenced to death! But he is innocence itself!... Merciful heavens!'

'But there is a way out, Ernestine,' the Senator continued, supporting her in his arms, 'there always is... Resist my passion no longer, grant me now the favour I ask of you, and I shall go directly to the judges... They are there, Ernestine,' said Oxtiern, gesturing towards the square outside, 'they have met to conclude this sorry case... I will go at once. I shall hand them the hundred thousand ducats, I shall swear that the mistake was entirely mine, and Madame Scholtz, who will drop all charges against Herman, will further declare that in the audit they carried out together the money was entered twice. In short, I shall save your lover... I shall do more: I will keep the promise I gave you and within a week I shall make you his wife... Say the word, Ernestine, and remember that there is not a moment to lose. Consider the money I shall sacrifice... think of the crime of which you are suspected... of Herman's desperate predicament... of the happiness that will at last be yours if you satisfy my desires.'

Ernestine. 'What! Submit to such a horrible fate? Is this the price I must pay to cancel a crime which neither Herman nor I ever committed?'

Count. 'Ernestine, you are in my power. The thing you fear could happen without your actively submitting to me. In giving the man you love back to you in exchange for a... favour which I could obtain unconditionally, I am doing more for you than I need to. Time presses... One hour from now and it will be too late... Another hour and Herman will be dead and your reputation will not have been spared... Think on this: by refusing me, you doom your lover without saving your honour, while by sacrificing your honour, upon which people place an illusory value, you will save the life of a man who is precious to you... more, you will have him back instantly in your arms... You are as deluded as your virtue is false, and you cannot hesitate without being culpably weak... you cannot waver without being guilty of an undoubted crime. By consenting, all you will lose is a thing of imaginary worth... By refusing, you sacrifice a man, and that man, whom you send to his death, is the human being you love most in the whole world... Make up your mind, Ernestine, decide. I give you just five minutes more.'

Ernestine. 'My mind is made up, sir. It can never be right to commit a crime in order to prevent another. I know Herman well enough to be quite sure that he would not wish to have a life for which I should have paid with my honour, and even more certain that he would never marry me after I had been so shamed. I should make myself guilty without making him happier, I would be culpable without saving him, for he would surely not survive such a mountain of horrors and slander. So allow me to leave, sir. Do not behave any more like the criminal I already suspect you to be... I shall go to Herman and die at his side. I shall share his dreadful fate and at least will perish worthy of him. I would prefer to die virtuously than to live in shame...'

At this, the Count became extremely angry:

'Leave my house?' said he, aflame with love and rage. 'Escape before I have been satisfied? Do not hope, do not even think of it, dragon of virtue!... Thunderbolts will destroy the earth before I allow you to go free without first having served my appetites!' he cried, and he took the helpless girl in his arms...

Ernestine tried to defend herself... but in vain... Oxtiern had turned into a demented beast prepared to take the most unspeakable liberties...

'One moment... wait a moment...' said Widow Scholtz. 'She may be putting up this resistance because she still has doubts.'

'That may well be,' said the Senator. 'We must convince her.'

And taking Ernestine by the hand, he dragged her to one of the windows which overlooked the square and flung it open.

'There, will you believe it now?' said he. 'Look and you will see Herman and the scaffold on which he will die!'

And indeed there stood the bloody gallows and the wretched Herman, about to lose his life, kneeling at the feet of a confessor... Ernestine recognized him... she tried to cry out... she gave a violent start... but her faculties failed her... her senses abandoned her... and she fell in a lifeless heap.

Then all of Oxtiern's wicked plans were put into immediate execution... He seized the defenceless Ernestine and, giving no thought to the state to which she was reduced, dared consummate his crime, dared vent the extremes of his lust on a virtuous young woman unjustly abandoned by heaven to suffer the most horrible indignities. Ernestine was dishonoured before she regained her senses. At the same instant the sword of justice descended on Oxtiern's rival, and Herman was no more.

After receiving attention, Ernestine at last opened her eyes. The first word she uttered was 'Herman,' and her first wish was for a dagger... She stood up, returned to the ghastly window, which was still open, and would have thrown herself out of it but was prevented. She asked for her lover but was told that he was dead and that she alone was responsible for his death... She shuddered... Her mind began to wander, words that made no sense escaped from her lips... were interrupted by sobs... only the tears could not flow... and it was only then that she was aware that she had served as Oxtiern's prey... She looked at him with fury.

'So, blackguard, it was you,' she said, 'you who robbed me of both my honour and the man I loved?'

'Ernestine, all this can be put right,' said the Count.

'I know,' said Ernestine, 'and doubtless it will. But now may I leave? Is your lust sufficiently slaked?'

'Senator,' exclaimed Widow Scholtz, 'we cannot let the girl go... She will inform on us. What does it matter to us if the creature lives or not?... Let her die. With her dead, our lives will be safe.'

'No,' said the Count. 'Ernestine knows as well as we do that laying a complaint would not help her. She may have lost her lover, but she can still ensure that her father makes his fortune. If she keeps her mouth shut, then happiness may yet smile upon her.'

'A complaint, Senator? Me, lay a complaint? Madame here may imagine that it is what I would like to do. But no, there is one kind of outrage a woman should never complain of... She cannot do it without degrading herself, and her admissions, for which she would be forced to blush, would prove more damaging to her modesty than any redress she obtained would be satisfying to her vengeance. So, Senator, open the door for me. You may count on my complete discretion.'

'Ernestine, you shall go free... I say again: your fate is in your own hands.'

'I know,' replied Ernestine boldly, 'and it is to those hands that I look to guarantee it.'

'This is most unwise,' cried Widow Scholtz. 'Oh, Count, I should never have agreed to participate in a crime with you if I had believed you capable of such weakness.'

'Ernestine will not betray us,' said the Count. 'She knows that I love her still... she knows that marriage may be the price of her silence.'

'Oh, do not be afraid, you need fear nothing,' said Ernestine as she stepped into the coach which awaited her. 'I am far too anxious to salvage my honour to stoop to such low expedients... You will be content with those I shall adopt, Count. They will do honour to us both. Farewell.'

Ernestine drove home. Her way lay though the square where her lover had just perished. It took her through the crowd which had just feasted its eyes on that fearsome spectacle. Her courage sustained her, her resolve gave her strength. She arrived at her destination. Her father returned at the same time: the dastardly Oxtiern had taken good care to ensure that he was detained elsewhere for as long was required for him to commit his crime. He saw his daughter's dishevelled state... pale, with despair in her heart, but dry-eyed nonetheless, and with a resolute expression on her face and a firmness in her voice.

'Let us find a private room, father. I must speak with you.'

'Daughter, you make me tremble with apprehension... What has happened? You went out while I was absent... there is talk of a young man from Nordkoping who has been executed... I had misgivings as I drove back, I felt most disturbed. Explain yourself... there is death in my soul...'

'Listen to me, father... hold back your tears' (throwing herself into the Colonel's arms). 'We were not born to be happy, father. There are some people whom nature creates only so that they might stumble from one misfortune to another for the whole of the brief span they must spend on this earth. Not all individuals can lay claim to the same portion of happiness and must bow to the will of heaven. But at least you still have your daughter. She will be the comfort of your old age, she will be there for you to lean on. The unfortunate young man from Nordkoping you have heard about was Herman. He has just died on a gibbet, before my very eyes... Yes, father, I saw it... they wanted me to see it and I did... He died a victim of the jealousy of Widow Scholtz and the demented fury of Oxtiern... But that is not all, father. I wish that all I had to inform you of was the death of the man I loved, but there is something even more cruel to tell... Your daughter has been returned to you dishonoured... Oxtiern....

even as one of his victims was being sacrificed... the blackguard defiled the other.'

At this, Sanders sprang furiously to his feet:

'That is enough,' said he, 'I know where my duty lies. The son of the good friend of Charles XII does not need to be told how to deal with a villain! Daughter, within the hour either I shall be dead, or you shall have satisfaction.'

'No, father, no,' said Ernestine, preventing the Colonel from leaving. 'I insist, in the name of all that you hold most dear, that you do not attempt to take our revenge yourself. If I were unfortunate enough to lose you, can you think how horrible my fate would be? All alone, with no one to turn to... left to the tender mercies of those monsters... how long do you think it would be before they sacrificed me?... Live for my sake, father, for the sake of your dear daughter who is so unhappy and can only look to you for help and comfort... who has only in the whole wide world your hands to wipe away these tears... Listen, I have a plan. It involves only a small sacrifice, which may not even be necessary if my cousin Sindersen has a brave heart. His fear that my aunt may give us the preference in her will is the only reason for the coolness that exists between us. I shall dispel his apprehensions. I shall sign a paper formally renouncing the inheritance. I shall win him round to my side. He is young and courageous, a soldier like you. He will call on Oxtiern, he will wash away my insult with the blood of that scoundrel. But since we must have satisfaction, father, then should he succumb I would no longer restrain your arm. You would in turn seek out the Senator and avenge both the honour of your daughter and the death of your nephew. In this way, the rogue who deceived me will have two enemies instead of one, and surely we cannot have enough?'

'But, Ernestine, Sindersen is very young to go up against Oxtiern.'

'Do not be afraid, father. Traitors are invariably cowards, and to vanquish them is not difficult... not that I regard our victory easy... This arrangement... I insist on it... Father, I have certain claims on you which are authorized by my misfortune. Do not refuse the favour I beseech... I ask it on my knees.'

'If that is what you wish, then I consent,' said the Colonel, raising his daughter to her feet. 'And what persuades me to yield to your wishes is the certainty that in doing so I shall, as you say, multiply the number of enemies of the man who has dishonoured us both.'

Ernestine embraced her father and hurried away to find her cousin. She returned shortly afterwards.

'Sindersen has agreed, father,' she told the Colonel. 'But to spare his aunt's feelings he asks most insistently that you say nothing of this business. She would never forgive herself for the advice she gave me that I should go to the Count's, though she did so in good faith. So Sindersen takes the view that we should say nothing to Aunt Plorman. He himself will keep out of your way until the matter is concluded, and you must do likewise.'

'Good,' said the Colonel. 'Let him avenge us at once. I shall follow hard on his heels.'

Calm was restored and Ernestine went to bed greatly pacified, it seemed.

The next morning Count Oxtiern received a note written in a hand which he did not know. It contained only the following words:

> No heinous crime is committed but receives its punishment. No odious injustice is perpetrated but is avenged. No modest maid is dishonoured but costs the life of either the villain who seduced her or the man who seeks to avenge her. At ten o'clock this evening an officer in a red uniform will stroll by the port, with a sword under his arm. He hopes to meet you there. If you do not come the same officer will come to your house tomorrow and blow out your brains.

The letter was delivered by a valet out of livery, and since he had orders to return with a reply, the Count handed him the same note on which he had written these four words: 'I shall be there.'

But far too much was at stake for the wily Oxtiern not to want to know what had happened at Widow Plorman's after Ernestine had returned, and he had spared no expense in securing the means of finding out. He learned the identity of the officer who would wear red. He also discovered that the Colonel had ordered his personal valet to find him an English uniform, because he wished to be disguised when he followed the man who was to avenge his daughter, so that he would not be recognized by him and would be able to fly at once to his defence should he by chance be vanquished. This intelligence was more than Oxtiern needed to hatch out a new scene of horror.

Night fell. The darkness was intense. Ernestine informed her father that Sindersen would leave in one hour's time and, feeling near to prostration, begged leave to retire. The Colonel, only too happy to be alone, wished his daughter goodnight and prepared to follow the man who was to do battle for her. He left the house... He did not know how Sindersen would be dressed, for Ernestine had not shown him the challenge which had been issued. Anxious to observe the mystery on which the young man had insisted and to avoid rousing his daughter's suspicions, he had not wished to enquire. But what did it matter? He continued on his way. He knew where the duel was to be fought, and was sure he would recognize his nephew. He arrived at the place appointed. No one had arrived yet. He began to pace up and down. Then an unknown man approached him. He was unarmed and had removed his hat.

'Sir,' the man said, 'are you not Colonel Sanders?'

'I am.'

'Then prepare yourself. Sindersen has betrayed you. He will not come to fight the Count, who follows me here hard on my heels. His business therefore will be with you alone.'

'God be praised!' exclaimed the Colonel with a cry of joy. 'That is the very thing I wanted most.'

'If you please, do not speak a word,' the stranger continued. 'This place is not safe. The Senator has many friends who might try to separate you... and that is not what he wants: he wishes to give you full satisfaction... So without saying one word, you must attack with spirit the officer in red who will come to you from this direction.'

'Good,' said the Colonel. 'Now, leave me. I cannot wait to cross swords...'

The stranger withdrew. Sanders took two more turns around the square, and at last, in the gloom, saw the officer in red advancing valiantly towards him. He was in no doubt that it was Oxtiern and bore down on him at once, sword unsheathed, fearing that an attempt would be made to separate them. The soldier defended himself in the same manner, without uttering a word and with extraordinary courage. Finally his brave resistance yielded to the lusty attack of the Colonel, whose unfortunate adversary fell mortally wounded to the ground. At the same time a woman's cry was heard, and the sound of it pierced Sanders's very soul... He bent over his opponent... he saw a face very different from that of the man he had believed he had been fighting... Great God!... He recognized his daughter!... For it was she, the courageous Ernestine, who had resolved to perish or take her own revenge, and who now, in a pool of blood, lay dying by her father's hand.

'This is a most sorry day for me!' cried the Colonel. 'Ernestine! It is you whom I have sacrificed to our honour!... A tragic mistake!... But who could have done this?'

'Father,' said Ernestine in a weak voice as she clung to the Colonel, 'I did not know it was you. Forgive me, father, for taking up arms against you... will you grant me your pardon?'

'Oh God! But my hand has dug your grave! Oh my darling girl, how many poisoned arrows must heaven shoot at us to bring us down?'

'All this is once more the work of the dastardly Oxtiern... A stranger approached me, sent by the monster. He said that to avoid our being separated I was to keep the strictest silence and attack the man who would be dressed as you are, that man being the Count... I believed him! Was there ever such foul treachery?... I am dying... but at least I die in your arms. Such a death is the sweetest I could be granted after all the ills which have overwhelmed me. Kiss me, father, and receive the final adieu of your unhappy Ernestine.'

With these words, she breathed her last. Sanders bathed her with his tears... but thoughts of vengeance pushed out grief. He left the bloody corpse, determined to seek redress through the law... and in the process either die or expose Oxtiern... for now he would work only through the justices... he must not, could not commit himself further with a blackguard who would surely have him murdered rather than stand and face him. Still covered in his daughter's blood, the Colonel threw himself on the mercy of the magistrates. He gave an account of the appalling chain of misfortunes he had endured, and revealed the full extent of the Count's infamy... He roused their pity and their indignation, and above all insisted on showing them the extent to which the tactics employed by the villain he now accused had misled them in reaching the sentence they had passed on Herman... He was given assurances that he would be avenged.

Despite the high standing the Senator believed he enjoyed, he was arrested that same night. Either because he believed he was safe from the consequences of his criminal actions, or because he had been misled by his spies, he was resting quietly at his house. He was discovered in the arms of Widow Scholtz, and both monsters were congratulating themselves on the success of the odious scheme by which they thought they had secured their revenge. The pair were led away to a felons' prison. The case was tried with the utmost rigour, in circumstances of the strictest justice. When questioned, the accused gave contradictory testimony and convicted each other... Herman's name was cleared and Widow Scholtz was sentenced to pay for her infamous crimes on the very scaffold to which she had sent an innocent man.

The Senator was given the same sentence. But the King mitigated the horror of the verdict by ordering him to be banished forever to the bottom of these mines.

Out of the estate of both guilty parties, Gustavus offered the Colonel a pension of ten thousand ducats and the rank of general in his service. But Sanders refused to accept anything.

'Sire,' he said to the monarch, 'you are too kind. If it is to reward my past services that you offer me these favours, they are too large and I cannot accept them... If it is to make up for the losses I have incurred, they are too small, Sire. Wounded hearts cannot be cured with gold or honours... I beg your Majesty to leave me some time to myself to grieve. Then soon I shall petition your Majesty for the only favour which would be fitting for me.'

'There, sir,' Falkenheim broke off, 'you have the details you asked for. I am sorry that we shall soon be forced to see this man Oxtiern once more. He will sicken you.'

'No one is more indulgent than I am, sir,' I replied, 'of all the errors into which our physical constitution leads us. I see wrong-doers who move among decent people as being like the anomalies with which Nature varies the beauties which ornament the universe. But this Oxtiern, and particularly Widow Scholtz, presumed too far on the understanding which human weakness may claim from the philosophers as their right. Worse crimes could not be imagined. In the conduct of both there are circumstances which elicit a shudder of disgust. To abuse a defenceless girl while the man she loved is killed... then to have her slain by her own father... these are refinements of horror which make a man feel ashamed to be human when he reflects that he must unfortunately share that epithet with such odious villains.'

I had no sooner spoken these words than Oxtiern appeared, bringing his letter. He was too sharp-eyed not to read in my face that I had just been informed of his misdeeds. He looked at me.

'Sir,' he said to me in French, 'pity me. Immense wealth... a noble name... reputation... those are the sirens which led me astray. Yet I have learned from my misfortune, have felt remorse, and am now fit to live among men without harming them or making them fear us.'

The unfortunate Count accompanied these words with a few tears which it was impossible for me to share. My guide took his letter, promising to see it was delivered, and we were making ready to leave when we saw the street filling with a crowd which bore down on the place where we were. We stopped. Oxtiern was still with us. Gradually we made out two men who were talking heatedly and who, on seeing us, headed in our direction. Oxtiern recognized them both.

'Oh God!' he exclaimed. 'What is this?... Colonel Sanders escorted by the chaplain to the mine... yes, that is our pastor who is heading this way and bringing the Colonel with him... Their business is with me, gentlemen... But how can this be?... Has my implacable enemy come looking for me even in the bowels of the earth? Is not my cruel suffering sufficient to satisfy him?...'

Oxtiern had not finished when the Colonel spoke to him.

'You are free, sir,' he said the moment he was near enough, 'and it is to the man you more grievously offended than any other on the face of the earth that you owe your pardon... Here it is, Senator, I have brought it with me. The King offered me promotions, honours... I refused them all... I wanted only your freedom... I have obtained it. You may come with me.'

'Oh generous mortal!' cried Oxtiern, 'can this be true?... I, at liberty... given my liberty by you?... By you, who even if you deprived me of my life could not punish me as I deserve to be punished?...'

'I was convinced you would now think along such lines,' said the Colonel. 'That is why I supposed there was no risk in restoring to you a privilege which it has become impossible for you to abuse any more... Besides, do your sufferings ease mine? Can I be happy because you are unhappy? Does your captivity cancel the blood spilt by your barbarities? I should be as cruel as you, and as unjust, if I thought so. Does imprisoning a man compensate society for the injuries he has done it?... That man must be freed if we want him to make amends, for when he is so kindly treated no man will refuse to atone, since all men would rather choose to do good than be forced to languish in chains. The most punitive arrangements devised in some nations by despots, and the rigour of the law in others, are disavowed by men of goodwill...* Go, Count, leave this place. I repeat: you are free.'

Oxtiern was about to throw himself into the arms of his benefactor: 'Sir,' said Sanders coldly as he pushed him away, 'there is no reason for gratitude, indeed, I have no wish to see you so grateful to me for doing something which I did solely for myself... Let us leave this place now. I am even more anxious than you to see you out of it, so that I may explain everything.'

Sanders, observing that we were with Oxtiern and having enquired who we were, invited us to go up to the surface with the Count and himself. We accepted. Oxtiern went off with the Colonel to attend to formalities connected with his release. Our weapons were returned to us and we were all hauled up.

'Gentlemen,' said Sanders once we were on the surface, 'would you be so good as to act as witnesses to what remains to me to communicate to the Count? You saw that I did not tell him everything in the mine, there were too many spectators...'

And as we continued to walk on, we soon found ourselves skirting a hedge which hid us from prying eyes. Then the Colonel, grabbing the Count by the collar, cried:

'Senator, now is the time for you to give me satisfaction. I hope you have the courage not to refuse me and that you also have enough wit to realize that my chief motive for doing what I have just done was the hope of a duel to the death.'

Falkenheim attempted to act as mediator and tried to separate the two opponents.

'Sir,' barked the Colonel, 'you are aware of the outrages I have suffered at the hands of this man. The shade of my dead daughter cries out for blood, and one of us shall not leave this spot alive. Gustavus has been informed, he knows what I have in mind—by granting me this villain's freedom, he clearly withheld his disapproval. So please let us get on with it, sir.'

And the Colonel, throwing his coat on the ground, drew his sword... Oxtiern did likewise. But he had no sooner taken his guard than he reversed his sword with his right hand and with his left held the point of the Colonel's. Then, falling on one knee, he offered him the hilt of his weapon.

'Gentlemen,' he said, looking in our direction, 'I take you both as witnesses of my action. I want each of you to know that I am not worthy of the honour of fighting with this respectable gentleman, but that I put my life in his hands to make free use of it, though I beg him to end it... Take my sword, Colonel, take it, I surrender it. Here is my heart. Drive your blade into it. I will help direct you to the target. Do not hesitate, I insist, and deliver the earth here and now of a monster who has been a stain upon it for too long.'

Sanders, surprised by Oxtiern's gesture, called on him to defend himself.

'I will not, and if you refuse to use the blade which I am holding,' Oxtiern replied without flinching and directing the point of Sanders's sword at his bare chest, 'if you do not use it to extinguish my life, then I tell you, Colonel, I shall run myself through even as you watch.'

'Count, blood must be shed, it must, I tell you!'

'I know,' said Oxtiern, 'and that is why I present my breast to you. Hurry now and do the deed: only from there must that blood flow.'

'This is not conduct that I can countenance,' resumed Sanders, as he attempted to free his sword. 'I must punish your villainy according to the laws of honourable combat.'

'You are an honourable man, and I am not worthy to accept such a challenge,' replied Oxtiern. 'But since you will not take your satisfaction as your duty requires, then I shall spare you the trouble...'

With these words he threw himself on to the Colonel's sword, which he had continued to grip in his hand, and blood spurted from his entrails. But the Colonel drew back his sword and cried:

'That will do, Count... Your blood has been spilled, I am satisfied. May heaven complete your punishment, for I have no wish to act as your executioner.'

'Then let us shake hands, sir,' said Oxtiern, who was losing a great deal of blood.

'No,' said Sanders. 'I can forgive your crimes, but I cannot be your friend.'

We made haste to bind up the Count's wound. The generous Sanders helped us.

'And now,' he told the Senator, 'now you may enjoy the freedom I have given back to you. Try, if you can, to make up for all the crimes you so wittingly committed by doing good deeds. Or if you do not, I shall answer to the whole of Sweden for the error I myself shall have perpetrated by handing back to her a monster of which she had already been delivered. Gentlemen,' continued Sanders, turning to Falkenheim and me, 'I have made the necessary arrangements. The carriage you will find at the inn which lies down that road was meant for Oxtiern alone, but it is large enough to take you both back. My horses are waiting for me in the opposite direction. I shall say farewell. I ask for your word of honour that you will give the King an account of what you have just observed.'

Once more Oxtiern attempted to throw himself into the arms of his liberator. He begged him to return his friendship, to live in his house, to share his fortune...

'Sir,' said the Colonel, rejecting his overtures, 'I have told you. I can accept from you neither benefits nor friendship, but I do insist upon virtuous conduct: do not make me regret what I have done... You say you wish to console me for my sorrows. The surest way of doing so is to change your ways. Every good action which, from my place of retirement, I hear you have committed will help to erase the deep and painful hurts which your crimes have engraved upon my heart. If you persist in your evil, each new piece of villainy you commit will conjure before my eyes the image of the daughter who, thanks to you, died by my own hand, and you will plunge me into despair. Farewell, let us part, Oxtiern. And pray God we never meet again...'

And so saying, the Colonel walked away... Oxtiern, in tears, attempted to follow, dragging himself after him... We stopped him and carried him, almost unconscious, to the carriage, which soon brought us back to Stockholm.

For a month the poor man hovered between life and death. At the end of this time he asked us if we would accompany him to the King, who asked for an account of all that had happened.

'Oxtiern,' said Gustavus to the Senator, 'you see how crime humbles a man, how it demeans him. Your rank, your fortune, your birth, all these advantages set you above Sanders, but his virtues have raised him to a height you will never attain. Enjoy the favours which, thanks to him, have been restored to you, Oxtiern, they have my blessing. I am convinced that after learning this lesson either you will punish yourself before I learn of whatever new crimes you commit, or that you will never again allow yourself to stoop so low as to perpetrate any.'

The Count threw himself at the feet of his sovereign, and swore that henceforth his conduct would be irreproachable.

He has kept his word. By many a deed, each finer and more generous than the one before, he has shown all Sweden that he has made amends for the errors of his ways, and his example has demonstrated to that wise nation that it is not always by despotic methods and cruel, vengeful punishments that men may be reclaimed and contained.

Sanders returned to Nordkoping. There he ended his allotted span in solitude, shedding tears each day for the hapless daughter he had loved so much, and finding his sole comfort for her loss in the flattering reports he heard daily of the man whose chains he had removed.

'O virtue,' he would sometimes exclaim, 'perhaps all these things had necessarily to come to pass to bring Oxtiern back to Thy temple! If that is so, I take comfort. His crimes will have brought grief only to me, but his good works shall benefit the many.'*

THE COUNTESS OF SANCERRE

or HER DAUGHTER'S RIVAL

An Anecdote of the Court of Burgundy

CHARLES THE BOLD, Duke of Burgundy, ever the enemy of Louis XI and perpetually embroiled in plans of revenge and ambition, had enrolled virtually all the knights in his states in his retinue and kept them at his side on the banks of the Somme.* There, with no other thought than to conquer or die and be at all times worthy of their leader, they forgot in his service the pleasures of their own domains. The courts of Burgundy were sorry places, and their chateaux deserted. Absent from the glorious tournaments of Dijon and Autun were the valiant knights who had once made them glorious. Their beautiful ladies, now neglected, no longer took pains to make themselves attractive, since there was no one to attract. They feared for the lives of the warriors they loved. Now only anxiety and worry were to be seen on faces once so radiant and so proud in better days, when so many brave champions had paraded their skill and courage in the lists wearing the favours of their consorts.

When he had left to follow his liege lord by enrolling under his flag and thus prove his zeal and loyalty, the Count of Sancerre,* one of Charles's finest generals, had urged his wife to devote herself exclusively to raising their daughter Amélie. She should, furthermore, have no qualms about actively fostering the tender affection young Amélie felt for the lord of the manor of Monrevel, who would marry her one day after worshipping her since childhood. Monrevel was then twenty-four years of age and had already undertaken several campaigns with the Duke. To mark his forthcoming marriage, he had newly obtained permission to remain in Burgundy, but his youthful spirit needed all the love which burned in him not to chafe at the delay which this arrangement meant for the advancement of his career at arms. But Monrevel, the handsomest knight of his century, the most engaging and the bravest, was as accomplished in love as he was in war. Favoured by the graces and the god of battle, he robbed the latter of the tribute demanded by the former and was turn by turn about crowned by the laurels which Bellona* heaped on him and decked with the myrtle which Cupid hung upon his brow.

And who more than Amélie deserved the moments which Monrevel stole from Mars? Words must fail anyone who would describe her... Indeed, how could one even begin to evoke that slender, supple figure whose every movement was grace personified, or that delicate and delightful face whose every feature expressed a world of feelings? But the beauty of this divine creature who had only just turned fifteen lay even more wondrously in her many virtues... candour, kindness, filial love... so that it was impossible to say what made Amélie the more enchanting, the qualities of her nature or the charms of her person.

But how could it be, alas, that a daughter such as this could have been born to a mother who was so cruel and possessed of so dangerous a character? Behind a figure that was still beautiful and a face noble and regal in its expression, the Countess of Sancerre hid a jealous, haughty, vindictive nature capable, in brief, of all the crimes to which passion may lead.

She was only too notorious at the court of Burgundy for the laxity of her morals and her love affairs, and there were few mortifications which she had spared her husband.

It was not without envy that such a mother observed the charms of her daughter grow before her very eyes, nor was it without a secret pang that she saw that Monrevel loved her. All she had managed to achieve thus far had been to ensure that what the young woman felt for Monrevel remained unspoken. Against the Count's wishes, she had always made her daughter promise not to admit her feelings for the husband her father had chosen for her. This astonishing mother, whose heart burned so fiercely for the man her daughter loved, felt it was some consolation that she had been able to make sure that he knew nothing of a passion which she took as a personal affront. But if she kept Amélie's desires firmly under control, as much could not be said of her own, and her eyes would long since have left Monrevel in no doubt, had that young warrior wished to heed what they said... and if he had not believed that being loved by anyone but Amélie would have been an affront rather than a joy.

For the last month, following her husband's orders, the Countess had welcomed young Monrevel to her chateau. During that time her every waking moment had been designed to conceal her daughter's feelings and make her own all too clear. But although Amélie remained silent, although she kept her feelings in check, Monrevel suspected that the arrangement made by the Count of Sancerre was in no way displeasing to her. He even allowed himself to think that Amélie would have looked with regret upon any other man who came forward hoping to make her his some day.

'Why is it, Amélie,' Monrevel said to her in one of those rare moments when he was not transfixed by the jealous gaze of Madame de Sancerre, 'how can it be that, although we have both been promised that one day we shall be husband and wife, you are not even allowed to tell me if the prospect pleases you or whether I may count myself happy to know it does not displease you? Imagine! The suitor who thinks only of how to make you happy is forbidden to know if he may even aspire to do so!'

But Amélie was content simply to gaze tenderly upon Monrevel. She sighed, but returned to her mother unaware of all she would have to fear from her if the feelings of her heart should ever be expressed by her lips.

Matters stood thus when one day a courier arrived at the chateau of Sancerre bringing news that the Count had died fighting under the walls of Beauvais on the very day the siege was lifted.* Lucenai, one of the Count's knights, wept as he conveyed this intelligence, which was accompanied by a letter from the Duke of Burgundy to the Countess. He asked her pardon if his current difficulties prevented his expanding on the consolations which he believed he owed her, and expressly enjoined her to follow her husband's wishes exactly in the matter of the union which the general had planned for his daughter and Monrevel, to proceed immediately with the wedding, and then, two weeks after the marriage had been consummated, to return the young hero to him since he could not, given the current state of affairs, deprive his army of a warrior as brave as Monrevel.

The Countess went into mourning, but said nothing of what Charles had urged in his letter. She was too opposed to his wishes even to mention the matter in public. She sent Lucenai away and exhorted her daughter more earnestly than ever to disguise her feelings, even to repress them entirely, since there were no longer any circumstances which required her to face a marriage... which would now never take place.

Once these measures had been taken, the jealous Countess considered herself free of anything which stood in the way of the unbridled passion she felt for the man who loved her daughter. She now occupied her mind entirely with discovering ways of cooling the young man's ardour for Amélie and of setting his heart ablaze for her own person.

Her first step was to intercept all the letters which Monrevel might write to Charles's army, and to detain him under her roof, keeping his love dangling on a string and leaving him a vague and distant hope which, thwarted at every turn, would keep him there and ensure that he grew more and more despondent. Then, having done so much to create his state of mind, she would exploit it to win him slowly round and make him see herself in a more favourable light. For, cunning woman that she was, she imagined that rancour would give her what she would never get from love.

Once she had made sure that no letter could leave the chateau without first being brought to her, the Countess began to spread rumours. She told everyone, and even darkly intimated as much to Monrevel, that when Charles the Bold had sent news of her husband's death he had urged her to arrange the marriage of her daughter with the Lord of Salins, whom he ordered to come to Sancerre where the match would be made. To Monrevel she added conspiratorially that such an eventuality would certainly not put Amélie's nose out of joint, since she had been smitten with Salins for the past five years. Having thus twisted the knife in the young man's heart, she sent for her daughter and told her that all her efforts were purposely aimed at detaching Monrevel from her. She urged her to support her in this matter, for she was absolutely opposed to the marriage, and said that once this was understood it would be better to find some excuse (such as the one she was using) than make a sudden break for which there was no obvious reason. But, she added, her daughter would not be any the worse off because, in exchange for this small sacrifice, she promised to leave her absolutely free to make whatever choice of husband she liked.

On hearing these cruel orders, Amélie tried to hold back her tears. But nature, stronger than prudence, forced her to go down on her knees to the Countess. She begged her, by all that she held most dear, not to part her from Monrevel but to carry out the wishes of a father she had adored, and whose loss she was being made to regret most bitterly.

This excellent young woman did not shed a single tear, but that it splashed salt on to her mother's heart.

'Well now,' said the Countess, making an effort to be mistress of herself, the better to enable her to discover her daughter's true sentiments, 'am I to take it that your misplaced feelings are so strong that you cannot sacrifice them? And if your Monrevel had suffered the same fate as your father, you would presumably have mourned him likewise?'

'Oh Madame,' replied Amélie, 'pray do not paint such a painful picture! Had Monrevel perished, I should soon have followed him. You must not think that my father was not any the less dear to me, and my sorrow at losing him would have been eternal, save for the hope that some day my tears would be stopped by the hand of the husband he had chosen for me. If I have gone on living it was for that husband; it was solely on his account that I have overcome the despair to which I was reduced by the terrible news we have lately received. Is it your wish that my heart should be rent by so many cruel jolts at once?'

'That is all very well,' said the Countess, who sensed that brutal methods would succeed only in stiffening the resistance of a daughter whom her plans made it necessary to humour, 'but if you cannot conquer your feelings you can still go on pretending to behave as I propose. Tell Monrevel you love Salins. It will be a way of finding out if his feelings for you are sincere. The only way of knowing where you truly stand with a lover is to unsettle him by making him jealous. If Monrevel becomes angry and deserts you, would you not be relieved to know you were a simpleton to love him?'

'But what happens if his feelings become stronger than ever?'

'In that case I might let you marry him. Surely you know the many claims you have upon my heart?'

And sweet Amélie, comforted by these last words, continued to kiss the hands of the mother who betrayed her, who in reality regarded her as her most mortal enemy... and who, while pouring healing salve on to her daughter's uneasy heart, nurtured in her own nothing but hatred and foul plans for revenge.

Meanwhile Amélie undertook to do as she was advised. Not only did she agree to pretend to love Salins, but she even promised to use this ploy to test Monrevel's heart to the limit, with the sole proviso that her mother would not take matters too far, but would call a halt when they were both convinced of Monrevel's love and constancy. Madame de Sancerre promised everything that was asked of her, and a few days later observed to Monrevel that it seemed most strange to her that, since he could no longer have any reasonable hope of marrying her daughter, he should wish to bury himself in Burgundy for such a lengthy period of time while the rest of the province was away fighting under Charles's banner. And as she said this, she adroitly allowed him to catch sight of the last lines of the Duke's letter which said, as we know: 'You will return Monrevel to me, Madame, for given the current state of my affairs, I cannot dispense with the services of so courageous an officer for long.' But the deceitful Countess was most careful not to let him see any more.

'So, Madame,' said Monrevel despairingly, 'it is true that you intend to sacrifice me. It is settled, then, that I must give up all thought of a delightful prospect which filled my life with such sweet anticipation.'

'In reality, Monrevel, had the plan been put into practice, the result would have been misery. Is not a man like you the last person who should marry a faithless wife? If Amélie ever allowed you to hope, then she most certainly deceived you, for her love for Salins is only too real.'

'Alas, Madame!' the young hero went on, with tears in his eyes, 'I ought never to have believed that Amélie loved me, I agree. But how could I ever have imagined she loved another man?'

And moving quickly from sorrow to despair, he continued angrily:

'No, no! She must not think she can abuse my trusting nature. It is beyond my power to endure such insults. Since she does not love me, since I now have nothing to lose, why should I set any limits on my vengeance?... I shall seek out Salins. I shall follow the rival who offends me, the man I hate, to the ends of the earth. He will pay for this affront with his life, or I shall lose mine by his hand.'

'No, Monrevel!' exclaimed the Countess. 'No, I cannot in all prudence permit such things! If you are rash enough to entertain ideas of this sort, it would be better if you went back to Charles, for I am expecting Salins to arrive here in a few days and I cannot allow you both to meet under my roof... Unless, however,' continued the Countess with a seeming afterthought, 'you ceased to be a danger to him by mastering your feelings. Now, Monrevel... if your eye had fallen on another person... I should have no reason to fear your presence in my chateau and I would be the first to urge you to remain here on an extended visit...'

Then, continuing immediately where she had left off and looking at Monrevel with eyes inflamed by passion, she said:

'Tell me, is Amélie the only woman under this roof who has the good fortune to please you? How little you must know of the feelings of those around you if you think that she is the only person here capable of having any idea of your true worth! How can you imagine that there are any solid feelings in the heart of a child?... Do girls of her age know what they think?... Do they know who they love?... Believe me, Monrevel, to love well calls for a little more experience. Is seduction conquest? Can you speak of conquering if your opponent is incapable of self-defence?... Oh, is not victory more sweet when those you have in your sights know all the ruses which might save them, but defend themselves against your attacks with only their heart and capitulate while seeming to resist?'

'Oh Madame,' interjected Monrevel who could see only too well where the Countess was leading, 'I do not know what qualities are required of anyone who would love well. But this I do know: Amélie, and she alone, has all the attributes which can make me worship her, and I shall never love anyone else but her in the world.'

'In that case, I pity you,' replied Madame de Sancerre caustically. 'Not only because she does not love you, but also because of your absolute certainty that your heart is immovable, I have no other choice but to separate you for ever.'

Having uttered these terrible words, she left Monrevel abruptly.

It would be difficult to convey the young man's state of mind in words. He was stricken by grief but also assailed in turn by anxiety, jealousy, and a thirst for revenge. He did not know to which of these sentiments he should give the most vehement expression, for he was imperiously solicited by all of them. Eventually he hastened to find Amélie.

'I have never stopped loving you for one moment,' he exclaimed, bursting into tears. 'I cannot believe it!... You have betrayed me!... Another man will make you happy... Another man will deprive me of the only possession for which, had I been emperor of the world, I would have surrendered my crown!... Amélie!...

Amélie! Is it true that you are unfaithful and that it is Salins who is to have you?'

'I am angry that you should have been told, Monrevel,' replied Amélie who was determined to obey her mother, not only to avoid making her angry but also to discover for certain if the young man loved her truly. 'But even though the secret of what must inevitably be is now out, I most certainly do not deserve your bitter recriminations. Since I never gave you grounds for hope, how can you accuse me of betraying you?'

'That is only too true, cruel girl, and I admit it. I never could kindle in your heart the faintest spark of the fire which consumed me. It was because for one moment I judged your soul by mine that I dared suspect you of a wrong which only love can cause... and you never loved me. Of what, Amélie, do I therefore complain? I accept that you have not betrayed me, that you have not sacrificed me. But you despise my love... you have made me the unhappiest man alive.'

'Really, Monrevel, I cannot conceive, given how unclear the situation was, how you can make so much fuss about love.'

'But were we not to be married?'

'It was what some people wanted. But was that a reason why I should want it? Must our hearts reflect the wishes of our parents?'

'And I would have made you unhappy?'

'When it came to the day, I would have let you see what was in my heart, and you would not have forced me to go through with it.'

'Merciful God, there I have my quietus! I shall leave you... I must go away... and it is you who delight in breaking the heart of a man whose greatest wish was to love you all his days! Well, I shall remove myself from your sight, faithless girl. I shall rejoin the Duke and find some swift means of eliminating myself from your presence permanently. Reduced to despair because I have lost you, I shall die at his side on the field of glory!'

And so saying, Monrevel strode away. Amélie had made a supreme effort of will to submit to her mother's intentions. Now that there was no reason to maintain the pretence, she burst into tears the moment she was alone.

'Oh Monrevel, I love you so! What must you think of Amélie?' she exclaimed. 'What sentiment will now replace in your heart all the feelings which responded to my love? How you must blame me, no doubt, and how richly I deserve your reproaches! I never said I loved you, it is true... But my eyes surely spoke volumes. If I delayed telling you out of prudence, my heart was still no less set on letting it be shouted abroad some day... O Monrevel!... Monrevel! What torture it is to be a woman in love who dares not admit her feelings to the man best qualified to kindle them in her heart... a woman who is forced to act a part... to substitute indifference for the emotions which consume her!'

The Countess came upon Amélie at this desperate juncture.

'I have done what you asked, Madame,' she told her. 'Monrevel is in despair. What else do you want?'

'I want this pretence to go on,' replied Madame de Sancerre. 'I want to see how strongly Monrevel is attached to you... Listen to me, daughter: he has never met his rival... Clotilde, the dearest of all the women who attend me, has a young cousin of the same age and figure as Salins. I shall have him brought to the chateau. He will be taken for the man who, so we claim, has loved you for six years. But his presence here will be a secret. You will only see him in private and seemingly without my knowledge... Monrevel will merely have suspicions... suspicions which I shall take good care to nurture, and then we shall be able make up our minds when we see his love driven to desperation.'

'But Madame,' replied Amélie, 'what is the point of all this pretence? You need have no doubt about Monrevel's feelings. He has just given me the fullest assurance of his sentiments, and I believe him with all my heart.'

'I regret having to tell you this,' the wicked woman went on, still keeping to her ignoble plan, 'but I have received news from the army that Monrevel is very lacking in the virtues of a chivalrous, valiant knight... It pains me to say it, but his courage has been questioned. I realize that the Duke is mistaken in this matter, but the facts are undeniable... he was seen to run away at Montlhéry.'*

'He, Madame?' exclaimed Mademoiselle de Sancerre. 'How could he be capable of displaying such weakness? You must not think it, you have been misled. It was Monrevel who slew Brezé...[1] He, run away?... I would not believe it if I saw it with my own eyes!... No, Madame, he set out from this chateau to take part in the battle. You

[1] Pierre de Brezé, Grand Seneschal of Normandy. He commanded Louis XI's advance guard on the day he lost his life.*

had allowed him to kiss my hand and this same hand pinned a bow of ribbon to his helmet... He told me he would be invincible... He carried my image engraved on his heart and he cannot possibly have dishonoured it... nor did he do so.'

'I know', said the Countess, 'that the first reports were to his advantage. You were kept in ignorance of those which came later... The Seneschal did not die by his hand: twenty soldiers saw Monrevel run away... But what difference can one more test make to you, Amélie? No blood will be spilt, for I shall put a stop to it before it comes to that... If Monrevel is a coward, would you wish to give him your hand? Besides, just remember that this is a matter which will be decided according to my good pleasure and that I have every right to impose conditions on you. The Duke now says that he is opposed to your marrying Monrevel and has asked for him to be returned. Now if, despite all this, I do indeed give way to your wishes, at least you should give some ground to mine.'

And so saying, the Countess walked out of the room, leaving her daughter facing fresh uncertainties.

'Monrevel, a coward?' Amélie said to herself through her tears. 'No, I shall never believe it... it cannot be... he loves me... have I not seen him with my own eyes expose himself to the dangers of the lists and, sure in the knowledge that I would reward him with a glance, vanquish every opponent who went up against him?... Those glances, which gave him courage, accompanied him across the plains of France. I was everywhere he looked, he felt my eyes on him as he went into battle. His bravery is as genuine as his love for me is sincere, and both these virtues are surely most generously present in a soul which will never be touched by anything impure... But no matter. It is my mother's wish and I will obey... I will say nothing, I will keep my heart hidden from the man who owns it entirely, but I shall never have any suspicion about his.'

Several days went by, during which the Countess prepared her stratagems and Amélie continued to play the role forced on her, however uneasy it made her feel. Finally Madame de Sancerre sent word to Monrevel that he was to come to her when she was alone, since she had something important to tell him... She had made up her mind once and for all to state her feelings at their meeting, so that she would have no regrets if Monrevel, by resisting her advances, drove her to commit criminal actions.

'Chevalier,' she said as soon as she saw him enter her presence, 'since you must surely now be as certain of my daughter's contempt as of your rival's happiness, I feel I must find some other explanation for your extended stay at Sancerre, when your commanding officer has asked for you and wants you at his side. So please speak frankly and tell me what it is that detains you here... Would it be the same reason, Monrevel, as the one which also makes me want to keep you with me?'

The young officer had long suspected that the Countess loved him, yet not only had he never mentioned the matter to Amélie but, bitterly regretting being the cause of it, he had also tried to hide it from himself. Pressed hard by the question which was now too clear for him to be in any doubt, he blushed and replied:

'Madame, you know what gossamer threads hold me here. If you would only condescend to tie them tighter and not seek to snap them, I would surely be the happiest man on earth...'

Perhaps it was a pretence, perhaps it was pride, but the Lady of Sancerre took his answer to refer to herself.

'My handsome, my sweet,' she said and motioned him to come nearer to where she was sitting, 'those threads shall be tied together whenever you wish... They have too long held my heart captive. They shall adorn my hands when you can show me how much you want them. Today I have no attachment, and if I should wish to lose my freedom a second time, then you know very well with whom I would do so...'

Monrevel shuddered when he heard these words, and the Countess, who did not miss the smallest of his reactions, now gave vent, like some harpy, to her unrestrained passion. In the most uninhibited terms she berated him for the indifference with which he had responded to her feelings.

'How could you blind yourself to the emotions which your glance ignited? Ingrate! How could you not know?' she exclaimed. 'Has a single day gone by since you were a boy when I did not openly parade my feelings, which you now treat with such disdain? Was there a knight at Charles's court who attracted me as much as you? I was proud of your triumphs, I wept for your disappointments: did you ever win a crown of laurels which my hand did not adorn with myrtle? Did your mind ever formulate a single thought, but that I knew instantly what it was? Did your heart experience a feeling which I did not share? Fêted wherever I went, having all Burgundy at my feet, I was surrounded by admirers and intoxicated by the sweet smell of success, and yet all my thoughts were of Monrevel, Monrevel had the monopoly of them and I despised everyone who was not Monrevel... And when I worshipped you, you turned your faithless eyes away... being head-over-heels in love with a girl who was still a child... sacrificing me to an unworthy rival... you even made me loathe my own daughter... I was aware of your methods, there was not one which did not cut me to the quick, and yet I could not hate you... But what do you hope for now?... Yet where love cannot succeed, perhaps your pique at being rejected will deliver you to me... Your rival is here. I can assure him of a prompt victory, tomorrow... my daughter is urging me to do so. What hope can remain to you? What wild optimism still prevents you from seeing things as they are?'

'The hope of dying, Madame,' replied Monrevel, 'dying of remorse for having started sentiments in you which it is not in my power to share, dying of the sorrow of being unable to inspire them in the only heart which will ever rule mine.'

Madame de Sancerre controlled herself. Love, pride, villainy, and vengeance worked too strongly in her for her not to feel an imperious need to dissemble. Where a frank and honest soul would have grown angry, a vindictive, deceitful woman was obliged to resort to cunning, and the Countess was duly artful.

'Chevalier,' she said, with feigned resentment, 'you inflict on me the first rejection I ever suffered in my life. While your rivals might be surprised, I alone am not: no, I shall be honest with myself... I am old enough to be your mother, Chevalier, and how, with such an impediment, could I ever hope to marry you?... I shall stand in your way no longer, Monrevel. I hand the honour of enslaving you to my fortunate rival. But if I cannot be your wife, I shall always be your friend. Surely you will not object? Cruel man, will you begrudge me that?'

'Oh, Madame! I fully recognize the nobility of your heart in your manner of proceeding,' replied Monrevel, who was taken in by these misleading words. 'Please believe', he went on, kneeling before the Countess, 'that all the feelings of my heart, other than those of love, will be forever yours. I shall have no better friend in all the world. You shall be both my benefactress and my mother, and I shall always devote to you each and every instant when, dazzled by my love for Amélie, I am not entirely hers to command.'

'I will be content with these crumbs, Monrevel,' the Countess went on, raising him to his feet, 'for everything to do with the person we love is very precious to us. Obviously sentiments more affectionate would have touched me more deeply. But since I must no longer think of aiming so high, I shall settle for the sincere friendship you swear you have for me, and I, in return, shall repay you with mine... Listen Monrevel, I shall now give you proof of the feelings I have sworn I shall have for you. It will be my way of showing my desire to see your love triumph and keep you permanently near me... Your rival is here: so much is certain. Being informed of Charles's wishes, how could I possibly have refused him entry to the chateau? All I can do for you... and remember, he has no inkling of your intentions... the best I can arrange is for him to appear only in disguise—actually, he is wearing it already—and for him to see my daughter only in secret. Now, how do you think we should proceed in the circumstances?'

'According to the dictates of my heart, Madame. The only favour which, on bended knee, I dare beg is your permission to go forth and fight my rival for my beloved as honour requires of a knight such as myself.'

'That way you will not succeed, Monrevel. You do not know the man you would go up against. Did you ever see him perform in the honourable career of arms? To his shame, Salins has always lived deep in his province, and only now, for the first time in his life, has he emerged from it to marry my daughter. I cannot think how Charles came to choose him, but it is what he wants... and there is nothing we can say. But I repeat, Salins is known to be a villain and will certainly not fight... And if he discovers your plans, if he were to work them out from your actions, then, Monrevel, I tremble for you!... Let us find another way, and keep our intentions hidden from him... Let me give this matter some thought for a few days. I will let you know what I decide to do. Meanwhile stay where you are. I shall circulate various rumours concerning your reasons for remaining here.'

Monrevel, only too happy with the little he had obtained, and never imagining for a moment that anyone would wish to deceive him, because his honest, feeling heart was a stranger to guile, knelt in thanks before the Countess and then withdrew, feeling somewhat heartened.

Madame de Sancerre used this time to give the orders which would ensure the success of her odious plans. Clotilde's young cousin, secretly introduced into the chateau in the guise of a household page, played his part so well that Monrevel could not help but notice him. At the same time four new valets entered the house. It was assumed that they were servants of the Count de Sancerre who had returned to the chateau after their master's death. But the Countess made a point of informing Monrevel that these unknown men were part of Salins's retinue. From that moment on he had virtually no opportunity of talking to Amélie. If he went to her apartments, her maids refused to let him in. If he attempted to approach her in the grounds or the gardens, then either she ran way or else he saw that she was with his rival. Such frustrations were too much for Monrevel's impatient heart. In the end, near to despair, he found Amélie alone. She had been left to her thoughts by Salins.

'Are you so unfeeling', he said to her, able to contain himself no more, 'that you so despise me that you will let me watch while you set the seal on the fatal alliance that will separate us? You could settle this whole affair yourself, for I am on the verge of winning your mother to our side, and yet it is you who strikes the blow that breaks my heart!'

Amélie, informed of the glimmer of hope that the Countess had held out to Monrevel, and assuming that this would all help to give a happy ending to the little drama she was required to act in—Amélie, as I was saying, stoutly kept up her pretence. She answered Monrevel, saying that he was perfectly free to spare himself the spectacle he seemed to find so painful, and that she would be the first to advise him to forget in the company of Bellona the hurts inflicted by Cupid. Still, despite everything the Countess had said, she was careful not to appear to cast aspersions on Monrevel's courage. Amélie knew him too well to have any doubts on that score, and loved him too much in her heart of hearts to dare even to joke about something so sacred.

'Then it is all over and I must leave you,' exclaimed Monrevel through his tears, as he knelt before her one last time. 'It is in your power to order me to go, and I shall find in my heart the strength to obey. May the fortunate man to whom I leave you know the value of what I relinquish in his favour! May he make you as happy as you deserve to be, Amélie. You will let me know how happy you are, that is the one favour I ask. I shall be less wretched myself if I know that you are content.'

Amélie found it impossible to hear these words and not be moved... Tears came unbidden to betray her. Monrevel held her close and exclaimed:

'O happy day! I have found a regret in a heart which I for so long believed was mine! Oh dearest Amélie, if you can shed a tear for Monrevel, then it is not true that you love Salins! Say one word, Amélie, just one, and then, however cowardly the monster who would take you from me may be, I shall either force him to fight or punish him for his poltroonery and for his temerity in aspiring to your hand.'

But Amélie had regained her composure. Feeling the threat of losing everything hanging over her, she was much too aware of how important it was to keep on playing her enforced role to dare weaken for one moment.

'I will not deny the tears you caught me shedding, Chevalier,' she said firmly. 'But you are wrong in your interpretation of their cause. A twinge of pity for you may have caused them to flow without love coming into it at all. So long accustomed to seeing you near me, surely I can be sorry to lose you without there being anything more tender to it than ordinary friendship?'

'Oh, merciful heaven!' cried Monrevel, 'you even rob me of the consolation which for a moment was balm to my heart! Amélie, how cruelly you treat a man who never did you any other hurt than to love you to distraction! Is it to your pity that I owe the tears which briefly made me feel so proud? Is that the only feeling I can expect from you?...'

They heard someone coming, and our two lovers were obliged to separate, one most certainly in despair, and the other with a heart heavy with the pain of such cruel duress... yet nevertheless very relieved that a chance happening had freed her of the need to keep up the pretence.

Several more days went by. The Countess made the most of them to marshal the last of her forces. Then one evening Monrevel, alone and unarmed, was returning from a distant corner of the gardens where his melancholy mood had led him when he was suddenly attacked by four men, clearly intent on leaving him for dead. His courage did not desert him in so dangerous a pass. He defended himself, drove back his adversaries who were pressing him hard, called for help, and succeeded in escaping with the assistance of the Countess's servants, who came running the moment they heard him cry out. Madame de Sancerre, informed of the danger he had just faced—the wicked Lady of Sancerre, who knew better than anyone whose hand had ordered the assault—asked Monrevel to call on her in her apartment before he retired to his own.

'Madame,' he said going to her, 'I have no idea who might want to threaten my life, but I did not believe anyone would dare attack an unarmed knight in your chateau...'

'Monrevel,' replied the Countess, observing that he was still heated from the fray, 'I cannot save you from these dangers. All I can do is help to defend you against them... My servants rushed to your aid: could I have done more than I did?... I told you: you are dealing with a villain. You will get nowhere by insisting on following the protocols of honour, for he will not respond to them and your life will still be in danger. I would most certainly prefer him to be far away from here, but I can hardly refuse my house to a man whom the Duke of Burgundy wishes me to receive as a future son-in-law, who loves my daughter, and who is loved by her. Do not be so unjust, Chevalier, for I have suffered as much as you. Consider how deeply involved I am, how closely bound I am to your fate. Salins is behind all this, I am sure of it. He will have enquired into your reasons for staying here when all the other knights are away with their lords. Unfortunately it is no secret that you are in love, and he has doubtless encountered wagging tongues... Salins wants his revenge and, knowing only too well that he cannot get rid of you except by committing a crime, that is what he is doing. Having failed once, he will try again. Dear Chevalier, I tremble at the prospect... I am more afraid for you than you are yourself.'

'Very well, Madame,' replied Monrevel, 'order him to abandon his disguise which no longer serves any purpose and allow me to go after him in such a way that he will be forced to answer me... Besides, why does Salins need a disguise if he is here at the behest of his sovereign lord, if he is loved by the one he came here for and is protected by you?'

'By me, Chevalier? I was not expecting to be so insulted... but no matter, this is not the time for defending myself. Let us deal only with your allegations, and when I have explained everything you will see whether or not I feel the same way about my daughter's choice as she does. You ask why Salins adopted a disguise. First, I insisted on it out of consideration for you, and if he persists with the deception it is out of fear for his person. He fears you, he avoids you, and he will only attack you by underhand methods... You want me to agree to let you fight. Believe me, he will not accept, Monrevel, I have already told you so, and if he finds out that this is what you intend, he will lay his plans so well that I shall not be answerable for your life. My standing with him is such that it has even become impossible for me to remonstrate with him for what has just happened: if you want vengeance, you must take it yourself, it is entirely your own affair. But I should be very sorry if you do not retaliate, as would be only right and proper after the despicable way he has behaved. When dealing with a blackguard, why should anyone respect the laws of honour? Moreover, once it is clear that he will not accept any challenge which you offer him as an honourable man, what methods are left to you other than those he himself uses? Should you not think of striking before he does, Chevalier? Since when has the life of a coward been so precious that no one now dares snuff it out except in formal combat? You fight a duel with a gentleman, but you order the death of the man who tries to assassinate you. May the example of your masters be your guide in this. When the pride of Charles of Burgundy, the same that now governs us, was offended by the Duke of Orléans, did he challenge him to a duel or did he have him murdered? He thought the latter course was best, he took it... and was himself the victim of the same fate at Montereau when the Dauphin had cause to feel aggrieved with him.* A man does not become a less chivalrous or valiant knight because he rids the world of a knave who intends to kill him... Yes, Monrevel, yes, I want you to have my daughter, I want her to be yours whatever the cost... Do not look too hard into the feeling which makes me want to keep you near me... the answer would probably make me blush... and my still convalescent heart... But no matter, you shall be my son-in-law, Chevalier, you shall indeed... Your happiness is what I seek, even if it is achieved at the expense of my own... So now will you dare to repeat that I protect Salins? Say it, sweet boy, and I shall be entitled to call you at the very least unjust, for not appreciating all I have done for you.'

Monrevel was deeply moved and, kneeling before the Countess, asked to be forgiven for having misjudged her... Yet he felt that murdering Salins was a crime of which he was not capable.

'Oh, Madame,' he wept, 'never could these hands strike at the heart of a living creature who resembles me! Murder, the most heinous of crimes...'

...'ceases to be a crime if it can save our life... But why this weakness, Chevalier? How out of place in a hero! What is it that you do, I ask you, when you go forth to do battle? The laurels you win, are they not earned by murder? You believe it is right to slaughter your lord's enemies, but you tremble to kill your own. What despotic law can put such widely differing interpretations on the same action? Do you not see, Monrevel, that either we must never try to take anyone's life at all, or if doing so may sometimes seem legitimate, then it is because it is justified by the need to avenge an insult?... But why am I telling you this, for what business is it of mine? Quake like the weak coward you are! If you fear to commit an imaginary crime, forget honour and abandon the woman you love to the arms of the monster who stole her from you. Watch as your wretched Amélie, seduced, despairing, and betrayed, languishes in the depths of misery! Hear her cry to you for help, while you, you craven wretch, would limply prefer to leave the woman you once worshipped to face a future of unending misery than to take the rightful, necessary steps to end the life of the vile man who would kill you both!'

The Countess, seeing Monrevel hesitate, proceeded to use every argument to smooth the way for the foul deed she was urging him to commit, and make him see that when such an action becomes so necessary, it is most dangerous not to carry it out. In short, she said that if he did not hurry, then not only would his life continue to be constantly in peril, but that he even ran the risk of seeing Amélie stolen away under his nose. For Salins, who could not fail to notice that she herself did not favour him, knew that he would please the Duke of Burgundy whatever methods he used to get his hands on Amélie, and might well carry her off at the very first opportunity, his task doubtless being made all the easier because she would be willing. In this way, she so inflamed the young knight's spirits that he agreed to everything and, kneeling at the Countess's feet, swore that he would end his rival's life with his poniard.

Thus far, the intentions of the perfidious Countess seem very suspect indeed. It is an impression which the hideous consequences will amply confirm.

Monrevel left her in her apartment. But his resolve quickly melted, and despite himself the voice of nature wrestled in his soul with what his vengeance would have him do. He decided he would determine upon nothing until he had tried all the rightful channels which honour demanded. Next day he issued a challenge to the so-called Salins, and within the hour received the following reply:

It is not my practice to fight for what belongs to me. It is for the man spurned by his lady to seek death. For my own part, I love life. Why should I not cherish it since all the moments which constitute it are precious to my Amélie? If you wish to fight, Chevalier, Charles has need of heroes. Go to him. Believe me, you are better suited to the exertions of Mars than the sweet pleasures of love. You will achieve glory by yielding to the first of these. But the second, without risk to me, could cost you dear.

Monrevel shook with rage when he read these words.

'The scoundrel!' he cried. 'He threatens me but dares not defend himself! There is nothing to hold me back now. Let us give some thought to safeguarding myself then devise some way of saving the woman I adore. The time for hesitation is past... But what am I saying?... My God, what if she loves him?... If Amélie has lost her heart to my unprincipled rival, can I regain her love by killing him? Will I dare go to her with my hands stained with the blood of the man she adored?... Today she thinks of me with indifference... but if I persist in this, she will look on me with hate!'

Such were the thoughts of the hapless Monrevel and the inner turmoil of his distraught mind, when, about two hours after receiving the reply we have just seen, the Countess sent word asking him to come to her apartment.

'To forestall your reproaches, Chevalier,' she said the moment he walked through the door, 'I have put the soundest measures in place to ensure that I am informed of everything that goes on. Your life is once again in danger. Two attempts on it are being prepared simultaneously. An hour after the sun has set you will be followed by four men, who will not let you out of their sight until they have stabbed you to death. At the same time, Salins will abduct Amélie. If I intervene, he will inform the Duke that I tried to stop him. That way he puts himself in the clear and points the finger at us both. You can avoid the first danger by taking six of my men with you as an escort. They are waiting for you at the gate... When it strikes ten, dismiss the men and go alone to the great vaulted hall which leads to my daughter's apartments. Exactly at the time I have given you, Salins will walk through the hall on his way to join Amélie. She will be waiting for him and they will leave together before midnight. Then, armed with this dagger... take it, Monrevel, I want to see you receive it from my hands... then armed as I say, you will take your revenge for the first crime and prevent the second. Be just, acknowledge that it is I who have supplied you with the weapon which shall punish the man you hate, I who will restore you to the woman you love... Now will you go on damning me with your recriminations?... This is how I return your contempt, you ungrateful wretch!... Go, hurry, take your revenge... Amélie will be in my arms, waiting for you.'

'Give me the blade, Madame,' said Monrevel, too angry now to hesitate any longer, 'let me have it: nothing now can stop me sacrificing my rival to my fury! I offered him the honourable way out but he refused, for he is a coward and must die like one... Give it to me. I shall do your bidding.'

Monrevel quitted the room... No sooner had he left the Countess than she hurriedly sent for her daughter.

'Amélie,' she said, 'surely we must now be as certain of Monrevel's love as we are of his courage. Further tests would serve no purpose. I therefore agree to your wishes. But since it is unfortunately only too true that the Duke of Burgundy intends you to marry Salins, and only too likely that he might be here within the week, the only course open to you now, if you wish to be Monrevel's, is flight. It must appear that he has abducted you, unbeknownst to me, and to justify his action he must invoke my husband's last wishes. He will deny all knowledge of the Duke's change of mind, marry you at Monrevel, and then gallop off to make his excuses to him. Your lover understands why these conditions are necessary and has accepted them all. But I thought it best to tell you before he spoke to you himself... Well, daughter, what do you think of the plan? Can you see any problems with it?'

'There would be many, Madame,' replied Amélie, with equal measures of respect and gratitude, 'if it were to be implemented without your approval. But since you have agreed to be a party to it, all that remains is for me to kneel and express my truest thanks for everything you have been so kind as to do for me.'

'In that case, there is not a moment to lose,' replied the wicked Countess, for whom her daughter's tears were a new affront. 'Monrevel has been told all the details. But it is essential for you to be disguised. It would be most unfortunate if you were recognized before you reach Monrevel's chateau, and even more undesirable if you encounter Salins, who we are expecting daily. Put these clothes on,' the Countess continued, handing to her daughter the costume worn by the bogus Salins, 'and go back to your apartment when the sentry on the watchtower sounds ten o'clock:[1] that is the time agreed, and at that moment Monrevel will come to you, horses will be waiting, and you shall both ride away...'

'Was there ever such a kind mother?' exclaimed Amélie, throwing herself into the Countess's arms. 'I only wish you could see into my heart and observe what feelings you fill me with... If only you could...'

'No, no,' said Madame de Sancerre, freeing herself from her daughter's embrace, 'there is no need for gratitude. If you are happy, then so am I. But we should only be thinking of your disguise.'

The time was fast approaching. Amélie put on the clothes she was given. The Countess took extreme care to ensure that she looked exactly like Clotilde's young cousin, whom Monrevel mistakenly believed was the Lord of Salins. She spared no effort until they could not be told apart. Finally the fatal hour sounded.

'Now go,' said the Countess, 'run, Monrevel is waiting for you!'

The beautiful Amélie, who feared that the need for a hurried departure meant that she would never see her mother again, put her arms around her and wept. The Countess, whose false heart enabled her to conceal the horrors she had planned, gave every outward sign of affection, embraced her daughter, and mingled her own tears with hers. Amélie tore herself away and made off in haste towards her apartment. She opened the door to the fatal vaulted hall, dimly illumined by a feeble light, where Monrevel,

[1] It was the custom of the time for the sentry posted in the lookout turret to sound a horn on every hour.

dagger in hand, stood waiting to kill his rival. Seeing a figure appear which the circumstances led him to assume was the enemy he was expecting, he suddenly sprang forward, struck out blindly, and left lying on the ground in a pool of blood... the woman he loved, for whom he would gladly have sacrificed his own life a thousand times over.

'Cur!' cried the Countess, who appeared at once carrying a flaming torch. 'This is how I avenge your scorn. Look now and see your error, and live with the knowledge... if you can.'

Amélie still breathed. Through her moans, she spoke these few words to Monrevel:

'My dear, my sweet,' she said, weakened by pain and the great quantity of blood that she had lost, 'what did I do to deserve to die by your hand?... Is this the union for which my mother prepared me? But I do not lay any blame on you. In these my final moments Heaven has revealed everything to me... Monrevel, forgive me from hiding my love from you. You must now realize what made me do it... at least may my last words convince you that no woman ever loved you more truly than I did... that I loved you more than I loved God, more than life, and that I die loving you.'

Monrevel heard no more. Prostrate on the ground over Amelia's bloody corpse, with his mouth on hers, he tried to revive her precious soul, breathing out his own which burned with love and despair... Convulsed in turn by tears and rage, he blamed himself and cursed the wicked perpetrator of the crime which his hand had executed... Finally, he rose furiously to his feet:

'What did you expect to gain by this vile, perfidious deed?' he said to the Countess. 'Did you think your horrible wishes would come true? Did you think Monrevel was weak enough to survive the woman he loved?... Get away, go! In the cruel state to which your crimes have reduced me, I cannot promise not to wash them away with your blood...'

'Strike!' cried the Countess wildly. 'Strike! Here is my breast! Do you think I value my life if the hope of having you has been taken from me forever? I wanted vengeance, I wanted to be rid of a hateful rival, and I have no more intention of surviving my crime than of surviving my despair. But let it be your hand which strips me of my life, it is by your hand that I wish to die... Well? What is stopping you?... Coward! Did I not offend you enough?... What is it that stays your anger? Find a spark to light the torch of your vengeance in the spectacle of the precious blood which I made you spill, and show no more mercy for a woman you must hate, although she cannot stop loving you!'

'Monster!' exclaimed Monrevel. 'Dying would be too good for you... I would not be avenged... Live, then, that you may be regarded with universal horror! Live, that you may be racked by remorse. Every creature that breathes shall know of the horrors you have committed and hold you in utter contempt... Every moment you will loathe yourself and find the light of day unbearable. But this at least you shall know: your wickedness will not prevent me from being with the woman I adore... My soul will follow her to the feet of the Almighty and we both shall invoke His wrath against you.'

With these words Monrevel drove the dagger into his heart. As he breathed his last, he held his beloved so close, clasped her to him with such strength, that no effort of human hand could separate them... Both were placed in the same coffin and were laid to rest in the main church of Sancerre, where true lovers sometimes go and shed tears over their tomb and are touched by the following lines, chiselled into the marble slab which covers them, which Louis XII* did not disdain to compose:

Lovers shed your tears, for once they loved, like you.
Though married they never were by holy law,
They exchanged their vows and to them were true
Until foul vengeance undid the oaths they swore.

The Countess alone survived her crimes, but did so only to repent for them all her days. She fell into the deepest piety and died ten years later, having become a nun at Auxerre,* leaving her community edified by her conversion and genuinely touched by the sincerity of her repentance.

EUGÉNIE DE FRANVAL

A Tragic Tale

TO instruct mankind and correct human manners, here is our only purpose in offering this tale. Let my readers reflect, as they read, on the immensity of the danger involved as they follow the progress of those who are prepared to stop at nothing to satisfy their desires. May they be persuaded that a sound upbringing, wealth, talents, and natural gifts are apt to lead people astray unless backed or turned to good account by self-control, sensible behaviour, a level head, and modesty: these are the truths whose workings we shall demonstrate. May we be forgiven for furnishing the monstrous detail of the appalling crime of which we force ourselves to speak. Could we inspire a loathing of such wrongdoing if we lacked the courage to show its operations raw and unadorned?*

It is rare that everything is perfectly combined in one human being to enable him to prosper. If he has been favoured by nature, fortune refuses to smile on him. If fortune showers him with its benefactions, nature has withheld hers. It would seem that the divine hand, both in its treatment of every human being and in its most grandiose workings, is bent on reminding us that the law of equilibrium* is the fundamental law of the universe, for it rules everything that happens, all the plants that grow, every creature that breathes.

Franval, who lived in Paris where he was born, had, in addition to an income of four hundred thousand livres,* the handsomest physique, the most attractive features, and the most varied talents. But beneath this seductive exterior lay all manner of vices and, regrettably, those which, once adopted and practised habitually, quickly lead to crime. A disorder of the imagination, beyond anything that can be described, was Franval's major defect: it is a flaw which no man can correct. The fading of a man's powers reinforces its effects: the less he is able to do, the more he wants to do; the less he acts, the more he invents. Each phase of life brings new ideas, and, far from cooling desire, surfeit has the effect only of stimulating him to even more deadly and sophisticated refinements.

As we have said, Franval possessed all the graces of youth and the talents which enhance it, and possessed them in abundance. But since he showed nothing but contempt for moral and religious obligations, his teachers had found it impossible to persuade him to adopt the least of them.

In an age when the most dangerous books find their way into the hands of children as easily as into the hands of their fathers and tutors, when bold systems of thought masquerade as philosophy, unbelief as strength, and libertinage as imagination, Franval as a boy observed that people laughed at his witticisms, then perhaps moments later that he was scolded for them, and then only the next moment praised again. Franval's father, a devout supporter of modish ideas, was the first to encourage his son to think *solidly** about all these matters. He allowed him to borrow the books which were likely to corrupt his mind most quickly. Given this circumstance, what tutor would have dared try to instil in him principles which were at variance with those accredited in the house in which he was required to give satisfaction?

Be that as it may, Franval was a mere boy when he lost both his parents. When he was nineteen years of age an old uncle, who also died a short while later, undertook to make over to him, when he married, the entire inheritance which was one day to be his.

Now, with such a fortune Monsieur de Franval should have been able to find a wife without difficulty. A great many eligible girls came forward, but since he had begged his uncle to find him one who was younger than he and had the fewest relations, his aged uncle tried to accommodate his nephew. He cast his eye in the direction of a certain Mademoiselle de Farneille, a banker's daughter, who now had only a mother living but a very real income of sixty thousand livres. She was fifteen and possessed one of the most dazzling physiognomies in Paris: it was one of those virginal faces wherein both innocence and promise are painted in the delicate features of Love and the Graces: shining blonde hair hanging down to her waist, wide blue eyes which spoke of tenderness and modesty, a slender, supple, willowy figure, skin like the lily, the freshness of roses, all the talents, a lively imagination, but also a manner tinged with sadness, a hint of that gentle melancholy which starts a taste for books and solitude. Such attributes nature seems to confer only on individuals for whom she plans disaster, as if to sweeten their bitter fate by allowing them to know sombre, affecting pleasure, which they go on feeling even as they suffer, and makes them prefer tears to the frivolous joys of happiness which are more passive and do not go as deep.*

Madame de Farneille, who was thirty-two when her daughter was married, was also a person of wit, attractive, but perhaps a little too reserved and austere. Eager to secure her daughter's happiness, she had canvassed the whole of Paris for views about this marriage. And since she had no relations to advise her, and only friends who were of the kind for whom nothing really matters, she was given to understand that the young man who had been mentioned as an eligible prospect for her daughter was, beyond a shadow of a doubt, the best possible match she could find in the capital, and that moreover she would be committing an unpardonable folly if she failed to conclude the proposed marriage. And so the wedding took place, and the happy couple, rich enough to set up in their own house, moved into it in the days immediately following their nuptials.

There was no trace in Franval's character of the vices of fickleness, dissoluteness, and recklessness which prevent a man from becoming mature before the age of thirty. He was entirely at ease with himself, liked a settled routine, and was supremely competent in the running of his household: for those matters, indispensable for a life of contentment, Franval had all the necessary qualities. His vices were of a quite different order, and rather the defects of middle age than the failings of youth—cunning, intrigue, malice, cruelty, selfishness, and a large capacity for deviousness and underhand dealing. All this he kept hidden, not only by the charm and talents of which we have already spoken, but by a silver tongue, a ready wit, and the most attractive outward show and manner. Such is the man whose portrait we have to paint.

Mademoiselle de Farneille, in accordance with convention, had known her husband for a month at most before becoming his wife, and was entirely duped by these false appearances. The days were never long enough for her to delight in his presence. She doted on him to such a degree that fears might have been expressed for the young woman's sanity, had not certain obstacles arisen to interrupt the smooth course of a marriage in which, she said, she found the only happiness she would ever want.

For his part, Franval, as philosophical about women as he was about everything else in life, thought of his delightful spouse with the greatest indifference imaginable.

'The wife who is ours to hold', he would say, 'is a creature who is assigned to us by convention for our use. She must be sweet-natured, obedient, and very docile. Not that I care much for the common notion of the dishonour that can be brought upon us when wives imitate our adulterous conduct. Still, we are never likely to be best pleased when others set out to usurp our rights. But the rest does not matter at all, for it adds nothing to our happiness.'

Given such sentiments in a husband, it is easy to predict that it was not roses which awaited the hapless girl who married him. Honest, considerate, well brought up, and endlessly anticipating the every wish of the only man alive who mattered to her, Madame de Franval wore her chains during the early years of her marriage without ever suspecting that she was a slave. It was plain enough to her that she was merely gathering up crumbs that fell from the table of married bliss. But, still more than happy with the scraps that came her way, her every thought, her sincerest wish, was that in the brief moments when she was allowed to express her love, Franval would at least find everything she believed was necessary to make her darling husband happy.

However, the best evidence to suggest that Franval was not always derelict in his duties is the fact that, in the very first year of their marriage, his wife, then sixteen-and-a-half years of age, was brought to bed of a daughter even more beautiful than her mother, whom the father instantly named Eugénie... Eugénie: simultaneously an abomination and a miracle of nature.

It is likely that Monsieur de Franval formulated the most odious plans for the child the moment she was born, for he removed her at once from her mother's care... Until she was seven Eugénie was raised by women whom Franval trusted implicitly. He limited their role to giving her a sound constitution and teaching her to read, and they took good care to avoid giving her any inkling of the religious and moral principles which a girl of her age should normally be taught.

Madame de Farneille and her daughter, utterly shocked by such behaviour, spoke reprovingly to Monsieur de Franval. He replied coolly that since his plan was to make his daughter happy, he would not fill her head with foolish delusions which had no other effect than to frighten people and were of no benefit to them whatsoever; that a daughter whose only need was to learn how to please others was best served if she ignored such fairy-tales and living fantasies which, by interfering with her peace of mind, would never add a single truth to her mind nor an extra grace to her body. Such comments were supremely offensive to Madame de Farneille, who grew more attracted to thoughts of Heaven as the distance she put between herself and worldly pleasures grew wider. A belief in God is a failing inseparable from the different ages of our life or the state of our health. When the winds of passion rage, a future which seems very remote from the present rarely causes anxiety. But when they blow more gently... when the end grows nearer... when all our faculties desert us... we return to the bosom of the Lord of which we were told as children. And if this second instalment of illusion is as fantastical as the first, it is also at least as dangerous.*

Franval's mother-in-law had no living relatives, very little influence of her own, and at the very most, as we have observed, only a few occasional, fleeting friends of the kind who would drift away if we ever put them to the test. Having to face up to a son-in-law who was young and well connected, she understandably assumed that it would be simpler to keep up her protests than to institute action through formal channels against a man who, if she dared cross him, could ruin the mother and lock up the daughter. With this in mind, a handful of reproaches were as far as she dared go, and she said nothing as soon as she saw that her objections would lead nowhere. Soon Franval, certain that he was the stronger, and observing that he was feared, dropped all restraint in whatever he did and, drawing the flimsiest of veils over his actions for the benefit of the public, proceeded directly towards his hideous goal.

On the day Eugénie reached her seventh birthday Franval brought her to his wife. That tender mother, who had not seen her child since the time of her birth, could not embrace and hug her enough. She held her for two hours clasped to her breast, smothering her with kisses and shedding unstoppable tears. She asked to know what toddler's talents she had acquired. But Eugénie had acquired none, save the ability to read, enjoy rude good health, and look as beautiful as an angel. There was a further shock for Madame de Franval when she discovered that it was only too true that her daughter was ignorant of even the most rudimentary precepts of religion.

'Surely, sir,' said she to her husband, 'you do not propose to bring her up fit to live only in this sublunary world? Pray stop and reflect that that she will dwell here below for a brief span, only to be cast thereafter into everlasting fire if you deny her knowledge which may enable her to meet a better fate at the feet of the God from whom she has received the gift of life.'

'If Eugénie knows nothing, Madame,' answered Franval, 'if every care is taken to hide these precepts of yours from her, she will never be unhappy. For if they are true, the Lord on high is too just to punish her for her ignorance, and if they are false, is there any point in telling her about them? With regard to the other aspects of her education, you must trust me. As of today I shall myself be her tutor, and I guarantee that a few years from now your daughter will outshine any child of her age.'

Madame de Franval tried to be firm, pleading from her heart as a way of reinforcing more rational arguments, and her tears indeed spoke for her. But Franval was unmoved and seemed not even to notice that she wept. He ordered Eugénie to be taken away, warning his wife that if she dared to interfere in any way whatsoever with the education he intended to give his daughter, or if she attempted to instil in her principles at variance with those he intended to teach her, she would forfeit all prospect of seeing her and he would send the girl away to one of his estates, where she would remain and never leave it. Madame de Franval, forced to submit, said no more. She begged her husband not to separate her from her dear treasure, and promised through her tears never to interfere in any way with the education which he had in mind for her.

From that day forth Mademoiselle de Franval was sent to live in a very elegant apartment, next to her father's, with a very capable governess, a deputy governess, a lady's-maid, and two little girls of her own age whose role was to keep her amused. She was given a writing-master, a drawing-teacher, tutors for poetry, natural history, elocution, geography, astronomy, anatomy, Greek, English, German, and Italian, plus instructors in fencing, dancing, riding, and music. Eugénie rose each morning at seven, whatever the season, and ran out into the garden, where she ate a thick slice of rye bread for her breakfast. She came indoors at eight, spent a few moments in the apartment of her father, who rollicked and romped with her for a while or taught her childish parlour games. Until nine she did the work she had been set. It was then that her first tutor arrived. She saw five in all by two o'clock, when she ate separately with her two little comrades and her governess. Her dinner consisted of vegetables, fish, pastries, and fruit: she was never given meat, soup, wine, liqueurs, or coffee. Between three and four Eugénie went back into the garden and played for an hour with her two little friends. They played tennis, ball, skittles, battledore and shuttlecock, or practised who could jump certain set distances. They were dressed in comfortable clothes according to the season: nothing cramped their bodies and they were never forced into ridiculous whalebone, which is as dangerous to the stomach as to the chest and, by hampering a young woman's ability to breathe, has the unavoidable effect of weakening the lungs. From four until six Mademoiselle de Franval was visited by more of her tutors and, since they were too numerous for them all to come on one day, the rest came the next. Three times a week Eugénie went to the theatre with her father, and sat in one of the boxes enclosed by a latticework screen which had been reserved by the year for her use. At nine she returned home and had supper, which consisted only of vegetables and fruit. Four times a week, between ten and eleven, Eugénie played with her little friends, read novels, and then went to bed. The three other evenings, when Franval did not dine out, she spent with her father in his apartment, and this time was devoted to what Franval called his 'lectures'. There he imparted to his daughter his ideas on morality and religion. On the one hand, he told her what certain men thought of these questions, and then, on the other, set out what he himself believed.*

Since she had a clever mind, a wide knowledge of many matters, a quick understanding, and passions which were already beginning to ignite, it is not hard to imagine the effect of such ideas on Eugénie. But the ignoble Franval's plan was not simply to form her mind, and his lectures rarely ended without setting her heart ablaze. This abominable man had found so many ways of pleasing his daughter, had manipulated her so skilfully, made himself so necessary to her education and her pleasures, and was so impatient to provide whatever she might find agreeable, that when Eugénie was surrounded by the most brilliant company she found no one as attractive as her father. As a consequence, long before he made his purpose known to her, the innocent, vulnerable girl had filled her young heart with all the feelings of friendship, gratitude, and affection which must of necessity lead to the most passionate love. For her, Franval was the only person in the world. She had eyes for no one but him, and was violently opposed to any circumstance which might separate them. For him, she would have willingly given not her honour nor her beauty, for such sacrifices would have seemed to her far too unworthy of the wonderful man she idolized, but her blood, her life, if her twin soul had asked it.

There was nothing comparable in the sentiments Mademoiselle de Franval had for her worthy, unhappy mother. Her father, artfully informing his daughter that, as his wife, Madame de Franval made demands on him which often prevented him from doing for his dear Eugénie all he would have liked to do, had found a way of filling his daughter's mind with far more hatred and jealousy than with the kind of deference and respect she should have felt for such a mother.

'Dear friend and brother,' Eugénie sometimes said to Franval, who would not have his daughter call him by any other names, 'the woman you call your wife must be very importunate. By always wanting you to be with her, she robs me of the joy of spending all my time with you. Don't deny it: you like her better than your Eugénie. Personally, I shall never love anyone who tries to steal your heart from me.'

'My dear girl,' replied Franval, 'no one in the whole universe will ever have a greater claim to it than you. The bonds that exist between that woman and your best friend are the result of custom and social convention, which I respect as a philosopher, but they shall never count for more than the ties that bind us two. You will always be the one I love best, Eugénie. You shall be the angel, the light of my life, the place where my heart is, and my reason for living.'

'Oh such sweet words!' replied Eugénie. 'You must repeat them often, dear friend. If only you knew how happy it makes me to hear you say such tender things!'

And taking Franval's hand, which she pressed to her heart:

'There,' she went on, 'I can feel them there.'

'Prove it to me by your tender caresses,' replied Franval, gathering her into his arms. And thus it was that the perfidious man, without a twinge of remorse, completed the seduction of his own unfortunate daughter.

Eugénie was then approaching her fourteenth birthday, the time

Franval had fixed upon to... consummate his crime. The very thought makes us shudder. But consummated it was.

[The day she reached that age,* or rather when her thirteenth year was up, they went into the country unaccompanied by relatives or any other unwelcome persons. For the day, the Count had dressed his daughter in the style of those virgins who in olden times were dedicated to the service of the Temple of Venus. At about eleven in the morning he led her to a voluptuously decorated parlour. The windows, hung with fine gauze curtains, let in a suffused light and the furniture was strewn with flowers. In the middle of the room stood a throne of roses. Franval handed his daughter to it.*

'Eugénie,' he said as he sat her down, 'today you are the queen of my heart. Allow me to kneel and worship you!'

'Worship me, brother, when it is I who am so in your debt? For it was you who created me, who made me what I am! Oh it is I who should rather kneel down to you.'

'Oh sweet Eugénie,' said the Count, as he took his place on the bank of flowers which he had chosen for the site of his triumph, 'if it is true that you are in any way in my debt, if the sentiments you display towards me are indeed what you say they are, do you know by what means you can convince me of your sincerity?'

'What means are they, brother? Tell me quickly and I will gladly employ them.'

'Eugénie, each and every perfection which nature has showered on you, all the charms with which she has made you so beautiful, all this you must sacrifice to me here and now.'

'But why do you ask this? Are you not my master to command it? Is what you have made not yours? Surely no one else can take pleasure in possessing what you have created?'

'You know what prejudices people have.'

'You have never hidden them from me.'

'That is why I have no intention of riding roughshod over them without your consent.'

'But do you not despise them as I do?'

'Very well. But I would not wish to behave like a tyrant or even less as a seducer. I want it to be from love alone that I obtain what I ask and what is yours to give. You know what the world is like. I have hidden none of its attractions from you. To prevent you from setting eyes on other men and allow you see no one but me would have been a cheap tactic, unworthy of me. If there is anywhere another man you like better than me, then give me his name now. I will travel to the ends of the earth to find him and thrust him into your arms. In short, my angel, I want you to be happy, I want your happiness much more than my own. The honeyed pleasures you can give me would mean nothing if they were not the expression of your love. So decide, Eugénie. The moment of sacrifice is nigh: it cannot be avoided. But you yourself shall name the man who shall perform it. I renounce all claim to the bliss which would be mine if that man were me... unless they were given with all your soul. But I shall remain worthy of your love. If I am not the one you choose, then by bringing you the man you love, I shall at least have won your affection, though not your love—if I am not Eugénie's lover, I shall yet be her friend.'

'But you shall be all these things, brother, all!' said Eugénie, now aflame with love and desire. 'To whom should I sacrifice myself if not to the man I adore above all others? Where in the whole world is the man who is more worthy than you of the modest charms which you desire... and which your fevered hands are now exploring with such ardour? Can you not tell by the passion with which I burn that I am as impatient as you to experience the bliss of which you speak? Take it, take your pleasure, my darling brother and best friend! Eugénie shall be your victim, for sacrificed by your hand she cannot but triumph!'

As may be inferred from what we know of the kind of man he was, the eager Franval had behaved with such delicacy only so that his seduction would proceed the more surely. Soon he completely dominated his credulous daughter, and when the last obstacles fell as a result both of the notions he had put into her head, which was receptive to ideas of all kinds, and of the enticing arts with which he now ensnared her in this ultimate phase, he completed his ignoble conquest. Thus it was that he himself became with impunity the thief of a maidenhead of which nature and his noble name had appointed him the protector.

Several days passed in mutual rapture. Eugénie, now of an age to know the pleasures of love, and emboldened by Franval's philosophy, took to them with zest. Franval told her all of love's mysteries, mapped all its paths. The more he multiplied his amorous tributes, the more enslaved his conquest became, until she would have received him with open arms in a thousand temples simultaneously.

She accused her lover of deliberately curbing his imagination, for she felt that he was holding back from her. She complained that she was too young and perhaps too innocent to be sufficiently alluring. And if she wished to be more knowledgeable, the reason was simple: so that no means of arousing her lover would remain unknown to her.]

They returned to Paris. But the criminal pleasures which the perverse Franval had found so heady had flattered his senses and his mind to such an extent that an infidelity, which normally ended all his other affairs, was out of the question to terminate this new liaison. He was besotted, and from his dangerous passion was to result his cruel desertion of his wife, who became, alas, his victim.

Madame de Franval was then thirty-one years of age, and at the height of her beauty. Her doleful air, induced by the sorrows which consumed her, merely added to her loveliness. Constantly in tears, prostrated by melancholy, with her beautiful hair carelessly spread over her alabaster breast, her lips lovingly pressed to a cherished portrait of her faithless husband and tyrant, she called to mind the lovely, suffering virgins painted by Michelangelo.* Yet she was far from suspecting what lay in wait to make her torment complete. The way Eugénie was being brought up, the vital matters of which she was kept ignorant or which were broached to her solely to make her detest them, the absolute certainty that her daughter would never be permitted to embrace those duties which Franval despised, the brief interviews she was allowed to have with her child, her fear that the bizarre education given to her would sooner or later drive her to criminal conduct, Franval's wild behaviour and the callousness with which he treated her daily, although she had no thought but to do his bidding and placed all her felicity in earning his good opinion and pleasing him: such, up to this point, were the sole causes of her affliction. But by what searing anguish would this tender, sensitive soul be overwhelmed once she knew the whole truth!

Meanwhile Eugénie's education proceeded apace. She herself had asked to continue to be taught by tutors until she was sixteen, and her talents, wide knowledge, and the way she grew in graces with each passing day... all this combined to lock Franval's fetters tighter. It was patently obvious that he had never loved anyone as he loved Eugénie.

The only part of Mademoiselle de Franval's routine that changed was the time allotted for 'lectures'. These private sessions with her father took place more frequently and went on until late at night. Only Eugénie's governess was privy to what went on, and she was far too reliable for there to be any need to question her discretion. A few alterations were made to the way Eugénie took her meals, and she now dined with her parents. Such a change in a household like Franval's meant that soon Eugénie was able to meet other company and be thought of as eligible for marriage. Several men asked for her hand. Franval, confident of his daughter's feelings and believing he had nothing to fear from such advances, had not, however, given sufficient thought to the possibility that the rush of proposals might eventually bring matters into the open.

In a conversation with her daughter, a favour often requested by Madame de Franval but rarely granted, Eugénie's tender mother informed her that Monsieur de Colunce had asked for her hand in marriage.

'You know him, daughter,' said Madame de Franval. 'He loves you, is young, personable and will be rich. He is only waiting for your answer... the answer that is yours alone to make. What am I to say to him?'

Taken aback, Eugénie blushed and said that she did not yet find the prospect of marriage appealing, but that her father should be consulted. She would respect his views and act accordingly. Believing that this response was entirely straightforward, Madame de Franval waited a few days, and at last finding an opportunity of raising the matter with her husband, conveyed to him the views of young Colunce's family, the intentions of the young man himself, and added what her daughter had said. Now as may well be imagined, Franval knew everything. But he dissembled, though he was not able to keep total control of himself.

'Madame,' he said brusquely to his wife, 'I must insist that you do not meddle in Eugénie's affairs. You have seen how careful I have been to keep her away from you, and it must surely have been perfectly clear that I wished matters concerning her future to be none of your business. I repeat my orders to you now and trust that you will never forget them again.'

'But what answer shall I give, since the request was made to me?'

'You will say that I am conscious of the honour done to me but that an uncertainty surrounding my daughter's birth makes it impossible for her to marry.'

'But sir, there is no such uncertainty. Why would you have me say something which is not true? Why do you wish to deprive your only daughter of the happiness she will find in marriage?'

'Has marriage made you very happy, Madame?'

'Perhaps not all women have made as many mistakes as I have in failing to keep your love, or else' (said she with a sigh) 'not all husbands are like you.'

'Wives—unfaithful, jealous, wilful, flirtatious, or sanctimonious—and husbands—false, inconstant, cruel, or tyrannical—there in a nutshell you have all the men and women in the world. You must not hope to hit upon a phoenix.'

'Yet everyone marries.'

'Yes, fools and idlers do. A philosopher once said that people only marry "when they do not know what they are doing or when they do not know what else to do".'

'So the whole universe must be allowed to come to an end?'

'You could say that. A plant which produces only poison cannot be uprooted too soon.'

'Eugénie will not be grateful to you for treating her with such excessive severity.'

'Does she seem taken with the idea of marrying?'

'Your wish is her command, she said.'

'Well, Madame, it is my wish that you should say no more of this marriage.'

And Monsieur de Franval left the room, renewing his most express command that the matter should never be mentioned to him again.

Madame de Franval did not fail to render her mother an exact account of the interview she had had with her husband. Madame de Farneille, shrewder and more familiar with the effects of the passions than her worthy daughter, immediately suspected that there was something most unusual behind all this.

Eugénie saw very little of her grandmother: an hour at most when there were visitors, and always in the presence of Franval. Wishing to find out what was going on, Madame de Farneille wrote to her son-in-law asking him to send her granddaughter to visit her one day soon, and allow her to spend the whole afternoon alone with her, as a distraction, she said, from the migraines which were so troublesome to her. He sent a curt reply, saying that there was nothing Eugénie detested more than the vapours, but that he would bring her as requested, though she would not be able to stay for long since she would be expected to return home to attend a physics lesson, a subject she studied with close application.

They duly called on Madame de Farneille, who did not conceal from her son-in-law the surprise she had felt on learning that the proposal of marriage had been rejected.

'I do not think you would have anything to fear,' she went on, 'if you allowed your daughter to tell me in her own words what exactly this uncertainty is which, so you say, prevents her from marrying.'

'Whether the uncertainty is real or not, Madame,' said Franval, somewhat surprised by his mother-in-law's persistence, 'the fact is that it would cost me a pretty penny if my daughter were to marry. I am as yet too young to make such a sacrifice. When she is twenty-five and of age, she will act as she thinks fit. But until then, she must not count on me.'

'And do you share the same sentiments, Eugénie?' said Madame de Farneille.

'Not entirely, Madame,' said Mademoiselle de Franval very firmly. 'My father has given me leave to marry when I am twenty-five. But I tell you, as I tell him, that I shall never avail myself of his authorization for as long as I live. For, given my outlook on life, it would merely ensure that I was perpetually unhappy.'

'Girls of your age do not have outlooks on life, Mademoiselle,' said Madame de Farneille. 'There is something very odd about all this, and I must find out what it is.'

'I urge you to do so, Madame,' said Franval, making ready to leave with his daughter. 'A good starting point would be to use your circle of church hangers-on to solve the riddle. When their mighty clerical minds have minced the matter exceeding small and you know the answer, perhaps you would be so good as to tell me whether I am right or wrong to say no to Eugénie's marriage.'

This sarcastic reference to the ecclesiastical counsellors who advised Franval's mother-in-law in matters spiritual was aimed specifically at one worthy man of the cloth, who must be introduced at this point, since he has a part to play in the events which will soon unfold.

He was spiritual guide to Madame de Farneille and her daughter, one of the most virtuous men in France, upright, charitable, and blessed with honesty and plain good sense. He was Monsieur de Clervil, who had none of the vices of his cloth but only gentle, altruistic virtues. The ever-ready prop of the poor, a true friend to the rich, and the comforter of the distressed, this saintly man combined all the gifts which make a man likeable with all the virtues of the man of feeling.

When asked for his advice, Clervil replied sagely that before any step was taken in the matter, efforts should be made to discover Monsieur de Franval's reasons for opposing his daughter's marriage. And although Madame de Farneille dropped several hints likely to start a suspicion of a state of affairs which was only too real, her prudent adviser rejected the idea. Considering it far too damaging to the good name of both Madame de Franval and her husband, he refused indignantly to entertain any such notion.

'Crime, Madame, is a most distressing thing,' this good man would say. 'It is really so implausible to suppose that any person of goodwill would deliberately cross the threshold of decency and throw off the restraints of virtue, that it is always with the greatest reluctance that I am prepared to harbour any such suspicion. We should be sparing with our accusations, for they are often the result of our own pride, the offspring of a secret comparison which is made in the depths of our soul. We rush to find evil in others so that we may be justified in feeling that we are better than they. But when the matter is properly considered, Madame, is it not preferable that a secret fault were never revealed at all, than that we should proceed at an unpardonable gallop and assume the existence of non-existent sins, and in so doing sully—groundlessly, but to our satisfaction—the good name of people who have committed no other crimes than those imputed to them by our pride? And can this same principle not be extended with advantage to everything else? Is it not infinitely less important to punish a crime than to prevent that crime from spreading? If it is allowed to remain in shadow, is it not as good as cancelled?* If it is made public, scandal will surely follow, and talk of it will awaken the passions of others who may be inclined to the same kind of transgression. The blindness inseparable from wrongdoing gives comfort to other guilty persons, who will hope that they will be more fortunate than the sinner who has been found out. It is not a lesson they have been taught, but a practical piece of advice that they have been given, and they proceed to commit excesses they would doubtless never have dared dream of had it not been for the scandal which, unwisely provoked and wrongly construed as justice, is nothing more than misconceived moral strictness or a cloak for our vanity.'

At this first conference he therefore settled for reaching an accurate understanding of the causes of Franval's opposition to his daughter's marriage, and of the reasons which led Eugénie to adopt the same way of thinking. It was decided that nothing should be done until these questions were clear.

'Well, Eugénie,' said Franval to his daughter that evening, 'you see? They want to separate us. Will they succeed, child? Will they manage to remove the sweetest chains I ever wore?'

'Never! You must never fear any such thing, my dear, darling friend! Those same chains which delight your heart are no less precious to me. You have not misled me. As you were busy forging them, you made it perfectly clear how offensive they were to ordinary morals and manners. I was not afraid to defy customs which, since they vary from country to country, cannot be considered sacred, and I welcomed my chains with open arms and added to them without guilt. There is no reason therefore why you should fear that I will ever cast them off.'

'Alas, who can tell? Colunce is a younger man than I am. He has everything to make a young girl love him. Eugénie, you must not be held back by a lingering, youthful aberration which surely prevents you from thinking clearly. The enchantment will fade as you grow older and wiser, and you will soon have regrets. You will lay the burden of them on my heart, and I shall never forgive myself for having been the cause of them.'

'No,' replied Eugénie firmly, 'I have made up my mind that I shall never love anyone but you. I should count myself the unhappiest of women if I were ever forced to marry. Me, marry?' she went on heatedly. 'Yoke myself to a stranger who would not have two kinds of love to offer me as you do, and would cut me down to the size of his feelings or at most of his desires! Neglected and despised by him, what would become of me thereafter? Would I turn into a prude, a bigot, a whore? Never! I would infinitely prefer to be your mistress, my dear. Yes, I would prefer a thousand times to love you than be reduced to playing in public any of those ignoble roles. But what is behind all this present commotion?' Eugénie went on crossly. 'Do you know what has caused it? What can it be? Is it your wife? Yes, that's it, she and her unrelenting jealousy. Make no mistake: there you have the only reason for the calamities which threaten us. Oh, I do not blame her. It is all very straightforward, all perfectly understandable: to keep you, a woman would stop at nothing. What would I not do in her place if someone tried to steal your affections from me?'

Unexpectedly moved, Franval took his daughter in his arms. She, finding encouragement in his criminal caresses and infusing her black soul with new energy, chanced to tell her father with unforgivable shamelessness that the only way of ensuring that they were not spied on was to provide a lover for her mother. This idea delighted Franval but, being more wicked than his daughter and wishing to open her heart gradually to those feelings of hatred for his wife which he hoped to plant there, he replied that such a revenge seemed to him far too mild, adding that there were many other ways of making a wife unhappy when she put her husband out of temper.

Several weeks went by during which Franval and his daughter finally reconciled themselves to implementing their original plan, which was designed to reduce the monster's virtuous wife to the depths of despair, rightly believing that before they graduated to even viler schemes, they should at least attempt to find her a lover. This tactic would not only provide the basis for all the other stratagems they had in mind but, if successful, would necessarily teach Madame de Franval not to pay quite so much attention to the failings of others, since she would herself be guilty of proven shortcomings of her own.

To set the plan in motion, Franval cast an eye over all the young men of his acquaintance. Having given the matter considerable thought, he found only Valmont* who seemed entirely suitable for his purpose.

Valmont was thirty years of age. He possessed handsome features, wit, a goodly measure of imagination, and no moral scruples whatsoever. He was therefore eminently qualified to play the role which he was about to be offered. One day Franval invited him to dine and, as the company rose from table, he took him to one side.

'My dear fellow,' said he, 'I have always considered you to be as gamesome as I am myself. The moment has come for you to prove that I am not wrong to think so. I shall ask you to prove your sentiments, and prove them in a very unusual way.'

'What does it involve? Explain yourself. You should never doubt my readiness to serve you in any way I can!'

'What do you think of my wife?'

'Utterly ravishing. If you were not her husband, I should have been her lover long before this.'

'Tactfully put and very delicate, Valmont, but there is no need for that sort of thing with me.'

'What do you mean?'

'Prepare to be amazed. It is precisely because you are my friend... precisely because I am Madame de Franval's husband, that I would like you to become her lover.'

'Are you mad?'

'No, just capricious, whimsical... you have known me long enough to recognize my moods. I want virtue to take a tumble, and I would like you to be the man to trip it up.'

'But this is folly!'

'Not another word. This really is the most rational thing...'

'You mean you seriously want me to...?'

'Yes I do, I insist. Indeed, I shall cease to regard you as my friend if you refuse me this favour. I shall arrange opportunities for you... many opportunities... and you will make the most of them. And when I am absolutely certain of how I stand, I shall, if I must, throw myself at your feet and thank you for your co-operation.'

'Franval, I won't be your dupe. There is something very strange about all this. I will have no part of it unless I know everything.'

'Very well... but I suspect that you have a few lingering scruples. I have no guarantee that you have the strength of mind to grasp and understand what is involved. You still have antiquated notions... a few trailing wisps of chivalry, I'd wager?... You would jump like a startled child if told you everything, and then you wouldn't want to help.'

'Me, jump? I am mortified you should think such a thing of me. See here, old friend, there is no dissolute behaviour under the sun, no debauched act, however extreme, which could make my heart miss a single beat.'

'Valmont, have you sometimes let your eye linger on Eugénie?'

'Your daughter?'

'My mistress, if you prefer.'

'Why you old rogue! Now I've got it!'

'This is the first time in my life I have ever observed a glimmer of intelligence in you.'

'You mean, on your honour, that you're in love with your own daughter?'

'Yes, old friend, as once was Lot. I have always had the greatest respect for Holy Writ, and was always told that we may get to heaven if we model ourselves on its great men... Ah, I can now understand what possessed Pygmalion... Are such lapses not universal? Was not mankind obliged to resort to such methods to populate the world?* And if it was not wrong then, how can it be wrong now? It is all so much folly! Does it mean that I should not be attracted by a pretty girl, just because I made the mistake of bringing her into this world? What justifies my staying close to her becomes the reason why I should keep away from her! Is it because she is like me, because she is my flesh and blood... that is, because she embodies everything required to start feelings of the most passionate love... that I must keep my distance?... This is pure sophistry, and utterly absurd! Such curbs on desire should be left to the clods and the fools: they were not meant for people like us. The attraction of beauty and the divine right of love do not recognize these futile human conventions. Their power overcomes them just as the rays of the new day's sun washes the earth clean of the mists which shrouded it by night. We must ride roughshod over these odious prejudices which are eternally opposed to our happiness. If they have sometimes seemed to make sense to the human mind, they have done so only at the cost of denying us the most gratifying pleasures of the body. We should hold them eternally in the deepest contempt.'

'You have convinced me,' replied Valmont, 'and I freely grant you that Eugénie must be the most delectable mistress. Her style of beauty is more vivacious than her mother's, and if she does not quite have that languishing look which your wife has, the kind that fills the very soul with sensual thoughts, she has a pertness that enslaves a man and, in short, is likely to bring anyone who resists her to his knees. Whereas the one appears to yield, the other demands surrender; what the first grants, the other offers... and to my mind it is the latter who is the more charming.'

'Yes, but it is not Eugénie I'm offering you but her mother.'

'True. But what is your reason for doing this?'

'My wife is jealous. She is being a nuisance and keeps a close eye on me. She wants to find Eugénie a husband. I must show that she has committed transgressions if I am to cover up my own. So you must *have* her... take your pleasure with her for a while... then betray her... and I must find you in her arms... and either punish her or use the evidence to buy peace on both sides on the basis of our mutual misconduct... But remember, Valmont, make sure that love stays out of the reckoning. Keep a cool head, sweep her off her feet, and make sure you stay on yours. If feelings get dragged into this, my plans will be shot to pieces.'*

'Never fear, she would be the first woman to warm up my heart.'

And so the two miscreants agreed on their arrangement, and it was decided that in the days immediately following Valmont would make his approach to Madame de Franval, with full permission to use any method he chose to bring the business to a successful conclusion, even if it meant revealing the nature of Franval's love, this being thought the most powerful means of persuading his worthy wife to seek her revenge.

Eugénie, who was made privy to the scheme, found it vastly entertaining. The ignoble creature even went so far as to say that if Valmont succeeded, then, if her happiness was to be as complete as could be wished, she would have to be personally assured of her mother's disgrace by observing the spectacle for herself, so that she could see that heroine of virtue surrender unambiguously to the attractions of a pleasure which she normally damned with such severity.

At last the day dawned when the most righteous and unhappy of wives was not only to receive the most grievous hurt that anyone can receive, but also be profaned by her vile husband by being abandoned by him and delivered into the hands of a man by whom he had volunteered to be cuckolded. It was an aberration! Such contempt for every decent principle! What can nature be thinking of when she creates hearts as depraved as these?

One or two preliminary discussions had set out how the scene was to be played. Valmont was, of course, on sufficiently friendly terms with Franval for his wife to have no reason to think twice about remaining alone with him, for it was a thing that had already happened several times without anything untoward occurring. All three were in the drawing room. Franval got to his feet.

'I must go,' said he. 'I have important business to attend to. I should leave you as well chaperoned by your lady's companion,' he added with a laugh, 'as I do in leaving you alone with Valmont. He is utterly trustworthy. But if he does forget himself, you must tell me. He and I are not such close friends that I should be prepared to relinquish my marital rights to him...'

And the shameless rogue departed.

After a few banal pleasantries which arose out of Franval's jest, Valmont observed that he found his friend much changed over the last six months. 'I have not really liked to ask him the reason for it,' he went on, 'but he has the look of a man with worries.'

'One thing is certain,' answered Madame de Franval, 'and that is that he makes other people worry a great deal.'

'Great heavens! What are you saying? Has my friend wronged you in some way?'

'If only we were still at that stage!'

'I hope you will enlighten me. You know how devoted I am... how utterly attached...'

'A succession of the most unspeakable breaches... with morality flouted and wrongs of every kind. You would never believe it: he receives the most flattering proposal of marriage for his daughter... and he will have none of it...'

At this point the cunning Valmont averted his eyes, with the air of a man who sees clearly, who is cut to the quick, who fears to say what he thinks.

'Come, sir,' Madame de Franval went on, 'are you not in the least surprised by what I have just told you? Your silence is very strange.'

'Oh Madame, is it not better to say nothing than to speak and plunge those we love into the deepest despair?'

'What riddle is this? Explain what you mean, I beg you.'

'How can you expect me not to shrink from removing the scales from your eyes?' said Valmont, impulsively reaching for the excellent woman's hands.

'Oh sir,' Madame de Franval continued animatedly, 'either you must not pronounce another word or else I insist that you say what you mean. The position you put me in is intolerable.'

'Perhaps less so than the state to which you have reduced me,' said Valmont and, turning to the woman he was intent on seducing, he gazed at her with eyes inflamed by desire.

'What is the meaning of this charade, sir? You start by alarming me, you then induce me to ask for an explanation, and next you dare to suggest that you can tell me things to which I must not and cannot listen, and in so doing you deprive me of the opportunity of hearing from your lips precisely what it is that worries me most cruelly. Speak, sir, speak, otherwise you will reduce me to despair.'

'I will therefore be less opaque, Madame, since you insist and although it pains me to cause you so deep a hurt. Let me tell you the cruel reason why your husband rejected Monsieur de Colunce's proposal. Eugénie...'

'Go on.'

'Well, Madame, Franval is besotted with her. He is now not so much her father as her lover. He would sooner be forced to end his life than give up Eugénie.'

Madame de Franval had not heard this appalling revelation to the end before being overcome by a malaise which robbed her of her senses. Valmont hastened to her assistance, and when his efforts were rewarded, he went on:

'You see, Madame, the price you have had to pay for the explanation you insisted on having? I would not for all the world...'

'Leave me, sir, let me alone,' said Madame de Franval who, after experiencing such a violent shock, was now in a state difficult to convey. 'I need to be alone for a while.'

'And you want me to leave you in this condition? The pain you feel I feel too, in my heart, and too cruelly for me to refrain from asking your permission to share it with you. I caused the wound. Allow me to heal it.'

'Franval in love with his daughter! My God! The creature I carried in my womb is the same who now tears me to pieces so mercilessly! Such an unspeakable crime! Oh sir, how can this be? Can there be any doubt...?'

'If I had doubts, Madame, I would have kept silent. I would have much rather told you nothing than alarm you unnecessarily. It was your husband himself who gave me confirmation of his infamous conduct. He took me into his confidence. Whatever this means, I beg you to remain calm. Let us concentrate now on finding a way of ending this situation rather than trying to explain it. And you have the means of doing so...'

'Oh, then waste no time and tell me what it is! This crime fills me with horror!'

'A husband with a character like Franval's, Madame, cannot be reformed by virtue. Yours has little faith in the chastity of women. He claims that everything they do to retain our good regard is determined by their pride or their physiology: it is designed more for their own satisfaction than to please us or snare us in their toils... Forgive me, Madame, but I shall not hide the fact that I think as he does in this matter. I never yet saw a case where it was with her virtues that a woman succeeded in overcoming her husband's vices. Now if you were to behave more or less as Franval has done, it might prove a more effective goad and be a better way of winning him back. The result would be undoubtedly to make him jealous, and love has been returned to so many hearts by this invariably infallible stratagem! Your husband would then see that the virtue which is his natural mode but which he has the effrontery to despise, is much more the result of his way of thinking than of waywardness or his physical constitution, and he will learn to value it in you once he thinks that you are capable of falling short of it... He imagines... he has even suggested that if you have never had lovers it is because you have never been propositioned. Prove to him that it is your decision whether to be propositioned or not, and your choice to seek revenge for his misdeeds and his contempt. Perhaps, judged by your strict principles, you will have committed a small sin. But what evils will you not have prevented! What a husband you will have converted! And at the cost of a small offence against the goddess you revere, what a rare votary will you not have ushered back to the fold of her temple? Oh Madame, I appeal only to your reason. By the conduct I have ventured to prescribe, you will win back Franval for ever, he will be yours for all eternity. At present he eludes you by behaving badly; he will escape you and never return. Yes, Madame, I guarantee it: either you do not love your husband or you must not hesitate.'

Madame de Franval, extremely taken aback by what she had heard, remained for some moments without replying. Then, resuming her role in the conversation, and recalling the way Valmont had looked at her and the first words he had spoken:

'Sir,' she said shrewdly, 'assuming I were to take the advice you have given me, in which direction do you think I should look so that my husband would be the most deeply mortified?'

'Ah! Dear, divine lady,' exclaimed Valmont, not seeing the trap which had been laid for him, 'why, towards the man who of all others loves you the most, a man who has worshipped you from the moment he first saw you, who now kneels before you and swears that he will be yours until the day he dies!'

'Go, sir! Get out,' Madame de Franval said peremptorily, 'and never appear in my sight again! Your ruse is exposed. You accuse my husband of crimes of which he is incapable merely to make it easier for your own treachery to pass. Know this: even were he guilty, the approach you have outlined would be too offensive to my feelings for me to adopt it for one moment. The failings of a husband can never justify the immorality of a wife, and should be an extra reason for her to behave well, so that the just man, whom Almighty God will find in the grieving cities which prepare to feel the weight of His wrath,* may, if he can, deflect from their heart the fires which are about to consume them.'

And so saying, Madame de Franval left the room, called for Valmont's servants, and left him no alternative but to go, which he did, heartily ashamed of his first advances.

Although this remarkable woman had seen through the ruse of Franval's friend, what he had said tallied so well with the fears harboured by both herself and her mother that she resolved to leave no stone unturned in her efforts to establish the truth of such cruel charges. She called upon Madame de Farneille, told her all that had happened, and returned home, determined to take the steps which we shall observe her pursue.

It was said long ago, and with ample reason, that we have no greater enemies than our servants. Ever watchful, invariably envious, it would seem that they seek to lighten their chains by exploiting any failings on our part which put us in their power and allow their vanity to claim, momentarily at least, a superiority over us which fate has denied them.

Madame de Franval managed to suborn one of Eugénie's maids. A safe haven, a pleasant future, and the semblance of a good deed were enough to make up the creature's mind. She agreed that the next night she would put Madame de Franval in a position where she would have no further doubts about her predicament.

The moment arrives. The unhappy mother is led into a side room adjoining the apartment where each night her faithless husband violated both his vows and Heaven itself. Eugénie was with her father. Candles still burned on a corner table, and were sufficient to light up the crime. The altar is prepared, the victim takes her place upon it, and the high priest follows... Madame de Franval, sustained only by her despair, her inflamed love, and her courage, breaks down the doors which bar her way and bursts into the apartment where, falling on to her knees and weeping at the feet of her incestuous husband, she cried:

'Ah, faithless man, you who are the cause of my life's unhappiness, who have treated me in a manner I did not deserve, whom I still love, despite the wrongs I have suffered at your hand, see my tears and do not cast me aside! I implore you to spare our hapless daughter who, led astray by her own weakness and your blandishments, believes that she will find happiness in lewdness and crime... Eugénie, Eugénie, will you drive a dagger through this body which gave you life? You must cease to be a willing party to a compact whose horror has been hidden from you! Come... come to me... See, my arms are open and ready to receive you! Behold your pitiful mother, who goes down on her knees before you and begs you to defile neither honour nor nature! But if you both reject me,' the despairing woman continued, holding a dagger to her heart, 'this is the means by which I shall avoid the punishments which you intend to inflict on me. You will be splashed by the blood I shed, and you will have only my pitiful corpse on which to consummate your crimes.'

That Franval's flinty soul was able to resist this spectacle will be only too easily believed by those who are beginning to understand what a villain he was. But that Eugénie's heart should remain unmoved is a thing inconceivable.

'Madame,' said this depraved daughter, in the most callous and cruel tone, 'I must admit that I cannot for the life of me connect your rational mind with this ridiculous scene which you are making here in your husband's rooms. Is he not the master of his own actions? And since he approves of mine, what right have you to criticize? Shall we speak of your indiscretions with Monsieur de Valmont? Do we interfere with your pleasures? Then be so good as not to meddle in ours, or else you must not be surprised if I am the first to urge your husband to take measures which will force you to...'

At this point, Madame de Franval's patience snapped. All her rage now turned against the ignoble creature who could forget herself to the point of addressing her in this manner. Rising to her feet in fury, she threw herself at her. But the odious, brutal Franval, seizing his wife by the hair, dragged her angrily away from his daughter, ejected her from the room, pushed her roughly down the stairs, and sent her tumbling, unconscious and bleeding, until she came to rest outside the door of one of her maids who, awakened by the horrible din, hurriedly removed her mistress from the rage of her persecutor, who had followed her down to dispatch his wretched victim. She was taken home, the doors were locked, and her hurts were tended. Meanwhile, the monster who had treated her with such frenzy hastened back to the side of his hateful companion, where he spent as peaceful a night as if he had not sunk below the level of the most ravening beasts by perpetrating such an execrable outrage... by committing actions consciously intended to humiliate... and so horrible, in short, that we are mortified to be forced into the position of having to disclose them.

The hapless Madame de Franval could now have no more illusions, not one to which she might have plausibly clung. It was only too clear that the love of her husband, the most precious thing in her life that she possessed, had been taken from her... and by whom? By the person who owed her the greatest respect... and had just spoken to her with the greatest insolence. She also suspected that the whole Valmont business was nothing other than a despicable trap intended to lure her into actual misconduct if possible or, failing that, to impute sins to her, to blacken her name, in order to provide a counterweight—and thus the justification—for the wrongs, infinitely more serious, which had been so shamelessly done to her.

Such was indeed the case. Franval, informed of Valmont's failure, had persuaded him to substitute duplicity and an indiscreet tongue for the truth; in short, to tell all and sundry that he was Madame de Franval's lover. And they had agreed between them that they would forge odious letters which would provide the most unequivocal proof of a liaison to which, in reality, Franval's hapless wife had refused to be a party. Meanwhile, Madame de Franval, in a state of despair, and suffering from injuries to various parts of her body, fell seriously ill. Her barbarous husband, refusing to see her and not even troubling to enquire after her health, left with Eugénie for the country, giving it as an excuse that since there was a contagious fever in his house he had no wish that his daughter should be exposed to it.

Valmont called several times on Madame de Franval during her illness, but was not admitted once. Closeted with her loving mother and Monsieur de Clervil, she saw no one. Consoled by such affectionate friends, who were so well qualified to take charge of her, and brought back to life by their loving care, she was, forty days later, well enough to receive callers. Franval brought his daughter back to Paris at that time, and arranged with Valmont to assemble weapons capable of neutralizing those which Madame de Franval and her friends seemed determined to direct at them.

Our villain called on his wife as soon as he believed that she was in a fit state to receive him.

'Madame,' he said coldly, 'you should be in no doubt of the interest I have taken in your condition, for I cannot hide from you the fact that it was the state of your health that you must thank for Eugénie's restraint. She had decided to bring the most acrimonious charges against you for treating her the way you did. However convinced she might be of the respect a daughter should have for her mother, she is sensible that a mother places herself in the worst possible light when she throws herself on her daughter, with a dagger in her hand. Violence of that sort, Madame, by drawing the attention of the authorities to your conduct, might one day lead inescapably to consequences for your freedom and your good name.'

'I was not expecting these recriminations, sir,' answered Madame de Franval. 'And when my daughter, after being seduced by you, makes herself guilty, severally, of incest, adultery, debauchery, and the most odious ingratitude to the mother who brought her into the world... yes, after such a tissue of horrors, I confess I never dreamed I should be the one to fear criminal charges. It needs all the artifice and malice that you possess, sir, to accuse the innocent by excusing the guilty with such bare-faced arrogance!'

'I am not unaware, Madame, that the pretext for the scene you made was the odious suspicions you dare harbour of me. But idle fancies do not prove that crimes have been committed. What you thought is false. What you did is unfortunately all too real. You were surprised by the reproaches aimed against you by my daughter concerning your liaison with Valmont. But, Madame, she uncovered the irregularity of your conduct only after it was known to all Paris. Your affair is no secret, and the evidence is unfortunately so overwhelming that people who speak to you of this matter are guilty not of slander but at most of an imprudence.'

'Me, sir?' cried his worthy wife, rising to her feet in indignation. 'I am involved in a liaison with Valmont? Merciful heavens! That is what you say.' (Here shedding copious tears.) 'Ungrateful man! So this is the reward for all my affection... what I get for having loved you so? Not content with abusing me so cruelly, not satisfied with seducing my daughter, you must also have the audacity to justify your evil deeds by imputing crimes to me which I find more terrible than death itself...' (Then collecting herself.) 'You say you have evidence of this liaison, sir. Then produce it, I demand that it be made public. If you refuse to let me see it, I will force you to show it to the whole world.'

'Absolutely not, Madame. I shall not show it to the whole world. It is not usual for a husband to cause a scandal in matters of this sort. He weeps over it, he hides it as best he can. But if you really insist on seeing the proofs for yourself, Madame, I would certainly not refuse your request.' (Here he produced a wallet from his pocket.) 'Sit down,' he said, 'this must be looked into calmly: ill-temper and angry outbursts would harm your case and not convince me. So please collect yourself and let us discuss the matter rationally.'

Madame de Franval, knowing of course that she was totally innocent, hardly knew what to make of these preliminaries. Her surprise, which was mingled with apprehension, held her in a state of violent emotion.

'First, Madame,' said Franval, emptying one side of the wallet, 'here are all the letters you have exchanged with Valmont over the last six months. You must not accuse the young fellow of duplicity or a loose tongue, for he is assuredly too honourable to show you so little respect. The fact is, one of his servants, more cunning than his master was careful, found a means of procuring for me this precious testimony of your extreme good conduct and lofty virtue.' (He leafs through the letters and scatters them on the table.) 'You will not mind,' he went on, 'if from among the usual prattlings of a woman... excited by a handsome man, if I select one which to me seemed brisker and altogether more direct than the others:

My tedious husband will sup tonight at his own little pleasure house with that repulsive creature. I can scarcely believe that I brought her into the world... Come, my sweet, and console me for all the vexations those two monsters cause me... Yet when I think of it, is it not the best turn in the world they do me in the present juncture, for will not their little affair prevent my husband from noticing ours? So let him wrap himself as tightly in his amours as he pleases. But he would be well advised not to think of trying to unwrap mine which make me dote on the only man I have ever loved in the whole world.

Well, Madame?'

'Well, sir, I can but applaud,' replied Madame de Franval. 'Each day adds to the impossibly high regard which you so handsomely deserve. In the past I have recognized many great qualities in you. But I confess I never knew until this moment that you also possessed the talents of forger and slanderer.'

'So you deny everything?'

'Not at all. I merely wish to be convinced. We will choose judges... experts. And, if you agree, we shall demand the severest punishment for whichever of us is guilty.'

'This is what is called barefaced effrontery. Still I would prefer that to hand-wringing. Let us continue. That you should have a lover, Madame,' said Franval, giving the second side of the wallet a shake, 'since you have a pretty face and a tedious husband, is surely a matter plain and unvarnished. But that at your age you should keep a lover, and at my expense to boot, is something which you will permit me to find much less straightforward. Yet here are notes for a hundred thousand crowns either paid by you or made out in your hand in Valmont's favour. Be so good as to glance at them, would you?' the monster added, holding them in front of her but without letting her touch them.

To Zaïde, jeweller,

In full settlement of the sum of twenty-two thousand livres, this being the outstanding account of Monsieur de Valmont, as agreed with him,

Farneille de Franval

'To Jamet, horse-dealer, six thousand livres...' That was for the coach and chestnut pair which today are Valmont's pride and joy. Yes, Madame, and this one is for three-hundred thousand, two-hundred and eighty-three livres and ten sous, of which you still owe a third after paying the rest as agreed. Well, Madame?'

'Sir, this is a complete fabrication and much too crude to cause me a moment's anxiety. I ask but one thing to silence those who have conspired against me, which is that the people for whom I am supposed to have signed these notes should come forward and swear that I have had dealings with them.'

'They will do so, Madame, you may count on it. Would they themselves have informed me of your conduct were they not of a mind to affirm what they have stated? But for me, one of them would have begun proceedings against you this very day.'

Tears began to flow from the wretched woman's lustrous eyes. Her courage gave way and she collapsed beneath an onslaught of despair which was accompanied by frightening symptoms: she beat her head against the marble walls around her and pummelled her face with her hands.

'Sir,' she cried, throwing herself at her husband's feet, 'since you are intent on making an end of me, I beg you do it by a method that is less slow and less horrible! Since my existence is a hindrance to your crimes, end it swiftly... do not drive me slowly to my grave... Am I guilty for loving you, for rebelling against your conduct which so cruelly deprived me of your love? Well then, punish me, unfeeling man, yes, take this blade,' she exclaimed, reaching wildly for her husband's sword, 'take it, I say, and pierce my heart for pity's sake! But let me at least die deserving of your respect. Let me take to the grave, as my only consolation, the knowledge that you believe me incapable of the vile actions of which you accuse me only so that you can conceal your own!'

She was on her knees, prostrate at Franval's feet, her hands bleeding and cut by the naked blade she had attempted to seize and plunge into her breast, ready bared, over which tumbled her dishevelled hair and which was wet with the tears she shed copiously. Never did sorrow seem more piteous or more expressive; never had its every detail appeared more affecting, more vivid, and more noble...

'No, Madame,' said Franval, parrying her action, 'it is not your death we seek... not yet... but your punishment. I can understand your contrition, your tears are no surprise to me, for you are angry at being found out. Your reaction pleases me, for it allows me to think you might mend your conduct... a change of heart which will doubtless be hastened by the fate I have in mind for you. I shall now leave you and give the matter my fullest attention.'

'Stop, Franval!' cried his distraught wife. 'You cannot make your dishonour common knowledge! You must not inform the public yourself that you are a forger, an incestuous father, and a slanderer!... You would like to be rid of me. Very well, I shall go far away from you. I shall find some safe haven where I shall forget even the memory of you. You will be free, free to commit your crimes... Yes, I shall forget you, if I can, cruel man, or if the painful thought of you cannot be expunged from my heart, if it pursues me still into the depths of my solitude, I shall not seek to blot it out, the effort would be beyond my strength, no, I shall not blot it out, but shall punish myself for my own blindness, and to the horrors of the grave I shall consign a heart which loved you too well!'

At these words, which were the last throw of a soul overwhelmed by affliction, the hapless woman fainted away and collapsed unconscious. The cold shadows of death touched the rose petals of her luminous complexion, which had already been withered by the hand of despair. What remained was a lifeless body which, however, was not yet abandoned by beauty, modesty, and demureness—all the charms of virtue.

The monster left her and hastened away to share with his guilty daughter the appalling victory which vice, or rather villainy, had dared score over innocence and misfortune.

Franval's odious daughter found his account vastly amusing. She would have liked to be present... the horror ought to have been made more horrible, Valmont ought to have overcome her mother's resistance, Franval ought to have discovered them together... If all that had happened, what possible avenue for self-justification would have remained open to their victim? Was it not vital to deny her every means of defending herself? There you have Eugénie.

Meanwhile Franval's unhappy wife, having only her mother to receive the burden of her tears, did not wait long before informing her of this latest aggravation of her miseries. It was now that Madame de Farneille supposed that the age, calling, and personal standing of Monsieur de Clervil might have some salutary effect on her son-in-law: nothing is as trusting as desperation. She therefore, as best she could, made that respectable man of God privy to all the details of Franval's disorderly life. She convinced him that what he had always refused to believe was true, and in particular persuaded him that with such a villain he should take care to use only arguments designed to appeal to the heart, not the mind. When he had spoken to the blackguard, she suggested he should then seek an interview with Eugénie, during which he would likewise use all the eloquence he judged appropriate to make the wretched girl see the abyss which stood open beneath her feet and, if it were possible, return her to the arms of her mother and the fold of virtue.

Franval, forewarned that Clervil would ask to see his daughter as well as himself, had time to collude with Eugénie and, when their plans were fully laid, he let Madame de Farneille's adviser know that both were ready to hear him. The gullible Madame de Franval placed all her faith in her mother's spiritual guide. Those who are desperate grasp hungrily at illusions and, to obtain the relief which reality refuses them, will use all the ingenuity at their command to imagine that their hopes will come true!

Clervil arrived at nine o'clock in the morning. Franval received him in the apartment where he was in the habit of spending his nights with his daughter. He had ordered it to be decorated with the greatest elegance imaginable, while at the same time maintaining an aura of dissipation which bore witness to his criminal pleasures... Positioned close by, Eugénie was able to hear everything, so that she might prepare herself for the interview which had been arranged for her in turn.

'It is only with the greatest fear of intruding, sir,' began Clervil, 'that I venture to stand before you now. Men of my calling are ordinarily so burdensome to persons like you who spend their whole lives surrounded by worldly pleasures that I chide myself for having agreed to the wishes of Madame de Farneille by asking your permission to speak with you briefly.'

'Pray be seated, sir. As long as you continue to speak the language of justice and reason, you need never be afraid of taxing my patience.'

'You are much loved by a young wife who has many charms and virtues. Now people say that you make her very unhappy, sir. She has only her innocence and candour to defend her, only the ear of her mother to listen to her grievances, and yet she cherishes you despite the wrong you have done her. You cannot fail to imagine the horror of her position!'

'I would prefer it, sir, if we came directly to the point, for I sense that you are beating about the bush. What is the purpose of your mission?'

'To reunite you, if possible, with happiness.'

'So, if I prove to be as happy as I in fact am, then you would have nothing further to say to me?'

'It is impossible, sir, that happiness can be found in crime.'

'I agree. But the man who, by dint of long study and sober reflection, has succeeded in training his mind not to detect evil in anything, to consider all human actions with the utmost indifference, to regard them all as the inevitable consequences of a power—however it is defined—which is sometimes good and sometimes perverse but always irresistible, and gives rise both to what men approve and to what they condemn and never allows anything to distract or thwart its operations, such a man, I say, as you will agree, sir, may be as happy behaving as I behave as you are in the career which you follow. Happiness is an abstraction, a product of the imagination. It is one manner of being moved and depends exclusively on our way of seeing and feeling. Apart from the satisfaction of our needs, there is no single thing which makes all men happy. Every day we observe one man made happy by the very circumstance which makes his neighbour supremely miserable. There is therefore nothing which guarantees happiness. It can only exist for us in the form given to it by our physical constitution and our philosophical principles.'*

'I do know that, sir. But while our mind may deceive us, conscience never leads us astray: it is the book in which nature has written all our duty.'

'But do we not do as we please with this spurious conscience of yours? It bends under the weight of habit, we mould it like soft wax which our fingers press into countless shapes. If this book of yours were as complete as you claim, would not all men have the same invariable conscience? From one side of the globe to the other, would not all actions have the same meanings for them? And yet is that really the case? Does the Hottentot tremble at what frightens a Frenchman? And does not this same Frenchman commit actions every day for which he would be punished in Japan? No, sir. Nothing in the world is real, nothing which merits praise or blame, nothing deserving of reward or punishment, nothing which is unlawful here and perfectly legal five hundred leagues away, in other words, there is no unchanging, universal good.'*

'You must not think so, sir. Virtue is not an illusion. It is not enough to say that a thing is good here and bad a few degrees of longitude distant to define it absolutely as a crime or a virtue, and then to stand firm and claim to have found happiness in the choice one makes between the two. A man's only true happiness lies in his total submission to the laws of his country. He must either respect them or be wretched, for there is no middle ground between breaking them and disaster. It is not, if you like, these things in themselves which spawn the evils that bring us down when we submit to them, knowing them to be forbidden. It is rather the injuries that these things, which may in themselves be either good or bad, inflict on the social conventions of the climate we inhabit. Certainly there is nothing wrong in preferring to stroll along the Boulevards rather than the Champs-Élysées. But if it was decreed by law that citizens were not allowed to walk along the Boulevards, then perhaps anyone who broke that law would be forging for himself the first link of an unending chain of miseries, though he had done only a simple thing in not obeying. Moreover, the habit of rejecting the ordinary constraints quickly leads to the most serious infringements and, proceeding from one piece of wrongdoing to the next, we come to the kind of crimes which are punished in all countries of the universe, crimes which inspire revulsion in all rational beings who inhabit the globe, at every pole you care to mention. If there is not a universal conscience for man, there is therefore a national conscience which directs the life we have received from nature, upon which its hand imprints our duty in characters which we erase at our peril. For example, sir, your family accuses you of incest. Now whatever sophisms may have been used to justify this crime to diminish its repulsiveness, however specious the arguments which have been advanced on this issue, however authoritative the backing they have been given by examples borrowed from other lands, it is nonetheless proven that this offence, which is a crime only in certain cultures, is extremely dangerous in nations where it is forbidden by law. It is furthermore beyond doubt that it can bring the most appalling complications in its wake and breed further crimes from this first offence—crimes, I say, which are calculated to be viewed by all with horror. Had you married your daughter on the banks of the Ganges, where such marriages are allowed, you would have probably committed a very minor evil. But in a state where these unions are forbidden, then by offering this repulsive spectacle to the public... and to a wife who loves you and who will be forced into an early grave by such a betrayal, you undoubtedly commit a most shocking action, a breach likely to unravel the most holy bonds of nature—those same bonds which, by making a daughter cleave to the father who gave her life, must therefore make him in her eyes the most worthy and sacred of all men. You force your daughter to despise duties which are so precious, you make her hate the mother who bore her in her womb, you give her weapons which, though you do not realize it, she may turn against you, you offer her no system of values, you instil in her no set of principles where your guilt is writ large... And if one day she raises her hand against you, you yourself will have sharpened the blade.'*

'Your style of argument, so different from that of men of your calling,' replied Franval, 'encourages me to be quite candid with you, sir. Now, I could deny your indictment. But I hope my frankness in opening myself up to you will oblige you to believe that my wife is also guilty of wrongs, for I shall set them out for you with the same truthfulness which I shall use to set out mine. Yes, sir, I love my daughter. I love her with passion. She is my mistress, my wife, my sister, my confidante, my friend, my only god on earth, for she has all the qualities which would compel devotion in any man, and with every beat of my heart I give her mine by right. These sentiments will last for as long as I live. No doubt I must justify them, since I am quite incapable of relinquishing them.

'The first duty of a father to his daughter is indisputably, as you will agree, to procure for her the largest portion of happiness possible. If he does not achieve this, he is in his daughter's debt; if he succeeds, he is above reproach. I neither seduced nor forced Eugénie, a point which is very remarkable, and you must not let it escape. I never hid her from the company of others and cultivated the blooms of marriage without disguising the thorns which lurk among their petals. I then offered myself. I left Eugénie free to choose. She had ample time to reflect. She never hesitated, but declared that she was happy only with me. Was I wrong, in wanting her happiness, to give her what, with full knowledge of the facts, she appeared to want more than anything else?'

'These sophisms justify nothing, sir. You ought not to have intimated to your daughter that the man she could not choose without doing a wrong could be the one to make her happy. However beautiful a fruit might look, would you not refrain from offering it to someone if you knew for sure that death lurked in its flesh? No, sir, you were thinking only of yourself in your odious proceeding, of which you have made your daughter both the accomplice and the victim. What you have done is unforgivable. And your virtuous, tender wife whose heart you are breaking so wantonly, what wrong do you believe she has done? What wrong, unjust man, other than loving you?'

'I am glad you raise the point, sir, and on this matter I trust you will be frank. I think I have some right to expect it after the candid manner in which I have confessed to the charges which have been made against me.'

And then Franval showed Clervil the forged letters and receipts which he attributed to his wife, and assured him that the documents could not be more genuine, and as real as Madame de Franval's liaison with the man they concerned.

But Clervil knew everything.

'Well, sir,' he said firmly to Franval, 'was I not correct when I told you that a mistake which may initially be regarded as being of no consequence in itself, may, by accustoming us to step across boundaries, lead us to the ultimate horrors of crime and wickedness? You began with an action which you regarded as insignificant, but can you not see all the vile things you have had to do to justify or conceal it? Believe me, sir, let us put these inexcusable abominations on the fire and forget, I beg you, that they ever existed.'

'These papers are genuine, sir.'

'They are false.'

'But you cannot be absolutely certain: are not your doubts sufficient to give me the benefit of them?'

'One moment, sir. I have only your word for believing them to be authentic, and you have every reason for not withdrawing the accusations you have made. I have only the word of your wife for believing them false, though it would also be very much to her advantage to tell me if they were genuine, if indeed such is the case. That is how I judge these matters, sir... Human self-interest, that is what carries people through everything they do, it is the motive of all their actions. Wherever I encounter it, the torch of truth is lit for me. This rule has never led me astray, and I have been using it for forty years. So will not your wife's virtue refute this disgraceful slander in the eyes of all? Is it with her honesty, is it with her candour, is it with the love with which she still burns for you, that a woman allows herself to commit such abominations? No, sir. These are not the first steps in crime. And since you know how crimes grow more serious by incremental leaps, you should be better skilled in directing its course.'

'You insult me, sir!'

'Forgive me. Injustice, slander, and depravity offend my soul so deeply that I am sometimes not master of the feelings which these horrors start in me. Let us burn these documents, sir, I earnestly beg you once more. Let us burn them for the sake of your honour and your peace of mind.'

'I never imagined, sir,' said Franval rising to his feet, 'that given the ministry you profess it was so easy to become the apologist, the protector of licentiousness and adultery. My wife has sullied my good name and her extravagance is ruining me—I have shown you the proof. You are so blinded by her that you would prefer to accuse me and make me into a slanderer than see her as a faithless, depraved woman! Well, sir, we shall let the law decide: all the courts of France will ring with the action I shall bring. I shall produce my evidence, I shall make my dishonour public, and then we shall see if you will still be so naive, or rather so stupid, as to wish to defend such a shameless creature against me!'

'I had better leave, sir,' said Clervil, also getting to his feet. 'I never imagined that the bizarre cast of your mind should so pollute the qualities of your heart, and that, blinded by unwarranted vengeance, you would be capable of coolly defending propositions which seem more like the ravings of madness. Sir, all this leaves me more convinced than ever that when a man rejects his first and most sacred of duties, he will soon be ready to abandon the rest of them. If reflection changes your opinion, be so good as to let me know, sir, and you will always find in your family, as in me, friends ready to welcome you back... But might I be allowed to speak for a moment with your daughter?'

'As you wish, sir. But with her I would advise you to use either a more golden tongue or else more convincing arguments if you wish to set before her your luminous verities, in which I was unfortunate enough to detect only mental blindness and specious reasoning.'

Clervil entered Eugénie's apartment. She was waiting for him in the most teasing, elegant *déshabillé*. The kind of immodesty which results from crime and self-abandonment ruled her gestures and her glance, and the perfidious creature, desecrating the graces which enhanced her beauty, encapsulated everything which inflames vice and outrages virtue.

Since it did not become an adolescent girl to enter into such deep arguments as a philosopher like Franval, Eugénie confined her remarks to ill-natured bantering, then imperceptibly graduated to the most brazen flirtatiousness. But quickly observing that her advances had no effect, and that so virtuous a man as this would never be caught in her snare, she neatly slipped the knots which held a veil over her beauty and appeared in the most provocative state before Clervil had time to realize what was happening.

'The wretch!' she shrieked at the top of her voice. 'Make the monster go away! But not a word of this crime to my father! Merciful heavens! I expected to be offered pious counsel and the hypocrite has designs on my honour!... Do you see,' she said to her servants, who had appeared in response to her screams, 'do you see in what state the blackguard has left me? There you have them, these gentle disciples of a God they defile! Scandal, debauchery, seduction, that is what their morality is made of! And we, poor dupes of their false virtue, we go on stupidly venerating them!'

Clervil, extremely aggrieved by such an outrageous scene, managed nevertheless to hide his anger. Unruffled as he passed through the people who gathered around him, he withdrew.

'May Heaven', he said calmly, 'preserve this unfortunate child... May she be made more pure, if such a thing be possible, and may no one beneath this roof seek to undermine, any more than I have, her virtuous sentiments which I did not come to blight but to resurrect in her heart.'

Such was the sole outcome which Madame de Farneille and her daughter saw from a negotiation of which they had conceived such high hopes. They were ignorant of the damage that can be done by the workings of the souls of criminals. Lessons which would be learned by others merely make them more determined, and it is in the precepts of goodness that they find the incitement to evil.

From this moment on relations on both sides grew even more poisoned. Franval and Eugénie clearly saw that Madame de Franval had to be made to accept that she had done wrong, and in such a way as to leave her no room for doubt. Meanwhile, Madame de Farneille, acting in concert with her daughter, thought very seriously of kidnapping Eugénie. They spoke of it to Clervil. This honest man refused to have any hand in dramatic proposals of this sort. He said he had been too ill-used in their affair to be capable of anything other than of pleading for mercy for the guilty pair. This he asked most particularly, and refused to undertake any further role or mediation. Such sublime sentiments! Why is such nobility so rare in men of the Church? Why were the robes worn by this unique individual made from a cloth which has become so debased?

Let us begin with the steps taken by Franval.

Enter Valmont once more.

'You are a fool,' Eugénie's criminal lover told him. 'You are not worthy to be my pupil. I shall hoist your incompetence high for all Paris to see if you do not perform any better with my wife this second time around. You must *have her*, my friend, well and truly *have her*, and I shall only be convinced when I see her humbled with my very own eyes. I must deny that hateful woman any excuse and any line of defence.'

'And if she resists?'

'Then you must use violence... I shall see to it that everybody is kept well away... Frighten her, threaten her, whatever you like... I shall interpret any means you use to succeed as particular favours to me.'

'Listen,' said Valmont, 'I will do what you propose. I give you my word that your wife will submit. But I make one condition, and if you refuse, our arrangement is cancelled. Jealousy must not enter into any of this, as you know. So I want you to give me a quarter of an hour alone with Eugénie. You cannot imagine how I will perform once I've enjoyed the pleasure of a moment's... conversation with her.'

'But Valmont...'

'I can understand your fears. But if you believe that I am your friend, then I cannot forgive you for having them. All I want is the pleasure of seeing her alone and of talking with her for a few moments.'

'Valmont,' said Franval, somewhat taken aback, 'you set far too high a price on your services. I know as well as you do how ridiculous jealousy is, but I worship the girl you are talking of, and would rather give up my fortune than her favours.'

'Don't worry, that's not what I'm after.'

Franval, realizing that among all his many acquaintances none was as capable of serving him so well as Valmont, was extremely anxious that he should not get away.

'Look,' said he, with a touch of ill-humour, 'I repeat: your services do not come cheap. Perform them in this way, and you will forfeit any claim to my gratitude...'

'Oh, gratitude is the price we pay for honourable services rendered. You will feel no gratitude to me for this particular service and, to boot, it will drive a wedge between us within two months... Look, my friend, I understand human nature... the aberrations... the transgressions... and the consequences they give rise to. Man is the most dangerous of all animals, in whatever situation you care to put him. I shall not fail to perform according to your requirements, but I want to be paid in advance. Otherwise I do nothing.'

'I accept,' said Franval.

'Very well,' replied Valmont. 'So now matters rest entirely with you: just say when you want me to start.'

'I shall need a few days to prepare,' said Franval. 'But four days from now at the most I shall be ready for you.'

Monsieur de Franval had raised his daughter in such a way that he was absolutely certain that it would not be through an excess of maidenly modestly that she would refuse to co-operate with the plans he had agreed with his friend. But he was jealous, and Eugénie knew it. She loved him at least as much as she was worshipped by him, and when she was informed of what was afoot, she confessed to Franval that she was extremely worried that the proposed tête-à-tête might take a serious turn. Believing he knew Valmont well enough to be sure that all he would get out of it was a few crumbs to satisfy his head and nothing to imperil his heart, Franval dispelled his daughter's fears and the preparations went ahead.

It was at this juncture that Franval was informed, by the reliable testimony of servants in his mother-in-law's house who were in his pay, that Eugénie was in great danger, for Madame de Farneille was on the point of obtaining an order for her removal. Franval convinced himself that this was Clervil's doing and, setting Valmont's plans temporarily to one side, he applied himself to finding a way of ridding himself of the vexatious cleric whose hand he erroneously detected behind this new manoeuvre. He dug recklessly into his pocket, and money, that all-powerful facilitator of every vice, was slipped into countless different hands until six inveterate footpads agreed to execute his orders.

One evening, as Clervil, who often dined with Madame de Farneille, was leaving her house alone and on foot, he was seized. He was informed that he was arrested by order of the government, shown a forged warrant, bundled into a carriage, and driven at high speed to the dungeons of a sequestered chateau owned by Franval in the heart of the Ardennes. There the unfortunate cleric was delivered into the keeping of the estate steward and described as a scoundrel who had attempted to kill his master. The most stringent precautions were taken to ensure that the hapless victim, whose only wrong was to have shown too much indulgence towards those who now used him so cruelly, would never again see the light of day.

Madame de Farneille was in despair. She was in no doubt in detecting the hand of her son-in-law behind this outrage. The time spent looking for Clervil meant that the business of removing Eugénie was somewhat delayed. Having only a small circle of friends and very limited funds, it was difficult for her to manage two such important affairs at once, and Franval's decisive move had sent her off on the wrong tack. As a result, she concentrated her efforts on the missing clergyman. But all her enquiries proved fruitless. Our villain had laid his plans so carefully that it was impossible to find any trace of him. Madame de Franval dared not question her husband: they had not spoken to each other since their last confrontation. But what was at stake was so important that it overcame every other consideration. Finally she mustered enough courage to ask her despotic spouse if his intention was to add to the outrages he had inflicted on her the affront of depriving her mother of the best friend she had in the world. The monster denied all knowledge of the matter, and even carried his hypocrisy to the point of offering to help in the search himself. He realized that to prepare the way for her audience with Valmont, he could help calm his wife's fears by repeating his word of honour that he would leave no stone unturned in his efforts to find Clervil. He therefore lavished kind words on his gullible wife, and swore that however unfaithful to her he might be, it was impossible for him not to worship her from the very depths of his soul. Madame de Franval, ever accommodating and gentle, and always happy when anything brought her closer to a man who was dearer to her than life itself, consented to everything her lying husband asked, anticipating his wishes, furthering them, wanting them too, without ever daring to turn the moment to her advantage, as she should have done, to extract from the brute an undertaking that he would improve his conduct and behave in such a way as not to plunge his long-suffering wife each day into a pit of suffering and despondency.

But even had she done so, would her efforts have succeeded? Would Franval, so devious in every action he had ever undertaken in his life, have been more sincere in an operation which he regarded as worth carrying out only insofar as it moved his own plans several steps forward? He would certainly have promised anything simply to have the pleasure of breaking his word; he might even have hoped to be asked to swear an oath to it, so that the pleasures of perjury would have been added to the list of his wicked enjoyments.

Franval, without a care in the world, now thought only of making trouble for others. Such, when challenged, was the vindictive, turbulent, impulsive nature of his character, for he constantly needed to recover his tranquillity at any cost, and to regain it would clumsily adopt methods most likely to deprive him of it once more. Did he succeed? All his faculties of mind and body were now directed solely at doing harm to others. And so, in a constant state of excitement, he was obliged either to spike the guns which he forced others to train upon him, or find other weapons to turn against them.

Everything was made ready to meet Valmont's conditions, and the interview, which lasted almost an hour, took place in the garden of Eugénie's apartment.

[There, in a marquee hung with decorations, Eugénie, naked on a pedestal, was got up as a native maiden wearied by the hunt, leaning against the trunk of a palm tree whose high fronds concealed an infinity of lanterns, so arranged that their light fell only on her body and showed off its beauty with the maximum of art. The kind of small stage on which this living statue stood was surrounded by a channel six feet wide filled with water, which served as a bulwark for the girl and prevented her from being reached from any direction. Valmont's chair was placed at the edge of this barrier. It was fitted with a silk cord. By pulling upon it, he could make the pedestal revolve in such a way that the object of his veneration could be viewed from every angle, and her pose was such that whichever way she was turned she remained constantly agreeable to behold. Franval, hidden behind a section of the decor in the grove, could see both his mistress and his friend. The spectacle, as had been finally agreed, was to last half an hour. Valmont took his seat... he was entranced, and declared that never had so many feminine charms been set before his sight, and he surrendered to the excitement which inflamed his senses. The cord, permanently pulled this way and that, filled each moment with some new comeliness. To which would he make his sacrifice? Which would he choose? He could not say, for everything about Eugénie was so beautiful! Meanwhile the minutes ticked by, as they always do in such circumstances. The hour struck. The Chevalier Valmont could contain himself no longer, and the tribute of his love fell at the feet of the god whose shrine was forbidden to him. A veil descends and we must withdraw.]

'Well? Are you satisfied?' asked Franval, rejoining his friend.

'She is the most delicious creature,' replied Valmont. 'But, Franval, a word of advice: never risk such a thing with another man. You should be thankful that I have sentiments in my heart which are your guarantee against all dangers.'

'I shall count on it,' replied Franval quite seriously. 'But now it is time to act without further delay.'

'I shall begin working on your wife tomorrow. You appreciate that I shall need a preliminary interview... then four days after that you will have what you want.'

They gave each other their word and then went their separate ways. But after an audience such as he had been granted, Valmont felt no strong desire to deceive Madame de Franval, nor to engineer a triumph for his friend of whom he had become only too envious. Eugénie had made too strong an impression on him to be ignored. He resolved to have her as his wife, whatever the cost. After mature reflection, and deciding that he did not find Eugénie's intimacy with her father an obstacle, he felt sure that since his fortune was as large as Colunce's, he was as well qualified to set out a claim to her hand. He supposed, therefore, that if he put himself forward as a husband he could not possibly be refused. If he acted promptly to end Eugénie's incestuous relationship, and convinced her family that he would succeed in so doing, then he would not fail to win the woman he adored... though not without one last confrontation with

Franval which, having every belief in his own courage and skill, he had every hope of winning.

He needed only twenty-four hours to make up his mind, and it was with his head full of these ideas that he called upon Madame de Franval. She had been informed of his visit. It will be remembered that at her last meeting with Franval she had virtually healed the breach between them, or at least, having been taken in by her husband's deviousness and cunning, she could no longer refuse to see Valmont. Even so, she had taken strong exception to Franval's documents, language, and accusations. But he had then seemed to attach little importance to them, and had completely convinced her that the best way of making him believe either that none of the charges were true or that the whole business was now in the past, was to see his friend as usual: to refuse, he told her, would merely confirm his suspicions. The best proof a woman could give of her honesty, he had said, was to go on being seen in public with the man whose name has been publicly linked to hers. Now all this was specious and Madame de Franval knew it. But she hoped that Valmont might clarify matters. Her need for an explanation, together with her reluctance to make her husband angry, had made her lose sight of every consideration which might reasonably have prevented any further contact with the young man. And so he came to the house, and Franval, making a hasty departure, left them together as on the previous occasion. The interview should have been spirited and lengthy. But Valmont, full of his plans, was brief and came directly to the point.

'Ah, Madame, the person you see today is not the man who made himself so guilty in your eyes the last time he spoke to you,' he said quickly. 'I was then an accessory to your husband's wrongdoing. Today I come to right those wrongs. You must trust me, Madame. I ask you to believe me implicitly when I give you my word that I have come here neither to lie to you nor to mislead you in any way.'

Whereupon he confirmed the business of the false documents and forged letters. He asked to be forgiven for lending himself to the deception, and informed Madame de Franval of the latest horrors that were demanded of him. To prove his honesty, he confessed his feelings for Eugénie, revealed everything that had been going on, and promised to put a stop to it, remove Eugénie from Franval's clutches, and carry her off to Picardy, to one of Madame de

Farneille's estates, provided that she and her daughter gave their consent and agreed to reward him by allowing him to marry the girl he would have thus plucked from the abyss.

Valmont's words, his confession, rang so profoundly true that Madame de Franval could not help but be convinced. Valmont was an excellent match for her daughter, and after the way she had behaved, could she expect a better offer? Valmont was prepared to take charge of everything. It was the only way of ending the appalling crime which was driving Madame de Franval to despair. Besides, could she not reasonably expect her husband's feelings to revert to her once the only liaison which could prove a real threat to both of them was ended? These considerations persuaded her and she acquiesced, but only on condition that Valmont gave her his word of honour that he would never cross swords with her husband, that he would go abroad after delivering Eugénie to Madame de Farneille, and that he would stay there until Franval's head had cooled sufficiently to console him for the termination of his illicit affair and for him to give his consent to the marriage. Valmont agreed to everything. For her part, Madame de Franval vouched for the support of her mother who, she assured him, would not try to impede the decisions which they took jointly. Valmont withdrew, apologizing once more to Madame de Franval for having committed against her all the wrongs her dastardly husband had demanded of him. The next morning Madame de Farneille, having been fully informed, left for Picardy. Franval, fully absorbed in his never-ending round of pleasures, fully counting on Valmont, fearing nothing more from Clervil, walked into the trap which had been set for him, displaying the same unsuspecting confidence that he so often hoped to find in others when he in turn schemed to make them stumble into his snares.

For the past six months or so Eugénie, now approaching her seventeenth birthday, had been going out frequently by herself or with other girls who were her friends. The evening before the day Valmont, as agreed with Franval, was to open his siege of Madame de Franval, she went unescorted to see a new play at the Comédie Française.* Afterwards she left, still alone, to fetch her father from an address where he had arranged to meet her, so that they could go on together to another house and take supper there. Mademoiselle de Franval's carriage had barely left the Faubourg Saint-Germain when ten masked men stopped her horses, opened the carriage door, laid hands on Eugénie, and bundled her into a post-chaise next to Valmont who, taking every precaution to stop her crying out, ordered the driver to press on quickly and was carried beyond the city limits in the twinkling of an eye.

Unfortunately it had not been possible to dispatch Eugénie's grooms and carriage. As a result, Franval was soon informed of what had happened. To cover his tracks, Valmont had counted on Franval's not knowing which road he had taken and on the two or three hours' start he would obviously have. Providing he reached the perimeter of Madame de Farneille's estate, he need do no more, because from that point on two dependable women and a carriage and post-horses stood waiting to whisk Eugénie to a spot just short of the frontier, to a place of safety unknown even to Valmont. He would immediately continue on to Holland, and return only for his marriage once Madame de Farneille and her daughter had sent word that all obstacles to it had been removed. But fate decreed that this careful plan would not succeed against the ghastly designs of our villain.

Franval, quickly informed, did not waste an instant. He went directly to the post-coach stables and asked for which routes horses had been ordered since six o'clock that evening. A berline* had left for Lyons at seven and a post-chaise at eight for Picardy. Franval did not hesitate. The Lyons coach was obviously of no interest to him, but a post-chaise bound for a province where Madame de Farneille had an estate was: it would have been folly to doubt it. Accordingly, he ordered the stables' eight best horses be put to the carriage he had arrived in, hired hacks for his men, bought pistols and loaded them while the horses were being harnessed and saddled, and flew like an arrow where love, despair, and vengeance led him. At the staging inn at Senlis he learned that the carriage he was pursuing had left only moments before. Franval ordered his driver not to spare the horses. For his sins, he caught up with the coach. He and his men, brandishing pistols, forced Valmont's postillion to halt, and the reckless Franval, seeing his enemy, blew his brains out before he could attempt to defend himself, laid hold of Eugénie, who had fainted, climbed into his carriage with her, and was back in Paris before ten the next morning. Quite untroubled by what had happened, Franval's only thoughts concerned Eugénie. Had the scoundrel Valmont tried to take advantage of the situation? Was Eugénie still faithful to him?

Were her culpable feelings for him tarnished? Mademoiselle de Franval soon put her father's mind at rest. All Valmont had done was to tell her of his plans and, buoyed up by the hope of marrying her, had refrained from profaning the altar on which he would one day make an offering of his most chaste love. Eugénie's assurances satisfied Franval. But what did his wife know of the conspiracy? Had she taken a hand in it? Eugénie, having had ample opportunity to ask questions, insisted that the entire plot was the work of her mother, on whom she lavished the most odious names, and added that the crucial interview, which Franval assumed Valmont had used to prepare the ground to serve his own purpose, was beyond doubt the moment when he had betrayed him so contemptibly.

'Ah!' cried Franval in a fury. 'Why has he not still a hundred lives so that I might strip him of them all, one after the other? And what of my wife?... She was the first to deceive me... a creature whom everyone believes so mild and gentle... an angel of virtue... Betray me, would you! Well, your treachery will cost you dear... My vengeance calls for blood, and if I have to I shall suck it with my lips from your perfidious veins... You must not worry, Eugénie,' Franval went on, still in a violent mood, 'there is no need for concern, you must rest. Go now and sleep for a few hours. I will keep an eye on things here.'

Meanwhile, it was not long before Madame de Farneille, who had posted spies along the road, was informed of what had happened. Knowing that Valmont had been killed and her granddaughter recaptured, she returned at once to Paris. Infuriated, she called a meeting of her advisers, who convinced her that Valmont's murder would deliver Franval into her hands, that his power and influence, which she feared so much, would be instantly eclipsed, and that she would be restored to her rights over both her daughter and Eugénie. But they also recommended that she avoid any whiff of scandal and, to avoid a damaging public trial, that she should seek a legal order which would keep her son-in-law out of circulation.

Franval was immediately informed of their advice and of the steps which would be taken as a result. Realizing at the same time that what he had done was known, and being informed that his mother-in-law was only waiting for his public disgrace to turn it to her advantage, he drove at once to Versailles, spoke to the minister, confessed everything, and in return was merely advised to take himself off to an estate he owned in Alsace, near the Swiss border. Franval returned immediately to Paris. He was determined not to be deprived of his vengeance, but to punish his wife's treachery and assert his rights over two women so dear to Madame de Farneille that she would never dare—it would hardly be sensible—to take action against him. He therefore resolved to leave for Valmor, the estate recommended by the minister, but only if, as I say, he was accompanied by his wife and daughter... But would Madame de Franval agree to it? Even if she felt guilty for what she might think of as her betrayal of him with Valmont, from which all that had happened had flowed, would she still go? Would she discount her fears and dare to place herself in the hands of an outraged husband? Such was the quandary in which Franval found himself. To find out where he stood, he went directly and called on his wife, who knew everything.

'Madame,' he said with the utmost composure, 'you have sunk me in a mire of troubles by your indiscreet, ill-considered conduct. But if I cannot condone its effects, I nonetheless approve its cause, which surely lies in the love you have for your daughter and for me. And since the first wrongs were mine, I have no right to remember yours which followed. You are the dearest, most tender half of my life,' he continued, falling on his knees before her. 'Will you accept a reconciliation which henceforth nothing shall jeopardize? I have come offering peace, and this is what I give into your keeping as an earnest of my intentions...'

And so saying, he laid at his wife's feet all the forged documents and the fake correspondence with Valmont.

'Burn it all, my dear, I beg you,' the hypocrite went on, weeping bogus tears, 'and forgive everything that jealousy drove me to do. Let us have an end to all bitterness between us. I have done great wrongs, I admit. But who knows if Valmont, in order to further his own plans, did not paint me to you in blacker colours than I deserve? Had he dared to say that I had stopped loving you... that you might not always have been the woman I loved and respected most in the whole universe... ah! dearest angel, had he dishonoured himself by uttering such calumnies, then how right I should have been to rid the world of a rogue and hypocrite like him!'

'Oh, sir,' said Madame de Franval through her tears, 'how could anyone imagine what cruel abominations you concocted against me?

How can you expect me to trust you after all the horrible things you have done?'

'I wish you still loved me, tenderest and most gracious of women! I wish you would berate only my head for the multitude of wrongs I have done, and accept that this heart, where you will rule forever, was never capable of betraying you. Yes, I want you to know that there is not one of my mistakes which did not bring me closer to you... The further I grew away from my dearest wife, the less I could see her in anything: neither my new pleasures nor my feelings could replace those which my inconstancy stole from me when it robbed me of her, and even when languishing in the arms of her living image, I regretted the original... My sweet, exquisite darling, where shall I find another soul like yours? Where else shall I enjoy the favours garnered in your embrace? Yes, I abjure my wicked ways... All I want now is to live only for you, to revive in your wounded heart the love which was so understandably stifled by wrongs... which I hereby renounce, even unto the memory of them!'

It was impossible for Madame de Franval to resist such tender words on the lips of the man she still adored. Can we hate what we have loved? With a soul as fine and delicate as hers, could this remarkable woman turn an unfeeling eye upon the man who meant everything to her and now lay at her feet weeping tears of remorse? She began to sob. Taking her husband's hands and pressing them to her heart, she cried:

'I have never stopped loving you, cruel man! Yet you have callously reduced me to despair! As God is my witness, of all the hurts you inflicted on me, the thought that I had lost your love or given you cause for your suspicions was the hardest to bear!... And who was it you chose to betray me with? My own daughter! It was with her hand that you stabbed me through the heart... Would you have me hate my own child, whom nature has made so dear to me?'

'Ah!' said Franval, his exaltation mounting, 'I want to bring her back so that she may kneel before you, I want her to abjure, as I do, her insolence and the wrongs she has done... I want her to be forgiven, as I am. Let all three of us think only of our mutual happiness. I shall restore your daughter to you... please restore my wife to me... and then let us go away!'

'Great heavens, go away?'

'My little... escapade has set tongues wagging... Tomorrow

might be too late for me... All my friends, the minister too, have suggested a visit to Valmor... Won't you consent to accompany me, my dear? Surely it is not at the moment when I kneel before you to ask forgiveness that you will break my heart by refusing me?'

'You are frightening me... You mean that what you did...'

'... is being treated as murder, not as a duel.'

'Oh God, and I am the cause of it all!... Give your orders... I am yours to command, dear husband... I shall follow you if needs be to the ends of the earth... Ah! I am the most unhappy of women!'

'Say rather the most fortunate, for every instant of my life shall henceforth be devoted to replacing with flowers the thorns I have strewn beneath your feet... Is not a quiet backwater enough for people who are in love? In any case, the move will not be for ever. Once my friends are informed, they will intervene.'

'But my mother... I would like to see her...'

'Oh you must not think of it, my dear. I have irrefutable proof that she is inflaming Valmont's family... that she herself, with their support, is calling for my ruination...'

'She is quite incapable of doing any such thing. Stop imagining all these vile horrors. She has a soul made for loving and is a stranger to duplicity... You never appreciated her qualities, Franval... Why could you not love her as I do? In her embrace we would have known heaven on earth, she was the angel of peace who offered salvation for the errors of your ways. But you were unjust and rejected her enfolding arms, which were ever open to your affection. By your unpredictability or your whims, your ingratitude or your dissolute habits, you deliberately cut yourself off from the best and most loving friend nature could have created for you. Well, am I not to be allowed to see her?'

'No, I beg you most earnestly! Every moment is precious. You can write to her, you can tell her how sincerely I have repented... Perhaps she will be won round by my remorse, perhaps one day I might win back her respect and affection. All this will pass and we shall come back... we shall return and savour her embrace of forgiveness and love... But now, my dear, let us leave... we must be gone within the hour... the carriages are waiting...'

Madame de Franval, deeply apprehensive, did not dare say another word and made her preparations: was not Franval's wish her command? The scoundrel hurried to his daughter and brought her to kneel at her mother's feet. The false creature prostrated herself as perfidiously as her father had done. She wept, she begged to be forgiven, she was forgiven. Madame de Franval embraced her. It is so difficult for a woman to forget that she is a mother, whatever wrong her children may have done her, for the voice of nature speaks so powerfully in a sensitive heart that a single tear shed by these sacrosanct creatures is enough to efface the memory of twenty years of delinquency and aberrations.

They set out for Valmor. Madame de Franval, still gullible and still blind, accepted the extreme haste with which the expedition was perforce undertaken as an adequate explanation for the small number of servants who accompanied them. Crime does not like to be seen, it fears all eyes: it is safe only when hidden beneath a cloak of mystery, and when it decides to act it wraps itself in its folds.

As they drove through the countryside there was nothing to cloud her expectations. Courtesy, attentiveness, deference, marks of affection on the one hand and, on the other, the most demonstrative love were given unstintingly, and it all captivated the hapless Madame de Franval... Although she was far from anywhere, far from her mother, deep in a horrible, wild country, she was happy because she had, so she told herself, the love of her husband and because her daughter sat constantly at her feet and thought only of ways of pleasing her.

The apartments occupied by Eugénie and her father did not adjoin. Franval's was situated in the furthermost wing of the chateau, while Eugénie's rooms were next to her mother's. At Valmor, propriety, regular habits, and chaste behaviour replaced in the most noteworthy degree the disorderliness of life in the capital. Each night Franval visited his wife, and the blackguard, in the presence of innocence, candour, and love, shamelessly nurtured her hope with his abominations. Too cruel to be disarmed by the artless, burning caresses lavished on him by the most delicate of wives, it was with the torch of love that the villain lit the brand of revenge.

Even so, it may be imagined that Franval's attentiveness to his daughter continued undiminished. Each morning, while her mother was being dressed, Eugénie met her father in a distant part of the gardens. She in turn received not only his instructions as to how she should behave in the circumstances, but also his favours, which she was certainly not prepared to surrender entirely to her rival.

They had not been a week in this sequestered haunt when Franval learned that Valmont's family had instituted the most serious proceedings against him, and that the affair would be treated with the utmost gravity. It was now impossible, he also learned, to pass the matter off as a duel, for unfortunately there had been too many witnesses. Furthermore, Franval was told, it was quite clear that Madame de Farneille was leading a coalition of her son-in-law's enemies and was bent on completing his downfall, either by depriving him of his freedom or by forcing him to flee France, so that the two beings she loved but from whom she was separated would be prised from his grasp.

Franval showed the letters he had received to his wife. She at once took up her pen to calm her mother, to try to persuade her to take a more sanguine view of the matter, and to inform her how happy she had been ever since misfortune had softened the heart of her hapless husband. Moreover, she gave her to understand that whatever steps were taken to make her return to Paris with her daughter would be to no avail, that she was resolved not to leave Valmor until her husband's case was satisfactorily settled, and that if the malice of his enemies or the stupidity of his judges secured a ruling which disgraced him, she was quite determined to leave the country with him.

Franval thanked his wife. But he had no desire to await the fate which was being decided for him, and he informed her of his intention to spend some time in Switzerland. He would leave Eugénie with her, and urged both of them not to leave Valmor until his future had been clarified. He added that whatever was finally decided, he would come back and spend twenty-four hours with his wife so that they might agree together on arrangements for their return to Paris, if there was nothing to prevent their doing so, or if there was, to make plans to find another place where they could live in safety.

Once these decisions were agreed on, Franval, breathing vengeance—for he had not forgotten that his wife's plotting with Valmont was the sole cause of his predicament—sent word to his daughter that he was waiting for her in a distant part of the grounds. Closeting himself with her in a solitary gazebo, he made her swear to follow unquestioningly the instructions he would give her, kissed her, and spoke as follows:

'Daughter, you are about to lose me... perhaps for ever...' (Observing Eugénie in tears): 'Don't worry, angel,' said he, 'you have it in your power to make our happiness flourish once more and ensure that, whether here in France or in another place, we shall be almost as perfectly happy as we used to be. I think I am right in saying, Eugénie, that you are as convinced as anyone can be that your mother is the sole cause of all our troubles, and you know that I have not forgotten my determination to be avenged. If I have hidden it from my wife, you have been told my reasons, you approved them, and you helped me fashion the blindfold which it was prudent to place over her eyes. The time is now ripe, Eugénie, and the hour to act has come: your safety depends on it, and what you are about to do will guarantee mine for ever. You will hear me out, I hope, for you are far too astute to be alarmed for a moment by what I am about to propose... Yes, daughter, it is time to act, to act without delay, to act without remorse, and what is done must be done by you. Your mother wanted to make you unhappy, she defiled the bonds of marriage which she would now reclaim, though she has forfeited all right to them. Since this is so, not only is she now no more than just another woman to you, but she is also your most mortal enemy. Now the law of nature which is most deeply engraved on our souls enjoins us to be the first to act and thus rid ourselves, if we can, of those who plot against us. This sacred law, which constantly spurs and prompts us to act, was not intended to make us love our neighbour more than we love ourselves. We come first, the rest follow, that is nature's way. Consequently, we need have no respect, no consideration for others if we are convinced that our misfortune or ruin is the sole end they have in mind. To behave any differently, my dear, would mean preferring others to ourselves, and that would be absurd.* But let us now come to the reasons which shall determine the course of action I recommend to you.

'I have to go away. You already know why. If I leave you here with that woman, then within a month she will be talked round by her mother and will take you back to Paris. Since you will not be able to marry after the scandal which will ensue, you can be quite sure that both those cruel women will assert their rights and pack you off to a convent, where you will weep eternal tears of regret for your weakness and our pleasures. It is your grandmother, Eugénie, who has initiated proceedings against me. She it is who has joined forces with my enemies to crush me into the ground. Such an initiative on her part can have no other purpose than to take you back, but can she have you back unless she keeps you under lock and key? The more acrimonious my case becomes, the stronger, the more credible the party persecuting us will be. Now you must be in no doubt that your mother is inwardly committed to that party, nor should you doubt that she will rejoin it once I have gone. Yet the coalition only wants my ruin so that they can make you the most miserable woman on this earth. It is a matter of urgency that we find ways of weakening it: detaching Madame de Franval from it would remove the mainspring of its energy. What if we changed the plan? Let's say I was to take you away with me? Your mother would be furious and immediately go back to hers, and from that moment, Eugénie, we would not know a moment's peace. We would be hunted and pursued everywhere. No country would have the right to give us sanctuary, and no refuge anywhere on the face of the globe would be sacred and inviolable in the eyes of the monsters whose fury would follow us everywhere. Are you aware how far the odious arm of despotism and tyranny can reach when it is driven by hatred and lubricated with money?

'But if, on the other hand, your mother were dead, Madame de Farneille, who loves her more than she loves you, and serves only her own purposes, would accept that her party was diminished by the loss of the one person who is her reason for belonging to it, and would withdraw. She would no longer encourage my enemies and would cease to stir them up against me. If that happened, one of two things would follow: either the Valmont business would be settled and there would be nothing to prevent us from returning to Paris, or else it would take a turn for the worse. This would mean that we would be forced to go abroad, where we would at least be safe from persecution by Farneille who, as long as your mother is alive, will have no other purpose but to make life impossible for us because, I repeat, she believes that her daughter's happiness can only be secured through our downfall.

'So whichever way you look at our situation, you can regard Madame de Franval as an ever-present threat to our peace and tranquillity, and her accursed existence as the greatest obstacle to our happiness.

'Oh Eugénie,' Franval went on ardently, taking his daughter's hands in his, 'dear Eugénie, you love me. Are you prepared to lose the man who idolizes you because you fear a course of action which is crucial to our interests? Oh my dear, gentle girl, you must decide. You can allow only one of your parents to live. Since one of us must die, you have only to choose which heart to pierce with your felonious blade. Either it shall be your mother or else you must give me up... no, more, you must cut my throat yourself... for how, alas, could I go on living without you?... Do you think I could tolerate life without my Eugénie? How should I survive the thought of the pleasures I might have tasted in your arms, delicious pleasures of which my senses would be deprived for ever? The crime, Eugénie, would be the same in both cases. Either you must kill a mother who hates you and exists only to make you unhappy, or murder a father who lives and breathes only for you. Choose, Eugénie, choose, and if I am the one you sentence to death, do not hesitate, ungrateful child, but put aside pity and rend this heart whose only fault was to have loved too much. I shall bless the hand that strikes me. I shall adore you with my last breath.'

Franval fell silent and waited for his daughter's reply. But she was deep in thought and seemed gripped by uncertainty... Then at last she threw herself into her father's arms.

'You are the one I shall love all my life!' she cried. 'Can you doubt which way I shall lean? Can you suspect my courage? Place the weapon in my hand, and she who is doomed by her abominable interference and my fears for your safety will soon be cut down by my avenging blade. Give me your instructions, Franval, tell me what I must to do, then go, since your salvation depends on it... I shall act in your absence. I shall keep you informed of everything that happens. But whatever turn our affairs take, once our enemy is dead I insist that you will not leave me alone here in this chateau... Come back for me or let me know where I can come to you.'

'My darling daughter,' said Franval, embracing the monster he had so thoroughly drawn into his web, 'I knew all along I should find in you those sentiments of love and courage which are indispensable to our mutual happiness... Take this case... there is death inside it.'

Eugénie took the fatal case and renewed her pledges to her father. Then the outstanding practical details were settled. It was decided that she would await the outcome of the trial, and that the planned murder would take place or not according to whether the verdict would find for or against her father... Then they separated. Franval rejoined his wife and had the audacity and hypocrisy to shed tears as he spoke, and the insolence to accept without demur the touching, ingenuous caresses showered on him by that angel from on high. Then, having confirmed that she would be quite safe if she remained in Alsace with her daughter, whatever the result of his trial, the scoundrel got on to his horse and rode away—away from innocence and virtue which had for so long been sullied by his crimes.

Franval settled in Basle. There he would be safe from any proceedings that might be taken against him and, at the same time, would stay as close to Valmor as possible so that in his absence his letters would keep Eugénie as firm of purpose as he required her to be... Basle was approximately twenty-five leagues from Valmor, but the roads, though they traversed the Black Forest, were good enough for him to receive news from his daughter once a week. As a precaution Franval had brought vast sums with him, more of it in letters of credit than ready money. Let us leave him to establish himself in Switzerland and return to his wife.

The intentions of that excellent woman could not have been purer or more sincere. She had promised her husband that she would stay on his estate until she received fresh word from him. Nothing would have persuaded her to change her decision, as she assured Eugénie every day... Unfortunately, Eugénie, too haughty to acquire the trust which her worthy mother was so well fitted to inspire in her, and continuing to replicate Franval's injustice, a tender plant which he kept well watered by his regular letters, could not imagine that she had a greater enemy in the whole world than her mother. However, this good woman did everything within her power to overcome the invincible aloofness which her ungrateful daughter nurtured in the depths of her heart. She lavished caresses and loving kindness on her, she looked forward tenderly with her to the happy return of her husband, and on occasions carried gentleness and consideration to the point of expressing her thanks to Eugénie and of giving her all the credit for her most welcome conversion. Then she would berate herself for being the innocent cause of the recent troubles which threatened Franval. Far from accusing Eugénie, she aimed her recriminations at herself alone, and holding her close asked her tearfully if she could ever forgive her... Eugénie's depraved heart was impervious to such angelic conduct, her perverse soul was deaf to the voice of nature, for vice had closed off all routes by which she might have been reached... Coldly disengaging herself from her mother's arms, she would stare at her, sometimes wildly, and say to herself, to keep up her courage: 'How deceitful this woman is... how perfidious... she caressed me on the very day she had me abducted.' But these unmerited reproaches were no more than the abominable sophisms with which crime bolsters itself when it sets out to silence the voice of duty. By ordering Eugénie to be abducted to serve for the good of the one, the peace of mind of the other, and the interests of virtue, Madame de Franval had managed to keep her true motives a secret. Such proceedings are objected to only by the guilty who are deceived by them, for they do not conflict with an upright heart. In short, Eugénie resisted all the tender overtures offered by Madame de Franval because she wanted to commit a foul deed, and not at all because of any wrongdoing by her mother who certainly had done absolutely nothing to harm her.

Towards the end of the first month of their sojourn at Valmor Madame de Farneille wrote to her daughter saying that her husband's case was taking a most ominous turn and that, since she feared that a very punitive sentence would be handed down, the return of Madame de Franval and Eugénie had become extremely urgent—as much to win round the public, among whom the most damaging comments were circulating, as to join forces with her so that together they might plead for some kind of arrangement that might draw the teeth of the law, by which Franval might be bound over but not sacrificed.

Madame de Franval, who had decided to have no secrets from her daughter, showed her the letter at once. Coolly, Eugénie looked her mother in the eye and asked her, in the face of this distressing news, what action she intended to take.

'I do not know,' answered Madame de Franval. 'But looking at the matter squarely, what is the point of our being here? Would we not be far more useful to my husband if we were to follow my mother's advice?'

'It is for you to decide, Madame,' said Eugénie. 'I am here to do your bidding and you may count on my complete obedience.'

But Madame de Franval, sensing from the curtness of this reply that her proposal did not appeal to her daughter, said that she would go on waiting and write again, and that Eugénie could be quite sure that if she were to depart from Franval's wishes, it would only be because she was absolutely convinced that she could be more useful to him in Paris than at Valmor.

Another month went by in this way. During this time Franval never stopped writing to his wife and daughter, and in return received from them letters which could not have pleased him more, for in his wife's he found the most unquestioning obedience to his wishes, and in his daughter's the most unquestioning commitment to the execution of the planned murder, if a development in his case required it, or if it looked as though Madame de Franval was about to yield to her mother's pleading. For, as Eugénie wrote in her letters, 'if all I continue to see in your wife is uprightness and plain dealing, and if the friends who serve your interests in Paris succeed in upholding them, then I shall return to you the mission you gave me, and you yourself shall carry it out when we are together, if you think fit at that time. However, if, despite this, you should order me to take action and consider it vital that I do so, then you may leave everything to me. On that you may depend.'

In his reply Franval approved everything his daughter had told him. But that was the last letter he received from her and the last he wrote to her. The next post brought no more. Franval grew concerned. And no more satisfied by the posts which followed, he grew desperate and, his impulsive nature making it impossible for him to wait, he immediately formulated a plan to return to Valmor himself to discover the reason for the delays which made him worry so cruelly.

He set out on horseback, attended by one faithful valet, counting on arriving on the second day late enough at night to be seen by no one. On the edge of the woods which screened the chateau de Valmor and, to the east, merged into the Black Forest, six fully armed men stopped Franval and his servant. They demanded his purse. The rogues were well informed and knew who their man was. They also knew that Franval, being implicated in some serious trouble with the law, never went anywhere without his wallet and a large quantity of gold. The valet tried to resist, and was left for dead under his horse's hooves. Franval, sword in hand, leaped to the ground, laid into the villains, wounded three of them, but was overpowered by the rest. They robbed him of everything he carried, though they were unable to relieve him of his sword. Once they had taken all he had, they made off. Franval pursued them, but the bandits rode away with their booty so quickly that he was unable to tell which way they had gone.

It was a wild night of high winds and hail. All the elements seemed to have united against the wretched man... There are perhaps times when nature, outraged by the crimes perpetrated by the miscreant she pursues, sets out to heap miseries on him with all the means at her disposal before finally gathering him to herself... Franval, half-naked but still grasping his sword, set forth from the ill-fated clearing as quickly as he could and directed his steps towards Valmor. Being unfamiliar with the approaches to an estate where he had resided only on the sole occasion when we observed him there, he lost his way along the gloomy tracks of a forest which was totally unknown to him... Weary to the point of exhaustion, weakened by pain, consumed by anxiety, buffeted by the storm, he flung himself to the ground where the first real tears he had ever shed in his life filled his eyes and overflowed.

'Ah, wretch that I am!' he exclaimed. 'Everything conspires to bring about my downfall at last... to make me feel remorse... remorse which would not have gained entry to my soul except it were put there by the hand of misfortune! Had I continued to be cradled by the comforts of prosperity, I would never have known what it was. My wife, whom I have outraged so grievously and who, even as I speak, is perhaps being made the victim of my barbarity... my adorable wife, are you still of this world which should take such pride from your life? Or has the hand of Heaven intervened to halt my horrible crimes? Eugénie, my too trusting daughter, too ignobly seduced by my abominable stratagems, has your heart been softened by nature? Has nature suspended the cruel consequences of my power and your weakness? Is it too late? My God, is there still time?'

Suddenly, the plaintive, majestic sound of church bells, dolefully rising into the clouds, reached him and amplified the horror of his fate... He began to tremble and feel afraid.

'What is that sound?' he cried, getting to his feet. 'Oh, unfeeling Eugénie, does it mean death? Or does it signal vengeance? Or is it the din of the Furies who have come from hell to complete their handiwork? Do these bells toll for me?... where am I?... can I bear to hear them?... Be done, Heaven above!... Make an end of this sinner...' (prostrating himself on the ground) '... Lord on high, grant that I might add my voice to those which are at this moment raised to you in supplication... Behold my remorse and your power, forgive me for rejecting you... and hear my prayer... the first prayer I ever dared offer up to you! Almighty God, protect virtue, protect the woman who was your sweetest image in this vale of tears, so that these sounds, these lugubrious sounds, may not prove to signify what I most fear!'

Franval, now quite distraught, no longer knowing what he was doing or where he was going, mouthing only broken words, followed the first path on which he stumbled... He heard someone approach... he gathered his wits... he strained his ears... it was a man on horseback.

'Whoever you are,' cried Franval, advancing towards the man, 'whatever you might be, take pity on a poor man driven mad by suffering! I am ready to end my life... Enlighten me, help me if you are a man and charitably disposed... help me to save me from myself!'

'My God!' replied a voice which was only too familiar to the desperate man. 'What? Are you here?... Merciful God, stay thy hand!'

And Clervil, for it was he, in the flesh—the worthy cleric who had escaped from Franval's dungeons and was sent by fate to meet the poor wretch at the lowest ebb of his existence... Clervil leaped down from his horse and threw himself into the arms of his enemy.

'Is it you, sir,' said Franval, holding the good man close, 'is it really you, against whom I have committed so many sins which lie heavy on my conscience?'

'Calm yourself, sir, compose yourself! I put aside the hardship I have recently endured, I forget the terrible treatment you were determined to inflict on me, for Heaven has granted that I might serve you yet... and I shall serve you, sir, in ways that are cruel no doubt but unavoidable... Come, let us sit... here, at the foot of this cypress, for only its baleful leaves are fit now to make a wreath for your brow... Oh Franval, I have such dreadful things to say to you!... Weep... for weeping will bring you relief, my friend... yet I have a tale to tell which will make you shed tears that will be more bitter still... your halcyon days are done... they have dissolved like a dream, and those which remain to you will be filled with suffering.'

'Ah sir, I understand... the bells...'

'... will convey to the feet of the Lord most high the homage and prayers of the sorrowing denizens of Valmor, to whom almighty God granted the boon of knowing an angel only so that they might pity and mourn her.'

Franval, turning the point of his sword and placing it on his heart, was about to snap the thread by which his life hung. But Clervil prevented him from committing this act of frenzy.

'No, no, my friend,' he cried, 'making amends, not dying, is what you must do! Listen to me. There is much to tell, and you must be calm if you are to hear what I have to say.'

'Very well, sir, speak. I am listening. Drive your dagger into my heart slowly, by degrees, for it is just that I should suffer as I have made others suffer.'

'I shall be brief in setting out what concerns me, sir,' said Clervil. 'After passing a few months in the gruesome cell to which you condemned me, I managed to soften my gaoler's heart. He unlocked my prison gates. I urged him most particularly to use every care to conceal the injustice you had done to me. He will never speak of it, dear Franval, not one word.'

'Oh, sir!...'

'Listen, I say again, for I have much else to say. On returning to Paris I learned of your ill-advised escapade and flight. I shared the tears of Madame de Farneille, which were more sincere than you ever thought, and I supported her worthy efforts to persuade Madame de Franval to bring Eugénie back to us, for their presence was more necessary in Paris than in Alsace... You forbade her to leave Valmor... she did as you commanded... she informed us of your orders and conveyed her reluctance to disobey them. She put off the moment of decision for as long as she could... Then you were found guilty, Franval, and guilty you are. You were sentenced to death for the crime of murder on the king's highway. Neither the canvassing of Madame de Farneille nor the steps taken on your behalf by your family and friends could deflect the sword of justice, and your cause was lost... your name is stained for ever... you are ruined... everything you own is confiscated...' (and, countering a second wild interruption from Franval) '... Listen, sir, I insist that you listen to me as an atonement for your crimes, I demand it in the name of God, whose anger may yet be assuaged by your repentance!

It was then that we wrote to Madame de Franval and told her everything. Her mother told her that her presence had become indispensable, and she sent me to Valmor to make her see finally that she must leave. I set out at the same time as the letter which, alas, arrived before I did. When I reached the house it was too late. Your ghastly plan had succeeded only too well. I found Madame de Franval on the point of death... Oh sir, was there ever such villainy!... But your sufferings move me greatly, and I shall cease to reproach you for the crimes you have committed... But that is not all. Eugénie could not bear the sight. When I arrived, her repentance was already all too visible in the bitterness of her tears and sobbing... Oh, sir, how can I convey to you the dread effect produced by that appalling spectacle?... Your wife about to expire and racked by the convulsions of agony... Eugénie, restored to the feelings of nature, uttering the most hideous screams, admitting her guilt, calling upon death, and ready to kill herself, one moment prostrate at the feet of the mother whose pardon she implored, the next clinging to her breast, attempting to breathe life back into her, to warm her with her tears, to melt her heart with her remorse. Such, sir, was the dread spectacle which presented itself to my sight when I entered your house.

'Madame de Franval recognized me... she gripped my hands, bathed them with her tears, and said a few words which I could scarcely hear, so faintly were they breathed out from her throat which was constrained by the workings of the poison... She forgave you... she prayed to God for you... and above all she asked pardon for her daughter... Now mark this well, unfeeling man: the final thoughts, the last wishes of the wife you tormented, were directed to your happiness. I did all I could for her. I made the servants do likewise. I sent for the best physicians. I spoke words of consolation to your Eugénie. I was moved by her horrible plight and did not think I could refuse her anything. But nothing helped: your most unhappy wife surrendered her soul, tormented... by convulsions... by agonies which words cannot express.

'It was then, sir, that I saw one of the prompt effects of remorse which I had never observed before that moment. Eugénie flung herself on her mother and died at the very same instant that she did. We thought she had merely fainted. But no, all her living faculties had been extinguished. Her organs, reeling under the shock of her predicament, had given out simultaneously... she had died of the violent shock which remorse, grief, and despair had administered to her system... Yes, sir, both met their end on your account. And these bells, whose sound still rings in your ears, are tolled to celebrate two women, both born to make you happy, whom your crimes turned into the victims of their affection for you, and whose bloody memory will haunt you to the grave.

'Oh my dear Franval! Was I wrong an age ago to urge you to climb out of the pit into which your appetites had cast you? And will you now blame, will you mock the defenders of virtue? Do you think they are mistaken to worship at its shrine, when they see what troubles and calamities are begotten by crime?'

Clervil fell silent. He looked at Franval and saw that grief had turned him to stone: his eyes were fixed and staring, tears streamed from them, but no words passed his lips. Clervil asked him to explain the state of undress in which he had found him. Franval told him briefly.

'Oh sir!' exclaimed that charitable mortal. 'I count myself fortunate, even in the midst of the horrors which surround me, that I can alleviate your condition. I was on my way to see you in Basle, to tell you everything and offer you the small wealth that I possess... Accept it, I beg you. I am not a rich man, as you know... but here are a hundred louis... my savings, it is all I have... All I ask of you...'

'Generous man!' exclaimed Franval, falling to his knees before this honest, exceptional friend. 'But great Heavens, what needs have I, now that I have lost everything? And you, whom I have treated so abominably, it is you who hold out your hand to help me!'

'Should we remember the injuries we have suffered when misfortune overwhelms those who raised their arm against us? The best revenge we can take against them in such circumstances is to offer comfort. And why should we add to their miseries when they are already lacerated by their own remorse?... Sir, there you hear the voice of nature. As you see, it is not contradicted by the sacred belief in a Supreme Being as you once imagined, since the promptings of the one are the holy laws of the other.'

'No,' answered Franval, rising to his feet. 'No, sir. I no longer have needs, for by leaving me this ultimate resource,' he continued, brandishing his sword, 'Heaven has shown me what use I must make of it...' (Staring at it.) 'It is the same, yes, my dear, my only friend, this is the very same weapon which my saintly wife tried to seize and turn against herself on the day I heaped vile accusations and slander on her... It is the same... Perhaps I shall find traces of her hallowed blood on it... It must be washed clean with mine... But let us go... Let us find shelter in some cottage and I will tell you my last wishes... and then we shall separate for ever.'

They set off and looked for a path which would lead them to some inhabited place... The forest continued to be cloaked in night... the sound of mournful chanting was heard, then suddenly the faint glimmer of torches dispersed the shadows and stained them with a horror that can be imagined only by sensitive souls. The tolling of the bells quickened, and to their lugubrious clangour, still scarcely audible, were added crashes of thunder which, silent until that moment, lit up the sky with flashes of lightning and punctuated the funereal dirge, still audible, with violent detonations. The lightning which furrowed the clouds and intermittently eclipsed the sinister flicker of the torches seemed to challenge the right of earth-dwellers to escort to her final resting place the body of a woman borne by a cortège. The scene inspired horror, breathed desolation... and was perhaps arrayed in nature's eternal mourning dress!

'What is this?' said Franval apprehensively.

'It is nothing,' replied Clervil, and he took his friend by the hand and began to steer him away from the path they were following.

'Nothing? You lie! I must know what it is...'

He sprang forward... and saw a coffin.

'Great God!' he cried. 'There she is... it is she! I know it! Almighty God has granted that I might see her again...'

At the bidding of Clervil, who realized that the poor wretch was not to be quieted, the priests withdrew in silence... Distraught, Franval fell upon on the coffin and from it bore away the sorry remains of the woman he had so mortally offended. He took her corpse in his arms, set it down at the foot of a tree, and threw himself upon it with all the frenzy of despair.

'Ah!' he raved. 'Your life was ended by my barbarity, sweet creature whom I still love to distraction! See, your husband prostrates himself before you and presumes to beg for your forgiveness and his pardon. You must not think he asks this in order that he might live, no no, but that the Almighty, touched by your virtues, might yet, if such a thing be possible, pardon me as you are pardoned... Blood must be shed, my dearest wife, blood must be spilled if you are to be avenged... and you shall be... But first see my tears, see my repentance. I shall follow you where you go, my dead darling... but who will receive my tormented soul unless you intercede for it? It is as unacceptable to God's love as it is to yours... Is it your wish that it be consigned to the burning fires of hell, when it repents so sincerely of its crimes? Only pardon, dear soul, forgive, and see what amends I make for them!'

And with these words, Franval, eluding Clervil's vigilance, grasped the sword he still held in his hand and drove it twice through his body. His corrupt blood coursed over his victim and seemed less to avenge than to defile her.

'Ah, my friend,' he said to Clervil, 'I am dying, but I die in the arms of remorse... Give an account of my deplorable death and my crimes to such friends as I have left. Tell them that this was the inevitable end that awaited one who was the joyless slave of his passions, a man so base that he silenced in his heart the cry of duty and nature. Do not refuse me a place in the coffin of my unhappy wife. Had I not repented I would not have deserved to have it, but my remorse has made me worthy to be granted this petition.'

Clervil respected the wretched man's last wishes, and the cortège resumed its progress. Soon an everlasting haven received the remains of a husband and wife who were born to love each other, born to be happy, and might have known untrammelled felicity if crime and its inevitable consequences, directed by the culpable hand of one of them, had not intervened to turn the roses of their life into serpents.

The honest man of God soon returned to Paris with the ghastly tale of each of these several catastrophes. No one lamented the death of Franval; the only feeling it aroused was outrage for his life. But his wife was mourned, bitterly mourned. For indeed, what creature could be more precious, more commendable in the sight of men than this woman who had cherished, respected, and cultivated all the virtues of this world only to find unhappiness and suffering at every turn?*

*If the brush-strokes I have used to portray crime disturb and distress you, then your redemption is nigh and I shall have accomplished what I set out to achieve. But if you find the truth they depict offensive, if they provoke you to curse their author... then, wretched reader, you have recognized your own self and you will never change your ways.**

APPENDIX I

DRAFT OF THE AUTHOR'S FOREWORD (1788) TO THE ORIGINAL COLLECTION OF HIS SHORT STORIES AND LONGER TALES*

THE obligation laid upon every writer to conform to the tone and style of the age in which he lives explains why the present author was virtually *forced* to make the serious tales of this collection extraordinarily sombre, and *constrained* to strike perhaps an over-free note in those scattered among them which he intended to lighten the general mood and uncrease the reader's brow. Everything degenerates with age. During the reign of Louis XIV the sensitive, subtle novels of Madame de La Fayette entertained a public still steeped in chivalry and courtly love which, having digested its Round Table romances, uncomplainingly took to the adventures of a heroine who kept her lover dangling for nine volumes before agreeing to a white wedding in the tenth. In those days, when books were few, readers had plenty of time to grow pale-cheeked as they perused this insipid stuff. Indeed, it is not too long since people modelled their wooing habits on the pattern laid down in these novels.

The Epicureanism of the likes of Ninon de Lenclos, Marion de Lorme, the Marquis de Sévigné and the La Fares, the Chaulieus, the Saint-Evremonds, in short, of the whole of that delightful company of souls who had been cured of the modish languors imposed by the god of Cythera and now began to think that, as Fontenelle later put it, 'the only good thing about love is the physical side of it', their Epicureanism, I say, somewhat altered the tone of fiction. Marivaux and Crébillon *fils* who came after them felt that the old style of languishing would not appeal to a century corrupted by the Regent, and accordingly wrapped immorality and cynicism in a style which was light, flowery, and often even philosophical. Perhaps they should have left it at that. But wit to a writer is what the stomach is to a gourmet. At first both are satisfied by simple dishes which, however, must steadily be improved by adding all the spices of Asia. Eventually Prévost appeared and, if we may make so bold, invented the true form of the novel. He alone had the art of maintaining interest in a multitude of invariably racy adventures which never allowed the reader's mind a moment's respite, but forced him to be caught up by that necessary state of tension which is the most solid way of ensuring that his interest stays gripped.

Prévost was the man who opened up the French language to the masterpieces of the English novel. Schooled by Fielding and Richardson, we learned from them that it is not always with virtue that we catch the reader's interest; that virtue is a fine thing to be sure, and that everything must be done to ensure that it triumphs; but we also saw that its victory is not a law of nature, merely a law by which we would like all men to abide, that it is in no way indispensable to fiction, that it is not even the rule which allows the reader's attention to be gripped, for when virtue triumphs, things being as they of necessity are, my tears dry up by themselves. But if, on the contrary, virtue, after being most sorely tested, finally succumbs to the repeated assaults of vice, then our hearts will not fail to be torn and, having brought us to the ultimate pitch of involvement, the author cannot fail to succeed. Yet if Richardson, after fifteen volumes, had brought matters to a chaste conclusion by converting Lovelace and allowing him to marry Clarissa quietly, then it might well be asked if readers, confronted by a novel which went in this quite different direction, would have shed the precious tears which we could not prevent the author extracting from us. It is therefore nature that must be captured by all who strive in this genre, and not morality, for however fine a thing morality may be, it invariably remains the handiwork of men, whereas the novel must always be a picture of nature.

Be that as it may, it is clear that in the wake of the novelists who wrote at the start or around the middle of this century, any author who wished to please his public had either to write as they had or else seek those stronger colours in nature which had eluded them. Crébillon's 'sweet love-talk' was not worth pursuing, but both the broad brushstrokes of the author of *Marianne* and Prévost's varied nuancing of light and shade were.

As to *La Nouvelle Héloïse*, it were best set to one side. It is a kind of unique masterpiece which cannot be repeated. All the imitations it has spawned are dreadful. Unfortunately people nowadays are not sufficiently convinced of this point, which explains why we are drowning in a stream of inanities allegedly drawn from Rousseau's novel. It is now impossible to read a single page of any of it because the authors of all these platitudinous reproductions, who have as little taste as brains, stupidly concluded that all it takes to be as perfect as the original is to add languor to two or three mildly risqué episodes. They had not the wit see that more than this is needed to produce a second *Héloïse*, nor did they have any sense that it is vital to own a blazing spirit like Rousseau's and a mind as philosophical as his—two things which nature does not bring together in one person twice in any century.

It must be conceded that in these tales which we here set before the reader, the impetuous tack we have given ourselves a licence to follow does not always accord with the moral values, as chaste as they are tedious, expressed in the anaemic stories of Monsieur d'Arnaud. But if we have not always been very virtuous, we have always been true. Now, nature is much more often bent than straight, and its twists and turns had to be followed. This we did. And who can boast, in writings of this sort, that he has shown virtue truly victorious unless the stratagems of vice which press it hard on all sides have not been strongly emphasized? Would Madame de Thélème in the story which bears her name* be so sympathetic if the merchant who deceives her were not an odious man? Would Monrevel provoke tears which are so delicious to shed had not the Countess de Sancerre been such a villainous woman? And finally, what would Lorenza be other than merely a woman harassed by a rival of Antonio,* if that rival were not at one and the same time her father-in-law and a depraved monster? etc.

Let us be plain. With time tastes grow blasé, minds decay, and the public tires of stories, romances, and comedies. An author has no alternative but to serve up his wares highly seasoned if he wishes to succeed. In several of these tales we have used a ploy which is quite new. Unfortunately the bigots will protest, however dramatic the effect which we feel justified in expecting it to produce. The basis of all stories, all novels, is the young woman loved by a young man of her own sort, who is crossed in her affections by a rival she dislikes. If this rival wins, then the heroine is, as people say, very unhappy. But in the present age (for the present must always be our starting point), and given the depravity of modern manners, must the denouement of novels which we have always known really go on driving young women to despair? In view of the generally acknowledged ease with which she can console herself for having married an unpleasant husband, need we feel particularly sorry for any girl who has been thrust into the arms of a man like that?... It was this consideration which led us to add a further dimension to the usual age and ugliness in our portrayal of the rival who disrupts the amours of the heroine. We gave him a touch of vice or lechery calculated to instil real fear into the girls he sets out to seduce, with the result that by this means these young women, finding themselves facing a fate infinitely more terrible than anything they have been made to fear hitherto, cannot help proving to be infinitely more interesting. An ugly old man who becomes the lord and master of a young woman may well make her the deserving object of our sympathies, as you will agree. Yet does her predicament amount to a full-blown calamity, when we reflect that a new wardrobe and a young lover can so easily make her forget her small, temporary trials? But if, on the contrary, either this rival lover or the husband she has already married should prove capable of unimaginable depravity, odious conduct, bizarre tastes, cruel and ignoble whims, and threatens to subject his young, defenceless victim to an unending sequence of mental and physical tortures, will we not quake as we watch while he succeeds? Cold-blooded readers will be scandalized by such wicked ways, though they are much too underused nowadays. But there is an altogether different thrill in store for readers who are warmer-blooded and more spirited and will lap up anything as long as it is interesting. Aware of how wayward nature can be, they will readily pursue her down the most tortuous paths with a view to studying people, understanding them, and shedding tears for the terrible things that invariably befall them if they fail to apply the principles of virtue to correct the influence of their capricious temperaments on their weak and pusillanimous souls.*

No doubt it was wise that monstrous examples of intemperance were kept well hidden in more virtuous, more honest times, when even the word 'love' was scarcely ever mentioned. But with the growing perversity of modern manners it has been possible to lift one corner of the veil, and say to mankind: this is what you have turned into, *you must change your ways, for you are repulsive, an abomination.*

Were people in the ancient world, or even since the age of chivalry, aware that the kind of depravity we have shown actually existed? Did authors deliberately exclude it from their portrayal of human nature? Yet did not Boccaccio, Bandini, the Duchess d'Alençon,* and our troubadours make extensive use of it, and was it not the reason why they proved so popular? To be interesting, a writer can nowadays call upon passions other than jealousy, vengeance, and ambition; he can pluck other chords in his reader's heart, and make them vibrate effectively. This new style of proceeding calls for discretion, and the most modest of women may read us without a shadow ever passing across her brow.

Yet we admit that there is a modicum of ribaldry in our facetious tales.* But as a man of sober judgement has observed: 'It is perfectly legitimate for an author to be merry in a tale, and even to take certain liberties which would be quite out of place in a serious work.'

It is a form of writing in which great men have not been ashamed to dabble. Sisenna, Roman praetor and scion of the illustrious Cornelian family, translated the licentious Milesian fables, and Petronius the consul amused us with the debauches of Nero.* Where is the censor so strict who could not smile at the frankness, the naivety of the scholar of Pergamum whom Saint Louis, however, would have gladly burned?* As we know, Boccaccio was accused of atheism because he wrote those delightful stories of his... but we no longer live under the thumb of the clerics, and the word 'atheist' has ceased to be a term of abuse. One other fault was found in him. 'Chi potesse contare' (said Boniface Vannozzi) 'quantè putanè ha fatto il decamerone rimmarebbe stupido et senza senzo'*—

another criticism we do not fear. 'Adhesso,' we might say, 'le putane sono fatte no che piu periculoso.'* Respectable ladies will therefore shed tears as they read our tragic tales. They will grace with a smile those which seem a trifle bawdy and, sure in the knowledge that all is meant to amuse, will not take fright or be corrupted. Ma per le puttane,* they will not venture any further down the ignoble path on which they have chosen to set their feet. In these facetious tales we shall not, therefore, have inflicted any harm on virtue, and we will most certainly not have given any encouragement to vice. That leaves the clerics, but no one listens to them any more... and the bigots, but they have their reputations to think of, and will not dare speak out. There remain the trifling, ephemeral authors or those half-baked assemblers of thirty volumes a year, who are either absurd compilers or ridiculous plagiarists who bring literature into disrepute. They grow apoplectic when they see that these tales of ours are written with scrupulous regard for a language which they themselves mangle every day, and that they grip the reader's attention by means other than their own tediously repetitious ploys. As a consequence, they may well stir up whatever trouble they can for us. But we despise them utterly. We stand too high above them even to see that they exist, we shall not even hear their snarls, nor shall we stoop to answer them. To speak of them or pay them the slightest attention would be to raise them from the mud to which their petty scribblings damn them to remain in perpetuity.

It only remains to point out that these tales are all new. None is modelled upon an existing source. Only one, 'The Enchanted Tower', has some historical basis, and a small element of another, 'The Marquise de Thélème', is a reminiscence of Madame du Noyer.* It will be seen from the frankness of this admission how far we are from trying the reader's patience by foisting borrowings or thefts on him. Whoever writes in this genre must either be original or steer clear of it altogether. We shall now set out the elements of the two tales we have mentioned which can be found in the sources we identify.

The Arab historian Abul-Coecim-Terif-Aben-Tariq, an author hardly known to our fashionable wits, said the following of 'The Enchanted Tower'. Rodrigo, a decadent king, was in the habit of summoning the daughters of his vassals to his court. Among their number was Florinde, daughter of Count Julian, whom he ravished. Her father, who was in Africa, received the news by an allegorical letter written by his daughter. He raised the Moors and returned to Spain at their head. Rodrigo knew not which way to turn. His coffers were empty and there was no place to hide. He decided to search the Enchanted Tower near Toledo, where he was told he would find vast amounts of gold. There he discovered a statue of Time holding a club poised to strike which, by means of words carved in stone, warned Rodrigo of the misfortunes which awaited him. The prince continued on his way and found an immense tank full of water, but no money. He retraced his steps and ordered the tower to be shut up close and locked. A thunderbolt carried it off, leaving mere vestiges. Despite these dire portents, the king assembled an army, fought a battle near Cordova which lasted one week, and was killed. No trace of his body was ever found. That is what history supplied. Let the reader now peruse our story and he may judge for himself whether or not what we have added justifies our contention that the story should be regarded as entirely ours.

As to 'The Marquise de Thélème', the reader who turns to volume 2, page 202, of the *Letters of Madame du Noyer* will find the story of a woman from Champagne who travels to Paris to take part in a court case. Soon it becomes clear that she will lose. A rich tax-gatherer who is infatuated with her offers to ensure that she wins, his price being her favours. She agrees and wins her case. When she returns home to her husband, guilt makes her ill. Her husband insists on knowing the cause of her melancholy. She admits everything. She is pardoned and told that what she did was well done. The woman is restored to health and subsequently lives as happily as can be with the husband she had offended. There you have the bald situation, the crude, comic outline on which we built one of our most tragic and absorbing tales. If our work is compared with the source we have indicated, it will be seen that we may rightly claim the honour of being the true originators of the story.

We had no guide for any of the other twenty-eight tales.* If the stories they tell do not please, the fault is ours alone, since no help from outside was sought to bolster our feeble talents. We would be considerably more confident of winning the approval of the modern public if we had imitated Richardson or Rousseau. But alas, our tales are our own, and consequently the reader who is closed in his mind need go no further. He will discover here nothing that is already well known and a boldness of outlook which may well not be suited to his tastes.

APPENDIX II

THE CONTROVERSY WITH VILLETERQUE

I

Review of *The Crimes of Love* by Villeterque,* in *Le Journal des Arts, des Sciences & de Littérature*, 30 vendémiaire, An IX (22 October 1800)

THIS is a detestable book from the pen of a man suspected of having written another even more loathsome.* I do not know, nor do I wish to know, whether this suspicion has any foundation or not. A reviewer is entitled to judge a man's books but not to accuse him. I would go further. He should defend an author who has such a terrible charge hanging over him until such time as he shall be found guilty and thereby becomes the object of public execration.

In a piece entitled 'An Essay on Novels' which precedes *The Crimes of Love*, the author sets himself the task of answering three questions: Why should this kind of composition be called a novel? In which nation should we look for its beginnings, and which are the best examples? And what, lastly, are the rules which must be followed if perfection is to be attained in the art of writing them?

I shall not linger over the first two questions, which have been admirably dealt with several times elsewhere and to which the author, with a show of apparent erudition which is in fact riddled with errors, gives the most comprehensively wrong answers. I shall concentrate on the principles of what he is pleased to call the progress of the art of writing them.

It is not, claims the author, the triumph of virtue which makes a work of fiction interesting. 'This rule is in no sense indispensable to the novel, nor is it even the principle which makes a work of fiction interesting. For when virtue triumphs, things being as they necessarily are, our tears dry up before they even begin to flow. But if, after it has been tested by the most severe trials, we finally see VIRTUE CRUSHED BY VICE, then our souls will invariably be tormented, and the book, having moved us immoderately, will indubitably attract the kind of attention which is the only guarantee of fame.'

Now is this not an attempt to give intellectual respectability to the infamous book which the author has disowned? And is not thus disowning only the infamy attaching to the loathsome form of that book tantamount to exposing oneself to the danger of seeming to adopt its basic tenets which, in the final analysis, can only mean a deliberate intention to show VIRTUE CRUSHED BY VICE?

Moreover, what useful purpose is served by these depictions of vice triumphant? They release the evil impulses of the wicked man. From the man who is good and stands firm in his principles, they extract cries of indignation. And from the man who is good but weak they draw tears of discouragement. These hideous pictures of crime do not even serve to make crime more odious. They are therefore both futile and dangerous.

These disastrous principles are so patently false that they are even disowned by the man who propounds them. In the story entitled 'Eugénie de Franval', the author observes: 'If a crime is allowed to remain in shadow, is it not as good as obliterated? If it is made public, disorder will surely follow, and the disorder it creates will stir the passions of others who are inclined to the same kind of transgression.'

Here the author contradicts himself, as must often happen when a man holds erroneous opinions.

I was unable to read these four volumes of disgusting horrors without experiencing a sense of outrage. The repulsion they inspire is not even compensated for by the author's style which, in this book, is lamentable, being invariably inflated and full of turns of phrase in the poorest taste, of misconceptions and trivial observations. There are a few pages which express views which are sound and based on the principles of justice. But such passages are, as it were, stuck on, and there is no sense that they have anything to do with what has gone before or comes after.

Do not imagine that the author is happy to settle for one crime per tale. He piles them high: this book is a tissue of horrors. Here, a woman is raped by her son, she kills him, sends her own mother to the gallows, marries her father, etc. There, a father raises his daughter according to the most execrable moral principles, lives with her, and persuades her to poison her mother, etc. And yet this is what the author calls 'the perfection' of narrative art!

You authors of novels, it is not in respectable society, nor in the events which happen and perturb or enhance our lives, nor is it in the perfect and subtle knowledge of the human heart that you must seek your subjects. It is in the history of poisoners, libertines, and murderers that you should look. Show us sinners who prosper, for the greater glory and encouragement of virtue!

Rousseau, Voltaire, Marmontel, Fielding, Richardson, etc., what you wrote was not fiction. You described manners, but you should have described crimes. You make virtue attractive by convincing us that it is the only road to happiness. That is not the thing at all! You should have shown VIRTUE CRUSHED BY VICE! That is how a writer instructs and pleases.

But you were not of the elect created by nature to paint her. You were never *her suitors from the moment she sent you into this world*. You have not *delved trembling into her depths to find the secret of her art*. You never had *a burning ambition to describe everything*, you never knew how to strike thirteen times with a dagger to good purpose. In your insipid works we find no mothers who strangle their children, no children who poison their mothers nor sons who rape them. Adieu Rousseau, Voltaire, Marmontel, Fielding and Richardson! Soon no one will read you any more.

2

The Author of 'The Crimes of Love' to Villeterque, Hack and Scribe[1]*

I have long been convinced that insults dictated by envy or some other even viler motive which reach us in due course on the foul breath of some miserable hack, should have no more effect on an author than the barking of a watchdog on a seasoned and sensible traveller. Feeling nothing but contempt, therefore, for the impertinent diatribe of the hack scribe Villeterque, I would most certainly not have taken the trouble to respond were I not so anxious to put the public on its guard against the never-ending defamatory scribblings of his tribe.

To judge by the brainless review Villeterque wrote of *The Crimes of Love*, it is clear that he did not read the book. If he had, he would not have made me say something I have never thought. He would not have taken isolated phrases, which no doubt someone else fed to him, and then truncated them to suit his purposes and give them a meaning they never had.

Yet Villeterque, though he had not read it (as I have just shown), begins by calling my volume 'destestable' and assures us, out of charity, that 'this detestable book comes from the pen of a man suspected of having written another even more loathsome'.

At this point, I challenge Villeterque to do two things which he cannot refuse me: first, to publish not isolated, truncated, mangled phrases but the whole sentences which would demonstrate that my book deserves to be called 'detestable', although those persons who have read it agree on the contrary that it is firmly rooted in the purest moral values; and secondly, I challenge him to PROVE that I am the author of this

[1] A reviewer is defined as an educated man, a person capable of discussing a book rationally, of analysing it, and of laying before the public a considered account of it which tells the reader what it is about. But the reviewer who has neither the wit nor the judgement required by this honourable calling, a man who compiles, reprints, defames, lies, slanders, and talks gibberish, and does it to earn his bread, now he is what I call a vulgar hack: and Villeterque is that reviewer. (See his review dated 30 Vendémiaire an IX, p. 90).

other, even more 'loathsome' book. Only a slanderer casts slurs on another man's probity in this way without offering any evidence. The truly honest man proves, names names, and does not stoop to allegations. Villeterque denounces but offers no proof; over my head he hangs a fearsome question-mark without explaining or specifying what he means. Villeterque is therefore a slanderer; Villeterque is therefore not ashamed to sound like a slanderer even before he begins his diatribe.

Be that as it may, I have said and I here swear that I have never written 'immoral books' and never shall. I do so again now, not to the scribbler Villeterque, lest it seem that I value his opinion, but to the public whose judgement I respect as much as I despise that of Villeterque.[1]

After this initial courtesy, the hack begins in earnest. Let us follow him, providing of course that disgust does not stop us in our tracks. For it is hard to follow Villeterque without feeling disgust. He makes us feel disgusted with his opinions, disgusted with his writings, or rather acts of plagiarism, disgusted with... But no matter, we shall hold our noses.

The gross ignoramus Villeterque asserts that in my 'Essay on Novels', beneath 'a show of apparent erudition', I fall into an infinity of errors. Would it not again be appropriate here to provide evidence? Of course, it helps to have a modicum of 'erudition' if you wish to point out errors of 'erudition', and Villeterque, who will shortly demonstrate that he even lacks all knowledge of scholarly books, is a long way from possessing the 'erudition' necessary to point out my errors. He therefore makes do with stating that I make mistakes without saying what they are. Certainly it is not difficult to criticize in this manner; indeed, I have ceased being surprised that there is so much criticism about and so few good books. And

[1] It is the same contempt which made me keep silent about the fantastic, defamatory nonsense put about by a man named Despaze* who also claimed that I am the author of the infamous book which for the good of morality must never be mentioned by name. Knowing the depraved reprobate to be an adventurer spewed out by the Garonne so that he might come to Paris and stupidly denigrate arts of which he had not the first idea, books that he had not read, and decent people who ought to have banded together and clubbed him to death, and fully aware that this obscure scribbler and complete blackguard had struggled to cobble together a handful of ghastly verses with only that purpose in mind, which the pauper hoped would yield him a crust of bread, I had decided to leave him to wallow shamefully in the humiliation and opprobrium into which his scribbling constantly plunged him, fearing to pollute my ideas by allowing them to float, even for one single moment, past such a disgusting creature. But since he and his kind have taken to imitating donkeys, who bray all together when they are hungry, I had no other alternative, to shut them up, than to set about them all, without distinction. That is what obliges me to drag them momentarily by the ears out of the mire in which they were sinking so that the public may recognize them by the badge of shame which decorates their brows. And now that this service has been rendered to the human race, I shall kick the whole lot of them back into the stinking sewer where their scurvy deeds and degenerate lives will keep them floundering for ever.

that is why most literary journals, starting with the Villeterque's, would be totally unknown if their editors did not force them on the public, like the printed puffs which quacks hand out in the street.

With my errors boldly established and comprehensively laid out, as can be seen, by the word of the learned Villeterque, who, however, dares not cite one example, our genial scribbler then turns to my ideas, and it is now that he grows deep, it is here that Villeterque thunders and flashes. He does not place his trust in the subtlety or shrewdness of his arguments. Instead, he is all lightning and thunderbolts. Woe unto him who is not convinced! Villeterque, alias Aliboron, has spoken!*

O *Vile stercus*!* O wise and learned one! I have said it before and will say it again, that long study of the great masters has convinced me that it is not always by showing the triumph of virtue that an author may hope to interest the reader of a novel or a tragedy, and that this rule, which is not to be found in nature or Aristotle or any of our literary legislators, is nothing more than a principle all men must respect for their common good and is not absolutely essential in a dramatic work, whatever its formal genre. But these are not my ideas which I put forward here: I have invented nothing. Read what I wrote, and it will be seen that not only what I reported at that point of my essay is no more than the result of the effect produced by my study of the great masters, but also that I have not followed the rule religiously, however sound and wise I believe it to be. For what, fundamentally, are the two mainsprings of all dramatic art? Have not all good authors told us that they are *terror* and *pity*? Now what can best create *terror* if not scenes of vice triumphant, and what is the source of *pity* if not the spectacle of virtue under attack? We must therefore either stop trying to interest the reader, or accept these two principles. That Villeterque has not read widely enough to be convinced of their importance is all too obvious. There is no point in knowing the rules of a particular art if you insist on writing *Fireside Tales* which put the reader to sleep, or copy out short episodes from the *Arabian Nights* which you then proudly publish under your own name.* But if Villeterque the plagiarist is ignorant of these principles, because he is ignorant of almost everything, at least he does not challenge them. And when, for his newspaper, he extorts a few free theatre tickets and sits in the complimentary seats where this bad penny is offered performances of masterpieces by Racine and Voltaire, then he might at least learn from seeing *Mahomet*, for example, where both Palmire and Séide die virtuous and innocent while Mahomet triumphs, or be persuaded by *Britannicus*, in which the eponymous prince and his mistress die virtuous and innocent while Nero continues to reign. He will see the same thing in *Polyeucte*, *Phèdre*,* etc., etc., and when he gets home and picks up his Richardson he will see to what extent the famous English novelist holds our attention by showing virtue under siege. These are truths which I should like Villeterque to accept and, if he were convinced, he would criticize less *biliously*, less *arrogantly*, in short less *foolishly*, those writers who implement them as our very best authors did before them. The problem is that Villeterque, who is not one of our very best authors, is not familiar with the works of great writers. The moment the bilious Villeterque's axe is taken off him, the poor man has no idea what to do. Nonetheless, let us listen to what this ingenious *penman* has to say when he speaks of the use which I make of these principles. It is in this area that the *pedant* is worth hearing.

I claim that for a book to involve and hold the reader, vice must sometimes be shown to hold virtue hostage. I assert this to be a sure recipe for any writer who hopes to grip his public: yet Villeterque uses this literary maxim to attack my morals. Verily, verily, do I say this unto you, Villeterque, though you are as asinine a judge of men as you are of their works. The idea I put forward here is perhaps the best advertisement for virtue that could be made. Indeed, if virtue were not so fine a thing, would anyone weep for the misfortunes which befall it? If I myself did not believe that it is the worthiest idol that mankind can worship, would I say to authors who write dramatic narratives: if you would inspire pity, be bold for a moment and attack the best that heaven and earth can offer, and you will see what savage tears your sacrilege will produce? You see, I write in praise of virtue while Villeterque accuses me of repudiating it. But Villeterque, who is obviously not a man of virtue himself, has no idea how virtue should be honoured. Only the followers of a given divinity may enter its temple, and Villeterque, who may acknowledge neither god nor creed, lives in sublime ignorance of such matters. But when, on the very next page, he asserts that, because I think like our great writers and honour virtue as they do, I provide irrefutable evidence that I am the author of the book where it is most comprehensively humiliated, it must be admitted that it is here that Villeterque's logic shines forth in its greatest glory! I demonstrate that unless virtue is shown in action, it is impossible to write a dramatic narrative of any worth. This I assert because I think and say that indignation, anger, and tears are the necessary response to outrages perpetrated against virtue and the suffering that virtue endures, and from this proposition, says Villeterque, it follows that I am the author of the execrable book which promotes the exact opposite of the principles which I profess and justify! Yes, absolutely the exact opposite. For the author of the book in question seems to give vice power over virtue simply out of wilfulness... and libertinage... a despicable ploy which he in no way feels bound to use to create dramatic interest. On the other hand, the models which I quote invariably do the contrary, and I myself—insofar as my modest talents allow me to emulate the best models—have never portrayed vice in my books other than in terms best suited to make it seem hateful. And if on occasions I have allowed it to achieve some success at the expense of virtue, I have only done so to make the latter more attractive and more appealing. In following an approach which is radically different from that of the author of the book in question, I have certainly not adolpted his principles. Since I abhor those principles and have no truck with them in my books, I have obviously not adopted them. And the inconsistent Villeterque, who believes he can prove my guilt by drawing attention to what exculpates me, is therefore nothing more than a craven slanderer who needs to be exposed.*

But what purpose is served by these pictures of vice triumphant, asks the hack? Their purpose, Villeterque, is to show scenes in which the contrary of vice is displayed in a better light, and this is more than sufficient to justify their usefulness. This raises the question: where does vice triumph in the tales which you attack with as much *stupidity* as *impertinence*? I beg leave to offer a very brief analysis, just to prove to the public that Villeterque has no idea what he is talking about when he claims that in these stories I allow vice to get the better of virtue.

Where is virtue better rewarded than in 'Juliette and Raunai'*?

If virtue is under siege in 'The Double Test', is vice seen to prosper? Absolutely not, since there is not a single vicious person in this story, which is in fact a sentimental tale.*

As in *Clarissa*, virtue succumbs, I concede, in 'Henrietta Stralson'. But in this story is not crime punished by the hand of virtue?

In 'Faxelange' is it not chastised even more robustly, and is not virtue freed from its fetters?

Does the fatalism of 'Florville and Courval' allow crime to triumph? All the crimes unwittingly committed here are simply effects of fate, which the Greeks gave as a weapon to their gods. Do we not observe daily the same misfortunes as those which afflicted Oedipus and his family?*

Where is crime more wretched and more roundly punished than in 'Rodrigo'?

Is not the tenderest wedding virtue's reward in 'Lorenza and Antonio', and does not crime fail utterly?*

In 'Ernestine', is it not by the hand of the virtuous father of the unfortunate heroine that Oxtiern is punished?

Is it not upon a scaffold that crime ends in 'Dorgeville'?*

Does not the remorse which drives 'The Countess de Sancerre' to her grave constitute revenge for the virtue which she violated?

Finally, in 'Eugénie de Franval', does not the monster I have described turn his blade against himself?

So Villeterque, you miserable hack, where is it that crime triumphs in my tales? If I can see anything in all this which triumphs, it is only your ignorance and your spineless appetite for slander!

And now I would like to ask my *contemptible censor* how he has the gall dismiss a book as *a compilation of disgusting horrors* when not one of the objections he makes turns out to have any grounds whatsoever. And once that is conceded, what emerges from the verdict delivered by this inept wordsmith? Satire without wit, criticism without discernment, and bile for no reason. And all because Villeterque is a fool, and because out of a fool only foolishness can come forth.

I contradict myself, adds the schoolmasterish Villeterque, when I make one of my heroes say things which are contrary to what I say in my preface.* You ignorant clod, did you never hear that a character in a dramatic story must speak in a way that is consistent with the personality he has been given, so that it is the character who speaks, not the author? It is perfectly simple: when this happens, the character, completely determined by the role he plays, may well express views which are the opposite of those expressed by the author when he writes as himself. Indeed, what kind of man would Crébillon have been if he had always spoken like Atrée? What kind of person would Racine have been if he had thought like Nero? What a monster Richardson would have been if he had no other principles than those of Lovelace?* Oh really, Monsieur Villeterque, you are truly very stupid! There, that is one example of a truth upon which the characters in my novels and I invariably agree whenever we, severally or together, happen to discuss your tedious existence. But now I am being inept. Why am I using argument when what is required is derision? Indeed, what else does a bone-headed booby deserve who has the gall to tell an author who has punished vice at every turn: 'Show me sinners who prosper. That is what you must do if you would be master of your art—the author of *The Crimes of Love* has proved it!' No, Villeterque, I neither said nor proved any such thing, and to convince you I hereby call upon the public, who are not stupid, as a witness to your stupidity. I said the exact opposite, Villeterque: it is the contrary which is at the heart of all my writings.

Our scribbler's abject diatribe ends with a very fine invocation: 'Rousseau, Voltaire, Marmontel, Fielding, Richardson, what you wrote was not fiction,' he cries; 'you described manners but you should have described crimes!' As if crimes were not a part of manners! As if criminal manners did not exist alongside virtuous manners! But this is too advanced for Villeterque, who has not got this far in his thinking.

In any case, why were these charges laid at my door? I have always had the greatest respect for the authors named by Villeterque, and spoke of them in highly favourable terms in my 'Essay on Novels'. Moreover, did not these same writers, whom I have invariably praised, also offer us crimes? Is Rousseau's Julie really a thoroughly virtuous girl? Is the hero of *Clarissa* a really moral man? How much virtue is there in *Zadig*, *Candide*, etc.?* Ah, Villeterque! I suggest somewhere that anyone who wishes to write and has no aptitude for it would be better off making shoes for ladies and boots for men.* I had no idea at the time that this piece of advice was meant especially for you. Take it, my dear fellow, take it, and perhaps you might make a half-decent cobbler, because one thing is certain: you will never be much of a writer. Never mind, Villeterque. People will always read Rousseau, Voltaire, Marmontel, Fielding, and Richardson. Your cretinous pleasantries will persuade nobody that I ever denigrated these great men, because, on the contrary, I never stop holding them up as models to imitate. But what will surely never be read, Villeterque, is you. First, because there is nothing you have written that will survive you, and secondly, because even if anyone did stumble across any of your literary plagiarisms, they would prefer to read them in the original, where they bloom in all their purity, than defiled by a pen as gross as yours.

Villeterque, you have talked nonsense, lied, piled inanity upon slander, heaped stupidity on top of hypocrisy, and all because you wished to avenge the anaemic, passionless authors for whose ranks your own tedious compilations fit you perfectly.[1] I have given you one lesson and I am prepared to administer another if ever you decide to insult me again.

D.-A.-F. SADE

3

From *Le Journal des Arts*, 15 nivôse, An IX (5 January 1801)

The author of a twenty-page tract launched against me in connection with my review of one of his books, CITIZEN SADE, retracts, in a written statement which I have before me, all remarks capable of giving me offence. Those who have read his execrable pamphlet may well find this to make insufficient amends. But those who know the author will be well aware

[1] The only known work—praise be!—of this scribbler is a book of *Veillées* which he calls 'philosophic', though they are in fact merely 'soporific'. It is a turgid affair, uncommonly dull and tedious, in which our pedagogue, always on his high horse, would have us be as stupid as he is by agreeing to view his elucubrations as discernment, his inflated style as wit, and his acts of plagiarism as imagination. But unfortunately, all we find on perusing these pages are platitudes when the man is being himself, and the worst possible taste when he is stealing from others.

that it is all the apology I can ever hope to get from him. I shall not mention here either the title or the contents of the tract, for reasons which those who have read it and respect the general opinion will approve.

Villeterque, former army officer and associate member of the Institut national

EXPLANATORY NOTES

AN ESSAY ON NOVELS

3 *the kings of France*: the common ancestor of the Romance languages (French, Spanish, Portuguese, Italian, Romanian, etc.) was popular (or 'vulgar') rather than classical Latin. In ancient Gaul Celtic influence persisted and ensured the dominance of Gallo-Roman, the language spoken during the reigns of the Merovingian and Carolingian dynasties, from the fall of the Roman Empire in the late fifth century to the end of the tenth, when the first surviving literary texts in Old French appeared.

4 *of deranged minds*: Sade echoes the anticlerical refrain of the *philosophes*, who were always eager to point out that superstition, the great enemy of the rational Enlightenment, was the product of fear and ignorance.

History of the Celts: Michel Delon confirms that Simon Pelloutier, in his *Histoire des Celtes* (1741), had argued that the Romans identified Hercules in the religion of the Franks by identifying the name with 'Carl' or 'Kerl', the word for a Frankish warrior.

5 *the scholar Huet*: Daniel Huet, *Traité de l'origine des romans* (1670).

Ezra . . . Chariclea: The Book of Ezra is a historical chronicle in the Old Testament. The story of the loves of *Theagenes and Chariclea* (*c.* AD 250–80) is attributed to Heliodorus of Ephesus.

6 *Golden Ass*: a novel by the Latin writer Apuleius (second century AD). By claiming to write 'in the Milesian style', he intended his fantastic tale to reflect the extravagant, bawdy manner and content of the Greek *Milesian Tales*, a popular, oral tradition supposedly invented by Aristides of Miletus (second century BC). According to the Abbé Jacquin (*Entretiens sur les romans* (1755), 40), these early authors found ways 'of making vice agreeable' which 'soon spread throughout the whole of Greece'.

Antonius . . . to hell: Antonius Diogenes (fourth century BC) is known only through the *Bibliotheca*, which summarized 279 ancient works which had been read by its compiler Photius (died *c.*891), patriarch of Constantinople. J.-L. Lesueur's *Diana et Dercillade* (1745) was an adaptation rather than a translation of the story.

totally forgotten: the story of Sinonis and Rhodenis was told by the Syrian-born Iamblichus in his *Babylonaki* (*c.* AD 165–80). In his 'pleasant fiction' the *Cyropaedia*, Xenophon (*c.*427–355 BC) 'gave a portrait of the perfect prince' (Jacquin, *Entretiens*, 45). *Daphnis and Chloe*, a pastoral romance by the Greek writer Longus (third century AD), was much admired and many times translated into the European languages, notably into French by Jacques Amyot in the sixteenth century. Eustathius, last of the Greek romance writers, was active in the second half of the twelfth century AD. *The Story of Hysmine and Hysminias* was a coarse retelling of *Kleitophon and Leukippé* (*c.* AD 150–200) by Achilles Tatius.

6 *category of novels*: Petronius (d. AD 66), supposed author of the *Satyricon*, and Varro (116–27 BC), author of the *Saturae Menippeae*.

so Lucan says: Lucan (AD 39–65) author of the *Civil War*. In Nicolas Rowe's version (1674), lines 447–9 of Book I read:

> You too, ye bards, whom sacred raptures fire
> To chant your heroes to your country's lyre,
> Who consecrate in your immortal strain
> Brave patriot souls in righteous battle slain,
> Securely now the tuneful taste renew,
> And noblest themes in deathless songs pursue.

wonders they performed: the history of the principal medieval narrative genres may be traced from the *chanson de geste*, which appeared in the mid-twelfth century, to the more sophisticated romances which continued into the fifteenth and beyond. An example of the former, the Latin *Chronicle of Pseudo-Turpin* (mid-twelfth century), supposedly an account of Charlemagne's Spanish campaigns by Turpin, archbishop of Rheims, was translated into French early in the thirteenth century. Tristan and Lancelot, who also first appeared in the twelfth century, were just two of the many chivalrous heroes of the immense cycle of Arthurian romance, while *Le Roman de Perceforest* (1314–40) linked the cycles of Alexander and Arthur and spoke of the Round Table.

7 *copied in Italy*: the troubadours were lyrical poets of Occitania who, in the twelfth century, promoted the ideal of courtly love. They were not responsible for any of the non-courtly *fabliaux*, short comic, often bawdy, narratives which were not dissimilar to the 'Milesian fables' (see note to p. 6). Most surviving examples date from between the late twelfth and the fourteenth centuries and therefore long after the time of Hugues Capet (938–96), founder of the Capetian dynasty, who was crowned king of France in 987.

written in France: Sade disagrees with Jean-François de La Harpe (1739–1803), critic and author of a *Cours de littérature* (1799–1805), who claimed that Dante (1265–1321) and Petrarch (1304–74) had standardized the Italian language before the printing revolution of the Renaissance. It is difficult to see why, given his dates, Alessandro Tassoni (1565–1635) should be included in Sade's list. Boccaccio (1313–75) was less indebted to the French *fabliau* than Sade asserts.

banks of the Lignon: the name of the river made famous by *L'Astrée* (1607–27), the interminable pastoral novel, set in fifth-century Gaul, by Honoré d'Urfé (1567–1625). It tells how the shepherd Celadon, banished by the shepherdess Astrée, finally returns and wins back her love. Particularly valued were the discussions of love, jealousy, and the passions generally which marked the beginnings of the enduring French interest in psychological analysis.

Gomberville . . . Scudéry: Marin Le Roy (1600–74), *sieur* de Gomberville, author of a popular 'heroic' novel, *Polexandre* (1619–37); Gauthier de Coste (*c.*1610–63), *sieur* de La Calprenède, playwright then author of *Cassandre* (1642–5), *Cléopâtre* (1646–57), and the unfinished *Faramond* (1661–3), all historical novels celebrating modern courtly ideals; Jean Desmarets de Saint-Sorlin (*c.*1600–76), playwright, poet, and author of the novel *Ariane* (1632). There were two Scudérys, Georges (1601–67), soldier and playwright, who had a hand in the novels, published under his name, of his sister Madeleine (1608–1701): *Artamène, ou le Grand Cyrus* (1649–53) and *Clélie, histoire romaine* (1654–60), which inserted modern salon values into perfunctory historical settings. Though immensely long (*Artamène* ran to 15,000 pages), they were greatly admired.

8 *by Herodotus*: before Xenophon (see note to p. 6), Herodotus (*c.*480–425 BC) had already presented Cyrus (560–529 BC), founder of the Persian Empire, as a great general and wise ruler in the first book of his *Histories*.

were by her: long before Sade's time, the gaseous romances of the seventeenth century had become objects of ridicule. Horace Walpole's correspondent Madame du Deffand considered them to be founts of boredom and absurdity. But the most comprehensive rejection of French romances was made in *The Female Quixote* (1752), by Charlotte Lennox (*c.*1729–1804), whose heroine, with unfortunate consequences, models her life on them as Don Quixote had striven to live up to the ideals of chivalry.

defines it exactly: see Part I, chapter 6 of *Don Quixote* (1604). Cervantes (1547–1615) published the second part in 1614, a year after *The Exemplary Tales*, a collection of stories.

Saint-Evremond: the *sieur* de Saint-Evremond (1613–1703), a cultured exponent of *libertin* ideas who lived for many decades in exile in England. Michel Delon has confirmed Sade's source.

Scarron's . . . Le Sage: *Le Roman comique* (1651–7), a satirical novel about a group of strolling players at Le Mans, by Paul Scarron (1610–60); *Le Diable boîteux* (1707), a satirical fantasy, and the picaresque *Gil Blas de Santillane* (1715–1735), by Alain-René Lesage (1668–1747).

the Polixandres: see note to p. 7.

9 *for her style*: the Comtesse de La Fayette (1634–93), author of novellas of great psychological depth which helped shape the French tradition of psychological analysis, notably *Zayde* (1670) and *La Princesse de Clèves* (1678). She was close to La Rochefoucauld (1613–89), author of the *Maximes* (1665), who took a hand in her writing as did, at her request, Daniel Huet (see note to p. 5) and Jean de Segrais (1624–1701), who helped cleanse her works of any lingering traces of the florid style of Madeleine de Scudéry, whom she had admired.

9 *Fénelon . . . any more*: in 1689 François de Salignac de la Mothe-Fénelon (1651–1715), later archbishop of Cambrai, became tutor to Louis XIV's grandson, for whom he wrote a number of educational works. These included a reworking of the *Odyssey* (*Les Aventures de Télémaque*, 1699), which was judged to be critical of Louis XIV's absolutist rule. This completed the disgrace of the author, who was finally exiled to his diocese for his close involvement with the Quietism of Madame Guyon, a mystical tendency within Catholicism which attracted the condemnation of the pope in 1699. Sade was wrong about the neglect of *Télémaque*. Regarded by many as a model of moralizing fiction, it had been reprinted some 250 times by 1820 and was translated into forty languages. However, he was not alone in disliking it. Madame du Deffand thought *Télémaque* 'deadly dull... full of precepts and prescriptions and empty of feeling, action and passion'.

she so richly deserved: Madame Gomez (1684–1770), daughter of the actor Paul Poisson. Her *Journées amusantes* (8 vols.) appeared between 1722 and 1731, and the nineteen volumes of her *Cent nouvelles nouvelles* between 1732 and 1739.

honour to their sex: Madame de Lussan (1682–1758) was an exponent of the narrative which was barely distinguishable from history; the Marquise de Tencin (1681–1749) was the author of two novels, *Le Comte de Comminges* (1735) and *Le Siège de Calais* (1739); the *Lettres d'une Péruvienne* (1747) was the only novel of Madame de Graffigny (1695–1758); and Madame Élie de Beaumont (1729–83) was the admired author of the *Lettres du Marquis de Roselle* (1764). Among the eight novels of Madame Riccoboni (1713–92), the *Lettres de Milady Catesby* (1759) was particularly admired for its style, sensitivity, and control.

10 *god of Cythera*: one of the Ionian Islands, Cythera was in Greek mythology sacred to Aphrodite, and by extension, was the poetic, allegorical island of Love. The persons named here were all sympathetic to the libertine or freethinking culture of the seventeenth century. Ninon de Lenclos (*c.*1620–1705) and Marion Delorme (*c.*1611–50) were both cultured women and the most celebrated courtesans of the age. The Marquis de Sévigné, who died in 1651 in a duel over another woman, was the husband of the celebrated letter-writer. Like the Marquis de La Fare (1644–1712), the Abbé de Chaulieu (1639–1720) was a *libertin* poet and a member of the debauched company which met at the Temple. For Saint-Evremond, see note to p. 8.

is the physical: this celebrated formula (erroneously attributed to Fontenelle on p. 305) was not an instance of Enlightenment cynicism but an attempt made in his *Discours sur les animaux* (1753) by the Comte de Buffon (1707–88), the leading naturalist of the day, to show the distance separating the simplicity of nature from the complications created by human desires and passions.

by the Regent: Louis XIV outlived his children, and on his death in 1715 was succeeded by his grandson, during whose minority France was ruled by Philippe d'Orléans as regent. After the austerity of the last years of the Sun King, the years 1715–23 are remembered as a time of political and economic instability, lax morality, and a new spirit of intellectual daring.

Crébillon . . . success: Crébillon *fils* (1707–77), the subtlest of the *libertin* novelists of the eighteenth century, published, among other works, *Le Sopha* (1742), *L'Écumoire, ou Tanzaï et Néadarné* (1734), and *Les Égarements du coeur et de l'esprit* (1736–7).

perfection of his art: Marivaux (1688–1763), known mainly as a playwright, was the author of two novels, both unfinished: *La Vie de Marianne* (1731–42) and *Le Paysan parvenu* (1734–35). He was frequently criticized for his over-precious style, which Voltaire famously described as so many 'butterfly's eggs laid in a spider's web.'

Voltaire . . . masterpieces?: Voltaire (1694–1778) wrote twenty-six prose tales, of which *Candide* (1759) and *Zadig* (1748) are the best known. They are examples of the philosophical tale, a form which Voltaire invented and which Sade also used for *Les Infortunes de la vertu* (*The Misfortunes of Virtue*, 1787), the first version of *Justine*.

La Nouvelle Héloïse: Julie, ou La Nouvelle Héloïse (1761), was the only novel of Jean-Jacques Rousseau (1712–78). It had an astonishing impact on the nation's sensibility and helped to change the course of fiction, since, Sade's plea notwithstanding, many novelists continued to follow where Rousseau had led.

Momus: in Greek mythology, the god of raillery and censure.

11 *rose-tinted tales*: the *Contes moraux* (1755–65) of Jean-François Marmontel (1723–99) set the tone and style of most short fiction until the Revolution. *Bélisaire* (1767) was his philosophical novel set in ancient Rome. Chapter 15, which contained a plea for the civil toleration of the Protestants, whose religion had been banned in France since the Revocation of the Edict of Nantes in 1685, caused a public scandal.

in English novels: Samuel Richardson was regarded primarily as moral writer who showed the passions in action in fully realized characters. He was greatly admired, and his influence on the French novel was considerable. Henry Fielding was considered too 'eccentric' to command the same respect, but had his supporters. Sade's list of English novelists surprisingly omits Laurence Sterne, whose *Tristram Shandy* made him famous in France in the 1760s.

12 *from the back*: the quotation has not been traced to Diderot, but it highlights a cardinal principle of Sade's view of the novel—that it must engage the affective faculties of the reader—which he further defends in his response to Villeterque: see Appendix II.

into our language: Abbé Antoine-François Prévost (1697–1763) translated Richardson's *Pamela* (1742), *Clarissa* (1751), and *Sir Charles Grandison* (1755–58), and did much to promote knowledge of English literature and life.

12 *divides and diversifies*: many eighteenth-century novels were digressive, with long, intercalated tales interrupting and sometimes displacing the main narrative. Sade commends Prévost for his management of the 'drawers' of the *roman à tiroirs*, of which *Manon Lescaut*, the seventh tome of the multi-volume *Mémoires d'un homme de qualité* (1728–31), is an example.

criticizes you: 'The Abbé Prévost's greatest failing is his inability to set himself a plan and stick to it. He simply presses on, forgetting his point of departure and with no idea of where he is going' (La Harpe, *Cours de littérature* (1799–1805), xiv. 142).

13 *of his rivals*: Prévost, who later in life became a professional translator and compiler, was also a prolific novelist. Sade mentions only a fraction of his output: the *Mémoires d'un homme de qualité* (1728–31), *Le Philosophe anglais, ou Histoire de Monsieur de Clèveland* (1731–39), *Histoire d'une Grecque moderne* (1740), and *Le Monde moral* (1760). Sade's admiration is surprising, for the sentiment and melodrama he commends were ridiculed later in the century by writers such as Diderot, who derided Prévost's overheated imagination in *Jacques le Fataliste*. But in a letter to his wife of 27 July 1780, Sade wrote: 'What a man! What a writer! That's the sort I would want to adjudicate and judge me, not the gaggle of idiots who have the impertinence to tell me what I should do!'

capturing it exactly: Claude-Joseph Dorat (1734–80), author of plays and verse, light in tone and precious in manner. Remembered mainly for *Les Malheurs de l'inconstance* (1772).

your beautiful Aline: Aline, heroine of *La Reine de Golconde* (1761), an elegantly written *libertin* tale by the Chevalier de Boufflers (1738–1815), which tells how a milkmaid, by the exercise of her charms, rises to become queen. In 1800 Napoleon removed Boufflers's name from the list of émigrés, and Sade does not pass up the opportunity to flatter France's 'Hero-Saviour'.

surpassed him: Baculard d'Arnaud (1715–1805), novelist and playwright, known especially for two dozen long tales, *Les Épreuves du sentiment* (1772–80), written in the 'sombre' vein which was a prelude to romantic gloom and gothic horror.

will be grateful: that is, for paper in which to wrap their spices. 'R——' is the prolific Restif de la Bretonne (1734–1806), once a typesetter by trade, who occasionally rolled up his sleeves and helped print his own books. In the 1790s he kept a press in his room and used it to print a number of works, including *Monsieur Nicolas*, his autobiography. Sade's contempt was of long standing. On 24 November 1783, he had scolded his wife for thinking of sending a book by Restif to him in prison, and in 1788 he had already used this jibe, saying that if Restif was lacking in Attic salt, the grocers of the new century could add pepper to his pages. In 1800 Sade was particularly venomous, because Restif had several times denounced 'the author of *Justine*' as a danger to public safety. A review in the daily

Journal de Paris (28 Oct. 1800) chides Sade for this 'diatribe' against Restif.

14 *as a model*: *Ambrosio, or the Monk* (1796), by Matthew Lewis (1775–18), and *The Mysteries of Udolpho* (1794) and *The Italian* (1797), by Ann Radcliffe (1764–1823), which had all appeared in French translation in 1797, are among the best-known examples of the English gothic romance. If Sade does not linger over these 'new novels', it was because, as an atheistical materialist, he considered the supernatural to be the product of superstition. Only with *Rodrigo*, his sole gothic tale, was he tempted to conform to 'the style of the age' (p. 305). His sociological explanation for their immense popularity, as an escape from unbearable reality, has a very modern ring.

15 *will not read him*: the metaphor is, to say the least bold, and Villeterque was duly scandalized: see p. 313.

16 *earning your living*: although Sade was not prepared to compromise his writing, and distances himself from the likes of the despised Restif, who lived by his pen, everything he had published since 1791 had been intended to make money.

17 *authors of the Encyclopédie*: the compendium of Enlightenment *philosophie*, whose publication (1751–72) was overseen principally by Diderot. The source of Sade's assertion is unclear. The article 'Dénouement', written by Marmontel, recommends that the best sort of ending is one in which 'crime succumbs and innocence triumphs'.

Antoninus . . . the Neros: the reign of Antoninus Pius (AD 86–161), who succeeded the Emperor Hadrian, was known as a time of peace and prosperity, while Titus Flavius Vespasianus (AD 39–81) is remembered as a liberal emperor who beautified the city of Rome. On the other hand, Nero (AD 37–68) was a tyrant who ruled by terror, as was the Byzantine emperor Andronic I (1122–85).

18 *lavas of Vesuvius*: sons of Heaven and Earth in Greek mythology, the Titans revolted against the gods and attempted to reach them by heaping mountains on top of each other only to be destroyed by Zeus' thunderbolts. Symbols of the awful power of nature for Sade's generation, volcanoes have an important place in his fiction. Etna is evoked later in 'Rodrigo' and reappears in *Juliette* (1797), where it is the setting of a stupendous climax.

Amboise': 'The Enchanted Tower' is the subtitle of 'Rodrigo', and 'The Conspiracy of Amboise' of 'Juliette et Raunai' (not included in this selection).

The Arab historian: having written the 'fifteen or twenty pages' of 'Rodrigo' based on a memory of something he had read, Sade wrote to his wife on 15 January 1787 asking her to look for the story in the works of Mme d'Aulnoy (*c.* 1650–1705), author of tales and romanced history. He thought she might also find it in the *Bibliothèque Universelle des*

Romans, a periodical which printed nothing but fiction. Michel Delon has traced Sade's source to the issue of October 1782. The version there was based on a tale by the Spaniard Miguel de Luna, who masqueraded as 'Abulcasim Tarif Abentarique'.

19 *from history*: 'Juliette and Raunai' is the first tale of *The Crimes of Love* (see note to p. 317). The vast *Histoire de France depuis l'établissement de la monarchie jusqu'au règne de Louis XIV* (1766–86) was begun by Velli, continued by Villaret to 1468, and completed by J. J. Garnier (vols. 17–30). A set of volumes 1–24 (to 1556) figures in the 1776 catalogue of Sade's library at La Coste, and volumes 23–30 are mentioned as being among his books at the Bastille in 1787.

Aline and Valcour: for the tale of the enchanted tower, see *Aline and Valcour*, letter 38. Begun at the Bastille in 1786, completed in June 1789, Sade's long novel was published, after many difficulties, in 1795 under the name of 'le citoyen S'. The pirated editions of which he complains were *Valmor et Lydia, ou voyage autour du monde par deux amants qui se cherchaient*, 3 vols. (Paris, An VII [1799]), which converted his letter novel into a third-person narrative; and *Alzonde et Koradin*, 2 vols. (Berlin [Paris], 1799).

20 *entitled J——*: i.e. *Justine*, of which a new edition was seized by the police on 18 August 1800, about a month before the publication of *The Crimes of Love*.

MISS HENRIETTA STRALSON

21 *Ranelagh*: by the Thames at Chelsea. The house and gardens were built by the Earl of Ranelagh (d. 1711), and were opened as a place of resort and entertainment in 1742. Regattas, balls, and masquerades were held there. It closed finally in 1803.

have her: a crude, direct expression which was part of the jargon of the *libertin*. Sade sometimes italicizes such phrases, to draw attention to them: see also pp. 31, 104, 240.

23 *the sort of talk I like*: Granwel sets out the code of the *libertin*.

Cecil Street: there was no Cecil Street. Sade never visited England, and the London landmarks he mentions (Covent Garden, St James's Park, etc.) were familiar to any French reader of the fashionable 'English' novels of the period. The same is true of his later reference to Newmarket (celebrated because of the English weakness for horses and gambling), and explains his erroneous belief that Granwel is able to travel from London to his estate on the Scottish borders without a change of horses: see p. 59.

25 *be contaminated*: the association of the country with natural goodness and the town with moral corruption goes back to ancient times. Its recent revival by Rousseau had turned it into a commonplace of theatre, poetry, and fiction.

28 *Italian castrato*: Giuseppe Millico (1737–1802), an Italian soprano castrato and composer. He sang for a season in Vienna (1772) and two in London (1772–4) before returning to Italy. His performance in Gluck's *Orpheus* was much admired, though Mrs Thrale was unimpressed by his pronunciation. 'Millico was set to sing these English words—I come my Queen to chaste delights—He sung them thus—I comb my Queen to catch the lice'. Emma Hamilton was later his pupil.

41 *very last time*: David Garrick (1717–79) took leave of the stage by playing a season of his favourite roles, which included Hamlet. He ended his farewell as Don Felix in Mrs Centlivre's *Wonder* on 10 June 1776.

43 *the celebrated Fielding*: in 1754 Henry Fielding, author of *Joseph Andrews* and *Tom Jones*, resigned his post as magistrate in favour of his half-brother Sir John Fielding (d. 1780). Although the latter was blind from birth, it was said that he knew 3,000 thieves by their voices. Sade seems unaware of his disability, for in the next paragraph the 'blind beak' solves the case before him with a glance at Henrietta.

45 *Hosden*: perhaps Sade's attempt at 'Hoddesdon'.

49 *altar . . . to his desires*: i.e. a bed. Such circumlocutions were a common feature of the *libertin* prose style. Though seemingly coy, they were consistently used by Sade as part of his general attack on religion.

FAXELANGE

69 *thirty-five-thousand livres*: in the second half of the eighteenth century a labourer might earn 300 livres a year, skilled workers 500, and lesser professionals between 1,000 and 3,000. Bourgeois incomes began at about 6,000 livres per annum and the lesser nobility at around 40,000. An annual income of 100,000 livres and more defined the wealthiest rank of the aristocracy. The Faxelanges are very well-to-do members of the upper middle class.

a general quality: the word 'romantic', yet to be included in Gattel's *Dictionnaire portatif* of 1797, had been imported from England, where it was used primarily to describe mountainous regions, beetling crags, and other wild landscapes.

72 *Pope in English*: Alexander Pope (1688–1744) was much admired in France as the voice of English classical poetry. His *Essay on Man* confirmed the philosophical optimism of Voltaire, who translated it in 1738. The choice of Pope at the Faxelanges' soirée indicates the intellectual nature of the gathering.

74 *the Vivarais*: the ancient name of the mountainous area of south-east France, a poor region, noted for civil unrest, and now broadly the equivalent of the *département* of the Ardèche. Sade's family estate at La Coste, east of Avignon, was situated in similarly hilly country.

the Minister himself: persons of rank and wealth had ready access to royal ministers at the court of Versailles. Any minister could be approached, though most applications were made to the Minister of Justice, whose powers covered the widespread forms of litigation which kept the legal profession gainfully employed.

83 *Pont de la Guillotière*: a bridge of this name, leading west to the Place Bellecour, still spans the Rhône.

the gibbet at Les Terreaux: the Place des Terreaux, near the Hôtel de Ville.

84 *a hundred thousand écus*: Franlo deducts his outlay of 100,000 francs from the 400,000 he has received, and estimates his profit (at 3 francs to the écu) to be 300,000 francs, or 100,000 écus.

central France: Sade here evokes the reign of terror of the gang of bandits led by Louis Mandrin, who was as famous in France as Dick Turpin was in England. He was finally captured and broken on the wheel at Valence in 1755, aged 31. The subsequent participation of Goé in 'the war presently being fought in Germany' (see p. 96) seems to confirm that this tale is set in the late 1750s: Sade himself had served in Germany in 1759 during the Seven Years War.

passion for gambling: before 1789 diatribes against gambling, from cards to horse-racing, were a staple of both the sentimental novel and of moralizing literature of all kinds.

85 *the Palais Royal*: built in 1629 by Cardinal Richelieu, who gave it to Louis XIII in 1636. It was the residence of the Orléanist branch of the royal family, but by the late eighteenth century it had long been a favourite haunt of gamblers and libertines.

86 *Hermitage wine*: a highly regarded wine from near Tain on the Rhône.

87 *the town of Tournon*: opposite Tain, 80 km. south of Lyons and 18 km. north of Valence.

90 *cannot get used to*: this was Sade's argument against moral absolutes. Custom and habit are all, as the 'degradation' of the bandits' women will soon confirm, and conscience is a learned response, a mechanism exploited by the weak to keep the strong in check.

die with style: the demands of these Roman ladies were used by many contemporary writers as a measure of the decadence of Rome. Sade may have found the idea in the *Encyclopédie*, article 'Homme'.

93 *that is my crime*: an argument to add to the defence of Madame de Franlo, who is forced to act criminally by circumstances. Sade devoted a tale, 'Dorgeville, or the Virtuous Criminal', to the notion that crime is relative, not an absolute.

95 *executioners in their ranks*: an observation not lost on those of Sade's readers in 1800 who had survived a decade of bloodletting. An example of his irony, to add to his authorial comment (p. 93) that heaven 'never deserts the innocent'.

97 *a home for foundlings*: in 1674 the Sisters of Charity began taking in foundlings in a house in the Faubourg Saint-Antoine, and in 1748 a

second home, nearer to the centre of Paris, was opened at the western end of the Parvis Notre Dame. It was here that Jean-Jacques Rousseau, originator of child-centred education, sent his five illegitimate offspring, who remained there until old enough to exercise a trade. In the 1770s around 8,000 children were abandoned each year at the 'Enfants trouvés', where conditions were so bad that only a few hundred of that number survived. It was, in reality, an effective infanticide agency.

the Carmelite Convent: in the rue d'Enfer (now the rue Henri-Barbusse in the fifth *arrondissement*). Sade's mother lived in the convent from perhaps as early as 1752, and died there on 14 January 1777. Renée-Pélagie was also a boarder from the time of Sade's arrest until 1780.

ambition of daughters: these are the wrongs of ambition of the title. Sade's moral excludes Franlo, whose downfall is also tragic in its way.

FLORVILLE AND COURVAL

98 *of 15,000 livres*: see note to p. 69. We learn later that Florville has an allowance of 4,000 francs, to which, on her marriage, Saint-Prât adds a similar amount.

the rue Saint-Marc: situated between the rue Montmartre and the rue de Richelieu, just inside the old city limits. The Convent of the Assumption, where Florville later boards, was close by. The location has no particular significance, except that, like the Abbé Prévost whom he admired, Sade uses occasional topographical references to anchor his fiction in physical reality.

101 *hospital for foundlings*: see note to p. 97.

103 *the voice of Mentor*: in Homer's *Odyssey* Odysseus is shipwrecked on Ogygia, the island of Calypso, where he is detained for seven years. Sade refers to Fénelon's version of the story, in which Odysseus' son Telemachus, accompanied by Mentor (in reality the human form adopted by Minerva, goddess of wisdom), goes in search of his father: see *Les Aventures de Télémaque*, bk. VI.

110 *give you a place*: it has been suggested that this woman was Marie-Constance Quesnet, Sade's companion and helpmeet from August 1790 to the end of his life.

111 *return for ever*: this remarkable paragraph begins with arguments which effectively refute the recent postmodernist contention that 'grand narratives', absolute values, and totalizing ideological principles are no longer possible. It continues with a thesis, first advanced by Pierre Bayle at the end of the seventeenth century, which separated morality and religion. He contended that a community of atheists would not degenerate into anarchy, but would generate moral and civil laws without which coexistence is impossible. Sade uses this argument as a defence of enlightened self-interest which, though not unconnected with Bayle's view, leads in a different direction.

114 *your faith?*: a paraphrase of Pascal's celebrated 'wager' argument in his *Pensées*.

your nerves: a rare glimpse in these stories of Sade's argument, rooted in Enlightenment materialism, which gave all ideas a physiological origin.

126 *think of me once more*: in this equable apology for atheism there is little trace of the 'fearsome stoicism' earlier attributed to Madame de Verquin.

127 *courage and reason*: Madame de Verquin's 'Epicurean' philosophy is defined less by her sensual tastes than by her more general belief that the purpose of life is the avoidance of pain, and especially the rational pursuit of pleasure in all its forms.

128 *VIXIT*: 'she has lived', a defiant motto intended to contrast with Florville's anguished belief in God.

132 *like the latter*: Sade gives a generous amount of space to the arguments in favour of belief, the better to counter them with the ironic contrast between the peaceful end of the sinner and the torment of the saint. His earlier 'Dialogue Between a Priest and a Dying Man' (1782) had made a similar point.

134 *the Furies*: in Greek mythology, the three ministers of the vengeance of the gods, who were directed to punish the guilty both on earth and in the infernal regions.

135 *at the time*: see the 'Essay on Novels', pp. 13–14.

138 *King of Sardinia*: by the Treaty of Utrecht (1713), Sardinia was acquired by Austria which, in 1720, gave it to the House of Savoy in exchange for Sicily. United with Savoy and Piedmont, it gave its name to a new kingdom, whose capital was Turin.

RODRIGO

147 *Taenarus*: Cape Taenarus, a promontory of Laconia, the southernmost point of Europe where, in Greek mythology, Neptune had a temple in the form of a grotto. It was believed to be one of the entrances to hell: through it Hercules dragged Cerberus from the infernal regions.

rivers of hell: the Hades of Greek mythology was believed to have three principal rivers. Sade's 'Agraformikubos', made up of Graeco-Roman elements, suggests 'a flat field', and perhaps therefore a wide, slow-moving stream.

153 *the Furies*: see note to p. 134.

154 *his own heart*: where the lion read Rodrigo a lesson in kingship, the eagle is a spokesman for republicanism. As stated here, both creeds defer to the moral universe which had no place in Sade's philosophy. Sade's nod in the direction of received opinion, also at work in the climax of his tale, was born of his fear of offending.

156 *produce only evil*: Sade prudently allows the eagle to have the best of an argument which invariably triumphs in Sade's novels. Rodrigo equates

the physical 'deflection' of the sun with evil, and concludes that what moralists called evil is a naturally occurring by-product of the workings of blind physical forces. By implication, crime, vice, and perversion are as much a part of the fabric of things as 'orderly' goodness and virtue.

divine friend of Jupiter: before Jupiter engaged upon his struggle with the Titans, the eagle brought him a thunderbolt. To recognize this service, the god made the bird his emblem. It is often represented with wings outstretched, holding the bolts of Jupiter in its talons.

157 *two kingdoms of Spain*: by this Sade means the Iberian Peninsula in general, composed of Spain and Portugal, not the specific union of the Two Kingdoms ruled by the Spanish King between 1580 and1648. The tale seems to be set at around the time of the Moorish conquest of Spain in the eighth century, though the historical setting is perfunctory.

158 *from the country forever*: the Moors were finally expelled in 1492.

ERNESTINE

159 *Alarics . . . Theodorics*: Alaric I (d. 410) and Alaric II (d. 507) were Visigoth kings. Attila (d. 453) was king of the Huns, while of several Theodorics, Sade probably refers to the king of the Ostrogoths (455–526), who invaded Italy in 488–90. Sade follows his contemporaries in attributing a northern origin to these rampaging barbarian invaders.

Gustavus . . . Charles XII: Gustavus I (1496–1560), founder of the Wasa dynasty, freed Sweden from Danish rule. He also embraced the Protestant Reformation and confiscated the property of the Catholic clergy, as the anticlerical Sade gleefully points out in his footnote. Christine II (1626–89) opened her court to learning and welcomed foreign scholars and thinkers, including Descartes. Charles XII (1682–1718) was an ambitious, bellicose king, who led Sweden into a series of northern wars.

160 *his anecdotes*: Prévost's description of a Swedish copper mine first appeared in *Le Pour et le contre*, a periodical which he edited between 1733 and 1740. Sade refers to its reprinted version in the *Contes, aventures et faits divers* published in 1764. Prévost never visited Sweden, and drew heavily on the account of his travels by the playwright Jean-François Regnard in 1681.

the Scythians: a word applied very loosely to barbarians who originated in north-eastern Europe and north-western Asia. In Sade's day ideas as fanciful as Ernestine's costume 'in the Scythian style' (p. 172) were entertained of them.

Falun . . . Sweden: on leaving Stockholm, the narrator travels 40 km. to Uppsala, then the 120 km. to Falun, a mining town and the largest in Decarlia, the old name for a province of central Sweden, and thence south to the iron mines of Taperg at the southern end of Lake Vättern. These sketchy details are the limits of Sade's bookish knowledge of Sweden.

160 *could supply*: after walking into an open-cast iron-ore mine, Regnard also descended by means of a cable into a much less noxious silver mine. He found galleries which were spacious and not cramped: 'It is another town beneath the town: here, there are houses, taverns, stables and horses.' Prévost, borrowing from Regnard, also reported that the mine contained 'settlements as regular as any occurring above ground and composed of many families, all with their own chief, judges, houses, shopkeepers, shops, ministers and churches'.

162 *Augustus to Cinna*: the clemency shown by Augustus to Cinna in Corneille's Roman tragedy *Cinna* (1640/1) is a byword in France.

Count d'Oxtiern: the name recalls that of Oxenstierna, one of Sweden's chief families since the sixteenth century.

the people and the King: during the reign of Adolphus Frederick (1751–71) Sweden was divided by two factions of opposing nobles: the 'Caps', who advocated peace and opposed royal absolutism, and the 'Hats', a bellicose party influenced by French ideas. In 1772, shortly after his accession, Gustavus III (1746–92) broke the power of the nobles by means of a supposed revolt, and restored the constitution suspended by the nobility since the reign of Ulrica (1718–20).

163 *in Norway*: Charles XII conquered the Danes, Russians, and Poles but was defeated by Peter the Great at Poltava in 1709. He fled across the Turkish frontier to Bender (now Tighina, in Moldavia), and remained with the Turks until 1715, when he returned to Sweden. He was killed by a stray bullet at the siege of Frederikshald.

province of Ostrogothy: i.e. Ostergötland. Nordkoping is Nörrkoping.

164 *Frederick . . . Adolphus-Frederick*: Frederick I, crowned in 1720, was succeeded in 1751 by Adolphus-Frederick, who died in 1772.

Countess de Sparre: Countess Ebba Sparre (1626–62), more celebrated for her beauty than her learning, was a particular favourite of Christine's. In 1653 Bulstrode Whitelocke, Cromwell's representative in Stockholm, was presented to 'La Belle Comptesse, the fayre Countess' of Sparre by the queen, who encouraged him 'to discourse with this lady, my bed-fellowe, and tell me if her inside be not as beautiful as her outside'. Certain of Christine's letters to her were published in the 1760s and revived speculation concerning her private life.

173 *Bellona*: variously believed to be the sister, daughter, or wife of Mars, Bellona was the Roman goddess of war.

191 *an innocent man*: one of many examples of Sade's irony, which he indulges particularly at the expense of religion and the law.

194 *to be suspected*: the wording suggests a reference to the 'law of suspects', introduced in September 1793, under which Sade, 'suspected' of a lack of revolutionary zeal, had been imprisoned in December of that year.

212 *men of goodwill*: Sanders's liberal penal ideas are somewhat paradoxical. They reflect both an optimistic view of human nature and the gloomier

argument that human nature can be controlled effectively only by carrots and sticks.

215 *benefit the many*: Sade's highly moral ending shows that even a 'criminal-by-constitution' may be redeemed by a policy of minimal retribution. It is an argument conditioned by his own experience of prison and his eternal readiness to blame others. In the melodrama based on this tale, Herman survives and shoots Oxtiern dead moments before he can put his cowardly scheme into operation. Although Ernestine has been dishonoured, he still asks for her hand: 'can the crimes of a scoundrel leave a stain on nature's finest handiwork?'

THE COUNTESS OF SANCERRE

216 *Charles the Bold . . . Somme*: Charles the Bold (1433–77), last duke of Burgundy, attempted to create a principality as powerful as the monarchy of the French king Louis XI (1423–83), his feudal superior. He forced concessions from him after the battle of Montlhéry, and later conducted several campaigns, among which was the siege of Nancy at which he was killed.

Count of Sancerre: Sancerre, some 40 km. north-east of Bourges, was at the western end of the Duchy of Burgundy, which finally came under the control of the king of France after the death of Charles the Bold.

217 *Bellona*: see note to p. 173.

218 *the siege was lifted*: in 1472.

224 *at Montlhéry*: near Évry, south of Paris. The battle fought there in 1465 was Charles the Bold's greatest success.

lost his life: Pierre de Brezé (*c.* 1410–65), appointed by Louis XI as his royal lieutenant (seneschal) for Normandy, died at the battle of Montlhéry. He was a distant forbear of Sade through his mother, a Maillé de Brezé.

232 *aggrieved with him*: the Countess confuses Charles the Bold, Charles VII, and an earlier Duke of Burgundy, Jean Sans Peur. It was the latter who ordered the death of his political opponent, Louis, Duke of Orléans, in 1407. After an attempted rapprochement with the Dauphin of France (Charles VII), Jean Sans Peur was assassinated in 1419 on the bridge at Montereau (Seine et Marne) by Tanneguy Du Châtel and the Dauphin's party.

238 *Louis XII*: king of France from 1498 to 1515. He left a unified France to his successor, and is remembered for his encouragement of the arts.

at Auxerre: on the Yonne, 100 km. south-east of Paris.

EUGÉNIE DE FRANVAL

239 *raw and unadorned?*: similar defensive disclaimers were made regularly by authors of novels dealing with 'free' subjects. See, for example, the

preface to *Roxana* (1724), where Defoe states that 'when vice is painted in its low-prized colours, 'tis not to make people in love with it, but to expose it; and if the reader makes a wrong use of the figures, the wickedness is his own'.

239 *the law of equilibrium*: a view, having no scientific basis, first propounded during classical antiquity, that by an undefined principle of 'compensation' the sum of good and evil cancel each other out. This law was advanced by, among others, the materialist Jean-Baptiste-René Robinet (1735–1820), whose *De la nature* (1761) was several times reprinted and augmented. There was a copy in Sade's library at La Coste in 1776.

of four hundred thousand livres: on this income, and the 60,000 livres later received by Mademoiselle de Farneille, see note to p. 69.

240 *think solidly*: i.e 'rationally', in the *libertin* jargon.

241 *go as deep*: an example of the masochistic idea, common to post-Rousseauistic and gothic authors alike, that melancholy has its own pleasures. Compare Herman's awareness of 'the sorrowing joy which can only find expression in tears' (p. 187).

243 *at least as dangerous*: the narrative voice, in this rejection of faith as an illusion born of and maintained by human weakness, belongs more to Sade than to Franval.

245 *what he himself believed*: plans drawn up, usually by men, for the education of girls were a characteristic feature of the French Enlightenment. Laclos had thoughts on the matter, and Madame de Genlis put the children of Philippe d'Orléans through a programme not too different from that sketched by Sade.

247 *The day she reached that age*: the passages enclosed by brackets here and on pp. 280–1 were omitted by Sade in 1800 for reasons of decency. They were reinstated from the manuscript by Maurice Heine in his edition of the *Historiettes, contes et fabliaux* (1926).

The windows . . . daughter to it: an example of the 'voluptuous' decors favoured by authors of *libertin* fantasies. The most inventive example is Vivant Denon's *Point de lendemain* (*No Tomorrow*, 1777).

249 *by Michelangelo*: Sade had a painterly eye and had admired the works of Michelangelo (1475–1564) since encountering him during his travels in Italy in the 1770s.

253 *as good as cancelled?*: an echo of the hypocritical Tartuffe's self-serving argument that 'sins committed in private are not sins at all' (Molière, *Tartuffe*, IV. v). Villeterque quotes this passage as an example of the contradictions in Sade's position, a charge which he vehemently rebuts in his reply (see Appendix II).

255 *Valmont*: the name of fictional heroes adopted since the 1770s by numerous authors, and not only by Laclos in *Dangerous Liaisons* (1782). In the *libertin* tradition such names and their variants (Valcour, Meilcour, Ceil-

cour, Lussac, Pressac, etc.) usually suggested a hero of cynical propensities.

257 *populate the world?*: the tribes of the Moabites and Ammonites sprang from the loins of Moab and Ammon, the sons of Lot by his daughters (Genesis 20: 36). In Greek legend the debauched women of Amathus gave the sculptor Pygmalion a revulsion for their sex. Instead, he transferred his affections to his own works, and fell in love with the statue he had carved of Galathea, whom the goddess of beauty brought to life. By her he had a son who founded the city of Paphos in Cyprus. Sade uses these examples from Christianity and antiquity to demonstrate the universal unreasonableness of the taboo against incest. He was not alone in using biblical examples to cast doubt on the purity of human origins. Many before him had pointed out that the progeny of the children of Adam and Eve must, by definition, have been the product of incestuous relationships.

258 *shot to pieces*: a recognition of the fact that the Sadean hero can operate only in a climate from which all human feeling has been eliminated. When it dawns on the likes of Granwel or Oxtiern that other people have feelings too, they lose the ability to be cruel, and see the enormity of their crimes.

262 *His wrath*: Abraham interceded for Sodom, one of the cities of the plain, and God promised not to destroy it if ten righteous men were to be found there. In the event, one such man, Lot, was allowed to leave before brimstone and fire rained down upon the city: Genesis 19: 20–33; 20: 21–5.

271 *philosophical principles*: a glimpse of Sade's argument, set out at great length elsewhere, that a philosophical understanding of the links between physiology and the mechanisms of desire and action brings freedom from the shackles of religion and other forms of superstition. He regarded the imagination as a crucial part of our 'physical constitution'. It stimulated desire and gave it urgency. Franval's physiology, however, is 'flawed' by an irremediable 'disorder of the imagination' (p. 239). Cf. pp. 248–9 and 115.

universal good: Franval uses several arguments advanced by *philosophes* and materialists to blur the distinction between good and evil. First, he claims that conscience is not an innate sensor for telling vice from virtue, but a learned response which is eroded by practice: a second crime is easier to commit than the first but more difficult than the third. He then undermines attempts to judge the morality of actions by the argument that actions are not absolute but relative. They are subject to time, place, and circumstance, otherwise it would not be bad to kill a neighbour but good to kill an enemy in time of war. Cf. p. 233.

273 *sharpened the blade*: Clervil accepts the relativist argument and is even prepared to concede that there is some truth in the current theory of the impact of climate on human behaviour. But he counters by saying that actions are defined as good and evil by just laws developed locally to suit

local conditions, and that contentment for all lies in obeying them. He also points to the biblical wisdom that we reap what we sow.

283 *Comédie Française*: created in 1680 by Louis XIV. It was the most prestigious of the Parisian playhouses and its resident company of actors was granted royal licences and privileges. It had various homes before settling at the Palais Royal in the rue de Richelieu. It is still the major venue for the classical French repertoire.

284 *berline*: a capacious, closed carriage, with four wheels, substantial springs, and glass windows. It was in such a vehicle that the royal family fled to Varennes in June 1791.

291 *that would be absurd*: the clearest statement of Sade's rejection of all forms of Christian morality and social ethics, and his justification of total freedom by the argument that unrestricted licence is 'nature's way'.

303 *at every turn?*: Madame de Franval's virtue, like Eugénie's sudden change of heart, goes unrewarded, just as Franval's blood has not avenged his wife but 'defiled' her body, nor has his sincere repentance earned heaven's pardon. Sade's splendidly melodramatic climax is an exercise in cynicism.

304 *never change your ways*: this moralizing address to the reader defines the grave and reflective character Sade intended his 'heroic and tragic' tales to have. It contrasts markedly with the mood of the shorter *historiettes*, *contes*, and *fabliaux*, for which he composed the following, more playful *envoi*: ' "Reader; I wish thee joy, peace, and health!" Thus did our ancestors of yore speak as they finished their tale. Is there any reason why we should fear to imitate their civility and candour? So I say as they did: "Reader, peace, wealth, and pleasure! If you have found any of these things in my ramblings, then prop me up in a prominent place on your bookshelf. If I have bored you, please accept my apology and cast me into your fire." '

APPENDICES

305 *AND LONGER TALES*: this foreword, written for a selection of tales which would mix 'serious' and 'lighter' moods, is a first draft of the more ambitious 'Essay on Novels'. It is included for the further light it throws on Sade's particular view of the role of virtue in literature, its defence of the libertine novel, and as an opportunity to hear something of Sade's unedited patrician voice—choleric, vituperative, and contemptuous of clerics, minor authors, and critics. Only references not explained in the notes to the 'Essay' are dealt with here.

307 *which bears her name*: 'La Marquise de Thélème, or The Effects of Libertinage' is included in Sade's *Oeuvres completes* (1966), xiv. 229–36. The impecunious Marquis de Thélème has been married to a virtuous and wealthy wife for six months when a man claiming to be her older brother, thought to have died in a duel, unexpectedly appears and claims

the family fortune. Her wealth is frozen by the lawyers and Madame de Thélème travels alone to Paris to contest the claim. She engages a lawyer named Saint-Vérac who is the agent of Fondor, a wealthy man of business and callous libertine. They resolve to block the Marquise's legal efforts. When she has lost all hope and is at her most vulnerable, she will be propositioned. If she rejects Fondor's advances, he will send her back penniless to her husband and divert the inheritance into his own pocket. But if she agrees, he will ensure that she wins her case and keeps her fortune. At this point the manuscript breaks off. Elsewhere Sade reveals that Madame de Thélème submits to Fondor, who is as good as his word. She confesses her fault, explains her honest motives, is forgiven, and lives happily ever after. See notes to pp. 309 and 310.

a rival of Antonio: 'Lorenza and Antonio', subtitled 'An Italian Story' and set in Renaissance Tuscany, precedes 'Ernestine, a Swedish Tale' in volume III. After allowing his son Antonio to marry Lorenza Pazzi, Carlo Strozzi, an admirer of Machiavelli, is consumed by lust for his daughter-in-law. He comes between husband and wife with lies, keeps Lorenza a prisoner, and is about to take by force what she will not give him freely when a melodramatic turn of the plot allows Antonio to come to her rescue. Antonio condemns his father to live and regret his crime, but Carlo refuses him the satisfaction and kills himself.

308 *pusillanimous souls*: Sade insists that his new 'ploy', which adds a 'further dimension' to the drama of the only situation he ever tackled (virtue endangered), was a conscious literary decision. He changes the staple formula by making the third person in the love triangle a predator who is sexually monstrous, vicious, and depraved, and often (though he does not say so here) incestuously inclined. While Sade clearly articulates the aesthetic of terror and pity, first articulated by Aristotle and exploited in the contemporary gothic novel, he also seeks to make his own obsessions artistically respectable.

Duchess d'Alençon: the widow of the Duke d'Alençon, then wife of Henri d'Albret, King of Navarre, is better remembered as Marguerite de Navarre (1492–1549), author of a collection of tales, *The Heptameron* (1559), which were inspired by *The Decameron*. By 'Bandini' Sade perhaps means Matteo Bandello (1485–61), author of tales also in the manner of Boccaccio.

facetious tales: Sade gave specific labels to his short fictions. The 'facetious' *historiettes* were brief and farcical, often centring on the sexual discomfiture of public officials, clerics, monks, and women. His *fabliaux* were extended *historiettes*, but similar in subject and mood, while the *contes*, which he often supplied with a subtitle (as in the case of 'La Marquise de Thélème'), were sober tales of innocence under attack from vice, complete with social and intellectual asides. These last are distinguishable from the stories of *The Crimes of Love* only by their length. See also note to p. 304.

308 *Sisenna . . . Nero*: Lucius Cornelius Sisenna (*c.*120–67 BC), friend of Varro and Cicero and best known as a historian and orator. On the Milesian fables, see note to p. 6. Petronius, satirist of the reign of Nero (AD 39–68), is generally recognized as the author of the *Satiricon*.

Saint Louis . . . gladly burned?: Louis IX (1215–70) created the administrative framework of modern France. Voltaire regarded him as an enlightened philosopher-king. A deeply pious man, he died of plague in Carthage while leading a crusade, a paradox which amused Sade, who reproduced a similar irony in 'Florville and Courval', where the devout Madame de Lérince dies unhappy while the sinning Madame de Verquin makes a peaceful end. Sade loathed Louis's narrow moral views, his friendliness to the Inquisition, and his intolerance of human sexuality. He was a 'a cruel, witless king whose every action was false, ridiculous or barbaric' (*Aline and Valcour*, in *Oeuvres*, i. 669 n.).

Chi . . . senza senzo: 'Anyone who tried to count how many women have been turned into whores by *The Decameron* would be left permanently dazed and brain-addled.' Bonifatio Vannozzi was an early seventeenth-century Italian divine.

309 *Adhesso . . . piu periculoso*: 'Consequently the dangers represented by whores are not made any more dangerous as a result.'

Ma per le puttane: 'And as for the whores . . .'

Madame du Noyer: Anne-Marguerite du Noyer (*c.*1663–1720), author of tales, pseudo-memoirs, and the *Lettres historiques et galantes* (1713) which Sade later gives as his source. He claimed that 'the basic situation has been so expanded, the original outline so embellished, that it is not possible to recognize the source from which it was taken'.

310 *the other twenty-eight tales*: i.e. the tales, mixed in tone, intended for the collection planned in 1788. In all Sade wrote about fifty stories: see the Note on the Text.

311 *Villeterque*: Alexandre-Louis de Villeterque (1759–1811), journalist, translator, author of five *drames* and the *Veillées philosophiques, ou Essais sur la morale expérimentale et la physique systématique* (1795), a book of 'experimental ethics and systematic physics'. An opponent of the individualism of Rousseau, he denounced self-indulgence and defined happiness as the discharge of moral and social duty. He was better fitted than Sade to survive the strict climate of the new century.

even more loathsome: i.e. *Justine*.

313 *Hack and Scribe*: Sade replied to Villeterque in this brochure, dated An IX, published between 22 October 1800, when the review appeared, and 5 January 1801, when Villeterque accepted Sade's less than wholehearted apology (see pp. 319–20 below).

314 *named Despaze*: Joseph Despaze (1776–1814), a native of Bordeaux, edited the short-lived periodical *Le Fanal* (1799), and published *Les Quatre Satires* (1800) which also offended the playwright M.-J. Chénier

and the poet Lebrun. It seems that Sade thought of suing Despaze for defamation, but never did so. The lines of the second *Satire* to which Sade objects imagine 'a friend of virtue' who peruses *Justine*, 'a black-hued book printed on the presses of hell'. He turns pale and exclaims: 'Why did not the monster who devised these dreadful scenes | Succumb 'midst the horror of tortures so obscene?'

315 *has spoken!*: Aliboron was the ass of La Fontaine's 'Les Voleurs et l'âne' ('The Thieves and the Ass') (*Fables*, bk I, xiii).

Vile stercus: Sade's play on his tormentor's name is no less crude for being dressed in Latin. *Stercus* (dung, ordure) was a word used by Horace, Cicero, and other Roman authors as a term of vulgar abuse.

under your own name: Villeterque's *Veillées philosophiques* maintained the didactic purpose of the supposedly homely *veillée*, a term used by the educationalist Madame de Genlis (1746–1830) for *Les Veillées du château* (1784), which contained plays written for the children of the Duke d'Orléans; and by Sade's bugbear, Restif de la Bretonne, author of *Les Veillées du Marais* (1785), allegedly imitated from Irish folk-tales. *Les Mille et une nuits* were translated by the orientalist Antoine Galland between 1714 and 1711, and had helped fashion the vogue for so-called 'oriental' stories. There were numerous complete and partial reprints of the text.

in Polyeucte, Phèdre: Mahomet (1742) by Voltaire, Racine's *Britannicus* (1669) and *Phèdre* (1677), and Corneille's *Polyeucte* (1641/2) were all tragedies.

317 *to be exposed*: it is difficult not to feel the weight of Sade's patrician rage in this rather confused paragraph. He sets out his literary credo frankly, but denies his authorship of *Justine* and disowns the ideas it expresses. It is his furious response to Villeterque's allegation that he was the author of *Justine*, an accusation potentially very damaging in the prevailing moral climate.

Juliette and Raunai?: '. . . or the Conspiracy of Amboise, a Historical Tale', first of the tales of *The Crimes of Love*. It is set in 1560, and Henri de Guise is infatuated with Juliette, daughter of the Protestant Baron de Castelnau-Chalosse. He imprisons the Baron and threatens to execute him unless Juliette submits to his will. Raunai, in love with Juliette since childhood, plans to change places with the Baron and, when her father is safe, Juliette will kill the prisoner she loves to prevent his being tortured. Guise has a sudden change of heart, releases the Baron, and blesses the marriage of Juliette and Raunai. Sade, admitting that he has not respected the historical truth, praises the ideal of tolerance which brought about the ending, and castigates the abuse of power which not only turns men into slaves but makes them criminals too.

a sentimental tale: 'The Double Test' is the second story in the collection. It tells how Ceilcour, a rich libertine, having decided to marry, tests two candidates. The Countess de Nelmours proves to be less interested in him than in his money. Baronne Dolsé genuinely loves him but dies, as does, three months later, Ceilcour.

317 *Oedipus and his family?*: an argument which carries less weight now than in 1800, when incest had become an almost routine ploy for playwrights and novelists.

fail utterly: see note to p. 307.

in 'Dorgeville'?: the opening tale of volume IV. Dorgeville is a 'virtuous criminal' because the hero commits incest unknowingly. Born honest and considerate, nature has equipped him to be unhappy, notes Sade. Cheated in business, he retires to the country to dispense charity. He rescues a young woman who is rejected by her seeming parents and marries her, only to discover that she is his lost sister and a murderess who intended to poison him for his money. She and her lover are arrested and executed. Sade concludes with an exhortation to the reader to respect 'our sacred duties'.

318 *in my preface*: see paragraphs 7 and 8 of Villeterque's review.

those of Lovelace?: in addition to the hero of *Clarissa*, Sade refers us again to Racine's *Britannicus* and to the tragedy of *Atrée et Thyeste* (1707) by Crébillon *père* (1674–1762), who owed his considerable success to the blood and horror in his mythological sources which he exploited to the full. In this play a father is invited to quaff a cup of his son's blood.

319 *in Zadig, Candide, etc?*: Sade was not alone in pointing out the contradictions of the sentimental novel. Fielding had written *Shamela* to mock the sordid calculation of Pamela, the heroine of Richardson's first novel, and many commentators had problems with Clarissa's ultimate taming of Lovelace. Of Rousseau's Julie, who becomes the mistress of her tutor, Voltaire had already tartly observed that 'Saint-Preux takes his pupil's virginity in lieu of wages'. Voltaire's own 'philosophical' tales reiterate the point that in real life, *pace* the literary theorists, vice is not punished nor is virtue rewarded. On the contrary, sinners prosper and innocence is no match for wickedness.

boots for men: see 'Essay on novels', p. 16.

MORE ABOUT **OXFORD WORLD'S CLASSICS**

American Literature

British and Irish Literature

Children's Literature

Classics and Ancient Literature

Colonial Literature

Eastern Literature

European Literature

Gothic Literature

History

Medieval Literature

Oxford English Drama

Poetry

Philosophy

Politics

Religion

The Oxford Shakespeare

A complete list of Oxford World's Classics, including Authors in Context, Oxford English Drama, and the Oxford Shakespeare, is available in the UK from the Marketing Services Department, Oxford University Press, Great Clarendon Street, Oxford OX2 6DP, or visit the website at www.oup.com/uk/worldsclassics.

In the USA, visit www.oup.com/us/owc for a complete title list.

Oxford World's Classics are available from all good bookshops. In case of difficulty, customers in the UK should contact Oxford University Press Bookshop, 116 High Street, Oxford OX1 4BR.

A SELECTION OF OXFORD WORLD'S CLASSICS

	Six French Poets of the Nineteenth Century
HONORÉ DE BALZAC	Cousin Bette Eugénie Grandet Père Goriot
CHARLES BAUDELAIRE	The Flowers of Evil The Prose Poems and Fanfarlo
BENJAMIN CONSTANT	Adolphe
DENIS DIDEROT	Jacques the Fatalist The Nun
ALEXANDRE DUMAS (PÈRE)	The Black Tulip The Count of Monte Cristo Louise de la Vallière The Man in the Iron Mask La Reine Margot The Three Musketeers Twenty Years After The Vicomte de Bragelonne
ALEXANDRE DUMAS (FILS)	La Dame aux Camélias
GUSTAVE FLAUBERT	Madame Bovary A Sentimental Education Three Tales
VICTOR HUGO	The Essential Victor Hugo Notre-Dame de Paris
J.-K. HUYSMANS	Against Nature
PIERRE CHODERLOS DE LACLOS	Les Liaisons dangereuses
MME DE LAFAYETTE	The Princesse de Clèves
GUILLAUME DU LORRIS and JEAN DE MEUN	The Romance of the Rose

A SELECTION OF OXFORD WORLD'S CLASSICS

Guy de Maupassant	**A Day in the Country and Other Stories** **A Life** **Bel-Ami** **Mademoiselle Fifi and Other Stories** **Pierre et Jean**
Prosper Mérimée	**Carmen and Other Stories**
Molière	**Don Juan and Other Plays** **The Misanthrope, Tartuffe, and Other Plays**
Blaise Pascal	**Pensées and Other Writings**
Abbé Prévost	**Manon Lescaut**
Jean Racine	**Britannicus, Phaedra, and Athaliah**
Arthur Rimbaud	**Collected Poems**
Edmond Rostand	**Cyrano de Bergerac**
Marquis de Sade	**The Crimes of Love** **The Misfortunes of Virtue and Other Early Tales**
George Sand	**Indiana**
Mme de Staël	**Corinne**
Stendhal	**The Red and the Black** **The Charterhouse of Parma**
Paul Verlaine	**Selected Poems**
Jules Verne	**Around the World in Eighty Days** **Captain Hatteras** **Journey to the Centre of the Earth** **Twenty Thousand Leagues under the Seas**
Voltaire	**Candide and Other Stories** **Letters concerning the English Nation**

A SELECTION OF **OXFORD WORLD'S CLASSICS**

ÉMILE ZOLA	**L'Assommoir**
	The Attack on the Mill
	La Bête humaine
	La Débâcle
	Germinal
	The Kill
	The Ladies' Paradise
	The Masterpiece
	Nana
	Pot Luck
	Thérèse Raquin

A SELECTION OF **OXFORD WORLD'S CLASSICS**

	Eirik the Red and Other Icelandic Sagas
	The German-Jewish Dialogue
	The Kalevala
	The Poetic Edda
LUDOVICO ARIOSTO	**Orlando Furioso**
GIOVANNI BOCCACCIO	**The Decameron**
GEORG BÜCHNER	**Danton's Death, Leonce and Lena, and Woyzeck**
LUIS VAZ DE CAMÕES	**The Lusiads**
MIGUEL DE CERVANTES	**Don Quixote** **Exemplary Stories**
CARLO COLLODI	**The Adventures of Pinocchio**
DANTE ALIGHIERI	**The Divine Comedy** **Vita Nuova**
LOPE DE VEGA	**Three Major Plays**
J. W. VON GOETHE	**Elective Affinities** **Erotic Poems** **Faust: Part One and Part Two** **The Flight to Italy**
E. T. A. HOFFMANN	**The Golden Pot and Other Tales**
HENRIK IBSEN	**An Enemy of the People, The Wild Duck, Rosmersholm** **Four Major Plays** **Peer Gynt**
LEONARDO DA VINCI	**Selections from the Notebooks**
FEDERICO GARCIA LORCA	**Four Major Plays**
MICHELANGELO BUONARROTI	**Life, Letters, and Poetry**

A SELECTION OF **OXFORD WORLD'S CLASSICS**

Ludovico Ariosto	**Orlando Furioso**
Giovanni Boccaccio	**The Decameron**
Matteo Maria Boiardo	**Orlando Innamorato**
Luís Vaz de Camões	**The Lusíads**
Miguel de Cervantes	**Don Quixote de la Mancha** **Exemplary Stories**
Dante Alighieri	**The Divine Comedy** **Vita Nuova**
Benito Pérez Galdós	**Nazarín**
Leonardo da Vinci	**Selections from the Notebooks**
Niccolò Machiavelli	**Discourses on Livy** **The Prince**
Michelangelo	**Life, Letters, and Poetry**
Petrarch	**Selections from the *Canzoniere* and Other Works**
Giorgio Vasari	**The Lives of the Artists**

A SELECTION OF OXFORD WORLD'S CLASSICS

ANTON CHEKHOV	Early Stories Five Plays The Princess and Other Stories The Russian Master and Other Stories The Steppe and Other Stories Twelve Plays Ward Number Six and Other Stories
FYODOR DOSTOEVSKY	Crime and Punishment Devils A Gentle Creature and Other Stories The Idiot The Karamazov Brothers Memoirs from the House of the Dead Notes from the Underground and The Gambler
NIKOLAI GOGOL	Dead Souls Plays and Petersburg Tales
ALEXANDER PUSHKIN	Eugene Onegin The Queen of Spades and Other Stories
LEO TOLSTOY	Anna Karenina The Kreutzer Sonata and Other Stories The Raid and Other Stories Resurrection War and Peace
IVAN TURGENEV	Fathers and Sons First Love and Other Stories A Month in the Country

A SELECTION OF **OXFORD WORLD'S CLASSICS**

Jane Austen	**Emma**
	Mansfield Park
	Persuasion
	Pride and Prejudice
	Sense and Sensibility
Mrs Beeton	**Book of Household Management**
Lady Elizabeth Braddon	**Lady Audley's Secret**
Anne Brontë	**The Tenant of Wildfell Hall**
Charlotte Brontë	**Jane Eyre**
	Shirley
	Villette
Emily Brontë	**Wuthering Heights**
Samuel Taylor Coleridge	**The Major Works**
Wilkie Collins	**The Moonstone**
	No Name
	The Woman in White
Charles Darwin	**The Origin of Species**
Charles Dickens	**The Adventures of Oliver Twist**
	Bleak House
	David Copperfield
	Great Expectations
	Nicholas Nickleby
	The Old Curiosity Shop
	Our Mutual Friend
	The Pickwick Papers
	A Tale of Two Cities
George du Maurier	**Trilby**
Maria Edgeworth	**Castle Rackrent**

A SELECTION OF **OXFORD WORLD'S CLASSICS**

GEORGE ELIOT	**Daniel Deronda** **The Lifted Veil and Brother Jacob** **Middlemarch** **The Mill on the Floss** **Silas Marner**
SUSAN FERRIER	**Marriage**
ELIZABETH GASKELL	**Cranford** **The Life of Charlotte Brontë** **Mary Barton** **North and South** **Wives and Daughters**
GEORGE GISSING	**New Grub Street** **The Odd Woman**
THOMAS HARDY	**Far from the Madding Crowd** **Jude the Obscure** **The Mayor of Casterbridge** **The Return of the Native** **Tess of the d'Urbervilles** **The Woodlanders**
WILLIAM HAZLITT	**Selected Writings**
JAMES HOGG	**The Private Memoirs and Confessions of a Justified Sinner**
JOHN KEATS	**The Major Works** **Selected Letters**
CHARLES MATURIN	**Melmoth the Wanderer**
WALTER SCOTT	**The Antiquary** **Ivanhoe** **Rob Roy**
MARY SHELLEY	**Frankenstein** **The Last Man**

A SELECTION OF OXFORD WORLD'S CLASSICS

ROBERT LOUIS STEVENSON	**Kidnapped and Catriona** **The Strange Case of Dr Jekyll and Mr Hyde and Weir of Hermiston** **Treasure Island**
BRAM STOKER	**Dracula**
WILLIAM MAKEPEACE THACKERAY	**Vanity Fair**
OSCAR WILDE	**Complete Shorter Fiction** **The Major Works** **The Picture of Dorian Gray**
DOROTHY WORDSWORTH	**The Grasmere and Alfoxden Journals**
WILLIAM WORDSWORTH	**The Major Works**